SOFT

Apocalypse

SOFT

Apocalypse

SF
FIC
MCI

Will McIntosh

Night Shade Books
San Francisco

First Edition

ISBN: 978-1-59780-276-5

Night Shade Books
Please visit us on the web at
http://www.nightshadebooks.com

The first one is for my parents, William and Blanche McIntosh.

Chapter 1: Tribe

Spring, 2023

We passed a tribe of Mexicans heading the other way, wading through the knee-high weeds along the side of the highway. Or maybe they were Ecuadorans, or Puerto Ricans. I don't know. There were about twenty of them, and they were in bad shape. One woman was unconscious; she was being carried by two men. One of the children looked to have flu.

A small brown man with orphan eyes and no front teeth spoke for them. "Por favor, dinero o comida?"

"Lo siento," I said, holding my hands palm up, "no tengo nada."

The man nodded, his head slung low.

Colin and I walked on in silence, feeling like shit. If we had enough to spare, we'd have given them something.

If you're not starving, but you may be in a month, is it wrong not to give food to people who are starving now? Where's the line? How poor do you have to be before you're not a selfish bastard for letting others starve?

"It's so hard to believe," Colin said as we crossed the steaming, empty parking lot toward the bowling alley.

"What?"

"That we're poor. That we're homeless."

"I know.

"I mean, we have college degrees," he said.

"I know," I said.

There was an ancient miniature golf course choked in weeds alongside the bowling alley. The astroturf had completely rotted away in places. The windmill had one spoke. We looked it over for a minute (both of us had once been avid mini golfers), then continued toward the door.

"You know what I'd pay money to see?" Colin said.

"Yes," I said. He ignored me and carried on.

"I'd pay to see a golf tournament for really terrible golfers, with a million dollar prize. The best part of watching golf is seeing guys choke under the pressure, digging up divots that go farther than the ball."

"Now that would be worth watching," I said, stepping around a small, decomposing animal of some sort. "By the way, we're not homeless, we're nomads. Keep your labels straight."

"Ah, yes, I forgot." Colin had always been a master of the sarcastic tone, even in grade school. He reached the door first, pulled it open and waved me through.

Given all of the bowling leagues I'd been in as a kid, it surprised me that the clatter of bowling pins didn't stir any nostalgic feelings. Maybe it was because this bowling alley was in semi-darkness. The only light was what filtered through the doors and windows.

A guy with a bushy beard was hunched to make his shot in the lane nearest the door. He missed the spare, then walked down the lane into deep shadow to reset the pins by hand.

This was promising; if they weren't even running the automatic pin-setters, they needed power badly. A half-dozen fans of various shapes and sizes were spread around, buzzing like model airplanes. They appeared to be the only things hooked up to the generator.

Colin stopped short. "Do you have the cell? I hope you brought it, because I forgot all about it."

I pulled the storage cell from my pocket and held it in front of Colin's nose.

"Well that's a relief," Colin said. "I was not looking forward to walking all the way back to get it. Let's take care of this and get out of here."

My cell phone jingled, alerting me to an incoming text-message. I jolted, dug the phone out of my pocket while trying not to appear as eager as I felt. I had to tilt the phone toward the windows to read it.

Miss you, the message said.

Miss you too. Love you, I typed back.

Sophia and I talked in awful clichés, but somehow words that made me wince when others said them seemed fresh and powerful when we said them. *Love you so much. Thought about you all day. I would die for you.* Pure poetry.

"You've really got it bad," Colin said. He was sweating like a pig, his shirt soaked dark down the center from his neck to his belly.

"I know. I know it's pointless, but I just can't get unhooked from her."

"You haven't suffered enough yet. Once you have, you'll get unhooked."

My phone jingled again. Colin chuckled.

Love you too, the message said. I put the phone away. It took effort. I could picture Sophia sitting at her desk at work, glancing at her phone, waiting for it to burble. Mine jingled, hers burbled. Actually, both of the phones were hers. She paid the bills, anyway.

It wasn't an affair in the usual sense of the word. She had too much integrity for that. I'd like to think I do as well, but she never made the offer, so I can't be sure. Maybe part of having integrity is surrounding yourself with people who have integrity, so that yours is never tested.

"All done?" Colin asked. "Now can we get this over with?" I followed Colin to the front desk, where a gray-haired woman was spraying disinfectant into blue and red shoes that lined the counter.

"Excuse me, are you interested in trading some water or food for energy?" Colin held up the storage cell.

The woman went on spraying.

"Excuse me?" Colin said, louder. She didn't look up.

A pair of bowlers put their scorecard down on the counter. The woman went right over and rang them up.

"Excuse me," we said simultaneously as she walked right past us and resumed her battle with stinky shoes. We looked at each other.

"Hey!" I said. Nothing. I looked around the alley to see if anyone else was witnessing this. Four people, evidently on a double-date, looked away as I looked at them. One of the women said something to the others and they laughed.

"Take a hint," someone shouted from one of the far alleys.

My heart was thudding. "You know, we've got eight other people depending on us. They're dehydrated and close to starving. We're not asking for a handout, just a fair trade."

The woman sprayed some more shoes.

"Come on Jasper, let's go," Colin said.

My phone jingled. We turned to go. I stopped and turned around.

"Fuck you, you ugly old bigot piece of shit," I said. She smirked, shook her head, but didn't look at me.

It was a long walk, across that gum-stained carpet to the doors. I suddenly felt so self-conscious I could barely walk—one of my legs felt longer than the other, and my hands were too big.

"Fucking gypsies!" someone yelled as the door closed.

Outside, a guy on a mountain bike rolled up, dropped a foot that skidded to a stop on the cigarette-littered pavement. He ignored us as he slung a bowling bag off his shoulder.

My phone jingled.

"Go ahead," Colin said. "I won't be offended."

The text message said, *What r u doing?*

I called Sophia and told her what had happened. She cried for me, and told me she loved me very, very much, and not to let it get to me, that I was a brilliant, wonderful person in a bad situation. I felt a little better. Sophia was good at making people feel better. The first time I ever met her, she was handing out Christmas presents to the children of illegals down by the river in Savannah. I was down there coordinating an effort to give the children tuberculosis shots, but I was getting paid.

Whenever anything bad happened, my first thought was to call Sophia. I don't know why—she didn't have much spare time to give me solace, between her job and her husband.

How do you look into the future when you plan to spend it with someone you don't love? It boggled my mind. It frustrated the hell out of me that she wouldn't leave him (because he was a nice guy and would fall apart if she left), even though she loved me, not him. Even though every fiber in our souls pulled us toward each other.

I had thought that same string of thoughts a thousand times, and still it kept looping, day after day, digging a pit in my mind. Shit.

We cleared a rise and caught sight of the rest of our tribe lounging in the shade on the grassy median of the highway. Jim had all six of our little windmills working, bless his soul. The guy was pushing sixty, twice the age of most of the rest of us, but he was always working. The windmills were set as close to traffic as possible to harvest the wind of passing vehicles. They spun pretty good each time a vehicle passed. The tribe had also spread a couple of the smaller solar blankets on the sunny spots in the grass, and pitched our tents.

Jeannie met Colin with a hug, and a "How'd it go?"

Cortez asked if I wanted to go to the Minute Mart with him and Ange to buy food. I told him I'd pass, that we only had two bikes, so they could travel faster alone. Truth was I didn't care much for Cortez, though I loved Ange to death. Cortez was too aggressive-salesmany for me, and had the sort of thick, meaty lips that would make any man look like a thug. I didn't understand what Ange saw in him, although I don't know, maybe I was just jealous because Ange was so damned hot and she was with Cortez.

I sat up against a tree and typed a message to Sophia as cars whooshed past and the windmills spun.

Thinking about you, I wrote.

Love u so much. Miss u like crazy. Going hm to sleep, she wrote.

Why did I always have the urge to find a printer and print out her messages? It was as if I wanted hard evidence, something I could show to someone to prove that this beautiful woman loved me. Am I that insecure? Some part of me is, yes, especially now that I'm a bum.

Another message came through:

Can I see u?

I could barely type fast enough. *Yes! Rt. 301 N, median strip, W of Metter.*

See you in 40 min. :) Can't wait!!!!!

I leapt to my feet, grinning like an idiot.

A passing truck slowed; a plastic fast-food cup flew out the passenger window and hit me in the neck. Soda splashed across my face and chest.

"Faggot!" a woman screamed out the window as the truck sped off. She had to be sixty.

"Fat ugly bitch!" I screamed, though she wasn't fat, and couldn't hear me anyway.

Jim handed me a filthy hand towel. "Don't let it get to you," he said in his calm Zen voice. I located the cleanest spot on the towel and wiped my chest with it.

"What the hell is going on?" I said. "We're not illegals. Now it's anyone who doesn't have a home?"

Jim could only shrug and return to his windmills. Well, our windmills. Everything was common property; everything was shared. Capitalism was a luxury we could not afford. It's amazing how quickly your deeply held values crumble when the cupboards are bare.

Thirty minutes later I spotted Sophia's silver Honda in the distance. I could barely stand to wait for the car to cover the distance between us. I stepped to the edge of the curb and watched as her face became distinct, a big smile on her beautiful brown lips. I hopped in before she came to a complete stop, reveled in the cool air as I waved goodbye to my tribe.

Sophia leaned over and gave me a wet kiss by my ear, struggling to watch the road at the same time. "Hi there."

"Hi," I said, taking her free hand in mine, enjoying the contrast of our brown and white fingers laced together. "How was work?"

"It sucked ass," she said. She always said that. But she also knew she was damned lucky to have a job. Accountants were mostly still employable, even with a forty-something percent unemployment rate (which didn't count the millions of refugees who were landing on beaches and hopping over fences every day). Sociology majors, on the other hand, were eminently unemployable. I should have listened to my parents. Although, come to think of it, when I was struggling to decide on a major my parents told me to follow my heart. There were eighty million artists, blackjack dealers, documentary filmmakers, florists, and fellow sociology majors who were very sorry they'd followed their hearts.

Sophia pulled into the Wal-Mart parking lot, parked in the far corner and left the car running, for the air conditioning.

"I brought you some things," she said. I loved her beautiful island accent. She twisted to pull a plastic shopping bag out of the back seat and toss it casually into my lap. She tried so hard to make it seem like nothing, to keep our relationship on equal footing. I opened the bag and peered inside: soap, bug spray, vitamins, aspirin, protein bars, and a twenty dollar bill. Whenever I saw her, she had supplies for the tribe. She was a god damned saint.

A waxy package caught my eye. I pulled it from the bag and smiled.

"Baseball cards?" Like an idiot, I used to buy them every spring—a rite of passage into baseball season left over from childhood. When we first met, when I still had a job and the world was as it had always been, I bought a pack in a coffee shop and opened them at the table, introducing her to the players as I thumbed through their cards. She'd been a cricket fan on Dominica—in desperate need, as I saw it, of an introduction to the greatest bat and ball game in the universe.

She laughed. "Subsistence rations."

I ran my finger across the foil seal, held the breach to my nose and sniffed. I shut my eyes, sighed as the smell of freshly minted baseball cards triggered fond memories. I pulled out the cards. They felt so clean and slick in my filthy hands. "Chris Carroll," I said, studying the first card. I flipped it over. "How'd he do last season? I didn't get to see many games."

And suddenly I was crying. Sophia threw her arms around me and cried with me. "I wish—" she said, but stopped herself. I knew what she wished. We stayed like that, huddled together, our wet faces buried in each other's neck.

"I only have until two, then I have to… go home," she said after a while. Which meant, that's when Jean Paul would be home, and even at such an indirect mention of her husband, that familiar cocktail of jealousy/hurt/despair lanced my stomach.

Sophia didn't lie to her husband about us. He was deeply hurt, and quietly angry, but he tolerated it, because he didn't want Sophia to leave him. In other words, Sophia had all the power in the relationship, whether she wanted it or not.

As I see it, there are four types of relationships. There are those where you're madly in love with someone, and her feelings are tepid. In that case she has the power, and you struggle to convince her to love you by trying to be witty and fascinating, forever seeking her approval for what you say and who you are, and grow increasingly pathetic in the process. That was where Jean Paul was.

There are those where the other person is in love with you, while you can only muster a warm and murky fondness for her. In this case you carry a knot of guilt, because you feel like a walking lie; you're forever trying to feel what you don't feel, and end up consumed by an existential emptiness, convinced that, not only can you not feel love for this person, you have become incapable of loving anyone. That's where Sophia was with Jean Paul, and why there was enough room in her heart for me.

Third, there are those where you're not in love with the other person, and she is not in love with you. There is a nice balance here; you're on the same page, so there is no need to struggle, no one feels like a loser and no one feels guilty. There is a sadness, though. When you look into someone's eyes and see the blandness you feel reflected there, it's hard not to wonder why you've chosen to be in a relationship that's the equivalent of a permanent Valium drip. This sort of relationship had always been my specialty, for reasons I don't quite understand.

Then there is the fourth type. You are madly in love with someone who is madly in love with you. This is the perfect balance, energy in harmony. This is the kind we all want—it draws you into the moment and keeps you there. You don't want to be anywhere else. The existential hum is silenced. Before I met Sophia, I'd never found one of these, and had begun to suspect they were mythical creatures, that I was as likely to happen upon a yeti as a woman who loved me as much as I loved her.

"We'd better get going," Sophia said. She reached toward the back seat again, handed me another plastic bag. "Keep this safe for when you need it."

It was a white dress shirt, wrapped in plastic and pinned to cardboard, and a lime-green tie. "For when you get an interview."

Still sticky from the soda flung at me an hour earlier, I wanted to laugh at the absurdity of that sentiment, but I didn't want to seem ungrateful of her gift.

"Watch out for immigration," Sophia said as she pulled onto the highway. "They're deporting homeless U.S. citizens to third world countries along with illegals."

"You're joking," I said.

"They're trying to defend it as retaliation for poor countries encouraging their people to come here. And they're getting lots of support from people on the right."

"Figures," I said.

"And avoid Rincon—they're lynching people, especially strangers."

"Oh, Christ. We had a trading partner there." Our list of reliable connections kept shrinking. Either the location was too dangerous, or they were going out of business.

"Uh-oh." Sophia slowed as we approached my tribe. There was a police car pulled partway on the median by our camp, its red light flashing. I convinced Sophia to go, kissed her cheek, and thanked her for the things she had brought, then rejoined my tribe, which was clumped before a middle-aged, red-haired cop.

"We're not doing anything illegal," Cortez was saying, "the energy from passing cars is just being wasted. We're not bothering anyone. We're just trying to make an honest living! Since when was that illegal?"

"Vagrancy is illegal here in Metter," the cop said. "Y'all need to move on."

"Move on *where*?" Cortez said. "We don't have homes."

"That's not my problem. You need to move outside the city limits." He pointed west, down the highway. "Six miles that way. You can pitch your tents there." Before anyone could protest further, he wheeled and headed toward his cruiser.

"Metter is closed, ladies and gentlemen," he said before closing the door. "Gypsies spread disease."

We packed up and started moving. It was Jim and Carrie's turn on the bikes; the rest of us hoofed it. Mercifully, it had clouded over and cooled a little.

"We need some sort of plan," Cortez said, throwing his free hand in the air. "This is no good, wandering around aimlessly. We need a better business model."

And what's the plan, what's our fucking business model? I wanted to shout. I kept my mouth shut. Cortez was always talking about angles and plans, but every day we still humped everything we owned somewhere else, looking for places to skim some energy, places to trade it for what we needed to live.

I caught up with Colin and Jeannie, and we slogged through the weeds. It was going to be a long six miles.

A dilapidated Saturn slowed, and the window rolled down. "Hey sweetie, let me see your tits!" a skinny black guy with bad teeth yelled.

Ange gave him the finger without turning.

"Hey," Jeannie shouted as the car rode off, "how do you know he wanted to see *your* tits? Maybe he was talking to me!"

Ange spun around, pulled up her shirt, and waggled her tits at

Jeannie. I'd never seen them before—they were smallish, but pretty fabulous, like Ange herself. I was disappointed when she dropped her shirt and turned back around.

"He may well have been talking to you," I said to Jeannie. "You have fabulous tits."

"Shut up," Colin said as Jeannie laughed.

"No, really," I persisted, "they're beautiful. Big, firm, Italian coconuts."

Jeannie laughed harder.

"No, really, stop talking about my wife's fabulous tits," Colin said over the laughter. They *were* fabulous, though Jeannie wasn't the type to yank up her shirt and waggle them. Which was a shame, really. She kissed Colin's cheek, still laughing, and trotted to catch up to Ange, giving her a little shove on the shoulder.

"You know what's wrong with that guy in the car, and all the rest like him?" I said.

"What?" Colin said.

"They don't masturbate often enough. They sacrifice every shred of dignity for the Lotto chance that some woman is going to respond to that shit and actually screw them, which would temporarily quiet the lizard brain that's screaming at them, because they don't shut it the hell up themselves by jerking off."

"Ah. That's profound," Colin said. "Thanks, I love talking about other men's masturbatory habits."

It started drizzling. Everybody scrambled. Some of us grabbed the tarps and spread them across the weeds, angling them so the rainwater formed canals and spilled toward one point. Others grabbed our plastic milk jugs and began collecting.

"We're a well-oiled machine, you know that?" Cortez said, his head tilted up to catch drops.

The rain fell harder. The tribe whooped.

Not ten minutes later, the flashing red light of officer asshole's cruiser was reflecting off the puddles in the road.

"What did I tell y'all?" he said as soon as his head was out of the car. "Pack all this shit up and move on, and I'm not gonna tell you again!"

"Please, officer, we need this water badly," Jeannie said. "We won't be here long, and we'll leave as soon as we're finished." The rest of us kept working.

The cop unsnapped his holster and took out his pistol. He held it at his side, angled just slightly in our direction. "I'm not gonna say it again."

We rolled up the tarps. Ange started to say something to the cop, who was watching us like a parent making sure the kids clean up their room. Four or five of us shot her a warning glance. She shut up. We got moving. Officer asshole drove away.

We tried to hurry, to get out of town before the rain let up, but it's hard to hurry when you're carrying a pack filled with forty pounds of shit and you're dehydrated.

"Hey!" Cortez said, pointing at a railroad track that disappeared into the woods to our right. "Why don't we head along the track? We can go a mile or two and set up camp. The bulls won't even know we're there."

Nobody had objections, so we climbed down a rocky gully and set out along the tracks. The gravel made for a bumpy ride on the mountain bikes, but for the rest of us it was easier than trudging through wet weeds.

The sounds of the highway receded, leaving nothing but the patter of rain. Long-leaf pines crowded close, littering the raised tracks with golden needles.

My phone jingled. *So wonderful 2 see u. U okay?* Both of us tended to suffer from severe post-visit depression.

I'm good. Run off by cop. On the move again.

Head west. Toward me. :)

"What's that?" Carrie said, pointing up the track. Someone was coming toward us, waving a sheet or something. The track began to hum as the figure came into focus.

"Oh, I don't fucking believe this," Ange said.

The guy was windsurfing on the track. He shifted from side to side, picking up the swirling winds of the storm, one side of his contraption lifting off the tracks, then the other, as if he were riding waves. The clack of well-oiled wheels grew louder as he approached.

We split to either side to let him pass. He waved, and pointed back the way he'd come. "About a mile," he shouted, then sped off on an energetic burst of wind.

"About a mile to what?" I said.

We stopped first, to harvest what water we could. The rain lasted another twenty minutes, then we pushed on with our milk jugs filled a few inches.

A mile on, another tribe was camped in a cleared strip created to allow power lines to run through. Four more of the railroad windsurfing contraptions were lined up beside the tracks. Most of the tribe were lounging in the shade, but a couple stood behind a folding table set up near one of the big, silver power line towers.

Two women hopped up to meet us, smiling and waving. One was in her mid-forties, though she may have been younger than she looked. Pale white skin is great when you're young, but it doesn't wear well, especially if you live in a tent and spend all day in the sun with no sunblock.

The other was probably twenty-five. She had a willowy-waifish look, tall and slim, reddish hair. Skinny as hell with no breasts to speak of, but damned sexy nonetheless. She had sort of an English look. I watched her walk toward us: she had a grace about her that made me wish I could sit and watch her all day.

"Are you here to buy weed?" the older woman asked, motioning toward the folding table.

"No, we just happened to be heading this way," Jeannie said.

"Where you heading?" the younger one asked.

"I don't think we know yet," I said. "We just got flushed out of Metter." I held out my hand to her. "Jasper."

"Phoebe, nice to meet you," she said.

The other woman introduced herself, and I immediately forgot her name. I suck that way sometimes.

A guy with a pointy red beard and wire-rimmed glasses came over to join us. "Have you heard rumors about a new designer virus that's going around?"

"No. Is it a bad one?"

The guy's tongue darted out, licked the corner of his mouth. "We don't know. Another tribe told us about it, but they only heard about it secondhand themselves. It's supposed to give you muscle-spasms."

"Terrific," I said. "You heard any news about what's going on out west?" Last we'd heard, a rogue army from Mexico had invaded southern Texas.

"We heard that U.S. troops had been sent down there, but we haven't heard what happened," Phoebe offered.

We went on talking for a while, and eventually just about everyone from both tribes were huddled in groups, exchanging news and information. It was amazing, really, how well and quickly tribes got along. They invited us to make camp with them and stay a while.

"She seems like your type," Colin said as we unpacked the tents from the bikes. "Kind of elven. I wouldn't be surprised if her ears were a little pointy."

"I must admit, she caught my eye. Made my heart go pit-a-pat." An image of Sophia, smiling wide, shot through my mind.

"You should go talk to her. Ask her out."

"Maybe I will."

But how do you ask a woman out when you have no car, no place to live, and no money to go to a movie, even if you could get there? I didn't understand the rules. Maybe there weren't any rules; maybe they were still being worked out.

I volunteered to wander over to their camp when Cortez suggested we ask if they had anything to store energy in, and anything besides drugs to trade. Ange thought trading for a little weed would be good for our dispositions (Ange had spent a year in rehab for coke, eight years ago, when she was fifteen), but she was voted down.

They didn't have anything for energy storage, so that was a bust, but I used the opportunity to sidle over to Phoebe and get chatting, and eventually I got up the nerve to ask.

"Hey," I said, trying to sound as if an idea had just occurred to me, "you want to go into town a little later, maybe get a candy bar, kick around downtown?" I always felt stupid asking a woman out, like I was trying to trick her into something. I had issues, no question about it.

"Okay," she said. Just like that.

"Great," I said, trying to sound pleased but not surprised. "I'll come find you in a while?" Something like "pick you up at seven?" might have been clearer, but neither of us had a watch, and I wasn't really going to pick her up in anything.

I dry-brushed my teeth with a dollop of the tribe's toothpaste, then busied myself talking with my tribe, all the while feeling guilty about Sophia. I didn't understand the rules there, either. Could I see other women, given that she was married and we weren't sleeping together? I guess the bigger question was, did I want to? At the moment, yes, I did. I wanted to do something normal for a change. I wandered back over to get Phoebe.

She had put on lipstick and eyeliner, and lots of perfume. I felt a wave of gratitude that she would make the effort to look nice for our date.

"Ready to go?" I said.

She nodded, and we walked off, climbing the rise to the tracks and heading toward Metter.

We went through the "Where are you froms" and "What did you used to dos" (she had a Master's degree in English lit—another unfortunate soul who had followed her heart), then talked music and movies. She had an easy confidence about her that, instead of radiating "I'm out of your league," took me along, made me feel confident as well. I liked her, and felt happy that I was able to feel something for someone besides Sophia.

Which got me thinking about Sophia, got me wishing that I was laughing with Sophia. As we walked, my mind kept wandering away from Phoebe, and I kept struggling to bring it back.

We split a microwaved burrito at the Minute Mart, and bought candy bars for dessert. When she reached into her bag to get money, I offered to pay, but she said that she was happy to split it.

We sat on the curb in the parking lot among scattered cigarette butts, beside the air hose for inflating tires, as far away from the stink of the gasoline pumps as we could get.

A scrawny little Chihuahua came out from behind a green dumpster and started barking at me, flying backward with the force of his barks. He was half-starved, and seemed outraged that no one was feeding him. I broke off a piece of my Butterfinger and tossed it to him. He scarfed it down, then immediately took up barking again. He darted forward and nipped at my feet. Phoebe found this hilarious, especially the fact that he wasn't bothering her at all, just me.

When we'd finished I popped back inside to use the bathroom. It occurred to me on the way out that it would be nice if I bought Phoebe something—a little gift of some sort. It would have to be really cheap, but I didn't want to get her a toy, or gum. It should be something thoughtful.

A rack of postcards caught my eye. I spun them around, rejecting aerial views of Metter, pigs talking to each other. There was one with hula dancers—clearly a stock photo from Hawaii. The caption read *Everything's Better in Metter*. Perfect.

"I bought you a gift," I said as we started walking.

She took the card, examined it, and laughed. "It pictures the famed Metter hula dancing troupe! Thank you."

The sky was dark blue. We passed a dilapidated Cinema 9 (which was probably now in reality a Cinema 2 or 3—no way they were showing movies on all of those screens), and I wished we could afford to see a movie. The last movie I'd seen had been with Sophia, probably six months ago. I'd kissed her in the dark, and she'd kissed me back, then after a moment she'd whispered, "I shouldn't," and squeezed my hand, and we'd watched the movie.

Sophia's smiling face returned to its usual position, as the screensaver of my mind, and now I felt guilty—like I was misleading Phoebe, because there was no room in my heart for her and she didn't know that. If she liked me, she was probably worrying about making a good impression, hoping this could lead somewhere. But it couldn't. Not now, anyway.

As if on cue, my phone jingled. I'd forgotten to take the god damned thing out of my pocket before we left, because it had been as attached to me as my ears for the past year.

"Do you have a call?" Phoebe asked.

"Text message," I said. "I'll check it later."

"Wow, how does your tribe afford a phone?"

"For emergencies and stuff," I muttered.

Phoebe reached out and took my hand; our fingers laced together easily. We reached the railroad tracks and headed into thick darkness and nighttime insect sounds.

Telling a lie is kind of like having a piece of food caught between your teeth. I tried to simply forget it and enjoy the date, but the whole date felt like a lie now.

"You know that text message? I wasn't being honest about it."

"I kind of figured. People don't usually jerk when their phone rings."

"The truth is…" What? I'm seeing someone else? I'm having an affair? "I'm emotionally involved with someone."

I told her about Sophia. She was cool about it, very understanding. We talked about it as if we were friends, and after making some thoughtful comments and suggestions, she told me that she was still recovering from a painful breakup. She'd been dating a guy, and he left her a few months ago. He was a black guy, and her parents had disowned her and kicked her out of the house over it, so she and the guy left town and caught up with a tribe formed by some of his old high school friends. And now he was gone, and she had no one but the tribe.

"The ironic thing is, I don't even smoke weed," she said. "I barely drink. Not that I judge people who do, but I've always been pretty straight-laced, and I find myself in a tribe that gets by selling drugs."

"Here I had you pegged as a wild child, getting high and living by your own rules."

"I'm more the read a good book while drinking tea type." I liked the way she said "tea." There was a British lilt to it.

We walked in easy silence. Soon we could hear music drifting from the dual camps. It sounded like heavy metal.

Phoebe slowed, tugged me to a stop. "We should say goodnight here, before we have an audience."

I wrapped my arms around her, and we kissed—a good, soft, date kiss. She was a good kisser. Her breath was sour, but I'm sure mine was too, probably worse than hers. We were getting used to smelling bad and having bad breath.

"This was fun," she said. "Thanks for asking."

"Can I get in touch with you somehow? Maybe we could get together again?"

"Hold on." She squatted on the track to rummage in her bag. She pulled out a pen and a scrap of paper, jotted a number, and the name Crystal. "This is the number of a friend. It might take a few days, but I always check in with her eventually. I'll send a message back through her."

We walked into camp holding hands, let our fingers slip apart as we reached the midpoint between our tribes, and each went to join our own.

"So how'd it go?" Colin asked as soon as I sat in the flattened wild grass.

"She's a really, really nice woman," I said. I watched Phoebe, standing with a few of her tribe mates, probably discussing the date as well. "Sophia texted me right in the middle of the date. I forgot to turn off my phone."

"Not good," Colin said.

The music was coming from their camp, and some of them were dancing. The forty-something woman whose name I forgot pulled Phoebe by the elbow and got her dancing. She danced a little awkwardly, shyly, maybe because she felt self-conscious that I was watching.

"I should be interested in her, but I don't want to lose Soph."

"Um, you don't have Soph," Colin said. "She climbs into bed with her husband every night. You climb into your tent with your trusty right hand."

"I'm a lefty," I said, but the joke was reflex. I was stinging from the image of Sophia climbing into bed with her husband. I saw them kissing, his hand on her bare breast, couldn't get the movie in my head to stop, even though the image was like lit cigarettes pressed to my eyes.

"I have to stop seeing her, don't I?" I said. And there it was. I'd never said the words before; I hadn't even allowed myself to think them. But this was killing me, it was torture.

"Yeah," Colin said. "If she won't leave her husband, what do you have? Phone calls and text messages. That's never going to be enough."

I nodded, my eyes filling with tears.

"I'm not saying Sophia's a bad person," he said. "Obviously she's a very good person, trying to do her best. But you have to do what's best for you." He stood. "I can see you're about to need someone to hold you and rock you and tell you everything will be all right, and I'm sure you don't want that person to be me," Colin said.

He went over to Ange, squatted beside her and said something. Ange looked over at me, then sprung up and headed my way. I was crying like a baby before she reached me, arms out, ready to enfold me.

"It's been almost two years," she said as she held me, "you don't want to turn around one day and realize ten years have passed, and you're still waiting by the phone. You're a wonderful guy. You deserve a whole person, not one you have to share."

But the whole person I wanted was Sophia.

"After you broke up with Tyler, how long did it take you to get over him?" I asked, speaking into her neck, which was wet with my tears.

"I never got over him. It got less painful, but even now, those emotions come crashing down sometimes, and it's like we just broke up."

I think everyone has a Sophia. When Ange first told me about Tyler, who she fell in love with when she was sixteen, she'd said "Don't get me wrong, I love Cortez, but Tyler, he sunk to my bones."

When you fall in love, really fall in love, the stakes are so high.

I took a walk down the tracks and called Sophia. She said she couldn't talk, which meant her husband was there.

"Can you take a walk. I really need to talk."

She was quiet for a long time. I knew she could hear in my tone, in my plugged up nose, that something was very wrong.

"I know what you're going to say. I don't want to hear it."

"I'm sorry," I said. "I'm so sorry."

I heard her close her front door. "Please don't," she said. She was crying, which made me cry harder. "You're the only thing in my life that makes me happy."

We talked for hours. I said if she was never going to leave him (I could never say his name, I just called him "him"), what was the point? She said she didn't know what the point was, she didn't need a point, she just needed to hear my voice every day. I told her we were just torturing ourselves.

In the end, she said she understood, but she still didn't want me to go. We told each other "I love you" about fifty times. And then I held a dead phone.

You go a little crazy after a breakup; you know you're a little crazy, that your thinking is all askew and can't be trusted, but you can't do anything about it besides wait it out. I've learned it's best not to make any substantive decisions during this time, because they're mostly going to turn out to be bad ones.

So I followed my tribe, one foot in front of the other, feeling bleak, tortured by guilt at the thought of the pain I was causing Sophia, knowing I could stop it by calling her and saying I was sorry and wanted things back the way they'd been.

We headed toward Vidalia, working rivers along the way with our hydropower collectors, roadsides with our windmills, spread solar blankets whenever we stopped and the sun was out.

"Nietzsche said 'What doesn't kill you, makes you stronger,'" Jim said to me as we slogged along another trash-strewn roadside.

"Yeah, right," I said. "How about radiation?"

Bob Marley came on the portable radio Cortez was carrying. I went over and stabbed the power button as that aching sadness ripped through me. Marley was one of Sophia's favorites. Cortez looked at me funny, but didn't say anything. They were all cutting me a wad of slack.

I'd loved Marley long before I met Soph. We used to play it during our high school poker games. That got me thinking of my folks, who put up with our loud late-night poker games in their basement, who had died in the water riots in Arizona. I turned the power back on. She couldn't have Bob Marley.

Cracks of gunfire sounded in the distance, and a police siren. Or maybe an ambulance siren. It occurred to me that I couldn't tell the difference. I looked around for Colin. The Winn-Dixie was getting close; I decided there wasn't enough time to get into the nuances of sirens.

The Winn Dixie was almost empty. Cortez and Jim and I went in—they were less likely to refuse our business if there were only a few of us. The sole woman at the row of checkout counters looked agitated as we pushed open the electric doors, but she didn't say anything. We set about shopping.

"Hey, what about these?" Cortez said, holding up a package of Oreos.

"We should stick to the list," Jim said, closing his eyes as he spoke—a classic Jim mannerism. "We can't afford to buy empty calories."

Cortez tossed them back on the shelf, huffing. "We've got to enjoy ourselves a little, or we might as well be dead."

A shrill voice up by the registers grabbed our attention. We hurried to the front of the aisle to see what was going on.

The checkout girl was tossing stuff into a cart, and she looked scared as hell.

"Stay!" she shouted, pointing at a woman standing near the entrance. "Don't come in, just stay!" The woman looked like she was in excruciating pain—she was moaning and gasping for breath, weaving noticeably, her hands dangling loosely at her sides.

"Jesus, what's wrong with her?" Cortez whispered.

"Here." The checkout girl pushed the shopping cart toward the woman. It rattled along part of the way, then veered into a cake mix display, knocking boxes to the floor. "Just take it and leave!"

The woman took a flaccid, spastic step toward the cart, then another. It was horrible, the way she walked. Her teeth were gritted in pain, her cheeks wet. She latched onto the cart, used it to steady herself as she jerked slowly, slowly toward the door.

Cortez ran to get the door for her.

"Are you crazy?" checkout girl screamed. "Stay away from her!" Cortez's sneakers screeched on the linoleum as he stopped short.

"What's wrong with her?" he asked.

"Just get out of here before I call the police."

"Fine, fine, we're going," I said. "But we need this stuff." It wasn't half of what we needed. "Just let us check out first."

"Twenty bucks. Leave it on the counter and go," she said without looking into the cart Jim was pushing. Cortez pulled a twenty out of the pocket of his jeans and dropped it on the counter. The checkout girl was looking off to one side, tears in her eyes, biting her bottom lip.

The rest of the tribe was resting in the shade of a Dollar Store.

"We need to get out of here," Cortez said to them, running ahead of Jim and me. "There's a virus here. A woman came in, she looked like a zombie—"

"Filthy gypsies! You did this." A skinny man with long hair and a Confederate flag t-shirt appeared around the corner of the building, from the front lot. He had the same horribly loose walk and agonized expression as the woman in the grocery store. And he had a pistol. My bowels loosened as he lifted it, his hand trembling viciously. Someone screamed.

"Kill you all. Every fucking last…"

The gun dropped from his rubbery grip and clattered to the pavement. He cried out in frustration, glared at us like we were the devil. Then he bent to retrieve the pistol and collapsed. He lay cursing, his nose and cheek bloody from pavement burn.

We ran. Carrie had grown up in Vidalia, and led us out behind the Dollar Store, through a small patch of woods and into a neighborhood. A few streets away there was a railroad track that would get us out of sight in a hurry.

"What *was* that?" Jeannie said.

"They're like zombies," Cortez said. "I swear, they move like zombies in a George Romero film."

"It's some sort of neurological disease," Jim said. "But a highly contagious neurological disease? I've never heard of such a thing."

Through the open window of a little yellow house, we heard

screaming. They were screams of agony—mindless, full-throated howls.

"This way," Carrie said, cutting between two houses. Weeds tugging at our ankles, we trotted, humping our packs, Colin and Jeannie bringing up the rear on the bikes.

Across the next street and down a ways was a little park crowded with a dozen people. They were wearing white masks and gloves, and they were filling a freshly dug hole with bodies wrapped in sheets. We cut straight across, running as fast as we could manage.

"Gypsies!" someone shouted from the park. Gunshots cracked. I heard that twanging ricochet sound you always hear in the movies. The railroad tracks were across the next street. We ran along the tracks, into the woods, glancing back and seeing no pursuit. We kept running until we were out of sight of the road.

We pitched camp below the track, then sat in a tight circle in the dark. Everyone was quiet, lost in their own thoughts. A siren keened in the distance.

"We have to stay out of towns as much as possible," Jeannie said. "That other tribe we camped with out here, they were much better at living in the wilderness than we are. We need better survival skills."

"That's not our thing," Cortez said. "We work the towns. We can't sell energy to squirrels."

"I don't think we can do that much longer. Our contacts are drying up. I think Jeannie's right," Colin said.

"There are two worlds now, and that one isn't ours," I said. I felt a falling sensation in my stomach. It wasn't ours any more. It really wasn't.

"We have to stop buying all our food at 7-Elevens," Jeannie said. "We have to start buying guns and fishing gear with the money we earn, not cell phone minutes."

"I'm not paying for the phone," I said.

"I know," she said. "I just mean we have to get tougher."

Tougher. I hated tough people. But she was right; if we didn't change we were going to die.

It had been a long, shitty day. We climbed into our tents as soon as it was dark.

I felt so utterly alone in my tent, even with my tribe all around me. Sleeping in tents in the woods was so different from sleeping in tents in town. The wild was an alien creature; a stark, silent reminder that there was no one to take care of us, that we were living in a ruthless world that would think nothing of it if we all died tonight. The crickets outside sounded metallic. I wanted to call Sophia so, so badly.

I threw my blanket off and crawled outside. It was too dark to go for a walk, so I stood in the middle of our little camp, staring at the stars through the dark treetops.

"I wouldn't want to be out there, dating again." I started a little. Cortez was sitting ten feet away, on a fallen tree trunk at the edge of camp.

"It's rough," I said, not really wanting to talk about my dating life with Cortez. Still, I went over and stood near him, not wanting our conversation to wake the others.

"It's not just that," Cortez said. "I've got the white man's curse." He held his hand up, his fingers three inches apart. I didn't understand. "I was always a nervous wreck the first time I had sex with a woman, because I wondered if she was laughing inside, when she first saw it."

Then I understood. I stumbled for a reply. "Wow. I can see how that would be nerve-wracking." Was he saying what I thought he was saying? Could he possibly be telling me something that personal? I wouldn't tell anyone, not even Colin, if I had a small dick.

And suddenly, I liked Cortez. He would probably risk his life for me if it came down to it. He was part of my tribe. I should cut him the same slack he cut me.

"Yeah, well. We all got our crosses to bear," he said, standing and brushing the seat of his pants. "Try to get some sleep if you can."

"Cortez," I said, holding out my hand. He took it, squeezed it hard. "Good talking to you, man."

I got up early, when the world was still a little gray. Everyone else was still asleep. I sat on the ground and looked through my photo album, at pictures of when I was a little boy. Mom and Dad on the teacup ride at Disney World, sunburned and laughing; Sis on the front lawn in her purple majorette outfit; me, missing a front tooth, at the plate in t-ball.

A woman hurried past our camp, up on the railroad tracks. She looked too scared to be out for exercise, but she was too clean to be a gypsy, and had no stuff with her.

"Hey!" I called to her quickly receding butt. "You all right?"

She glanced back, jolted to a stop. She stood panting, hands on hips, as if she wasn't sure if she was all right or not, or maybe she wasn't sure if she could trust me.

"We're harmless," I said, holding up my photo album as if it was proof of this.

She paused another heartbeat, then climbed down the slope to our camp. She was small, with an eager, slightly aggressive look. She stopped about twenty feet from me.

"What are you doing out here by yourself?" I asked.

"Are you coming from Vidalia?" she said. I nodded. "I'm from Vidalia. I'm getting as far away as I can."

Some of the other tribe members poked their heads out of the tents to see who I was talking to.

She was a doctor. Another doctor in town had tried to pack up and leave when things started getting ugly, and now he was sleeping in the city jail when he wasn't treating patients. She'd bolted before dawn, taking nothing that might raise suspicion if anyone saw her. She said her name was Eileen.

She told us that the virus acted like polio, but spread like influenza. The victims slowly lost feeling, starting in the extremities. If paralysis reached the torso, they suffocated.

"It's horrible, you have no idea," she said. "Half the town has it. Young children and old people usually die. Stronger people survive, but end up paralyzed. People are either leaving town or holing up to avoid being exposed. There aren't enough people to bring food and water to the infected, so the victims have to go outside to find food and water, until they can't any more. Then they die of dehydration."

I poured her half a Styrofoam cup of water, walked it halfway and put it down. Eileen thanked me and retrieved it. She held it with two hands as she drank, to stop the cup from shaking.

"There was nothing I could do," she said. "I can't help them! This is not a normal virus; it spreads too fast. It's got to be engineered."

"Who would engineer something like that?" Colin asked.

Eileen shrugged.

"Could be insurgents looking to overthrow the government. Or the government," Jim said.

"Look, can I buy supplies from you? I have cash," Eileen said.

We sold Eileen some things, and she went on her way.

Around midday we began to hear gunfire—not the occasional shots we'd become used to, but sustained automatic weapons fire. Military gunfire. We looked at each other, confused.

"Oh, jeez," Colin said. "They're cleaning out Vidalia."

I could picture it—soldiers in yellow hazmat suits, going door to door, killing everyone. That's exactly how this government would deal with the outbreak.

We reached Statesboro by late afternoon. Cortez and Charlie volunteered to try buying supplies at Wal-Mart while the rest of us went downtown to sell energy to some of our reliable trading partners.

Getting downtown meant winding through a series of what used to be middle-class neighborhoods. It was hard to figure out what to call the classes now, though. There was the starving, the almost starving (us), the dirt poor, the poor, and (as there always are) the filthy rich.

We passed a group of kids playing immigration and illegals. The kids playing the illegals jabbered in mock-Spanish as they were handcuffed with plastic six-pack rings and taken away.

A guy in a sweat-drenched t-shirt came out of his garage and stared at us, his arms folded across his chest.

"What do you want here?" he called.

"We're here to mow your lawn," Ange said. An old joke, but a few in our tribe laughed anyway.

"Move on, you fucking gypsies, no one wants whatever you're selling," the guy shot back. He was wearing those black hipster-doofus glasses that were big fifteen years ago.

Ange gave him the finger.

"When did lawn mower jokes start?" I asked Colin.

"Hmm." He thought about it. "I'm gonna say the summer of '19. Really poor people stopped mowing a couple years earlier, but that year was the biggie. I think the first jokes were about watering lawns though—" Colin stopped walking. "Oh shit."

Two more men had come out of the garage, clutching rifles. One of them tossed an empty beer can into the weeds and stormed up the driveway.

"You think you're funny?" he said, getting right in Ange's face, blocking her from continuing. This guy wasn't wearing glasses; he had muscles, and a swagger. Everything about him screamed "angry war veteran."

Ange didn't say anything.

"Well?" the guy said. "You think you're funny?" He smacked her across the face, hard.

Barely skipping a beat, Ange spat in his face. From thirty feet away I could see rage light up the guy's eyes as he wiped a spot just under his eye with the back of his wrist.

"We're leaving now, we're leaving now," I said, edging toward them. "We're sorry." My heart raced as the guy turned his glare on me.

"You go right ahead and leave. That's a smart idea."

He grabbed Ange's wrist and yanked. She screamed, dug in her feet, clawed at the fingers clamped to her wrist.

We all ran to help her. The third man took a few quick steps forward, raised his rifle and aimed it at Colin's chest. Everyone stopped.

The guy with the glasses grabbed Ange's other flailing arm. They dragged her, screaming, down the driveway and up the concrete stoop. The third guy, a short, bald guy, backed toward the door, pointing his rifle at one of us, then another.

"If you know what's good for you, you'll move on," he said from the top step. He lowered the rifle and followed them into the house.

Inside, Ange screamed.

"Somebody help!" Jeannie cried. She was facing a scrum of onlookers that had formed across the street. None of them moved.

"Oh shit. What do we do?" Colin said.

"I don't know," I said. "We have to stop them. We have to."

Colin nodded. He was huffing like he was out of breath. "How?"

Inside, Ange screamed, "Let me go."

"Somebody call the police," Jeannie called.

"Already did. Five minutes ago," a teenaged girl said.

I scanned the street in both directions. Nothing. There was a bark of hoarse laughter inside the house. I took a few quick steps down the driveway.

"I wouldn't," someone shouted from across the street.

"There!" Jim shouted. A police car was heading toward us. We waved frantically at it; it seemed to be crawling.

The cruiser's side window opened. Cool air wafted out. "What's going on?" a cop in dark sunglasses asked calmly, looking us up and down.

We all answered at once, pointing at the house. Ange's screams were muffled, as if someone was holding a hand over her mouth.

"How many men?" the cop asked.

"Three," I said.

"Armed?"

I nodded. "At least two rifles. We have to hurry."

The cop shook his head. "Three armed men? You think I'm Wyatt Earp or something?"

"Please. Please officer," Jeannie said. "We'll help you."

He shook his head again. "You shouldn't of screwed around with them." He rolled up the window.

"Call for backup!" I shouted. The cruiser pulled away. Jeannie pounded on the back of it, pleading for him to stop.

I looked at Colin. Sweat was pouring down his filthy face. "We have to go in there," I said.

Colin nodded. "I know."

"What do we have to fight with?" Jim asked. He was standing at my shoulder.

"Here," Jeannie said, holding kitchen knives and utensils. I grabbed a black-handled butcher knife, my hand shaking.

There weren't enough knives for everyone. Jim grabbed a rusted shovel off the driveway, Edie grabbed a two-pronged barbecue fork out of Jeannie's outstretched hand.

"Some should go in the garage door," Colin said. "We need to hit them all at once." He looked at me. "We have to do this. We can't let up." He looked so scared. I nodded, not sure if I could do it for real. I wished Cortez was here. Cortez was the action guy, we were the sarcastic clowns.

We ran to the doors. I eased the screen door open, flinching as it squealed, and saw them in there. They were circled around Ange, who was on the dining room table; her shirt and bra were on the floor in pieces. One of the men had her arms pinned, another was tugging her jeans off as she thrashed and screamed. They were grinning, joking, taking their time. A part of my mind kept insisting this was a movie, but the knife felt so real in my sweaty fist.

The guy with the glasses looked our way and shouted a warning. He grabbed the rifle leaning against the table. I froze in the doorway.

"Go," Colin said. I went.

Jim came crashing through the side door, shovel raised. The guy swung the rifle around just as Jim hit him. The rifle went off, but missed.

I reached the bald guy just as he got his hand on the other rifle, and stabbed him near the collar bone, felt the knife sink.

He screamed. I couldn't believe I'd just stabbed someone. He raised his free hand to ward off the knife and I stabbed again—hard this time—down through his hand, slicing between two fingers. The knife sunk halfway to his wrist.

They're so sharp, I thought.

He shouted something, but I didn't understand because it was garbled and wet. Edie was behind him, and the barbecue fork was in his back. The guy's split, bloody hand hit me in the face as he turned. He dropped to one knee, then fell, scrabbling on the floor like a roach sprayed with insecticide.

I spun and saw Jim slam the shovel down on the back of the struggling war vet's head. Jeannie was on the vet's back, trying to hold him down. There were a half-dozen bloody wounds in his back. Both Jim and Jeannie were crying hysterically. Jim brought the shovel down again and the vet lay still.

Colin and Carrie and Ange were staring down at the third guy. The plastic hilt of a steak knife was buried in his throat, in that spot where you give people tracheotomies. There was a spray of blood across Colin's face. There was blood everywhere. The TV, which was playing a DVD of some stupid comedy, was splashed with it. The bricks on the fireplace were speckled with it. A framed picture of a clean-cut family was lying on the floor, drenched in it.

We ran, past the dumbfounded stares of neighbors gathered on the sidewalk in front of the house.

"I keep thinking of *Lord of the Flies*," I said as we walked.

"We didn't have a choice," Colin said. His wavery tone was not terribly convincing.

Jeannie was taking it the hardest. She cried and cried. Her eyes looked haunted.

No animal instinct had taken over as we stormed that house. We had remained a bunch of scared suburban college graduates doing the last thing in the world we could ever imagine doing. *We have to get tougher*, Jeannie had said a million years ago. Well, we were tougher. Hooray for us.

My phone jingled; a rope of adrenaline ripped through me, clearing my sinuses and sending my heart racing.

I'm sorry. I know you asked me not to. Have news! Call me? Miss you so much.

Can't. Not right now.

The phone jingled again within seconds.

Pls meet me? Pls? It's important.

I was aching to see her, but I couldn't face her. I couldn't tell her what we'd done.

Another time. Soon.

A moment later, it jingled again.

And then again.

I need to see u!

We arranged to meet.

I read the messages over a few times, the way I always read Sophia's messages, looking for nuances I might be missing, drinking in every last scrap of meaning. Then I put the phone away.

I don't have much of a poker face. Before I'd even gotten in her car I was crying. She held me close, waited while I told her between sobs.

She told me we'd had no choice, that we'd done the right thing. She said she would have gone in with us to save Ange if she'd been there. But she hadn't been there; she hadn't stabbed people while they screamed. There was so much distance between intent and action. I'd had no idea how much until I had to act.

The screensaver in my mind no longer held a picture of a beautiful smiling Sophia, it held a screaming man, his hand sliced between two fingers, nearly to the wrist.

"I have a job interview arranged for you in Savannah. It's not much, just working in a convenience store, but it's a start." She was so remarkably clean, her clothes so crisp and new.

"I can't leave my tribe," I said. "They need me now; we need to stick together."

"No," she said, pulling me to her, holding me tight. "You have to come to Savannah. You can help them more that way. You can get an apartment and they can all stay with you and look for jobs."

You can get an apartment. Not "we." Three's a crowd, after all.

"I can't leave them now."

"How will any of you ever get out of this if you refuse to ever separate?"

"I don't know."

She pressed the interview information into my hand. "Just go to it."

I took my phone out of my pocket and held it out. "I'll always love you, Sophia. Always."

Fresh tears rolled out of her dark eyes. "No. I don't want it."

"I can't answer it any more."

"So don't answer it."

I kissed her, long and deep, and for the first time since we'd been in that movie theater, she let me. Then I got out of her car and headed into the woods to find my tribe.

So don't answer it, she'd said. But I knew I would. If she called, I'd answer.

There was a cypress swamp below the tracks, trees with roots like melting wax, branches draped in Spanish moss. I threw the phone in a high arc. It ricocheted off a tree and splashed in the brown water.

Chapter 2:
Art Show

Fall, 2024 (Eighteen months later)

The buttery-sweet smell of the candy bars made me a little nuts as I stacked them in the wire receptacles near the register. I fantasized about squatting behind the counter, out of sight of Amos the Enforcer, and scarfing a few down. But I couldn't afford to lose my job, and besides, I couldn't steal from Ruplu. Weird as it was to have a nineteen-year-old boss, the guy was gold, and I owed him for hiring me. Plus my momma taught me not to steal.

Having so many different colorful packages in my line of sight hurt my brain after a while. Racks of chips and crackers, gums and sodas, cigarettes and beer, energy packs and water filters, magazines, 3-D porn—there was barely a square foot of blank space for my eyes to rest on.

Amos stared out the window, arms folded, pistol tucked into his belt.

"How's it going, Amos?" I said.

"Just fine. Just fine," he said without turning his head. Amos wasn't much on talking. His qualifications for the job seemed to be that he owned a gun and was eager to use it.

The door jingled. An incredibly skinny woman came in, her hair so white it looked blonde, two fingers clutching a cigarette. She wandered the aisles, whispering to herself. From behind, you could easily mistake her for a girl in her twenties. If you did, her shrunken, wrinkled, toothless face would give you a jolt when she turned around. She walked with the knock-kneed energy of a godflash addict, which she probably was. She grabbed a packet of malted milk balls and brought them to the counter.

"I'm doing fine," she said, holding out a five, taking a pull on her cigarette, not noticing that I hadn't actually asked.

"That's good to hear," I said, handing back her change. Amos watched her go, alert to any sign of a grab and dash.

Another woman put a box of tampons on the counter, opened her overstuffed purse and dug through it.

"Twelve seventy-six," I said. It still felt strange to hear my voice say convenience store cashier things, to watch my hands accept payment and make change from the register. I had figured I was done with these sorts of jobs the day I graduated from Emory.

The woman gave an exasperated sigh, pulled a couple of things out of her purse and set them on the counter: Wallet. Key ring. Heat Taser. She continued searching.

"Wouldn't your money be in the wallet?" I asked.

She smiled. "You'd think so, but no." Her bra strap was hanging out of her shirt sleeve. "Um, could you put that in a bag?" she said without looking up.

It took me a second to get why she was asking me to do what I was obviously going to do in a moment anyway. A seven a.m. purchase of tampons at a convenience store. Emergency. She didn't relish everyone in the store knowing about her urgent feminine needs. "Oh." I snared a plastic bag from under the counter and stuffed the tampons into it. "Sorry."

"Thanks."

"No problem."

"Ah!" She handed me a twenty.

"I guess there are certain items that need to be bagged immediately," I said as I snared coins out of the till with two fingers.

"Yes. Tampons, pregnancy kits…"

"Pornography," I offered.

"Good one," she said, pointing at me. She was pretty in a slightly harsh, Eastern European sort of way. Dirty-blonde hair, her front teeth crooked but white. A little older than me, thirty-three or so.

I tried to think of something else to say, but my mind was suddenly a vast wasteland. I thought we were flirting. I was pretty clueless when it came to flirting, but I thought maybe we were, and I was dropping the ball.

"Do you live around here?" she asked.

"About four blocks away, on East Jones," I said, silently counting the bills into her hand. "Where do you live?"

"Southside."

"Wow, you're far from home." Southside was a good four miles away. Usually I was leery about long-distance relationships, but it was so easy to look into her blue eyes; it felt like I could go hours without blinking if I could just keep looking into them.

"I was in class. SCAD."

The Savannah College of Art and Design. Great reputation, outrageous tuition, no scholarships. Rich girl. I was probably misinterpreting polite kindness for flirtatious interest, given my station in life. I was wearing a name tag, for god's sake.

"What are you studying?" I asked.

"Graphic design. Change of career—I worked in corporate recruiting for ten years."

"Interesting." There was another awkward pause. She hovered, waited for me to say something. The only other customers in the store were puttering in the back, searching for just the right flavor of Gatorade. Amos was staring into the street, watching for marauders.

"You ever make your way down here at night, to see bands or anything?" I asked. Why not, what did I have to lose?

"No. Too rough around here at night. I tend to hang out in Southside."

"Mmm," I said. If she knew the question was meant to test the waters, she wasn't biting.

"You should come to Southside some time," she said, shrugging the shoulder that had lost its bra strap.

"Where would I go, if I came to Southside?"

She shrugged and smiled. "Snowstorm is fun."

"You think you'll be hanging out at Snowstorm Saturday night?"

"Possibly," she said as she slung her purse over her shoulder. She waved, winked, and headed for the door. I was impressed—almost no one can wink without it seeming hokey and contrived, but she pulled it off.

My nineteen-year-old boss appeared on the sidewalk outside; he and the girl whose name I forgot to ask passed each other in the doorway.

"Hello, hello," Ruplu said, grinning as he joined me behind the counter. "All is well?"

I nodded.

"Good. It's payday. How many hours did you put in this week?" He opened the register.

I never had to remind Ruplu it was payday. "Forty-four," I said. He counted two hundred forty-two dollars onto the counter. It was amazing, the way the guy trusted me. It was reckless. Lots of people thought they were reckless—fast drivers, kick boxers—but trusting a stranger to tell you how many hours he'd worked, that was truly reckless, and I admired him for it.

I namaste'd Ruplu and headed for the exit, squeezing the bills inside my pocket and fighting back tears. I tended to cry on payday. The first time Ruplu counted out those bills I blubbered like a babe. A job. My parents would've found a way to be proud, even if the job did involve mopping floors and stacking tins of sardines.

I'd known I was going to miss my parents terribly when they died, but I didn't realize *how* I'd miss them. When something interesting happened, one of my first thoughts used to be how I had to call my folks in Arizona and fill them in. They had been omnipresent observers to the unfolding of my life. That day three years ago, when my sister called to tell me they'd been killed in a water riot, it was as if my third eye had been shut. No one was watching over my shoulder any more.

The street smelled damp and vaguely fecal. It had rained earlier; the people camped on the sidewalks were wet and miserable. Savannah was a magnet, pulling people to its streets clutching filthy blankets and packs filled with whatever they could carry from whichever small town they'd come. It was a relief to no longer be one of them, to be able to bathe occasionally (even if the water was cold), and to change my clothes occasionally (even if the clothes came from the Salvation Army thrift shop). It was nice to be in a place where a professional woman might want to go out with me.

I cut through Chippewa Square—the center of the universe as far as my life was concerned—and passed through the shadow cast by General Oglethorpe's statue. A little boy was walking along the concrete skirting at the base of the statue, kicking garbage off it in a sort of game. Kids made me nervous—I had no idea what to say to them, didn't understand their language.

There are twenty-four town squares in Savannah, most canopied by stands of the Live Oaks dripping Spanish moss—but Chippewa Square had always been special to me. I stopped and sat for a moment on the bench where my parents had gotten engaged thirty years ago—a ritual I'd begun the day I learned that they'd died. Only a few dappled spots of sunlight filtered through the branches of the massive live oaks that canopied the square.

A pigeon wobbled up to me hopefully, like I might pull out a bag of breadcrumbs. When was the last time anyone had fed a pigeon? How did they still remember that we used to? After a minute it wandered away, pecking at pebbles and popsicle sticks.

I stood, letting my fingers linger for a moment on the rough wood of the bench. Time to go home. I crossed the street, out the other side of the square, and headed down Bull Street.

All of the houses on our block were in disrepair, but the one that housed our apartment took the cake. The celery-green plaster on number five East Jones was cracked in places, exposing the original brick beneath. Our iron railing was not as ornate as most in the neighborhood, and it was canted at an angle. A little historical plaque said the house had been built in 1850. The yellowed Neighborhood Watch sign in one of the first-floor windows—replete with silhouette of a cloaked burglar—was a nice touch.

The screen door squealed when I opened it. Colin was in the living room. "That virus is spreading." He motioned toward the TV.

As if Polio-X wasn't enough, now there was a flesh-eating virus to worry about. From the brief clips of victims on the news, it did not look pleasant, and the only way to treat it was to cut out the infected areas before it spread, which didn't sound pleasant either.

"If they ever catch the people who release these things, they should have them sodomized by Clydesdales on national TV," Colin said without a hint of a smile.

"Are they saying anything new?" Jeannie asked, gliding out of their bedroom. She stopped to stare at the screen of the old 2-D TV that'd been one of our first purchases after we'd saved enough for rent.

Colin muted the sound. "Just that it's not airborne, so masks aren't any help, and to wash your hands a lot," Colin said.

"Have they said any more about Great Britain and Russia?" I asked Colin.

"No. It's all about the virus."

Since the trade winds had sputtered last fall, the temperatures in Britain had been plummeting, and Britain was not taking kindly to Russia's decision to suspend all natural gas sales outside their borders. Britain's navy was cruising up and down Russia's border, and there had been some skirmishes. Britain had no chance in a war against Russia unless others jumped in, but I guess with tens of thousands of their people freezing to death, they were desperate.

We'd become total news junkies since getting the TV. Hard not to be when something awful was always going on.

"Every day it's something else," Jeannie said. "I'm so tired of it."

"Things have to get better soon," I said.

"It's been years," Jeannie muttered. She went over to our little kitchen corner, opened the chest that served as a kitchen cabinet, and peered in. "Does anyone mind if I eat a couple of rice cakes and some peanut butter?"

"No problem," I said. It probably wasn't necessary any more, to get an okay before you ate something, but it was a habit from our tribe days that we couldn't quite shake.

Colin switched off the TV. "Jasper, what do you think about running the a/c for ten minutes before we go to sleep? Jeannie and I were thinking it would be worth it, to have it cool to get to sleep."

I shrugged. "Sounds good to me." We were getting by; I guess we could afford to buy a little more energy.

It was a long bike ride to Southside, but I had plenty of time.

I headed up Bull Street, cutting through the middle of the squares, looking at all the houses that used to be pretty when I was a kid. They called this the Historic District back then; it used to be the most expensive part of Savannah. Now they just called it downtown.

I tried not to reminisce about my life before things went bad, but sometimes I couldn't resist. It's hard to stifle memories when everything around you is heavy with your past. How could I walk down Bolton Street, past the house where I'd grown up, without seeing my dad washing his truck in the driveway? We'd been in Clary's diner the night I told my parents I was switching my major from business to sociology. There'd been a baseball card store on the corner of Whitaker and York where John Kelly—who'd been my best friend in sixth grade—and I would buy twenty-year-old packs of baseball cards and open them on his stoop, our hands shaking, hoping to pull out a valuable rookie card. It was almost inconceivable now, the luxury of blowing fifteen bucks on a pack of baseball cards, but back then there always seemed to be enough money, an endless flow that just showed up from Mom's purse, or from doing some easy afterschool job. Looking back, it seemed as if everyone was well-off; even the poorest kids could afford to buy a Big Mac at McDonald's.

I stopped, dropped one foot to the pavement at the entrance to one of the alleys that stretched behind every row of houses as the roar and rattle of a muffler announced that a decrepit Volvo was pulling out. An old woman in the passenger seat looked at me, nervous eyes peering behind wire-rimmed glasses, her head bobbing a palsied rhythm.

The alley was scattered with homeless shelters. That's what people had taken to calling the big green trash cans stamped *City of Savannah* that now mostly lay on their sides with people's feet sticking out of them, amid heaps of trash and lumps of fly-ridden shit.

I didn't dare cut through Forsyth Park, so I took the sidewalk along Whitaker. The tic tic tic of a central a/c unit caught my attention. I marveled at the sound, at the audacious expenditure of energy, cooling all of the rooms in an apartment at once. The shift in ambient sound was subtle as you moved uptown, the proportion of popping gunshots to humming machinery changing with each block.

Screams of a man in terrible pain burst from an open second-story window. I pedaled faster—thinking of the reports of the flesh-eating virus and silently wished the poor bastard well.

I hadn't been to Southside in a long time. Very little had changed. In fact, if anything it looked nicer than it had the last time I'd been there. Through the tall steel gates surrounding the passing neighborhoods I could see that some of the lawns were mowed. I didn't venture too close to the gates, lest some private police take offense at my shabby clothes (the best I owned, for my trip to Southside), and beat me for being in the wrong part of town.

A car honked behind me. I moved to the side of the road and it whooshed past. I stayed by the side—there were more cars on the road up here, even a few trucks and SUVs.

When choices have to be made between oil to fuel luxury cars and oil for fertilizer to feed starving people, the choice is obvious: the oil goes to fuel the cars. Now that energy was scarce, consuming it ostentatiously was a status symbol. Leaving your porch light on announced to the world that you could afford to leave your porch light on.

Sometimes I hated these people, who lived so comfortably while the rest of us barely got by. Maybe I hated them because I always figured I would be one of them, I don't know. We had nothing, and they had so much more than they needed. But they were just people, doing what people do, which is to try to keep what they have.

It cost me eight bucks to get into Snowstorm. If I hadn't biked five miles to get there, I wouldn't have paid it, and as it was I felt guilty. I didn't have any business spending that kind of money when Jeannie was asking permission to eat some peanut butter. I went through big double doors and up a ramp that led to the club.

I couldn't believe my eyes. I'd stepped into the Alps. There were ski slopes that rose out of sight, piles of snow all over, snowmen with drinks clutched in frozen hands. People were dancing on a frozen pond. It had to be holographic, but it was so perfect, so solid, that it took my breath away. I made a conscious effort to keep my yokel mouth from dropping open and strolled through the place like I'd seen it all before, but I hadn't. I hadn't realized how much the world was still progressing. Even through this awful time, people were still inventing things. I just wasn't seeing it, just like people in third world countries never saw it.

There were cool rich kids everywhere, their hairstyles as varied as the flavors at Baskin Robbins: dreadlocks and Mohawks, Betty Page cuts, pigtails, red-and-white barber pole specials.

There was an Alpine bar perched in the corner thirty feet above the floor, on an icy cliff. It didn't appear to be a holo, because the guys sitting at the bar weren't that attractive. It looked like the place I'd be most comfortable. I watched a dude with blond little-Dutch-boy hair step on a steel plate that lifted him up to the bar, and I followed suit.

I took a stool next to a guy in his sixties with droopy red eyes and thinning white hair. There was a TV mounted among the bottles behind the bar, tuned to MSNBC. They were showing refugees pouring into California from Arizona and New Mexico.

"I just came from there," the guy said, to no one in particular.

"From California?" I asked.

"Arizona," he said.

"I've heard things aren't good in Arizona."

"It's bad in Arizona," he said.

A big-eared guy in a business suit turned around. "It's bad everywhere, man," he said.

The old guy fixed him with a shaky stare, his face a little blue from the flickering TV screen. "Mister, you got no idea what bad is. You want bad? There's no water there. None. Everyone with a car left months ago. They drove right over the bodies lying in the—"

"Okay! All right! Shut the fuck up, will you?" The guy turned away. "Christ in heaven."

"It's bad in Arizona," the guy said, shaking his head. We sat quietly for a while, watching the soundless TV, listening to the music.

Most Americans hadn't known what suffering was until the depression of '13. In school we used to hear about the so-called "Great Depression," as if having a lot of unemployed people who were reasonably well-fed was this terrible holocaust. We were wimps. We're not any more—we've learned how to eat bitterness, as the Chinese say.

"I've heard things are even worse in China," I said.

"China?" the guy said. "Let 'em rot in hell. My nephew died over there. Let 'em rot." He took a drink, shook his head. "This isn't how things are supposed to be. I had mutual funds for retirement. I had my house and my card games, money for whores."

I scanned the crowd, looking for my SCAD woman, but instead my attention was drawn toward a black woman on the ice pond dance floor, her hands over her head, her hips gyrating in tight circles.

Sophia.

She was dancing with two other women, gyrating her hips frenetically—whining, they called it on the islands. She looked incredible.

I went back to ground level, heart in my throat, and threaded through the crowd. As I approached, the music changed suddenly, from contemporary to Island Thump, as if I'd walked through an invisible membrane that held in sound. Another New Thing. I stopped a dozen feet from the dance floor and watched.

When she recognized me she stopped dancing, mouthed a silent "Oh my God." She didn't seem to know what to do. Finally, she came over.

"Hi."

"Hi," I said. "What are the odds?"

"I don't know, I'm not good at math," she said, breathless from dancing, her nostrils flaring like a colt's. "I'm nervous. My legs are shaking."

"Mine too."

"How're you?"

"Much better. Thank you for getting me the job. It changed our lives. Jeannie found a little work too, at a salvage center, stripping parts. Colin gets work on the docks sometimes."

"That's wonderful!" Sophia smiled, but there was distress in her eyes. I'd imagined this moment a hundred times. Now I couldn't think of anything of substance to say.

"I'm sorry things worked out the way they did," I said.

She shrugged. "Life is. What are you gonna do?"

"I guess."

A tall, slim black man in a white silk shirt approached us holding two drinks in tall flute glasses. "Do you want another?" he said to Sophia.

"Oh, thanks," she said, taking it. "Um, Jasper, this is Jean Paul." Her husband was five inches taller than me, and better looking.

I nodded. He stared back with a smirk. "My mipwi," he said.

"What does that mean?" I asked, looking to Sophia.

"It means," she considered for a moment, "his competition."

How the hell was I supposed to respond to that? Jean Paul smirked down at me. "So, did you follow my wife here?" He didn't open his mouth wide enough when he talked. It made him seem shifty. You couldn't trust someone who rarely lets you see his front teeth.

"I'm meeting someone," I said. "I have a date." I scanned the bar, praying for a sign of the SCAD woman so I could escape from this nightmare with some dignity. Sophia was managing a smile, but looked uncomfortable as hell. I stared hard at a woman tucked in a nearby booth, with three other women. Her hair was up, but I thought it looked like her. I'd only seen her once for a minute or so. She turned a little and I got a better look: yes, that was her.

"There she is," I said. I told Sophia it was good to see her, nodded tightly to her husband, and headed for the table, feeling their eyes on me. The music shifted again, to an old Carbon Leaf song. My dad used to love Carbon Leaf.

"Hello," I said, standing over the table. All four women looked at me.

"Oh, hi," she said. She was dressed in a long, white peasant dress with ruffles on the sleeves. She looked good.

"Thought I'd check out your hangout," I said.

"Right. How are you?" she said, not making any attempt to stand.

"Good, great. How are you?"

"Fine. How'd you get out here?"

I shrugged. "Bike."

"Great. Well, it was good seeing you again." She turned back toward her friends.

I hovered for a second, then I turned. Sophia's husband was watching. He said something in Sophia's ear; she glanced at me, said something back to Jean Paul, frowning, and turned to join her friends at a bar tucked into a snowbank.

I glanced back toward the table where my "date" was sitting, in the feeble hope that I'd misinterpreted her brush-off and she would suddenly be interested in me the way she'd been at the convenience store. She kept her gaze pointed straight across the table, toward her friends. Why had she struck up that conversation with me? What was the wink about, if I wasn't worth a lousy five-minute conversation? Was she embarrassed to admit she knew me in front of her friends?

I walked back over to her table. Finally, she looked up at me. I cast about for a clever put-down, but my mind had gone blank.

"I can't help wondering why you invited me here," I finally said.

"I didn't invite you. I don't even know you." She gave me the lip curl, the one that said I was a pathetic pest.

I puffed out a sarcastic breath. "Yeah."

The woman across the table from her stood and gestured past me. "Mickey!"

A second later a guy dressed in a black t-shirt was at my elbow.

"He's harassing us," the girl said, pointing at me.

"I am not," I protested.

Without a word the guy grabbed me by the neck and the elbow and yanked me away from the table. I tried to yank free, shouted at him to let go as he propelled me through the bar, toward the red exit sign in the corner. Everyone in the bar was staring. I spotted Jean Paul, laughing. Sophia stood next to him, her head down. The bouncer shoved me through the door, into the sticky-hot air of the street. Two girls hanging out on the sidewalk laughed as I lurched forward before regaining my balance. The door slammed closed behind me.

I unchained my bike from the rack and pushed off into the street, watched the road wind under my front wheel, my face still red. I swerved to avoid the porcelain remnants of a shattered toilet, ran over a fast food paper cup.

My hands on the handlebars looked strange, unfamiliar. I felt vaguely numb, and wished there was some way to wash away that feeling.

Jean Paul was probably still laughing. Sophia hadn't even tried to intervene. My only solace was that I would probably never see either of them again.

Bright lights and voices on a side street caught my attention. I took a right and rolled by a little crowd lounging outside a freshly painted storefront with big windows. It was an art opening. Christ, there were still art openings uptown.

What the hell. I didn't want to go home, didn't want to hear Colin ask "How'd it go?" I didn't want to recount the humiliation that even now made it hard for me to look passing strangers in the eye. I needed to get lost in distraction for a while. I pulled onto the curb, chained my bike to a street sign, and wandered in through the wide open door.

The gallery was a dimly lit, cavernous room that had once been a dairy, or an auto showroom, or something like that. A line of ghostly, featureless, emaciated figures made of papier-mâché were mounted to the high concrete walls. The figures were all facing the back of the gallery, and were posed as if they were moving, marching toward some faraway destination that they did not have the strength to reach. It was an eerie scene, lifelike despite the otherworldly look of the anonymous figures. They reminded me of my tribe, and made me wonder what I was thinking, coming to this part of town thinking a SCAD woman was interested in dating me.

There was a commotion at the front of the gallery. I turned to see a priest standing in the doorway holding an assault rifle in one hand, an unlit cigar in the other. He looked like he was part East Indian or Arab. His dyed white hair was set in a sumo wrestler's bun.

"Outside. Everyone outside," he said, waving the rifle in a sweeping motion toward the back of the room.

The people nearest him scurried away. I retreated into the shadows at the back of the gallery. There were stacks of folding tables and chairs in the corner—I considered trying to hide behind them, but it wasn't much of a hiding place. A woman cried out.

"Everyone out the back door!" the priest said.

The back door flew open and everyone poured out. I followed, into a dark alley.

There were two men waiting in the alley wearing round gas masks over mouth and nose.

"Against the wall," one shouted, gesturing with a gas gun. He was dressed in an old-fashioned army officer's uniform—epaulets on the shoulders and color-coded commendations embroidered on his chest. The other was dressed in a mailman's uniform. I stood facing the brick wall.

"What's happening?" a woman sobbed.

"Shut up. Turn around. Face the wall," the mailman said. He wasn't really a mailman—I'd heard stories about a gang, a violent political movement called the Jumpy-Jumps, who dressed in outfits and hurt people, and these guys fit the bill.

I heard the guy dressed as a priest come out the back door. He said something I couldn't hear to the woman lined up closest to him. She murmured something back.

I only had three dollars on me. If these guys were robbing us, I wondered if they'd be angry that I didn't have more. I didn't have a watch or a ring, nothing of value.

I jumped at the sound of a gunshot. Others cried out, startled. I looked over and saw the woman crumple to the pavement, blood leaking from her temple. I turned my head the other way, pressed my cheek against the rough brick and stifled a sob.

"God, what is this?" a man said. I couldn't see him; I was afraid to turn and look. The priest said something to him, low and emphatic.

"What?" the man against the wall said. "I don't understand what you're saying to me. I don't understand what you want."

The priest said something else.

"Please. I don't understand."

I heard the squeal of a gas gun. Then someone falling, and strangled vomiting. People screamed. Someone was trying to answer a question from one of the other men with guns.

I didn't understand what was happening; it sounded like they were interrogating people, but not giving them a chance to answer.

The priest walked passed me, went to the person next to me—a black guy in his forties. I strained to listen to what he was asking the guy. If I knew what the questions were, maybe I could figure out the right answer, the response that would convince him not to kill me.

Part of me knew there were no right answers. This was just how they did it, to make it more awful.

I risked glancing around, to see if I might be able to run for it. The alley was long and desolate. They would have plenty of time to shoot me before I reached cover.

"How many graves are in Saint Bonaventure Cemetery?" the priest asked.

"I don't… please, don't kill me," the black guy said.

The priest walked away. He came back a moment later carrying a bucket.

He stopped beside me.

"How many graves?" he asked. His mouth was close to my ear, his breath tickling my neck.

I wanted to tell him he'd made a mistake, that he had been questioning the guy next to me. He poured the bucket over my head. It stank—it was piss, or sewage.

He took a step back, looked me up and down. "Where do you live?" he asked.

"East Jones Street," I said quickly. I was relieved to know the answer. I wanted to cooperate. I craved his approval.

He raised the gas gun, held it to the side of my nose.

"How many steps is it from here to the Oglethorpe Mall?"

"I don't know what the right answer is."

"Are you ready to die?"

"I don't want to die."

The blast from the gas gun was coming. He was almost finished with the precursors, then he would push the black mask on the end of the gun over my face and pull the trigger. I tried to think of some way to stretch it out, to get him to ask me more questions, to switch to someone else, even if only for a moment. I didn't want to die. Through my terror I found myself trying to grasp that this was real. There would be a very painful few moments of dying, and then my life would end.

"Eat this." He held a plastic lid up to my face. There was a stringy, slimy, whitish thing on it, with lidded eyes, little arms curled in toward a torso. It was a fetus, maybe a rat fetus, or a cat. I lifted it off the lid with my tongue, and I ate it. It was horrible; it was chewy and slimy. I bit what may have been the head, and felt fluid squirt across my tongue. I swallowed dramatically, so he'd know that I'd done what he told me.

"How many cats prowl this city?"

"I'm not sure," I whimpered.

He smacked me in the back of the head, hard. "Run away now," he said. "We're not killing mice in rags today."

I was running before his words fully registered, my shoulders pulled toward my ears, waiting to feel bullets rip into my back. I sprinted out of the alley, turned down the street with the rush of wind in my ears and a horrible taste in my mouth. I was making some sound as I ran, a sound I didn't recognize and before this moment wouldn't have believed was within my vocal range.

A few blocks away I spotted two police officers on horseback. I waved and shouted to get their attention.

"They're killing people, behind an art gallery!" I pointed back up Abercorn.

"Where?" a female officer asked.

I pointed. "Three blocks up, I think, then right—"

"That's not our jurisdiction."

"No, but three men with guns are lining people up in an alley and shooting them! Right now!"

"Get lost," the officer said. She made a clicking sound, kicked her horse in the ribs. In a nonchalant tone she picked up the thread of whatever conversation they'd been having when I interrupted.

I looked back over my shoulder, heard distant gunshots. What could I do to help those people who'd only gone to look at art? Nothing. I could do nothing. I could save myself.

I was afraid to go back for my bike, so I ran as long as I could, then I walked. As I got close to home I stopped at a table set up in the alley off Drayton and bought a bottle of home brew with my three dollars. The guy didn't ask why I was shaking so badly, or why I stank of piss. The alcohol washed some of the rancid taste out of my mouth.

Colin and Jeannie weren't home. I didn't want to be alone; I couldn't even bring myself to go inside to change, because our apartment was dark and I was afraid. I headed toward Ange's.

The pattering of water behind a wrought-iron gate caught my attention. I stopped and peered through the gate at a perfectly manicured garden. The shrubs were trimmed in perfect arcs; there was an oval reflecting pool in the center. In the pool was a statue of a woman perched on the edge of a fountain, drinking, sharing the flow with birds in flight. It was so calm, so beautiful. I would have given anything to spend an hour in there.

I kept going, swigging from my bottle every few steps.

When I reached Ange's house I pounded on the door with the flat of my fist.

Chair, the guy in the wheelchair, opened it. He called to Ange. She took one look at me, shouted my name, and burst forward, tilting off-balance. She'd been drinking, too.

"What happened? Are you all right? Are you hurt?" She touched my arms, my sides, looking for wounds. I didn't know how to describe what had happened. I did, but I didn't know how to make it not sound humiliating. I felt like I'd been raped.

Ange led me to the bathroom, past roommates trying not to stare, which was worse than if they'd stared. She reached behind the shower curtain and turned on the water. I got in, still dressed, and splashed water on my face. The water at my feet was sewer brown as it slid down the drain.

"Do you want to tell me what happened? It's okay if you don't," Ange said from outside, her words a little slurred.

I ran my fingers through my filthy hair. "I stopped at an art opening uptown," I began. I unbuttoned my shirt with trembling plastic fingers, peeled it off and let it drop.

"Go ahead, honey," Ange said. "I know it was bad. You'll feel better when you tell it."

I told it. I gagged and almost vomited when I got to the part about being forced to eat the fetus. I opened my mouth to the precious water, let it spray my gums and teeth, then rinsed and spit.

The shower curtain drew back, and Ange stepped in. She was naked.

She pressed her face into my neck.

"This is just a thing, okay?" she said. "A little distraction. Just some grown up fun. Okay?"

"Okay," I said.

We stumbled out of the tub, letting the water dribble onto the ancient Formica, our legs moving in step like slow-dancers. We fell onto Ange's mattress soaking wet.

Maybe it's shallow and male, to be able to set aside something awful because a woman takes off her clothes, to forget that retching death-gag echoing through the alley and instead focus on erect nipples. I don't care. It worked. Ange transformed those first hours from hellish to tolerable.

And I think it worked like an aspirin administered right after a heart attack, minimizing the long-term damage. There was going to be damage—no one sees what I saw and walks away clean—but Ange slipped an aspirin under my tongue just when I needed it most.

I knew it would cost us later. Some women know they can't do the friends-with-sex thing without getting emotionally attached. Other women think they can do it, but they really can't. That's it—all women fit into one of those two categories. But I wasn't totally opposed to the possibility of it turning into more than friends-with-sex, so maybe it would turn out okay, for a while, at least. Right then I didn't care.

I dragged myself out of Ange's bed at six a.m., feeling the grit of old wood under my feet. I'm not good at mornings. The dog-eared posters covering Ange's walls were not quite perceptible in the hint of gray light filtering through the blinds.

Ange rolled over, opened her eyes.

"I have to get to work," I whispered.

She nodded, took a big breath and let it out. "You doing okay?"

"I'm good," I said. I got out of bed, headed for the door.

"Bye, sweetie. I love you, but I don't love you."

"I love you, but I don't love you, too," I said. I considered kissing her goodbye, decided that was a bad idea, and slipped out.

Two of Ange's roommates—Chair and an Indian guy named Rami—were in the living room, hunched over the coffee table, which was covered with charts and notes. Chair blocked my view of the table, gave me a look that made it clear I should keep moving. They always seemed to be working, but they didn't seem to be students. I had no idea what they did. I needed to remember to ask Ange what these guys were doing.

I walked in the street; it was easier than navigating the homeless asleep on the sidewalks, hugging their possessions.

On York I passed an emaciated little girl sitting on a stone curb, her chin on her knees, ten feet from a woman selling walnuts out of an old doorless refrigerator tipped on its back. A woman appeared around the corner of Whitaker Street and waved to the little girl. The woman had just swallowed something. She ran her tongue over her teeth, then smiled at her little girl, held out her hand for the girl to grasp.

I cut through Chippewa Square, rounded the corner onto Liberty, and stopped in my tracks.

The front of the Timesaver was a sea of broken glass. I broke into a run, flew into the Timesaver and found Ruplu sitting on the counter, staring at his ransacked store.

"Amos is dead, they've already taken him away," Ruplu said, gesturing at blood streaked across the floor by the window. He turned and looked at me with red-rimmed eyes. He'd probably been there half the night. "Can you work a double shift and help me get things back in order?"

"As long as you need me, I'm here" I said. Work was just what I needed right now; something to get lost in. I went to the supply closet and pulled out a broom.

"Can I ask you something? Do you think they did this because I'm Indian?" Ruplu asked.

"Yes and no," I said. "People around here hate foreigners, so your store becomes an appealing target. They also hate rich people—"

"But I'm not rich," Ruplu interrupted. "My family lives in a six-room house, nine of us. This store doesn't make that much."

I swept loose chips of glass wedged under the beverage cases that long ago used to be refrigerated. "I know, but they don't understand that. They don't want to understand it. They wanted what was inside your store, so it becomes a handy excuse."

I stopped at the puddle of blood. Both the broom and the mop would only smear the blood. I looked around, spied a busted bag of kitty litter on a low shelf. I retrieved the bag and poured it over the blood. Poor Amos. He probably didn't even get a chance to draw his

gun. I realized now that he was just for show, that when someone
really wanted to rip off the Timesaver, all it took was a few sweeps
from an assault rifle.

"I pay the local Civil Defense people eight hundred dollars a month
to protect the store," Ruplu said, piling cases of soda that the thieves
had not had time to cart away. "Do they offer to make reparations
when I tell them my store was shot up while it was supposed to be
under their protection? No. They just remind me that my next eight
hundred is due in four days."

"I think Civil Defense is starting to be more of a problem than a
solution in this city," I said.

"I think you're right. And they're not my only problem." Ruplu sat
on the stack of soda cases. "Every week, there's less and less merchandise I can get delivered. No more coffee. Pepsi doesn't distribute this
far south starting in November. No aspirin in months." He shrugged
his helplessness. "What can I do?"

"I've been thinking about that," I said. "Maybe you should look
into making deals with locals to sell their things—peanuts, preserves,
home-made blankets, things like that."

Ruplu nodded, thinking. "The problem is locating these people
and arranging all these separate deals. It takes all the time just to
run the sales end."

"I could work on that end—"

Ruplu shook his head. "I can't afford to pay you for that many
more hours," he said.

"Pay me whatever, or nothing," I said. "This job saved my life; I'm
grateful to you, I'll do anything I can to help your store be successful."

I thought Ruplu was going to cry. He clapped me on the shoulder,
gulped back tears.

"You are my good friend," he said. "All right. If I make money from
business you find me, I share some with you. Okay?"

"Sounds good," I said. We shook hands.

Ruplu clapped me on the shoulder again, and I got back to
work.

I felt a little taller as I swept. I didn't want to feel too tall, because
a man had died here this morning, but I couldn't help but feel some
hope rising. This could be a door opening for me, a chance to do
more than count change into people's palms. If I could help Ruplu,

I knew he'd give me my fair share of the profit. I could become sort of a limited partner.

My head was spinning from the last twenty-four hours. I felt great and awful, exhausted and exhilarated. Afterimages of Ange in the shower were superimposed with the priest feeding me from a beverage lid. Now the puddle of blood where Amos had fallen swirled with this opportunity. I guess I needed to take my joys where I could find them, and the hell with the notion that it was selfish to be happy amidst suffering. There was always suffering.

Chapter 3: Rock Star

Winter, 2027 (Three years later)

Pulaski Square was uncharacteristically crowded with teens and tweens and early twenty-somethings. They reminded me of pigeons, the way they milled aimlessly on the lawns and brick walkways, as if hoping to happen upon something interesting—a pizza crust or an errant cheese doodle.

"Think she's coming?" an acne-stricken kid said to his friend through a neon purple virus mask.

His friend, who had stripes of lamp black above and below his eyes to match his black mask (who could keep up with the pointless shit that passed for current teen fashion?), shrugged.

"Who's supposed to come?" I asked.

"Deirdre," the kid with the lamp black said. He pulled a pack of cigarettes from his sleeve pocket.

"Who's Deirdre?"

"Flash singer. The best." He lit the cigarette, pulled his mask up to his forehead, took a puff, blew smoke into the Spanish Moss hanging overhead in an "Ain't I so cool" way. "It's going around there's gonna be a flash concert here."

"Oh," I said. That I could probably do without. I nodded, the cool dudes nodded back, and I continued through the crowd.

"Jasper!"

I turned. "Cortez!" I pushed through the crowd to get to him, grabbed him in a bear hug. "Shit, I can't believe it! I didn't know you were back in the city."

"Yeah, about six months now," Cortez said, clapping me on the shoulder. He was dressed in a black t-shirt, black puffed pants. His head was shaved.

He was living with his dad, working security jobs when he could get them—mostly temp bodyguard stuff for semi-rich guys trying to impress their dates. Turned out he was on a job now—security for the flash concert that was indeed happening.

The rumble of the crowd on the west end of the square rose in pitch.

"Gotta go!" Cortez said. "Stick around, let's have a beer after."

So I stuck around.

A scrum of kids began chanting "Deirdre." It spread, rising in volume. The crowd parted on the other end of the park, and there she was, surrounded by guys in black. Everyone cheered.

Deirdre was small, almost childlike. She was wearing six or seven pink neck rings that accentuated an ostrich-neck, and a black skin-tight leotard that accentuated enormous breasts. Her eyes bulged a little, her meaty lips formed an eager "o." She was one of those women who was extremely sexy without being particularly pretty.

The stage was a bunch of two-by-fours on milk crates, hauled in by her roadies, along with amps, portable spotlights, and a generator. Deirdre paced, staring at the ground as they set up.

There was no introduction or anything. The amps squealed to life, there was scattered cheering, and Deirdre hopped onto the little stage and came to life.

Shit, did she come to life.

It wasn't that she was a great singer—she had a decent voice, sure, but it was her energy that hooked you. Her voice was so *loud*; there was so much raw force behind it that you kept expecting those bulging eyes to explode. She flew around the stage, leaping, spinning, dancing, seeming to defy gravity on her tiny fuel-injected frame.

Her songs were angry and violent. Lots of things blowing up, lots of fucking, lots of death and despair and infidelity. She was a perfect voice for the times.

After every few songs, roadies circulated with plastic buckets, collecting money. Cortez stood beside the stage with the other men in black, his arms folded across his chest, looking all tough. It was strange reconciling this Cortez with the one who'd been part of my homeless band, my tribe, five years ago. He'd put on a good twenty pounds of muscle; though part of that was probably because he was eating more regularly now, and wasn't walking miles every day.

After Deirdre's final song, she bowed primly and left the stage to roaring applause. One of the bodyguards pulled off his t-shirt and handed it to her, and she put it on over her leotard. It came down to her knees. They headed off as the roadies gathered the stage and equipment.

Cortez said something to Deirdre as they walked. She nodded, and Cortez broke off and headed toward me, grinning.

"Come on," he said, "we're gonna meet them at the after party."

The after party was at a bar called The Dirty Martini. At least it used to be called The Dirty Martini, before it went out of business. The front picture window was boarded up; the olive green bar, thick with dust and grime, was the only piece of furniture. Kerosene lamps hung from the rafters.

We got ourselves drinks and set up near the bar. Cortez asked if I'd seen Ange around, and I told him we were still in touch from time to time. I hated bending the truth like that, but what would be the point of telling him we'd had a friends-with-occasional-sex thing going for over a year? He might still have feelings for her. I caught him up on Ange's progress on her Ph.D.

"She ever mention me?" Cortez asked. He saw me hesitate, waved off my answer. "Never mind. She probably still hates me like running pus."

Their breakup had been about a bunch of little things, though the tipping point had come when Ange was accepted into the biotech doctoral program on a full scholarship, and Cortez didn't fully embrace the idea. Ange's take was that Cortez was threatened by it. Cortez said she used an offhanded comment he made about it not seeming practical as an excuse to break up with him. In any case, it hadn't been the sort where you keep in touch. I knew how that was, and, given that no punches had been thrown in either direction, I didn't feel a need to take sides. As far as I was concerned there were no bad guys when it came to breakups. Bad guys had guns, and forced you to eat things. I'd tell Ange I bumped into him. I doubted she would care much if Cortez and I became friends again. Ange didn't seem to care who I was dating, let alone who my friends were. It amazed me how well she could handle the friends-with-sex thing; she never expected anything more from me than a good friend could expect, and she never gave any more, either.

Cortez and I talked about the tribe, about the days when we were even poorer then we were now, about how humiliating it'd been to be homeless, and, finally, about that day, when the tribe had been forced to kill. It had been almost seven years, but I still rode a black wave at the mention of that day.

That's when Deirdre made her entrance.

She'd changed clothes: from upper thigh to just below her armpits she was wrapped in a continuous strip of black leather. It must have been fifty feet long when it was unraveled. I thought for a moment about what it would be like to unravel it, then allowed reality to kick in. She was out of my league. I'm strictly minor league—double-A, maybe triple-A if I stretch. Deirdre was playing in the majors.

A cadre of fifteen-year-olds circled her, sputtering about how she was pure poison, brilliant, vascular. She passed through them like they were gypsies asking for a handout and made her way to the bar, stopping right near me and Cortez. My stomach did a little somersault, the way it does when you're near someone famous, which made me feel a little stupid, given that she was a chick who performed on two-by-fours in the park for handouts.

An older guy, kind of short, with shiny shoes that announced he was a rich guy stepping outside the gates to slum, handed Deirdre a plastic cup of the home brew they were serving before she could ask for one.

"She's okay," Cortez said, gesturing toward Deirdre. "Pays on time," he held up his cup, "lets you party when you're working for her as long as you don't overdo it. She's a little wild, but she's okay."

Deirdre was asking Mister Shiny Shoes if he had any blow. The guy answered that he didn't, but he had cash if Deirdre had connections.

Cortez said something to me.

"Good, good," I answered, trying to listen to Deirdre's conversation. The guy said that he thought Deirdre was very sexy, and that he wanted to fuck her, and handed her his business card. She took it like it was a dead rat.

"She's a good singer," I said to Cortez. When your cognitive capacity is taken up by another task, the words that come out of your mouth tend to border on the inane. The guy was saying how he was good friends with Mayor Addams.

Deirdre ran her tongue along the inside of her cheek as if she was trying to dislodge something trapped between her back teeth, then suggested he go find the mayor and fuck him instead.

"Deirdre!" Cortez said as she broke off from the dumbfounded friend of the mayor. "I want you to meet my good friend Jasper. Jasper saved my ex-girlfriend from being raped by three war vets with rifles. Stabbed them to death with a kitchen knife."

"Now, that's interesting," she said, looking me up and down languidly, hands on hips. "You don't look like a killer. Is Cortez bullshitting me?"

"I wish he was," I said. "I'm not particularly proud of it. And it wasn't just me—there were five of us. And the vets with rifles had their pants around their ankles, and their rifles were leaned up against a china cabinet out of reach."

"Were they? How brave of you."

"Thanks," I said. "Maybe I can work as a bodyguard at your shows, in case someone unconscious looks like they may eventually wake up and get out of hand."

Deirdre burst out laughing. She looked straight into my eyes for a long moment, her eyes sort of sparkling. I struggled not to break eye contact, feeling like it was some sort of test. "I think I'm going to like you."

My legs had turned to jelly. I was grinning like an idiot and couldn't think of anything to say.

Music started up, heavy on bass. "Deirdre!" someone called.

"Stick around," Deirdre said over her shoulder, "I'd like to hear more about you stabbing people." With her back to us, it was safe to stare.

Cortez and I drank, and bonded, and drank more. Our eyes burned in the blue smoke of hand-rolled cigarettes.

"I should have looked you up before this," I said. "Funny how you just lose touch with good friends." "Good friends" was probably a stretch, but the drinks were making me feel all warm and nostalgic.

"Don't worry about it," Cortez said, "I could've looked you up too. We get caught up in things."

"Hey! Cortez's friend!" Deirdre shouted from across the room. "Come party with me!" She waved me over. Cortez gave me a shove in her direction. As soon as I reached her she slid her arm under mine. Suddenly I felt eleven feet tall.

"So what do you do?" Deirdre asked me.

"I manage a convenience store," I said. It was sort of true.

"Did you keep stabbing the rapists until they were all dead, or did you stop once they couldn't fight back?"

"They kept fighting back until they were dead. Although I guess at some point they switched from fighting for advantage to fighting not to die."

Deirdre's eyes narrowed. "I like that. Do you have a pen?"

"No, I don't."

A woman interrupted us. She was tall, with a way-short blue skirt and long, bright magenta hair.

"You know those rings I was telling you about?"

"Yeah?" Deirdre said, extracting her arm from mine.

"Chetty's found a connection."

"Oh really?"

Suddenly I was on the outside of the conversation looking in—an all-too-familiar situation for me. Evidently my moment in the sun had ended. I'd had enough booze that I was willing to take one last stab, though. I touched Deirdre's shoulder. She turned.

"Do you have a phone?"

She nodded absently, pulled a business card out of an unseen pocket and handed it to me. It was a nice card, with an electronic window that scrolled photos of Deirdre performing. I waved an unseen goodbye and left her to her talk of rings, clutching the card tight.

"Can't I just text her?" I asked.

"No," Ange groaned. "*Call* her." Somehow she was following the conversation while simultaneously reading a microbiology textbook, one leg draped over the arm of the folding chair.

"Call her," Jeannie agreed.

I'd spent an hour on my front porch composing and deleting text messages before Ange and Jeannie showed up. Now I wished I'd sent one of those messages before they got here. "But it's awkward, and scary," I said. "She's a little scary."

"That's part of the reason you do it. Look," Ange closed her book, craned her neck to look at me, "if a man doesn't have the courage to walk up and ask me out without a lot of tap dancing, I know there's no way it's going to work. He's got to have a backbone."

"So it's like a hoop I'm supposed to jump through," I said, while mentally filing away what Ange had just said. Was that why she never let things escalate between us? Was I not confident enough for her?

"It's a bar you have to be able to jump over," Ange countered.

"Jasper, it sounds like she's a pretty confident woman," Jeannie said.

"Yes. She's incredible," I said. She was the most dynamic, cool, confident, ballsy, exciting woman I'd ever met; it made me dizzy to imagine being with her.

"Then you've got to call," Jeannie said. "You know how much men like breasts? Women like confidence as much as men like breasts. Especially confident women."

"Oh," I said. I was clearly a little autistic when it came to the nuances of love and dating.

Out in the street, two twelve- or thirteen-year-old boys, one carrying a syringe filled with red fluid—blood, or more likely food dye—approached a third, younger boy in a mask playing in an abandoned truck.

"Hey, c'mere a minute," the boy with the syringe said, leaning in the broken driver's side window, "you got a dollar I can borrow?"

"Hey," I yelled over. "Get lost, leave him alone."

The kid pulled his head out of the window. All three of them looked my way. "What's it to you?" Needle boy said.

I reached for a baseball bat propped by the door. They moved on.

"Thanks, mister," the kid in the truck said when they were out of earshot.

"No problem," I said, looking down at my phone.

"Do women like Deirdre even date?" I asked. "It's hard to imagine walking her to the door and kissing her goodnight."

"Only one way to find out, sweetie," Ange said. She was back reading her book. How could this not bother her? I'd been eager to tell Ange about Deirdre, hoping she would be at least a little jealous.

"Crap," I said. I climbed down the creaky porch stairs and went into the narrow alley beside our house to have some privacy, then paced a while, memorizing the first couple of things I would say to get the conversation going.

I dialed her number. My heart was rocketing—I was going to stumble all over my words.

The phone rang, then again. It clicked; my sinuses cleared from the rush of adrenaline before I realized it was her voice mail.

"This is Deirdre." The phone beeped. It took me a second to realize that was the whole message.

"Hi, Deirdre," I said, "this is Jasper, we met last night at the bar. I was wondering if you might want to go out sometime—"

"No!" Ange shouted from the porch. "Not 'sometime.' Name a day." I didn't think she could hear me.

"So, just call me if you get this, and maybe we can go out Friday?"

"Not maybe!" Ange called.

"Bye," I said into the phone and disconnected. "Thanks!" I shouted at Ange. "Now I sound like a complete idiot, and there's a woman in the background critiquing my message as I leave it. That ought to go over well!"

Ange burst out laughing. "Aw, honey, I couldn't make it too much worse than it was going to be anyway."

Deirdre didn't call back. I waited three days, my stomach somer-saulting every time the phone rang. I decided to send a text. Screw Ange and Jeannie's advice. There was nothing wrong with texting.

Does your non-reply mean "fuck off," or is there a possibility I could still convince you to go out with me?

Her lack of a reply was a reply in itself—I knew that—but I was so wound up in fantasies of me and Deirdre that I couldn't let it go, couldn't just walk away without trying. I paced the porch. I had a meeting in two hours with a woman who was interested in selling her fruit preserves in Ruplu's store. I would probably spend the two hours wearing down the wood on the porch. I couldn't concentrate on anything else. I sat on the moldy weight bench and stared down the alley, at the rusty grill tangled in chest-high weeds next to a rotting outbuilding, a small stack of two-by-fours leaned against it, some do-it-yourselfer's long-forgotten ambition.

My phone jingled. My palms sweated as I read the reply:

Ok. Friday at 6. Don't be boring.

I leapt to my feet, threw my fists in the air. I had a date with Deirdre. Me—she was going out with me. Not shiny-shoed I-know-the-mayor, but me. And she'd answered my *text message*, not my phone message. Ange and Jeannie did not know as much as they thought about dating.

I got to work immediately—I sat on the porch and mentally rehearsed interesting things to say, imagining what Deirdre would say back, as the sun sank behind the DeSoto Hilton, its sign emblazoned at the top of the building, just visible over the houses across the street.

The first thing Deirdre said after opening the door was "What's your name again?"

I told her. She nodded. We started walking. I had no idea what to do with my hands; they suddenly felt all wrong just dangling there.

"I was thinking we could go to the Firefly Café," I said, stuffing them into my back pockets.

"I don't want to go to a restaurant," Deirdre said.

I was speechless for a moment. "Well, what would you like to do then?" I finally asked.

Deirdre thought about it. "Let's get some apples and some Lucky Charms, and find a way up to the roof of the Hilton and watch the city from up there."

I hoped the vast confusion I felt didn't register on my face. Apples and Lucky Charms? "You're a woman with very precise tastes," I said.

"Yes, I am."

I was already feeling in over my head with this woman. I needed to relax, to play along with her. "I've got to admit, your plan sounds more fun than mine."

Deirdre grinned, and looked at me for the first time. "Good."

We headed toward Wal-Mart on the east side of town, winding around camped-out tribes of homeless, stepping over people sleeping in filthy clothes.

"Scary stuff, what's going on between Russia and China, huh?"

Deirdre looked at me blankly. "What?"

"You didn't hear?" I said. "Russia dropped a nuke on Chinese troops massed at their border."

"A nuke? That seems excessive."

"Hey, honey, kill the loser and come marvel with a real man," a dude with gang scars on his neck called. He was sitting on a porch swing hung under stark steel fire escape stairs. I cringed as Deirdre gave him the finger without even looking. Mercifully, he stayed put, and we kept moving.

Wal-Mart was packed, probably because of the nuclear exchange between China and Russia. Every time there was a disaster, no matter how far removed, people flocked to the Wal-Mart to buy stuff. And not just water and flashlights, but Barbies and bath mats, tube socks and dental floss as well.

I thought that was a fairly entertaining observation, so I mentally rehearsed it a few times, then said it to Deirdre.

"People are pretty fucking stupid. Especially in the south," she said as she yanked a plastic produce bag from the dispenser and dug her delicious little fingers into the apples.

A little Hispanic guy eyed Deirdre up and down as he went by. Guys had been gawking since I picked her up. Each time it happened I felt a childish swell of pride at being with her.

There was a buzzing in the crowd over by the broccoli and bell peppers, so I went over to investigate. A Wal-Mart employee was crossing out prices and writing in new ones by hand with a black marker. Higher prices—like twice as high. A security guy hovered close to her, a pistol holstered in his red Wal-Mart belt.

The buzzing got louder.

"What the fuck?" I said. Normally I would say "What the hell?" but I was trying to keep up with Deirdre.

Over in the bread area a group of angry shoppers had surrounded an employee who was also shadowed by a security guard. This guy was middle-aged and male, so I figured he must be management. I went over to listen.

"Hey, I'm very sorry," he said, "the new viral crisis has caused disruptions in shipping, and we can't predict when distribution and delivery will return to normal. Prices will be higher until then. It's not under our control."

I ran back to Deirdre, who was picking out apples. I yanked the plastic price rectangle out of its holder and handed it to her. "I'll get the Lucky Charms—don't let the bitch with the marker get this."

No one had gotten to the cereal aisle yet. I ran up and down, looking for Lucky Charms, certain that Cocoa Puffs or Gummy Grabbers would not be acceptable. I spotted them low on the shelf, grabbed two boxes and the price rectangle, and met Deirdre up at the register.

"Twenty-four sixty," the girl at the register said. It should have been about fifteen bucks.

"No," I said. I showed her the price labels. "See—they haven't raised the prices on these yet."

"They haven't posted them, but they're already in the system," she said.

"That's bullshit!" I said. "You can't raise the prices at the register without posting them first!"

"I just work here," she said, just as loudly. "You think I like this? How am I going to feed my little boy?"

We stared at each other for a moment. She was chewing gum—probably her last piece for a while, because it was now about three bucks a pack, and she had her little boy to think about.

"This is bullshit!" I repeated.

Deirdre fished an apple out of the bag, reared back and fired it toward the produce department. "Bullshit!" she shouted.

She had a good arm. The apple sailed over the management guy's head and nailed a shelf of bread, sending loaves scattering. She grabbed two more apples. A security guy ran toward us, fumbling with the clasp on his holster.

Deirdre threw an apple at him. He ducked.

"Bullshit!" a young guy in surgeon's scrubs two registers down screamed. With his shoulder-length white hair, he was clearly not a surgeon—he was a Jumpy-Jump. He hurled a can of soup at the security guard. It hit the guard above the eye. The guard doubled over, clutching his face while the Jumpy-Jump reached for another can.

Deirdre threw more apples, rapid-fire, toward the back of the store, laughing with delight.

Over in produce, the Hispanic guy threw a pear at the security guy, who was still doubled over. Blood was dripping onto the linoleum from between his fingers. The Hispanic guy grabbed another pear from an enormous pyramid of them and hurled it toward the registers. He grabbed another and took a bite.

The Jumpy-Jump whipped items from his cart at the checkout girl behind his register. She was ducked down, hands covering her face, screaming.

There were things flying everywhere.

A shot rang out, then screams, then angry shouts and more shots. The Jumpy-Jump ducked behind a rack of impulse items, pulled a pistol with a silencer, and squeezed off a shot.

A security guard ran from the back of the store, his gun pointed in the air. A fat guy threw a TV, box and all, at him. It missed, crashed into a clothing rack, and spewed ugly v-necked shirts into the aisle. The Jumpy-Jump shot the guard in the chest.

"Let's go!" I said to Deirdre.

"Are you kidding?" she said. She was laughing like this was a Three Stooges film.

The management guy was down; four or five people stood over him, their fists rising and falling. The price-change girl was down too. At first I thought her head was splattered with pink bits of brain, then I realized it was watermelon.

It occurred to me that the mob might kill all of the employees.

"Stay here," I said to Deirdre.

She shrugged. "Whatever." She licked at the white creme center of an Oreo she'd pulled from the shelf of impulse items.

I crawled along the front of the checkout aisle. "Hey," I said to the checkout girl huddled on the floor below her register, "lose the vest!" I pantomimed pulling it over her head. She nodded, pulled off the blue employee vest and flung it toward the rest rooms. I ran along the registers and told the other checkout people.

By the time I got back to Deirdre, the shooting was over—people were either looting or smashing things, and no authority types were around to stop them. A beer-bellied guy in hunting fatigues, running toward the sporting goods department, slipped in a puddle of blood and fell on his ass.

The big crane game by the entrance crashed to the floor, spilling stuffed animals and cheap watches. The tweenaged girls who'd tipped it dove to retrieve their prizes. There were old people, mothers with kids, you name it, all filling shopping carts.

"Come on," Deirdre said, tugging me toward the free stuff. I ran to get a shopping cart.

We took our ill-gotten booty to Deirdre's place—a penthouse condo in one of the historic houses on Gaston, with high ceilings and a big old chandelier. High on the adrenaline of having started a riot, she wasted no time in introducing me to the world of sex with Deirdre.

She liked it fast, furious, and violent, just like her music, just like her life. It was filthy, and I loved it, because she loved it, and I was with a rock star that hundreds of guys wanted to be with, and that was so cool.

Yes, she had started the riot, and yes, people had died. But (I reasoned as I ran my hands over her body) she'd only thrown apples, which was playful, really. Others had turned it violent.

Afterward, I lay there panting, one arm wrapped across Deirdre's lightly freckled shoulders.

"Go home," Deirdre muttered into her pillow. "I hate sleeping with someone in the bed." The sweat on her pale white neck hadn't even dried yet.

I gathered up my wrinkled clothes and pulled them on (except my socks, because I could only find one and didn't dare dig around in the blankets), took a long last look at Deirdre—one leg straight, one bent, her back rising and falling with easy, even breaths—and headed home.

"Put the damned phone away," Colin said, shouting from the roof. "This is gonna turn into Sophia all over again."

"Deirdre's not married," I called up to him, but I stuffed the phone into my jeans pocket, and picked up the shovel.

She hadn't returned my call. I could barely see the dirt in front of me, what with flashbacks of the night before last dancing before me.

I heard Jeannie shout something to Colin.

"Jeannie heard on the radio that Wal-Mart isn't reopening for weeks," Colin said. "People are squatting in the building, and the company has to fly in a security force to take the store back before it can restock."

"Maybe this will boost business at the convenience store," I said. "We may actually profit from Deirdre's stunt." I finished filling the big plastic bucket, motioned to Colin. He hauled it up, grunting with the effort as the bucket danced and swung at the end of the rope.

It was getting dark; a couple more bucketsful and we'd have to call it quits.

"Oh. That's just lovely. And here I thought the Jumpy-Jumps were responsible for digging all the holes I keep tripping in."

Deirdre was leaned up against a light post. Her outfit was reminiscent of an S&M dominatrix: black and red, plenty of leather, plenty of straps. No mask. Deirdre never wore a mask. She strutted over on spiked heels, took in the excavation with hands on hips.

Suddenly I felt all filthy and sweaty. I'm not a macho enough guy for manual labor to make me seem manly. Clean and scrubbed is a much better look for me.

"Now, you've just got to be Deirdre," Colin called down.

Deirdre looked up, shielding her eyes. "And you've got to be someone I don't know."

Colin laughed.

"What are you doing up there?"

"We're making a vegetable garden," Colin said. "Some young hoodlums went and ruined the Wal-Mart, so now we have to grow our own food, someplace where others can't get at it." Although that meant no longer spreading the solar blanket up there to offset our energy bills.

Deirdre pressed a finger to her lips and grinned. She turned to me. "You want to come out and play, or do you want to stay in your sandbox?"

"Give me five minutes," I said, leaning the shovel against the porch railing.

"You kids have a good time, but don't stay out too late," Colin called after me as I trotted into the house.

I pulled off my clothes and jumped into the shower. The icy water made me gasp. I was busting inside. Deirdre had come to find me! I wasn't boring!

I was dried and dressed in moments, knowing that Deirdre probably wasn't good at waiting.

"I've got a show at midnight," she said as we started walking. "We've got—"

We both gawked at what had come around the corner.

It was a stripped-down car, little more than seats on an axle, pulled by a whining, barking pack of dogs. A cardboard "Taxi" sign was taped to the front.

"No way," Deirdre said.

It made sense, really. There were plenty of dogs. Hell, they were all over, like big rats. We watched as the taxi rolled out of sight.

"You walked over here alone?" I asked.

Deirdre looked at me like I was an idiot.

"It's just that the streets are so dangerous," I said.

"Yeah? And?"

I shrugged. She had a point. People seemed way more willing to take risks now than when I was a kid. Maybe it was because we didn't expect to live as long as our parents did.

Was that it? Did we think: Why not risk it, I'll probably be dead soon anyway? Yeah, we did. When I was a kid I was sure I'd live to ninety, maybe a hundred. I'd been adjusting that estimate downward ever since. Now I figured that unless things got better, I'd be lucky to reach fifty.

"What do you want to do?" I asked.

Deirdre shrugged. "Surprise me."

Surprise Deirdre? Shit. Maybe we could walk a tight-rope between the Hilton and the Saint John the Baptist Church belfry. Or dynamite the Savannah Bridge and watch it crash into the river. She'd like that. I was tempted to suggest a restaurant.

I glanced at Deirdre: she had an eager, hyper look on her face. It was becoming apparent that Deirdre was a woman of many moods, and that they cycled through her quickly and unexpectedly.

Surprise Deirdre. I took her hand, headed down East Jones and through Troup Square, trying to think.

Someone had wrapped a length of electrical cord down a busted out lamppost in the square, like Christmas garland only colorless. I'd almost forgotten about Christmas. It was soon; I wasn't sure exactly what the date was. Somewhere in the teens. In keeping with the Christmas theme, the big marble statue of John Wesley that sat atop his tomb in the center of the square had been spray painted red and green, except for his face, which was painted black. At least I thought it was his tomb. I'd never actually read the brass plaque embedded in the concrete below the statue.

Tombs. Now, that was something Deirdre might like.

"Come on." I took Deirdre's hand and drew her down Abercorn.

"Hmmm," Deirdre cooed as we crossed Liberty and walked toward the locked gates of Colonial Park Cemetery.

She ignored my attempt to boost her and scrabbled over the fence. I gripped the rough, rusty iron and climbed in after her. White headstones glowed vaguely in the tree-canopied darkness, chipped and crooked like giant teeth. Crepe myrtle, barkless and shiny, twisted toward the sky.

Deirdre stepped over a fallen lamppost, headed toward the concrete wall that marked the far end of the cemetery. I followed, wrapped my hands around her waist when I caught up to her. She was staring up at the rows of lost tombstones, mounted along the wall.

"What're those doing up there?" she asked.

"Soldiers came through here during the Civil War, pulled them out of the ground and tossed them around. The residents didn't know which went where, so they couldn't put them back."

"I don't know why people care so much about dead bodies anyway. What's the difference where someone is once they're dead?"

I slid my palms up her sides, wrapped them over her breasts. She looked back at me over her shoulders, smiling. "You want to fuck me in a graveyard?" She scanned the graveyard as I slid my hands under her shirt.

"This way," she said, taking my hand and leading me over a low fence enclosing two rows of concrete tombs that looked like coffins set aside to be buried later. There were eight of them in the little family plot. One of them was much smaller than the rest—suitable for a four- or five-year-old child. Deirdre chose that one.

I strolled down York Street toward Deirdre's condo, enjoying the cool weather, my hand in my pocket holding my pay. I loved the feel of the thickish wad of cash in my pocket. Six hundred forty dollars—not a bad week's pay. I wouldn't be moving into the gated district any time soon, and Deirdre probably made ten times what I did, but still, it was nice to be making enough that I could buy a newspaper if I wanted.

I wanted to think that my improved fortunes were part of a larger economic recovery, but it was hard to tell. To me, things seemed a *little* better, but there were still plenty of homeless, and the stock market just kept sinking. If the government knew what the unemployment rate was, they weren't saying, but on the news an economist had estimated it was close to sixty percent. Angling my face toward the sun, I decided I would stop fretting and be glad

I wasn't one of them. Things were going well, all things considered, and I should appreciate it. Deirdre and I were at a point in our relationship that it was assumed we'd see each other every day, and I was catching glimpses of a softer woman underneath the edgy, intense exterior.

I paused beside a huge Sanitation Department dumpster that sat abandoned on the corner, shaded by a live oak. There were two guys staring up at Deirdre's condo from across the street—a short old guy with the remnant of what must have been a prodigious beer gut when French fries were cheap, and a short younger guy who looked disturbingly like a gnome.

The gnome spotted me approaching, gestured me over.

"Feast your eyes," he whispered.

Deirdre was gardening on her terrace, completely naked. Her nipples brushed the dark soil as she filled in a hole, patting the earth vigorously, her immense satisfaction easy to read on her face.

"Yeah, I've seen her naked before," I said.

The gnome looked at me, confused. "She's done this before?"

"No, that's my girlfriend."

"Shiiit," he said, grinning. "You're lucky."

"I know," I said. I got a better grip on the plastic bag that contained my photo album and headed for the door, fishing Deirdre's key out of my pocket.

"Honey, I'm home," I called.

Deirdre lifted her head, peered at me through the sliding glass door. She got up, brushed her knees and ass, opened the door. "No you're not. Your home is on Jones Street." She pressed up against me, gave me a tongue-first kiss.

"You must have missed the tone I was going for. It was meant to be ironic. Well, not exactly ironic, or sarcastic exactly. But it was meant to have a tone."

"What the fuck are you talking about?" she said, smiling.

"I don't know," I said. I headed toward the terrace. The two guys were still standing across the street. The gnome waved. I waved back. "So what are you planting?"

"Peppers. Hot ones—all sorts. I love peppers."

"Ah. No tomatoes? No spinach?"

"Nope. Just peppers. I don't like all those other vegetables." She curled her lip as if eating vegetables was comparable to licking mold off the shower curtain. "Who were you waving to?"

"The two guys who were watching you from across the street. Nice guys. They weren't jerking off or anything. Very polite about it."

"Really?" Deirdre said, moving to the glass door to see. She laughed. "They were watching me? I didn't even notice."

The gnome waved again, tentatively. Deirdre waved back. We moved away from the window.

"You coming to the concert tonight?" Deirdre asked.

"Wouldn't miss it," I said.

"Cool." She turned on her 3-D TV, threw herself onto the couch, propped one leg on the coffee table, the other on the couch.

"You don't have a concert tomorrow, right? Everyone's planning to go to the beach."

"Right. Who's everyone?"

"Colin, Jeannie, Ange, Cortez," I ticked off. "You up for it?"

"Sure," she said, though she didn't sound enthused. Deirdre didn't seem to like hanging out with my friends, and, though she knew lots of people, she didn't seem to have many friends of her own.

I held up the plastic bag. "Remember when I said I'd show you my childhood photos? Want to see?"

Deirdre took one of the albums, started flipping through the pages. I was excited about showing them to her. To me it was like catching someone up on where you'd been, who you were.

"Do you have any?" I asked.

She shook her head. "Nope."

I waited for her to elaborate, but that was evidently her answer in its entirety. "How come?"

She sighed impatiently. "Because I don't want to remember my god damned fucking childhood." She closed the album. "Maybe I'll look at these later?" She retrieved the remote, flipped through the channels.

"Okay. No problem." Deirdre hadn't told me anything about her childhood; now it was clear why. I stashed my albums under the couch, adding one more item to my mental list of things I should be grateful for.

At the concert that night tingles ran down my spine as I watched Deirdre perform her dark magic. Afterward people surrounded her, asked her to hang out.

"Nah," Deirdre said, pressing close to me. The sensation was exquisite. "Come on." She splayed her fingers low for me. I laced mine between hers. Her palm was cool and soft and full of promises.

We headed toward her apartment.

"Razors, Deirdre! You cut to the bone," a kid called out as we passed. It was the kid with the lamp black around his eyes. He didn't recognize me.

Most of Deirdre's audience was so young. Most weren't even old enough to remember what the parking meters lining the street were for, or what the rusty signs meant.

No Parking this side
Saturday 12:01 - 4:00 a.m.
Sweep Zone

The street surely could use a good sweep.

We climbed the steps to Deirdre's apartment. I stood behind her, my arms wrapped around her waist, looking down on the top of her head as she unlocked the door.

"Want to hear something?" Deirdre said, kicking off her shoes and pulling a CD from a long shelf.

"Sure. Is it a new song?"

"Nope." She popped it into the player.

"Savannah 911: What's your emergency?" said a woman's voice.

"Is that real?" I asked. Deirdre shushed me, nodding.

"Someone just broke in here… they stabbed me and my kids, my little boys," another woman said. It was real. No one could fake the anguish and adrenaline in that tone.

"Who? Who did it?" the 911 operator said.

"My little boy is dying."

"Hang on, hang on, hang on," the operator said.

"I have a whole collection of them," Deirdre said. A vein in her neck, running over a stretched tendon, pulsed. "They're not easy to get."

"Oh my god, my babies are dying."

I should have told her to turn it off. I should have sprung from the bed, stabbed at the buttons on the CD player until the voices went silent, but I didn't want Deirdre to think I was… what? Weak. Uncool.

Deirdre unbuttoned her shirt. I leaned in and kissed the soft skin plumping at her cleavage.

"He's dead. Oh, no. Oh, no. My babies are dead," said the woman.

Deirdre's lip was curled. "I don't ride bikes."

"Well, we can't walk," I said. "The beach is ten miles; everyone else would be heading home by the time we got there."

Her fists were clenched on her hips, one knee bent. "Then go, I don't care." Of course she didn't mean it. If I left her and went with my friends, she wouldn't talk to me for days. I looked up into the branches overhead, feeling trapped. It was so rare that we did anything fun. I didn't want to miss it.

"Well, how else can we get there?" I asked.

Deirdre didn't answer. A woman with a cane who was way too young to have a cane struggled along the opposite sidewalk. Her legs were twisted, looking as if they might come out from under her at any minute. She paused to admire a small pack of dogs tied to a parking meter. They yipped and barked and wagged their tails, eager for the attention. It was the dog taxi—the owner was sitting on the curb, fanning himself with a piece of cardboard. He said something to the woman that I couldn't hear.

"Ooh!" Deirdre said, pointing. "That's how." Before I could protest she had crossed the street.

She used her charms (lots of "pleeease?" while standing closer to him than was technically necessary for the negotiation to take place) to whittle the guy's price down to $20. That wasn't bad. Not as cheap as the nothing it would cost to bike there, but not bad.

I texted Ange to alert the gang that we'd meet them there, then climbed into the hollowed-out Mustang convertible as the driver hitched the team.

The dogs were pretty hilarious. They weren't like a dogsled team, all lined up and pulling in a disciplined manner—more like the keystone cops, bumping into each other, biting ears, pulling at the wrong angle. They didn't seem to mind the work, probably because they were getting fed, and had someone telling them they were good dogs.

Occasional traffic passed us on the single-lane causeway out to Tybee Island. Refugee tents were set up alongside the road, beside the golden marsh that stretched for miles.

"This was a good idea," I said. "It's a great way to see the marsh."

Deirdre nodded. "Told you." A car beeped behind us, then roared past. Deirdre gave them the finger as they passed, with a sweet smile on her face.

The gang was lounging outside Chu's Beach Supplies when we arrived. Ange went right up to Deirdre like they were old friends. Cortez patted me on the shoulder and called me "bro." Ange had almost backed out when I told her I'd invited Cortez, but he was a friend, so I didn't think he should be left out.

The beach was packed with homeless people, leaving no space for us to spread the towels we'd brought. Strung out in a line, we stepped from one meager spot of white sand to the next and made our way to the ocean. Ange had a bottle of home brew that passed hands as we ran in the surf, splashing, laughing.

Deirdre and I swam out a few hundred yards and fooled around. The roar of the waves was distant; sea gulls screeched overhead.

"I almost expect to hear a lifeguard's whistle, see him waving us in because we're too far out."

Deirdre just laughed. She pulled off her t-shirt, pressed against me. A big wave lifted us up, dropped us down.

"This kicks ass," she said. She looked back toward shore. "Let's go get more of Ange's juice before it's all gone."

Ange was sitting on the shore, talking to Jeannie, not noticing me at all, but I still felt a little guilty about cozying up with Deirdre in front of her. Christ, we'd slept together on and off for, what, three years? It felt weird.

We rode the waves to shore. Deirdre pulled her t-shirt back on at the last possible minute, not that it helped much, given how wet it was. She made no attempt to tug it loose so it was less revealing.

I liberated Ange's jug from Cortez and took a long swig, then went off with Colin down the beach.

"So you really like her, huh?" Colin asked.

"I don't know," I said. "She's high maintenance, but it's never boring." I thought of her collection of 911 recordings, and felt an uneasy twinge that had been nagging me since that night. "Why?"

"I'm just asking," he said.

"You don't sound like you're just asking."

"Well, that's as may be. I'm still just asking."

We stopped, looked out toward the tiny cargo ships dotting the horizon.

"A lot of my attraction to her is the excitement of her being so dark and edgy and hot, I admit."

"I'm not saying anything," Colin said.

The sand sucked at my feet as we stood. I let them get buried until they were completely covered by the surf, then pulled them out.

"It's nice being with someone, even if it's not your soul mate. It sucks being single sometimes," I said.

"There are pluses and minuses to both."

I watched a seagull drift on the wind overhead, barely moving, like it was running in place. "What are the minuses to finding your soul mate?" I asked.

"You worry. I worry about Jeannie all the time. I probably average two nightmares a week about Jeannie dying."

"I never thought of that," I said.

"There are so many ways people can die now. If she died, I'd never get over it." He shook his head emphatically. "Never. You could bury me with her."

"Yeah." We watched little white birds dart in and out of the surf, plucking whatever it was they ate out of the sand. "We've been really lucky, you know? Nothing awful's happened to any of us."

"Jasper?" a woman called. I turned. She was standing at a distance, uncertain. I recognized her, but I couldn't place where I knew her. She was slim and pretty, tall, curly red hair.

"Hi," I said. Who was she?

She came over, smiling. "I don't know if you remember me. Phoebe. Our tribes crossed paths outside Metter four or five years ago, and we hung out one evening."

"Of course, yes, I remember," I said. Colin wandered off, wading into the water while Phoebe and I talked. She was here with a friend, looking for work in the beachfront restaurants. She'd had a job at Wal-Mart until it closed. Hearing that made me feel guilty, given the role I'd played in Wal-Mart's demise. Phoebe looked great—the last time I'd seen her she'd been half-starved and probably had lice, and had still looked good. Now, she looked almost elegant.

"I tried to call you, a few months after, but the number you gave me was disconnected," I said.

"Crystal died. My friend with the phone." She kicked at the wet sand with her toes.

"Sorry to hear it.

Deirdre, head down, was making her way toward us. I panicked, feeling like I was being caught doing something wrong.

"So what are you up to?" Phoebe asked.

"I got a job in a convenience store." I waved to Deirdre, as if I'd just noticed her. "Here comes my friend Deirdre."

I introduced them, still feeling like I'd done something terribly wrong. Phoebe asked Deirdre what she was up to, which was the polite way to ask what sort of work she did, if any, given that so many people didn't actually have jobs.

"I'm a rock star," Deirdre replied.

Jeannie was flagging us. I used it as an opportunity to say a quick goodbye to Phoebe. I stole a glance back as we walked away. Phoebe was looking out at the ocean.

"Who was that?" Deirdre asked as we headed back to our party.

"I met her once when we were nomads," I said. We caught up to Jeannie and Colin.

"We're hungry. We were thinking of going to that burger stand," Jeannie said. In fact Ange and Cortez were already on their way, winding through the maze of people. The rest of us headed after them.

"Do you realize," I said as we caught up to Ange and Cortez, "that this will be the first time we've eaten in a restaurant since before our tribe days?"

Jeannie laughed. "Did you take a good look at the place when we passed it? There are no seats—you stand over the table and eat microwaved French fries."

"Still, it's technically a restaurant. We're moving up in the world."

Ange put her arm around my neck and held the bottle up. "To moving up in the world." She took a swig, handed it to me. She was completely toasted. Good for her.

Cortez came up close behind us. "Keep your eyes open," he said under his breath. "There are some guys who I think followed us off the beach."

I glanced over Cortez's shoulder. Two scruffy guys were lounging outside the rest rooms. They didn't seem to be looking our way.

A dog ruckus erupted in the other direction: the taxi's dogs were barking angrily and snarling. A terrified yelping cut through the rest of the commotion. We hurried over.

Three of the taxi dogs were mauling a much smaller dog—not much more than a puppy. The taxi guy was trying to control them, pulling on one harness only to have the two other dogs fill the gap. Ange raced right into the melee, screaming at the dogs to stop. She grabbed a big pit bull by both ears; it spun around and snapped at her. She jerked her hand away. I grabbed one of the loose leads and yanked a shaggy black mutt out of the pile. Cortez and Jeannie jumped in, and a second later we had them all away from the puppy.

Ange lifted the puppy gently and cradled it. "Poor little guy. Are you okay?" It was whimpering pathetically, but it didn't look badly hurt—just some chew marks on its ears.

"I tried to stop them," the taxi driver said. "I was feeding them and the little one tried to get at their food."

"He's starving," Ange said, taking a closer look at the little black pup. She took one of the puppy's paws and shook it. "You want some French fries? Hm?" The puppy's ears went down and it licked her hand.

It was getting dark. We asked the taxi guy if he would mind sticking around for a while longer, and he said he would, for an extra five. Seemed fair enough.

We cut over to the next street, where the burger joint was.

My mind kept wandering back to my chance encounter with Phoebe. If I wasn't dating Deirdre, I would have asked for her number. I'd had a great time with her that night. I was regretting that I was with Deirdre, and that made me feel like a complete flake, given how I'd dreamed of being with Deirdre just six weeks ago. I felt childish for being so fickle. I was damned lucky to be with Deirdre—a lot of guys would give their souls to be with her.

Still, that bad feeling nagged me.

"Watch it. Stay close." Cortez had come up right behind us.

I glanced around, not sure what he was talking about. Then I spotted the two guys from outside the rest room. They were heading in our direction, laughing and goofing around. One of them had had a run-in with the flesh-eating virus—one side of his face was all but missing. As we reached them they walked up to us.

"Hey, you got a light?" the one with the mauled face said. He had a red rebel handkerchief tied around his head, and couldn't have been more than five-six.

"Sorry, bro, none of us smoke," Cortez said.

"How about a dollar and I can buy a lighter?"

Cortez fished in his pocket and pulled out a dollar. He held it out.

"How about twenty, so I can buy a couple of packs too?" His companion chuckled.

"Sorry, that's all we got. We ain't rich people," Cortez said.

"You got more than a buck," the lead guy said. He reached into his back pocket and pulled a knife. "Empty out your pockets."

"Bullshit," Deirdre said. I gave her a look, trying to shut her up, but she went on cursing as the rest of us dug into our pockets. Jeannie reached to hand over her money.

Cortez blocked her hand with his. "Put it away."

The guy glared at Cortez. "You want to die? Is that it?"

"Back away," Cortez said to us.

Colin and I exchanged a startled look—what the hell was Cortez getting us into? "Let's just give them the money," I suggested.

"Relax, everything's copacetic," Cortez said. "Just move back. Give me your shirt first."

I wasn't going to argue. I pulled off my shirt and pushed it into Cortez's hand. He never took his eyes off the guys, who looked more eager for a fight than for the money. We backed up as Cortez wrapped my shirt around his left hand.

Cortez struck an impressive karate pose—hands out front, squatting slightly—and floated toward the lead guy, who was grinning and waving his knife like it was a snake with a mind of its own.

Back in the peanut gallery, Deirdre was shouting for Cortez to kick their asses. I told her to shut up, but she ignored me.

Cortez lunged, his wrapped left arm leading. The guy slashed at Cortez and missed. Cortez kicked him in the knee. The guy went down. Immediately. Cortez did a stunning 360-degree spin and kicked the second guy in the chest, then reversed his spin and hit the guy in the throat with the edge of his hand.

The guy he'd kicked in the knee had gotten up. Cortez dropped, spun, swept the guy's legs out from under him, then stomped on the hand holding the knife as soon as he hit the pavement. The guy screamed; the knife clattered onto the sidewalk.

"Let's go," Cortez said, arms wide, corralling us away. We ran.

"Man, Cortez, I didn't know you were that good," I said as we reached the taxi guy.

Cortez stifled a grin, shook his head. "I been practicing. What else do I have to do?"

"Watch it," Colin said, steering Jeannie around bricks and glass.

It was unsettling to watch your city die. My mom had once bought a painting from the art gallery that used to be in the building we were passing—the one that had spit the bricks and shards of glass onto the sidewalk. Was the city dying, or just resting before it rose and dusted itself off? Surely one day it would come back. Soon, I hoped. I missed fresh paint. Only the trees kept their color. I tried to soak it in, letting my eyes linger on the leaves. Bright color was like a vitamin I was deficient in.

"Oh, jeez," Colin said, turning his head pointedly away from a homeless guy sitting in the eave of a stairway. At first I didn't understand, then realized the guy was masturbating into a rolled up newspaper.

"Charming," Jeannie said.

A guitar riff started up in the distance. "Hurry, it's starting," I said, picking up the pace. Above the wall of overgrown azalea ringing Chippewa Square, smoke wafted into the Spanish moss.

We made it to the square just as Deirdre's voice split the night:
"So sorry about the wheelchair,
But why should I clean my carpet
For a man who can't even fuck me
When there's always more dogs than bones?"

She reached down with her free hand and stroked the long mike. The crowd whistled and cheered. Deirdre grinned lasciviously.

"That's just beautiful. I'm getting all teary-eyed," Colin said. Jeannie laughed, wrapped an arm around his waist as we settled into a spot inside the square. The crowd was huge. The daylight was beginning to fade; Deirdre was bathed in the light of a lamppost, her eyes closed.

"What's that you say?
There can still be sex after Polio-X?
Then walk on over and spread my legs,
Cause I ain't carrying you.

"If you can't come to bed
Wheel your crippled ass home.
Cause there's studs lined up to take your place
There's always more dogs than bones."

The crowd ate it up. Except for the kids in wheelchairs.

But that was Deirdre's appeal, I think—she called it like she saw it. You got her unfiltered thoughts.

She launched into the next song. I didn't recognize it, and given that I was now Deirdre's biggest fan, I knew it must be a new one. It opened with a recording—a 911 call. The woman Deirdre had played for me, screaming into the phone. Then Deirdre began a ballad of sorts, a story about a group of gypsies walking a street in a suburban neighborhood.

No, she wouldn't, I thought.

She did, though.

"Oh, my god," Jeannie said as Deirdre described Jeannie holding out the knives and each of us taking one. She didn't use our names, but she described it all just as it had happened. Just as I'd described it to her. She'd set a collage of 911 recordings in the background to accompany her, a chorus of frantic souls screaming for help.

Jeannie sobbed, buried her face in Colin's chest.

"I'm sorry, I didn't know about this," I said.

Jeannie looked at me. "What do you mean, you didn't know about it? Where'd she get all of those details?"

"Well," I said, swallowing, "I told her about it, but not to use in a song."

"Well, what did you *think* was going to happen when you told her? She doesn't care about us, she only cares about her career."

Colin leaned in close to Jeannie's ear. "You want to go?" he whispered. Jeannie nodded.

"I'm really sorry," I said as Colin led Jeannie away.

I watched Deirdre gyrate onstage, my heart pounding with anger. She'd used me. The thing was, it didn't even surprise me that she'd used me, and why should it? That was Deirdre; she didn't even pretend she wasn't self-centered. The question was, what was I doing with her? She didn't relate to people in the normal way—showing interest in what they did, offering something of herself… she didn't do any of that.

The knot that had been in my stomach for weeks unclenched. I was done with her, I realized, and I was relieved.

"Did you hear my new song?" Deirdre asked after the concert.

"Yeah, I heard it." I started walking. I wanted to get away from the adoring crowds. "That was an awful thing for us. I don't appreciate you capitalizing on our suffering."

Deirdre's mouth fell open. "I thought you'd like it," she said.

"No," I said, stopping to face her. "I didn't like it. And I may have lost my best friends over you."

Deirdre glared razors. "That's right, *your* friends."

"What's that supposed to mean?"

"You think I don't see the expression on their faces when they're talking to me?"

"What expression?" I said.

She balled her fists on her hips and got right in my face. "The one that says there's an inside joke that I'm not getting, because I'm it. 'Look at the stupid little whore, she thinks she's our friend.'"

I looked at Deirdre, at her bulging, furious eyes and marveled at how utterly mismatched we were. How had I missed that before?

I hadn't missed it, I'd just ignored it. I loved the *idea* of Deirdre so much that I'd blocked out the actuality of Deirdre. It wasn't just Deirdre's music that was perfect for the times; Deirdre herself was perfect for the times. Dark and violent. Unpredictable. Infused with primordial energy. I, on the other hand, was not of these times. I was a great water beast, trying to dance the Watusi on fins. There seemed no better time to end things—Deirdre was furious at me anyway. She'd probably thank me at this point.

"I think it might be best if we stopped seeing each other," I said.

Deirdre's eyes opened wide with surprise. "What? We're just having a fucking argument."

"It's more than that," I said, feeling self-conscious about having this conversation in public. I paused while two girls with dyed white hair passed. "We're just very different. We like different things. We see things differently."

"Different, huh?"

I nodded.

She stood with her arms folded, staring at the sidewalk. "Fine. Get your skinny ass out of my sight before I cut your throat."

"No problem," I said. I turned to go.

"For once I try to do the right thing," she called after me. "I pick the stable guy, not the bomber dude. And what happens?" It sounded like she was crying, but I didn't turn to look. I just kept walking.

You'll overlook a great many flaws in a woman if she's famous, and has a great body. Actually, either quality alone might lead you to overlook a great many flaws, but *together*... together she could be a complete psychopath and you might overlook it. Which is what I'd done, and those were my excuses.

"Don't worry about it. It wasn't your fault. She was a nut," Colin said.

"It *was* my fault, because she was a nut from the beginning. I knew that, and I still shot off my mouth to get her to go out with me."

A siren screamed in the distance.

"Okay, it is your fault," Colin said. "But it's not like you poisoned our dog or something. Lots of people out there are hurting people on purpose."

"There is that, I guess. I don't poison people's dogs."

"Indeed. A dog-poisoner you're not," Colin agreed.

The chains holding the porch swing creaked as I dragged my foot back and forth.

It hadn't really been about Deirdre's body, or her fame. It was because she was cool, and the cool girls never liked me. If I had my photos, I could flip to one where I'm in Forsyth Park sitting on my bike. Completely by chance, Minnie Jameson is in the background, sunning herself on a towel. Minnie had been cool. The only time she'd ever talked to me was to ask me to try to buy her cigarettes at Kroger, and when I'd refused, she'd turned up her lip (much the way Deirdre did) and called me pathetic.

"I left all my photos in her apartment," I said. "If I give you a key, will you go over and get them for me?"

"What if she's there?"

"That's why I want you to go. She'd stab me if I knocked on her door and asked for those photos."

"She'd stab me, too."

He had a point. I was sick about my photos, though. There was no telling what she'd do with them, and they were the only photos I had from my childhood, from a time when life was normal and everyone had a place to live and an Xbox.

We sat in silence, staring out into the street, listening to the creak of the porch swing, the crickets, and the occasional gunshot.

Chapter 4:
Dada Jihad

Summer, 2029 (Eighteen months later)

A cop was doubled over, clutching a parking meter, puking on the sidewalk as a half-dozen onlookers wearing white virus masks gawked from a safe distance. Ange and I were on the bottom step of her porch, thirty feet away. Ange cursed and turned her head. I kept watching. I didn't want to, but somehow I couldn't turn away.

The puking went from a trickle to a sudden bursting-hydrant gush, then back to a trickle. It spattered in a six-foot swath, steam rising as the hot sidewalk boiled it. The cop made awful guttural sounds when the vomiting slowed enough, as though his intestines were about to spill onto the sidewalk as well.

"What is it?" a gray-haired woman asked.

The bald guy next to her shook his head. "I don't know. It's a bad one." They took a half-step back.

The vomit turned pink, then red. There were gasps and "oh my gods" from the crowd.

The cop's eyes bulged as the puke lost its thickish chunky quality and became smooth, bright red blood. He dropped to his knees, weaved as blood stained the front of his blue uniform a deep purple, then collapsed to the pavement.

"Jesus Christ," Ange said as a few final spasms squeezed the cop dry. He lay still, his eyes vacant. In the distance, a siren warbled, growing closer.

We went inside. Chair, one of Ange's housemates, had been watching through the window. A skinny, bald, bow-legged guy in his fifties stood next to him. The guy had a backpack slung over his shoulder, and he was crying. As we came in he swept his shirtsleeve across his eyes and gawked at Ange, starting at her toes and slowly climbing to her dark green eyes.

"Wow, would I like to make love to you," he said, not a hint of flirtation in his level tone, as if he were reporting on the weather.

Ange fixed him with her best bitch stare. "Yeah, thanks, let me get back to you on that."

"A new one," Chair said, motioning toward the cop with his chin. "Got to be engineered. Too quick to be a natural virus." Ange nodded. Chair was wearing shorts; I tried not to stare at the elaborate black steelwork of his long-nonfunctioning bionic legs. Even Chair was putting vanity aside in the scorching heat. Chair sighed, rotated his wheelchair in a tight circle. The skinny guy followed him toward the coffee table. His walk was loose, his arms swinging like he owned the freaking world, and he was now sporting a shitass grin.

"Who's he?" I asked Ange. She shrugged.

"You going to introduce us to your friend?" Ange said to Chair.

"This is Sebastian," Chair said over his shoulder. He parked across from the sofa and looked at me. "That's about all I can say in casual company."

Ange gave him an impatient tisk. "Jasper doesn't know any local government officials or Jumpy-Jumps, Chair. Don't be so fucking clandestine."

"Don't play it like this is no big deal, Ange. This is fucking clandestine stuff. No offense, but Jasper, you need to go." He waved me off like a cop directing traffic.

I shrugged, headed for the door. Ange grabbed my t-shirt and tugged. "No, you're fine. I pay rent here too." She turned back to Chair, hands on hips. "Look, I'd trust Jasper with my life. Whatever you tell me, I'm going to tell him anyway, so whatever the big secret is, just fucking tell us, will you?"

Chair tapped the arm of his wheelchair with a dirty fingernail that badly needed trimming. "I hope you trust him with your life, and ours too, because that's what you're doing." He nodded tightly. "Fine. Sebastian is a delivery man from the Science Alliance in Atlanta." He raised his eyebrows significantly behind delicate eyeglasses that looked absurd on his mastiff head.

I'd read about the Science Alliance—an underground group of smart people who'd gone rogue. They were aggressively taking matters into their own hands, trying to tackle some of the world's many problems. The federal government disliked them almost as much as the Jumpy-Jumps. Suddenly I had doubts about wanting to stay and hear what the guy had to say.

"Shit, you're kidding," Ange said. "You don't look like an eco-terrorist."

"I don't feel like an eco-terrorist," Sebastian said, shrugging.

Ange dropped onto the couch and swung her legs onto the coffee table, forgetting that one of the table legs was broken. It collapsed into a three-point stance. "Shit," she whispered. Uzi trotted into the room, hopped on the couch next to her, circled a couple of times and dropped like a stone, pushing his ass right up against her. I sat next to Uzi. The couch was coated with dog hair

"You know," I said. "If you pull something and get caught, you won't go to jail; the cops'll just drag you into the street and shoot you."

"No doubt," Chair said. "The stakes are high."

"The potential costs are high," I persisted. "I don't get how the benefits match those costs. What do you think you're going to accomplish?"

"The benefit is saving two billion lives, maybe three. Is that worth risking your life? About four billion people are going to die if things stay business as usual. If we can do our part to cut that in half, is it worth the risk?"

"We don't know for sure that billions of people are going to die," Ange said.

"Yeah, we do," Chair said. "For sure."

"We do," Sebastian chimed, nodding.

"It's all based on stochastic models," Ange said. "It's incredibly speculative."

Chair glared at her. "How many times do scientists have to be right before people give them a little credit? And you of all people, about to get your doctorate, should have some faith in them." He snared the remote from the arm of the couch, stabbed the power button. CNN came on. The president was having a news conference. The president always seemed to be having a news conference; I couldn't imagine when he had time to run the country, or what was left of it.

Almost on cue, the TV jingled and a text message scrolled across the bottom of the screen:

Ange. I want to see you. I'm free Monday, Tuesday, or Thursday for dinner. Can we meet one of those nights? Charles.

"Oh, god dammit," Ange howled. "'I want to see you.' Like I'm his fucking servant instead of his student."

Chair ignored the message. "They keep warning us, and we just keep carrying on as usual, and things keep getting worse. 'We have to keep the economy going,' the president says, while the fucking ocean is lapping at our ankles and we've got troops spread out over six different fronts in a never-ending war—"

"Okay, fine. I know the score, I don't need a lecture," Ange said.

The screen door squealed and slammed. "Damn, what happened out there?" Rami breezed into the room, carrying a stack of news-papers. He emptied a different newspaper dispenser every day to protest their editorial policies. These people didn't make a lot of sense to me. My friends and I were in the "keep your head down and try not to get it cut off" camp of surviving this mess. People like Chair got gassed. I was surprised he was still alive, and it scared the shit out of me that Ange was sharing a house with him and these other would-be rebels.

As Chair introduced Sebastian to Rami, I got up and hovered in the doorway, making it as clear as possible that I wasn't part of this meeting. I hoped Ange would follow my lead, but she stayed on the couch.

"You know I'm in," Rami said when he learned who Sebastian was. "So what's in the bag?"

"I have two deliveries for you." Sebastian unzipped his backpack. Uzi trotted over, stuck his nose into the pack and snuffled, probably hoping it was filled with bacon.

"Uzi, get your butt over here," Ange said. Uzi just wagged his tail.

Sebastian pulled something from the pack with a flourish, held it between thumb and forefinger. He was giggling. There was something definitely wrong with this guy. "Bamboo root," he said. It was a cone-shaped tannish nub, crowned with four or five tiny lemon fingers, reaching skyward. "It's engineered to spread like crazy. It can push through blacktop, even concrete if it's not too thick. And it's fast—you won't believe how fast."

"Nature taking back its territory by force. I like it," Rami said. "The authorities will suspect the Jumpy-Jumps. It's got their whimsical sensibility."

"Without the sick surprise at the bottom of the box," Chair said.

"We want to coat entire urban areas with it, in one coordinated attack, to bring commerce to a grinding halt. We'll plant it at night, in places where it will cause maximum disruption—busy roads, shopping plazas, tourist attractions."

"Wait a minute," I said, taking a couple of steps back into the living room. "How does this save lives? It sounds like you just want to add to the chaos."

"We need to slow things down," Sebastian said. "Otherwise the U.S. is six to twelve months away from an exchange of nuclear weapons with at least one other country, probably more, and we'll be under martial law, and things will get really nasty. So we clog the roads so vehicles can't operate, keep the military busy, slow the violence in the streets."

"Couldn't that stall food transport?" I asked. "People might starve."

"It could make transport difficult, but people shouldn't literally starve. Some may."

"That's pretty fucking cold," Ange said.

"Depends on how you look at it," Chair said. "Are a few thousand lives lost now worth saving a few billion later?"

I wasn't sure I liked that logic, but I kept my mouth closed. It was clear they weren't particularly interested in hearing dissenting opinions.

"What's the other delivery?" Rami asked.

Sebastian smiled wide, spread his arms. "You're looking at him!"

Chair frowned. "You're the other delivery?"

Sebastian nodded.

"So what can you do?" Rami asked.

"It's not what I can do, it's what I carry. In my blood." He fished around in his backpack, pulled out a plastic bag attached to a thin tube. He pressed the end of the tube against the crook of one elbow, demonstrating that it was for drawing blood. "It's a virus called Doctor Happy, and it's guaranteed to take the fight out of anyone infected with it."

It was scorching hot by afternoon—hot enough that it would cost a week's pay to keep the place cool, so they moved to the canopied roof. Other people arrived, mostly young rebellious types with interesting haircuts. One brought a boombox and cranked up some Necrobang. I kept expecting them to boot my ass out, but they didn't.

Sebastian bled himself while others sat hunched over pairs of VR gloves, embedding short pins in the leather fingerpads. Including Chair and Rami, I counted eleven members of the infection gang. I only knew one of them—Cortez—but Ange seemed to know most of them. It didn't surprise me that Cortez was here. Lately he seemed kind of lost, hungry for some direction. He spent a lot of time hanging out with shady gang types.

Ange watched the operation; she seemed ambivalent, caught in a nether-region between me and Chair. I stepped up behind her. "This whole thing smells like a Jumpy-Jump operation," I said.

The plan was to spread the virus pretty much at random, trying to target males, and anyone who looked pro-business or pro-government. Sticking those who would benefit most from the virus—gang types, political leaders, police—was deemed too risky.

Ange nodded absently. "I know. But these are the good guys. I feel like I should have faith in them."

"I don't have much faith in that guy." I gestured toward Sebastian, who was bouncing to the beat while he bled through a tube.

"I don't know what the fuck to make of that Homer." She folded her arms, blew a damp strand of hair out of her face. "I think I'm going to offer to be a spotter. Watch that no cops catch on to what's happening."

I wanted to point out that the getaway driver was no more moral than the guys who robbed the bank, but I knew better than to argue with her.

Rami broke out a quart of home-brewed grain alcohol, the sort that you could buy on any street corner these days, and passed it around. Chair nodded to the beat, watching people who had movable limbs with only a hint of envy. "Carpe diem," he shouted over the music, "but never forget that we're partying on the fucking *Titanic*." He took a long swig from a soiled plastic cup.

I wasn't convinced that things were going to get worse. It felt like we had already hit bottom, or were near it anyway. It was hard to ignore police puking blood on the sidewalk in front of your house, but most of the talking heads on TV thought that things would get better soon—that the stock market would recover, the Jumpy-Jump movement would be crushed, the warm wars we were fighting across the globe would end, that we'd get a grip on melting icecaps. Things hadn't gotten any better over the past five years, but they hadn't gotten much worse. We just needed to wait it out. Spreading happy viruses and planting voracious bamboo didn't sound like the right move at all.

"You two ready to roll?" Cortez put an arm around Ange's shoulder. It made my jealousy radar jangle, but Ange had told me a dozen times that she wasn't interested in starting things back up with Cortez.

"I think I'm gonna take a pass," I said. Cortez shrugged like it was all cool to him. Ange waved, and blew me a kiss.

I headed uptown to Gaston Street, to visit a woman who wanted to talk about selling honey in Ruplu's store. We tended to work on commission, partly to minimize cash outlay, and partly because when the store was robbed, the losses weren't all Ruplu's.

I passed two guys wearing CD armbands—Civil Defense. Everywhere you looked they seemed to be popping up, and every other blank concrete surface either had a poster encouraging you to volunteer, or a stencil of their logo—an eagle in flight, carrying a rat in its claws. The rat was supposed to represent the Jumpy-Jumps, and criminals of every ilk, but more and more it seemed the substantial fee Ruplu was paying the CD protected Ruplu from the CD itself, not the so-called bad guys.

The honey woman shook my hand with both of hers. She was old—eighty at least. I was pretty sure the sundress she wore had been made out of old curtains. She took me to the roof of her house, which had a three-sided corner dormer with a steep peaked roof, hugged by an ancient red brick chimney.

I didn't know anything about bees and wasn't particularly interested in learning about them, but the woman gave me an enthusiastic, long-winded dissertation on beekeeping and her hives. Afterward we went down to her living room to talk about the details. She said she could supply about thirty jars a week during the season. I held the sample jar she had given to me up to the light streaming in through the curtainless picture window. Little chips of honeycomb, dust, and even what looked to be a bee's wing were suspended in the golden goo. It still made my mouth water, but I'd found that people would pay way more for things that looked mass-produced.

An old Mickey Mouse coloring book was stuffed in a magazine rack by the woman's reclining chair. I pulled it out, took a good look of the image of Mickey on the cover, then held the coloring book up and pointed at Mickey. "Here's what I'd like you to do. Take this book to Mark Parcells at Whitaker Print Shop, and get him to make labels with this picture and 'Mickey Mouse Honey' on them. The honey will sell much better that way."

"Oh," the woman said, sounding less than enthused. "But isn't that a copyright violation?"

I chuckled, shook my head. "Disney isn't going to bother you, I promise." Ah, the good old days, when Disney had the time and energy to sue people for selling unlicensed products.

If there was any bright side to The Decline (as the media often referred to it), it had to be the neutering of corporate America. Back in the old days they were such a huge presence; today it took all of their energy and resources just to produce their products and get them onto store shelves.

Pleased to have secured another product for the store, I headed home. If I'd been able to whistle worth a damn, I might have whistled.

Bull Street was almost deserted in the afternoon heat. From an open second-floor window, an old woman with no front teeth stared at me, her mouth curled in suspicion. She reminded me of my great aunt, who had believed for the last ten years of her life that I and all the rest of her relatives were trying to kill her.

Two blocks ahead, a woman turned the corner and headed in my direction. It was Deirdre.

I bolted into the doorway of an abandoned storefront. Why I was hiding, I couldn't say. Deirdre still had all of my childhood photos (assuming she hadn't burned them). I should have confronted her, maybe twisted her little arm behind her back until she told me where they were. Instead I did my best to fold into the crack between the door and the boarded-up window.

What had she done with my photos? Sometimes I still lay awake wondering. There had been no cut-up pile greeting me when I finally built up the nerve to use my key to sneak into her place while she was out. No charred corners mixed with the ashes in the fireplace (showing a tantalizing hint of a sneaker; the ornament-laden branches of a Christmas tree...). They were just gone. Did she toss them in a dumpster? Did she still have them? I missed them to my bones. I had no proof now, that I had a past, that I'd once been a child. I never would have guessed it would hurt so much to lose them. Evidently Deirdre had.

Deirdre strutted past, oblivious to my cowering form. I was not afraid of her, I told myself. I just didn't want to deal with her. I waited a couple of minutes, then went on my way, still thinking about her.

At home I found Colin and Jeannie parked in front of the TV, watching the news. We might as well ditch the remote—our TV was always tuned to MSNBC. With times so dark there was always something new, always people dying. Egypt was systematically exterminating the population of the rest of Northern Africa. Why? Because the population of Northern Africa ate. Fewer people meant less competition for food and energy, and Egypt had the biggest guns. Bad as it was in the U.S., some other parts of the world were turning into nothing but giant concentration camps and killing fields. It was both mesmerizing and depressing.

I took a deep breath and turned away from the TV. I would have liked to go to sleep, but Colin and Jeannie were sitting on my bed watching TV, so I went into their room to do a little bookkeeping for the store.

"I have to say, Cortez was a natural," Ange said. "He'd stop to look at a table of sorry-looking pistols, then turn and bump into some guy in an expensive suit, grabbing the guy's shoulders like he was steadying himself. The guy didn't even flinch from the stick. He was slapping people on the back, even pulled it off with a couple of cops and soldiers."

Uzi tugged on his leash, panting and wagging his tail, trying to pull Ange across the street toward Jackson Square and its Live Oaks. "Uzi, no," Ange said, as if that would faze him. He lived to pee on those massive trunks.

"You want me to take a turn?" I offered, knowing she didn't. Ange shook her head. "Are we talking regular U.S. soldiers from Fort Stewart, or those private mercenary guys?" I asked.

"Regular. He's not suicidal."

There were more people in the park than usual. More adults, anyway. The kids were always there, playing their incomprehensible game, jumping among big colored dots laid along the squares and sidewalks, alternately frowning in concentration and laughing like hell, dousing each other with industrial-strength water guns, rolling dice the size of baseballs. Now there were also groups of adults, sitting in circles, cooking in pots on open fires, laughing their heads off. They were infected with Doctor Happy.

Doctor Happy had made the local evening news three days after Chair and Sebastian's infection party. They called it a strange new virus that results in "disorientation, amotivation, and giddiness." Sebastian had said the government wasn't going to like this virus at all. Authoritarian types are uncomfortable with people altering their consciousness—they'd rather see them vomit blood.

An ultralight helicopter buzzed overhead, casting a drifting shadow on the street. Probably some rich jerk going for a martini at Rooftop Elysium.

"What I wouldn't give for a rocket launcher," Ange said, her neck craned.

"Maybe you'll have one of your own once you get your Ph.D.," I laughed. "At the very least you'll be able to live in a gated community."

Ange glared at me. "I'd never become one of them. I'd live in a better place, sure, but never in one of those obnoxious gated fortresses." Ange kicked a soda can out of her way. "It doesn't matter anyway, because I'm not getting my Ph.D."

I stopped in my tracks. "What?"

She let her head loll back until she was staring at the sky. "I had that meeting with Charles, my thesis advisor. A *dinner* meeting, of course. At the Pink House."

"Typical," I muttered. The Pink House was a silk tablecloth, sniff-the-wine-cork place.

"Yeah. It was his usual shit—the grope-hug greeting, reaching over to brush my hair out of my eyes, all the sexual innuendo crap. I asked if we could schedule my defense, and he said no, he thinks I need to run another fucking study. Then he pulls out his appointment calendar and says his wife will be out of town the first half of next week, and why don't I come over to his place Tuesday night for dinner, to discuss the new study?"

Uzi strained hard on his leash, eager to get moving. We continued walking.

"It suddenly hit me that he's not going to let me defend my dissertation until I let him fuck me." She started to say something else but choked up. I waited as she took a few deep breaths and got herself under control. "He's going to throw one obstacle after another in front of me, make me sit through a thousand excruciating dinners, because that way he has power over me."

A Jumpy-Jump lounged on a stoop up ahead, watching us approach. Watching Ange, really. He was dressed in a mock-mailman outfit, the "U.S. Mail" shoulder patches executed in ornate calligraphy.

"For four years I've been dreaming of walking across that stage, with my whole family—even my bitch grandmother—watching. What do you think of your crank-addict loser, drug-rehab dropout, gypsy granddaughter now, you old bag? I wouldn't even have to say it out loud. Probably none of them but my mom and Cory would actually show up, but the fantasy works better when they're all sitting in a row on those metal folding chairs, watching."

"That's a big dog for such a little peanut," the Jumpy-Jump said as we drew near. We kept our pace steady. I'd seen the guy around—he was ethnic, maybe East Indian. Long braided hair. He spoke with the singsong accent that Jumpy-Jumps evidently had invented out of thin air.

"Where are you two and your big dog so urgently needed?" He stood lazily, not exactly blocking the sidewalk, but impeding it. Ange veered into the street, cutting a wide path around him, and I followed her lead.

"I'm talking to you, don't disappear me," he said. He moved to block our path.

Uzi snarled and lunged. Ange held his leash tight; the Jumpy-Jump leaped clear of Uzi's snapping teeth.

A heartbeat later, there were blades all over the Jumpy-Jump, jutting from his belt, his boots. He clutched what looked like machetes in both fists. "You think your big dog can protect you?" There was blood and a ragged gash on his thumb—Uzi had just caught his retreating hand.

I grabbed the leash and helped Ange drag Uzi backward. He was barking and snapping, scrabbling to get at the man. We just kept pulling, retreating the way we'd come, until Uzi finally relented and reversed direction as well.

"I can fuck you any time I want, Little Peanut," the Jumpy-Jump shouted at our backs. "Right here on the daylight street. Strip off your false security and live in constant fear, where you belong."

We ran five blocks before slowing.

"I hate that I can't walk the streets without being afraid. I hate it," Ange hissed.

"I know," I said. My heart was still thumping like mad. "What's wrong with those people? And what happened to the police? Or even the Civil Defense? What happened to their whole thing about taking back the streets?"

"Now they all just look out for themselves," Ange said. "Just like Charles."

A street sweeper rumbled along a side street, churning up plywood and cardboard shelters, its whooping alarm warning tenants to get clear or be swept up with their houses.

"Have you complained to the Department Chair about him?"

Ange nodded. "I was there this morning. She says there's nothing she can do, that I should switch advisors. But Charles is the only botanical biotech person left on the faculty, so I'd have to start my dissertation over in a different area. When I told her I couldn't afford to start over, because my financial support ended this year, she suggested I let him fuck me."

"You've got to be kidding me," I said.

Ange shook her head. "She said when buildings are being bombed and politically outspoken faculty are disappearing in the middle of the night, 'small incivilities' don't mean much."

"I can guess what you said."

"I bet you can," Ange said. She stopped in front of the Savannah College bio building. "This is where I get off." She waved. "Bye, sweetie."

I waved back. No public displays of affection. Somehow we'd made it work for four years, the friends-with-sex thing. Probably because neither of us had met anyone, or really wanted to meet anyone at this point. Things with Ange were comfortable and easy. Uncomplicated.

Truth be told, I was beginning to doubt that I would ever find someone to love in any case. I suspected that the sort of relationship I was looking for just wasn't possible any more, that it was an artifact from the time when those photographs I missed so much were taken. There was a line drawn in my memory that separated my life before The Decline from my life after. I imagine everyone has that line. Everything else had changed after The Decline; there was no reason to think that love had some special dispensation.

I headed home. The sun was low in the sky, filtering through the twisted, moss-covered branches of the oaks, adding a gold tinge to the red brick path. I felt so bad for Ange. She was so close. A two-hour defense, three signatures, and she had a Ph.D. She could teach at a university, or continue her research for an agro corporation. The stakes were so high. Once upon a time if you didn't make it into a lucrative career, there were plenty of semi-lucrative alternatives. Now it seemed as if the divide between rich and poor was a chasm. There was no middle class any more. On one side there were the rich—safe and comfortable, living in luxury—and on the other, on our side, it was a challenge just to stay alive.

As I approached Jackson Square, I stopped short. Sebastian was sitting on a bench in the square, with the Jumpy-Jump who had threatened us a half-hour earlier. They were laughing like old pals. Sebastian spotted me and waved; the Jumpy-Jump turned, smiled.

"Little Peanut's big brother! Come join us."

I headed toward the bench.

"You two know each other?" Sebastian said as I approached.

"Yes indeed," the Jumpy-Jump said. He held out a bandaged hand without getting up, looking amused, as if we'd shared a joke rather than an altercation. I ignored his hand.

"We began our song with the wrong note, I fear." He dropped his hand, stretched out on the bench and sighed contentedly. "So, Mister Peanut, what do *you* think of our Dada Jihad?"

I'd read everything I could about the Jumpy-Jump movement

since that night at the art show. It had started in Detroit, after the Foxtown Massacre, when the police broke up a protest using nerve gas. A Native American street singer named Dada Tanglefoot began preaching a weird mix of anarchism, Zen, and Dadaism that spoke to the people. Tanglefoot was assassinated in quick order, probably on orders from the feds, but her words spread like a virus through the poor and angry neighborhoods. As far as I could tell, the actual doctrine was incoherent bullshit. Maybe Tanglefoot's teachings had gotten tangled as it passed from person to person.

"I understand why you're angry, but I don't think much of killing random people," I said. "What do you expect to get out of it?"

"Me?"

"Jumpy-Jumps, I mean."

"We don't expect anything." He shrugged, his eyes twinkling.

"It doesn't make sense."

"Does anything make sense? It's all absurd. We're just unleashing some vicious absurdity to underscore the point." He stood, made a peace sign. "Sebastian, it was a pleasure."

Sebastian returned the gesture. "Same here, Rumor."

"Down is up, and sinners are saints, Mister Peanut," Rumor said as he turned to leave.

"My name is Jasper."

"Down is up, and sinners are saints, Jasper."

Rumor stood at the edge of the square, waiting for a truck to pass, before sauntering between two abandoned gas hogs and across the street.

"Why were you talking to that asshole?" I asked Sebastian. "He threatened Ange and me just half an hour ago, waving a machete at us. If Uzi hadn't been there we'd probably be lying dead with our throats cut.

"I'll talk to pretty much anyone." Sebastian said.

"Well hooray for you."

He met my sarcasm with a big grin. "If you always keep things amiable you minimize the chance of ending up in the street with your throat cut."

"Nothing minimizes the chances of getting your throat cut when it comes to Jumpy-Jumps—they'll happily cut you open and pull your guts out while they sing you a love song."

Sebastian laughed delightedly. "You almost sounded like a

Jumpy-Jump when you said that."

I smiled. It was difficult to hate the guy too much because of his demeanor. "So, what's it like? The virus."

"It's invigorating."

"Invigorating? So, you're happy all the time, and you don't want to hurt anyone? You'll even have a friendly chat with a terrorist? It sounds like a lobotomy."

"Oh, no." He clasped his hands together and held them to his heart. "It's the exact opposite of a lobotomy. You glimpse the infinite. Just a glimpse, but that's enough. If I were cracked open any wider I might go mad—we're not built to experience all that emptiness."

"Oh, now I get it. You're basically on a permanent acid trip." I gave him the peace sign. "Peace, love, all-is-oneness."

An ultralight copter buzzed low over the square. Sebastian waited till it passed before answering. "That's about right, I guess."

"How did you get infected?" I asked.

"I volunteered."

"You're shitting me. You volunteered to be infected with an incurable virus? Why would you do that?"

Sebastian sighed. "My wife and daughter were raped and killed in front of me during the Atlanta gas riots." He gave me a wan smile, as if he were talking about an old friend he missed. "I was going to hang myself; what did I have to lose?"

How do you respond to something like that? "I'm sorry." It was all I could think to say.

A tall, scrawny girl hurried past carrying a bucket of water, her body canted to compensate for the weight.

"What did you do in Atlanta?" I asked.

"Research and development. I'm a virologist." He closed his eyes, turned his face up to the sun. "I led the team that developed Doctor Happy."

"So what are you doing here? Why aren't you back there working on other fabulous new viruses?"

He made a face like he'd just bit into something foul. "I don't want to sit in a concrete room under artificial lights all day. I want to be around people, in the sunlight."

"Well, if it's people and sunlight you're looking for, you came to the right place."

The night of the bamboo party, Chair and his entourage dressed as homeless people, which basically meant getting a little dirtier than usual, looking a little more hopeless and depressed than usual, and taking along a couple of trash bags of what looked like their belongings. Only instead of just their belongings, the trash bags contained bamboo roots and containers of gray water, wrapped inside belongings.

The crickets were in full stereo as Ange, Cortez, and I crossed MLK and walked up the on-ramp to I-16. Vehicles rumbled past occasionally, the drivers taking no notice of us. It was nice to be invisible; I thought maybe I should haul a bag of shit around with me all the time.

"Do you ever find yourself envying Sebastian?" Cortez asked.

"Shit, no," Ange said. "I crave a good buzz as much as anyone, but I want to come down after." There was a slight breeze; it was almost bearable tonight.

"But nothing would ever bother you again. Doesn't that sound even a little tempting?"

"It's virus-induced," I said. "Those little fuckers are doing things to his mind." We reached the interstate, walked alongside, staying in the weeds well away from the road.

"Yeah. I'd never do it to myself, but still, sometimes I envy the bastard's peace of mind," Cortez said as he looked up and down the interstate. He dropped his trash bag and squatted, pulled a garden trowel from his pack and dug a hole in a bald spot. Ange dropped a bamboo root in the hole, pushed dirt around it. Ange had decided to participate fully in this operation; she said it didn't feel as much like rape as spreading Doctor Happy had. I, on the other hand, was there solely because I was afraid for my friends' safety, and there was safety in numbers. Plus I didn't have anything else to do. Colin and Jeannie were having a date night, and no one else was around.

Cortez poured water over it from an old soda bottle. We headed back toward the on-ramp. It had taken all of thirty seconds.

"How are you doing with that asshole Charles?" Cortez asked as we walked.

Ange filled him in on the latest; Cortez looked more pissed with each word. I peppered Ange's monologue with the occasional "Can you believe it?"

"You want me to take care of him?" Cortez asked when she'd

finished. "I can soften his dick in a hurry."

Ange looked tempted. "He deserves to be hurt, but I don't think that would help. Thanks, but no, I have to do this myself."

Cortez looked disappointed. "Let me know if you change your mind."

Ange stopped short, holding out her arms. "Shh. Listen to that."

We listened. Splitting, popping, crackling sounds lit the air, as if the entire city was built on ice that was giving way. It was an eerie, awesome sound. The other teams had been hard at work.

"Unbelievable," Cortez said.

We headed up Abercorn, under a canopy of oaks that cloaked the sky, as sirens began to compete with the hungry sound of awakening bamboo.

The effect was breathtaking. Broughton Street, the main retail strip, was completely impassable, choked with bright green bamboo stalks. Just as Sebastian had said, they pushed through the asphalt like it was cardboard.

The air smelled of blooming azaleas and piss. A group of young Dada wannabes in mock police, cowboy, and FedEx outfits strutted toward us, each sporting his own signature cool-walk. I put my arm across Ange's shoulder protectively. She smiled; I knew what she was thinking: she had a seventy-pound dog with her, and Uzi had no qualms about putting a hurt on someone, whereas I had once eaten an unidentified fetus, and did all but thank the Jumpy-Jump who fed it to me.

On Drayton Street two kids, a boy and a girl, were dragging clumps of cut bamboo along the brick sidewalk. They turned into an empty lot between dilapidated buildings.

"Good job, Emma; good job, Cyril!" an old man said. He stood next to a half-finished bamboo hut, canted but looking impressively sturdy. That was probably Grandpa; Mom and Dad and Grandma were likely dead. This was probably not how Grandpa had planned to spend his retirement.

In Jackson Square, more bamboo huts and curtains. On Bull, a group of homeless, mixed with cleaner people who were probably Doctor Happy victims, cheered on the bamboo as it chewed up Bull Street and surrounded police headquarters on Victory Drive. Machete-wielding cops and soldiers chopped at the sprouting bamboo in the blazing May heat; another ran a ditch-digger around the perimeter of the outbreak. They looked hot, and pissed off.

"Very nice, very nice," Ange said. She was reading a report texted from Sebastian. "And listen to this: a priest in Southside is being charged with spiking the sacramental wine with his Doctor Happy-infected blood. Wonderful." Ange had clearly drunk the Kool-Aid.

Some of those infected seemed to feel it was their duty to give it to others—biological evangelists, spreading the word of peace and joy and all-night street parties. Mothers poked their children with bloodstained pins while they slept.

On Whitaker, a tank was easily tearing through the bamboo outbreak, blazing a trail for troops and shoppers. But there weren't many tanks in Savannah, and tonight Sebastian and his followers would plant more bamboo.

The news was now reporting Doctor Happy outbreaks in the northeast and west. There were bamboo outbreaks happening all over the world—China, Europe, South America. I hadn't realized how large the Science Alliance's operation was. Sebastian wouldn't say whether all of these outbreaks had originated with his group in Atlanta, or even whether their group was a cell in a larger group. They had to be part of a larger group, to be able to pull off such a massive stunt.

There was a party raging in Pulaski Square. Twenty or thirty revelers were pounding on drums and trash cans while others circled them, doing some sort of square dance, hooking arms with each other. There were also at least two couples having sex right in the open. Opposite the square three cops stood on the sidewalk in front of a drug store, automatic weapons dangling from their fingers.

I caught a glimpse of movement on the roof above where the cops were lounging: hands, dropping something. A white oval plummeted, hit the sidewalk with a splat right at the cops' feet. Blood spattered everywhere. A blood-bomb? That was a new twist. It drenched the cops, the sidewalk, the side of the building. The cops lifted their weapons, pointed them all over, looking for an assailant. Then they seemed to notice that they were covered in blood. They wiped frantically at their eyes and lips, looking scared as shit.

Shouts and laughter erupted from the crowd of partiers. The square dance dissolved; some of the revelers trotted toward the cops.

"Welcome to reality!" someone shouted.

A lanky guy wearing nothing but a loincloth that looked like a diaper ran up to one of the cops and patted him on the shoulder as others crowded around, cheering.

The cop pressed his automatic weapon into the lanky guy's gut, and fired. The guy staggered backward. Before he hit the pavement the other cops were spraying gunfire into the looming crowd. Screams lit the air; people crumpled, slammed into each other in the frenzy to escape.

"No!" Ange and I shouted simultaneously. Ange moved toward the melee; I grabbed her elbow and yanked her away, toward cover.

One cop's head suddenly snapped back; chips of scalp and brain sprayed on the drug store window. The cop went down as the window shattered. I looked around, trying to figure out who was firing on the cops. I spotted the flash of a muzzle from inside a copse of bamboo half a block behind us.

Two men stepped out of the bamboo—Jumpy-Jumps, with rifles raised, peering through scopes. The other two cops convulsed, their already blood-soaked bodies blossoming fresh as they fell to the pavement. It wasn't taking the Jumpy-Jumps long to turn these new developments to their advantage.

Back home, I showered before joining Colin and Jeannie in the living room to watch the news. We watched footage of hundreds of Jumpy-Jump gunmen swarming the bamboo-choked streets of Chicago, then of a tank firing on insurgents in San Antonio. The Dadas were taking advantage of the chaos, spreading even more chaos.

What terrified me most were not the images, but the reporters' voices. The usual calm, even cadence was gone, replaced by shrill, breathless, unpolished descriptions that gave me the feeling that they might drop their microphones and run at any moment.

"I wonder if Sebastian's Nobel laureates expected *this*?" Jeannie said as we watched.

"The way Sebastian talks, they have it mapped out down to where each body is going to fall."

"Let me see the phone," Jeannie said to Colin, wriggling her fingers. She called Ange and asked her to ask Sebastian if this was all part of the plan. Jeannie pulled her mouth away from the phone. "He says it draws energy away from the large-scale conflicts that are bubbling, and weakens the central government, and that in the long run those are good things."

I'd heard this sort of crap before, from politicians. Whatever the results of their policies, they used some sort of tortured logic to argue that it was really a good thing.

I was struggling to get a sense of whose side I should be on. By nature I tended to favor anyone who took on the establishment. The establishment had proven that it was good at acting like it knew what it was doing, but was utterly incompetent underneath that façade. On the other hand these scientist-rebels seemed to be taking huge risks, treating the world as if it were a giant laboratory. Neither side seemed like a safe bet, and that was disconcerting.

I drifted off to sleep with my window open, serenaded by the ubiquitous crackle and pop of the bamboo, which drowned out much of the gunfire, and the screams of the night victims.

By morning, things had quieted considerably. We watched the news reports. The Jumpy-Jumps had melted back into the general population. The bamboo was still spreading.

The burble of the phone woke me. Our phone was so old that it didn't play music any more; instead it made a tone-deaf warbling sound.

"Jasper?" It was Ange; she sounded beyond panic.

"What happened?" I asked, adrenaline rushing through me, burning away the muddle of sleepiness.

"Uzi's gone."

"He's gone? From where?"

"I tied him to the bike rack and went into the grocery store, and when I came out he was gone."

"Is the leash gone too? Did he break it?" I got out of bed, pulled a pair of jeans from the mound of clothes I'd worn yesterday.

"No, it's gone too."

"He still could've pulled loose. He's probably nearby."

"He wouldn't run away, even if he got loose. Not Uzi."

"But he must have," I said. "Who would steal a big old mutt?"

Ange started to cry. "I don't know. But he's gone."

"I'm on my way," I said. "I'll bring Colin and Jeannie. We'll find him."

I ran to get Colin and Jeannie. A lost dog—it was the sort of old-fashioned problem you didn't often get to tackle these days. For a second I pondered the possibility that the bamboo outbreak had stifled food supplies to the point that people were kidnapping dogs and eating them, but that didn't make sense. There were plenty of strays out there if you wanted to eat dogs, and besides, no one would tangle with a big, mean-looking dog like Uzi.

"Shhh, shhh, we'll find him," I said, my arm wrapped around Ange as we sat on the steps of her house. The sun would be down in a few hours. I knew what Ange was thinking: Uzi would be alone, in the dark.

An electric wheeming announced that Chair was coming around the corner. Ange stood, stared expectantly at the corner.

Chair was alone. He looked at Ange hopefully as he rounded the corner; she shook her head no. He pounded the arm of his wheelchair. Sebastian, Colin, Jeannie, and a few others were still out. There was hope.

"He's okay," I said. "There are a thousand strays wandering the streets. No one would take him, he just got loose. We'll find him."

Just as I spotted Sebastian, alone, heading toward us, I heard a pitiful whine from the other direction. I snapped my head around, seeking the source. It had come from the square, but there was nothing there.

I began to suspect it was my imagination, but then I heard it again. Ange heard it, too. She leapt from the stoop, calling Uzi's name. I was right behind her.

We spotted him in the street across the square. He was moving slowly, slowly, his head hanging almost to the pavement.

"Uzi!" Ange screamed. Uzi howled miserably; Ange launched herself toward him. Uzi stopped at the edge of the square. There was something terribly wrong with him. He looked… twisted. As we closed the gap I saw something dangling from his stomach.

It was a wire.

I grabbed Ange's shirt from behind and pulled, shouting for her to wait. She struggled to get free, screamed at me to let go, then she managed to break my hold.

"Wait!" I shouted, chasing her.

"What's wrong with him? What's wrong with him?" Ange shouted as she wrapped her arms around Uzi's big head. He licked her face feebly.

I squatted, examining the wire. "Oh, Christ. Get back! Get away!" I screamed at her.

"What's wrong with him?" Ange screamed back.

Sebastian appeared, wrapped his arms around Ange's waist and pulled her backward; her feet bounced over the curb and across the grass as she struggled to get free.

I pushed Uzi; he fell onto his side in a pathetic heap, howling in pain. Ange screamed his name. His underside had been shaved, and there was a long, ragged incision on one side of his belly.

"Bomb!" I heard myself yell. I wasn't sure what to do. I wanted to run, wanted to get far away from Uzi, but I couldn't just leave him there, howling in pain.

I tore open the incision, pushed my hand inside Uzi and fished around until I felt something hard, something that didn't belong inside a dog. Ange was screaming at me from across the street, asking over and over what I was doing to him.

I pulled the bomb out of Uzi, leapt to my feet, and hurled it down the street. A trailing wire spun in the air. The device hit the pavement, bounced twice, then lay still.

An explosion ripped the air, throwing up fire and dust and chips of asphalt. I was knocked backward. Pebbles rained down on me.

Then Sebastian was leaning over me, cradling my head. He asked if I was okay. My whole body was throbbing. I looked down at it, afraid there would be some bloody hole in me, but everything looked fine. I turned to locate Ange.

She was hunched over Uzi, who gave one final, misguided attempt at a lick that missed badly, then twitched and lay still. Ange held his head and rocked him.

With Sebastian's help I got to my feet, went over to Ange.

"Are you all right?" I asked.

Ange grabbed my hand, clutched it hard. "No." She kissed Uzi's nose, gently lowered his lifeless head to the ground, and stood. A crowd had formed in the square. Ange scanned them, standing at a distance in their white masks.

"You," she said. Her voice was shaking with rage.

And then I saw him, our Dada neighbor, wearing his fucking mailman outfit and sporting a fucking maskless grin like his horse had just finished first by a fucking nose.

Ange stormed into the square with me right behind, pushed through the crowd until she was right in Rumor's face. "Did you do this?" she screamed. "Did you?"

He shrugged. "Who put these sharks in the water? Hard to say."

Ange lunged at him, tearing at his eyes with a clawed hand. Rumor grabbed her by the throat, spun her around and slammed her to the ground. She hit the ground hard, his hand pinning her throat.

I launched myself at him. I had no plan, no idea how I could hurt him—I just went for his throat. He cuffed me aside like a mosquito, a blow to my temple that made me see stars.

"Unclench those little fists," I heard Rumor say to Ange as I struggled to my knees. He let go of her throat; air squealed into her lungs. Rumor stood, turned his back to us. "You're not going to live long in this world, Little Peanut," he said.

Ange struggled to a sitting position as I crawled over to her. She screamed in rage and lunged to her feet to go after Rumor again, but I held her firm.

"He'll kill you without a second thought," I said. "We can't fight him head-on, not even if Cortez was here."

I looked at Uzi, sprawled on the sidewalk, his lips pulled tight in a rictus snarl. Uzi. Who was more innocent in all this than Uzi?

I hated feeling so powerless. Once, there would have been police cruisers filling the square, courts to prosecute this bastard, and prisons to put him away. Now, whoever was most willing and able to kill had all the power.

Beyond Uzi a young boy was laying down colored dots, smiling under his mask, water gun clutched in one hand. The game went on, whatever the tragedy of the moment. He raised his gun, test-squirted a girl standing forty feet away from him. I watched the water spurt in a tight, perfect arc...

"Chair," I said, my voice calm. He rolled closer to us. "Stay with her a minute?" Chair nodded.

I dug into my pocket, pulled out a twenty and approached the boy with the water gun. "I'll give you twenty bucks for your gun," I said, holding the bill between two fingers.

His eyes opened wide. "Okay." He grabbed his gun by the muzzle and held it out to me. I gave him the bill, said thanks, and headed inside Ange's apartment with the gun.

There was a half bag of blood in the fridge. I emptied most of the water from the gun and poured in the blood. Some of it missed, spilling across my knuckles, and over the plastic base and trigger of the gun. I rinsed my hand and the gun.

Rumor was still outside. He was talking to an Asian woman who seemed thrilled by his attention.

"Rumor," I said. He turned, dropped his head in a "you again?" gesture. I raised the water gun.

Rumor laughed like he'd never seen anything so funny. "Are you going to shoot me, Little Peanut's brother?"

I shot him right in the face. He went on laughing as he turned his face from the spray, wiped his eyes. He stopped laughing when he saw that his hands were covered in blood.

"My name is Jasper," I said. "My friend's name is Ange. Her dog's name was Uzi."

I ran, because it would be hours before he would lose the will to kill me. As I crossed the square, a gunshot cracked, then another. I sprinted up York, jumping over homeless bedding down for the night. I glanced back and spotted Rumor slowing to a walk, the gun at his side. All that weaponry probably made it hard to run.

"Jasper!" someone called. It was Ange, running like hell through a back alley. She must have cut around on Abercorn. I waited for her, then we ran together until we had put some distance between us and Rumor.

"Thank you," she said. She wiped away tears, which were immediately replaced by new ones.

"I'm sorry. I know it won't bring him back."

She nodded, wiped her nose with the back of her sleeve. "You got him, though. You made him pay."

Her phone jingled. She pulled it out, held it close to read a text message.

"Shit. It's from Charles: 'Ange, We had a dinner date, correct? Did you forget?'" Fresh rage poured into Ange's eyes.

"Just tell him you had a personal tragedy, and you'll have to do it another time," I suggested. Charles seemed like the last thing Ange needed to worry about right now.

She stopped walking, stared at her sandals. "I don't think so." She hugged me briefly. "He picked the wrong day to crawl up my ass."

"What are you going to do?"

"I don't know yet. I'll see you later," she called as she headed up Drayton.

Blood sloshed inside the water gun as I turned and headed in the opposite direction.

Behind a wrought-iron gate, a middle-aged man in an expensive power-suit supported a girl in her early teens who was vomiting onto an azalea bush in full bloom. The man was saying "Oh no" over and over. The vomit began to turn pink. I moved on.

I needed to disappear for about twelve hours. That wasn't a problem; I had a lot of work to do in the store.

"What did you do to him?" I asked Ange, sitting on the edge of her bed. She was lying on the bed, one leg canted, staring out the window.

"I beat him," she said.

"You hit him?"

She nodded absently. "Repeatedly. I think he probably had to go to the hospital, but I didn't stick around to find out."

Under other circumstances I would have laughed, but this was a somber time. In one day Ange had lost her closest companion and abandoned her greatest hope.

"Every few minutes I realize Uzi isn't with me, and I worry that I left him tied somewhere," she said. "Then I remember all over again that he's gone."

I nodded, not sure what to say. Maybe nothing needed to be said. Pain has its own half-life; words don't change that.

There was a knock on Ange's bedroom door. "Ange?" Chair pushed the door open a crack. "There's someone here to see you."

"Who?" she said.

Chair led her down the hall. "You've got to see for yourself." I hopped off the bed and followed.

Ange froze at the front door. I caught up, looked out the open window.

Rumor was sitting on the steps. There was a puppy asleep in his arms. He gestured with his chin for Ange to come out, and, after a moment's hesitation, she did. I followed. Rumor stood, smiled at me. The smile looked bizarre on his face, because it wasn't a sneering, sarcastic smile; it was warm, wide, genuine.

"Hello, Little Peanut," he said to Ange. His eyes were glassy, almost glowing. "I hope this little one will ease some of your pain." Gently, he folded the puppy into Ange's arms. "I'm very sorry for what I did."

Ange didn't look at the puppy, she just held it, stiffly. I was surprised she didn't push it back at Rumor. I wanted to. There are situations where an apology and a puppy just aren't good enough, and to me, this was one of those situations. Rumor didn't deserve our forgiveness; if it wasn't for Doctor Happy he'd still be terrorizing us, for no other reason than because he could.

Rumor turned to me. "Thank you." He bowed his head, turned to leave, then paused. He reached into the pocket of the hunting jacket he wore, and set a vial on the porch railing. It was filled with blood. "If you ever decide to join us, I wish you would use my blood—"

"I don't want it," Ange said.

"Maybe you won't, but keep it, just in case." He headed down the steps. "Who knows how dark this night will get."

Chapter 5:
Soft Apocalypse

Fall, 2030 (One year later)

I passed a lithe cormorant of a woman trying on gas masks at a street kiosk. She was gazing intently into a little round mirror mounted on a telephone pole, and wearing a cute round avocado-colored mask. I loved the way she moved, loved her librarian glasses and her buzz-cut. Was she too good-looking for me? I wasn't sure.

The lanky beauty left my field of vision. I continued scanning, assessing each woman I passed as a potential girlfriend, labeling them as "yes" or "no" in a heartbeat. I couldn't help it. All of the other features of the world receded—all the beautiful crumbling architecture, the colorful street vendors, the black diesel stink in the air—all of it shrank into the background as I obsessively evaluated each woman I passed, testing my heart for flutters, getting a sense of her from her walk, her expression, the bob of her breasts.

Not that I'd ever approach a woman on the street; I hated guys who did that. For me it served as some sort of rehearsal—practice for identifying my soul mate when she arrived. Or maybe it was a way to reassure myself that there were women in this city who could reignite that flame, if I could meet them.

Reignite? I wondered if I'd really ever had that flame ignited. Sophia had lit me up like the highlight screen at a baseball stadium, but that had never been a real relationship. Ange? Maybe. I could never quite put my finger on my feelings for Ange. Not that it mattered, given her feelings for me. Deirdre? Sometimes she was like a song stuck in my head, even two years later. Small, childlike, fish-faced Deirdre. What had she done with my photos?

Ange was probably the closest. I wondered what she was up to. We'd never officially "broken up," if that term was applicable given our arrangement, but she spent so much time with her housemates that I barely knew her any more. Maybe she was seeing someone. Maybe Rami—they seemed to spend a lot of time together.

I slowed as I passed Jittery Joe's Coffee, hoping against hope to score a cup. The "No Coffee Today" sign still hung on the board outside, as it had for the past three weeks. And there was a new, smaller sign below it: "No Milk." I continued on, caffeine-free, toward my speed-date appointment.

I spied a sexy pair of legs in the crowd, strutting my way. I got a jolt when her face came into view. She was a survivor of the flesh-eating virus. One whole side of her face was caved in; the damage trailed down her neck, disappearing inside a silk blouse. I did my best to hold my smile when she glanced my way, but it felt stiff. Poor woman.

There was a bamboo outbreak on Gaston. I stopped to watch. Street doctors were tearing up the pavement with jackhammers, circling the affected area, racing to set up rhizome barriers before the bamboo could spread. Four Civil Defense officers with heat-rifles surrounded the perimeter, along with half a dozen of those little mechanical bodyguard rat-things, as if Jumpy-Jumps were going to try to interrupt their little street cleaning operation. Real terrorists didn't give a shit about bamboo.

I tapped my waist-pouch to make sure my fold-up gas mask was there, just like the government public service cartoon taught us.

"ID?" An acne-scarred man in combat fatigues barked at me as I reached the gates leading to the rich part of town. There was a body lying nearby, half in the street, half on the sidewalk, one foot twisted at an odd angle. Vehicles swerved to avoid it.

I stood still while the guy scanned my eyes with his little silver wand. It bleeped. He glanced at the readout on the screen clipped to his thick utility belt.

"Okay," he said, waving me on. I wasn't sure what the criteria were for entry into Southside. Lack of a criminal record? Not on any government watch lists? That I had a job?

When I reached the SpeedMatch outlet on Victory Drive I dawdled outside, pretending to tie my shoe on a bench. I ducked through the revolving door when no one was looking. I felt like such a loser going in there—much like I used to feel when I was eighteen, skulking into porn shops. It'd been years since I'd resorted to a dating service. I couldn't believe I was doing this again. And I couldn't really afford it, but it was the only good way I could meet a bright, educated woman, given where I lived.

It was humbling to be starting over from scratch at thirty-five. How many more women would I have to tell all of my stories to—my funniest anecdotes, what music I like, how I got the scar over my eye? Three more? Eleven? Everyone else in the world seemed able to find someone long before they hit thirty-five, even if those relationships didn't always last forever.

"I'm here for the ten o'clock," I said to the receptionist, who sported the thick makeup of a woman too young to realize that sometimes less is more.

She led me to my room, showed me how to download my vitals and bio-video from the boost I'd brought, helped me put on the VR equipment, then shut the door behind her. My palms were sweating.

The VR landscape was hackneyed but impressive: I was sitting in a burgundy reading chair on a slate patio, in the center of a beautiful formal garden. To my left, water tattered from a winged water nymph reaching toward the sky from the center of a fountain. A bed of perfect yellow tulips bobbed in a slight breeze on the other side. The garden was in a valley, surrounded by towering white mountain peaks; a waterfall burst from a cave in one mountain, crashing into a lake in perfect white-noise harmony with the fountain.

"Five minutes till your first date," a mellifluous female voice informed me from out of the sky. I wondered if women heard a man's voice.

"Mirror, please," I said, and checked to make sure I didn't have a piece of dandruff dangling from one of my eyebrows. Everything was shiny and perfect inside the VR environment except us daters—exact replication of what you had was all you got.

"Thank you." The mirror disappeared. Mirrors aren't good things to have around on blind dates; the process makes you self-conscious enough.

In the air to my left, my first date's vitals appeared, along with the lie-detector readout, currently flatlined. Her name was Maura (though that didn't mean much; lots of women didn't give their real names to minimize the lunatic stalker factor). She was thirty-six, a physician, lived in Trenton. Liked Fuzz-Jazz and Postal music, and freerunning. I took a few deep breaths, readying myself for thirty-eight three-minute dates.

Maura materialized in the chair across the table. She had bushy brows and a pointy chin. Long, thin nostrils that you couldn't help but see into when you looked at her. Kind of aristocratic looking. Interesting.

"Hi Jasper. I have a few questions that I like to ask, then if you want you can ask me questions." She talked fast, but with three minutes that was par.

"Sounds fine," I said. Suddenly my nose itched; I resisted scratching it. Scratching, or any sort of face-touching for that matter, doesn't convey the best first impression.

"How many times have you cheated on a wife or girlfriend?"

I gawked at her. She had to be joking. What kind of an opening question was that?

"Less than twelve," I finally said.

She looked at me the way my grade school teachers used to when I was being bad and I knew it.

"Is your salary statement accurate?"

"Sometimes." It wasn't like my salary was all that impressive. If I was going to lie, I would have done better than what was listed. Maybe what she was asking was, "What are you doing here, given your pitiful salary? You're obviously a poor downtowner."

"Do you have any bizarre sexual interests?"

"Define bizarre."

I knew her type. She'd had some bad dating experiences and now she focused more on what she *didn't* want than what she did want. Avoidance dating. She was already angry with me for the thoughtless things I would potentially do if we dated.

When she finished I asked her a few questions: Have you ever stolen a shopping cart from a grocery store? What's your favorite Drowned

Mermaids song? You don't know the Drowned Mermaids? Hmm. That could be a problem. I pretended to jot a note; she didn't seem to realize I was being sarcastic. Maura faded away. I scratched my nose with a vengeance.

Next was Victoria. She was too fat: big and boxy—a rectangle over disproportionately skinny legs. As we talked I chided myself for being shallow, then I snapped back at the chiding voice: attraction matters; it's not the only thing that matters, but it matters, and I'm not going to pretend it doesn't matter to satisfy my less-than-attractive female acquaintances, who don't want it to matter. A girlfriend had to be reasonably attractive, or at least reasonably attractive to me. I found gangly women with overbites terribly attractive. Also nerdy women—shy, socially awkward librarian types really did it for me.

When Victoria faded I downloaded her bio-video out of courtesy. I probably wouldn't watch it, but she seemed nice and I didn't want to hurt her feelings. A few seconds later she downloaded mine as well.

The next woman materialized, interrupting my reverie. She was in a wheelchair.

The first time I'd done this speed-dating thing, I'd figured the difficult part would be trying to seem clever and kind and confident, all in the space of three minutes. But the truly difficult part was masking disappointment and disinterest.

For the third time today, I struggled to keep a stiff smile pasted on my face as we danced through the "nice to meet yous."

From the rubbery, slight movement of greeting she made with her hand, Maya was a victim of Polio-X, that top 40 dial-a-virus that swept the nation in '23. She had some nerve, I thought, getting on a dating service, inflicting us with guilt for rejecting her because she had a disability. Then I got hold of my irrational lizard brain and realized how incredibly unfair that was. She wasn't twisting anyone's arm. But there was no way I could be with her. A wheelchair was just too much baggage. I was not the sacrificing type, willing to wipe a woman's butt if that's what she needed. It just wasn't me. Maybe I'm not giving and self-sacrificing enough to ever have a truly successful relationship. At least I was honest about it.

"So you're an economist?" I said, seeking a polite topic that would pass the time, while hopefully conveying that I thought she was interesting, but that I wasn't interested. "Any insights to offer on the current state of affairs? When do you think the market's going to turn around?" Not that I had a dime to invest in the market.

"Wow, that's kind of a personal question, don't you think?" Her voice dripped sarcasm—she saw what I was doing, and was calling me on it.

I laughed uncomfortably.

"It's not going to turn around," she said. "It's going to get worse, and then it's going to collapse completely."

I laughed uncomfortably again.

"You think I'm kidding," she said.

"It's got to turn around eventually."

"No it doesn't," she said. "It didn't for the dinosaurs."

"Okay," I said. Next she'd probably tell me about the end of days, and ask if I'd made my peace with Jesus Christ.

"I can see you don't believe me," she said, gesturing toward the lie-detector, not unkindly.

"It's not a question of believing. I can see you believe what you're saying, and I'm sure you're good at what you do, but how sure can you be about something like this? Honestly?"

"Every Nobel Prize-winning economist who's still alive is sure of it," she said. "The economy is slowly collapsing. Remember all those dire warnings about global warming, overpopulation, resource depletion, the rain forest, nuclear fallout, save the whales? Any of that ring a bell?"

"Uh huh," I said mildly. I'd evidently picked the wrong topic. How much time did I have left with her? One minute, forty-six seconds.

"They weren't kidding. Billions of people are going to die before this is over." She gestured at my lie-detector readout with her chin. I looked at it. Ninety-seven percent honesty. Not even a hint of exaggeration. Billions of people, she said. It was the same estimate that Sebastian had given, back when he was convincing people to make our lives even more miserable by planting voracious bamboo.

She had an interesting face. Big, wide mouth showing lots of teeth—what I'd always thought of as a shark-mouth—and scary light blue eyes, like see-through gossamer fabric draped over sky. If it wasn't for the wheelchair. Well, if it wasn't for the wheelchair she'd be out of my league. I suppose if I was okay with the wheelchair, it would be one of those reasonable tradeoffs that we all pretend don't really enter into love and relationships: she settles for a somewhat immature, big-nosed, skinny guy, and I get a woman who is more attractive than I could reasonably have hoped for, but in a wheelchair, with arms and legs that were mostly useless.

"Why haven't they warned people?" I asked, not really wanting to hear the answer, but needing to say something because I'd been silent for three or four seconds.

She laughed. "They've been shouting it from the rooftops for years! There was an article in the *New York Times* just a few weeks ago. Nobody listens to academics. Smart is passé."

It was a reasonable argument. And for the past ten years things had only gotten worse. Blackouts, war, fifty-seven varieties of terrorists, water shortages, plagues. It reminded me of a story about frogs: if you put them in an open pot of water and turn on the burner, they just sit there and boil to death, because they're not equipped to recognize and respond to gradual changes in water temperature. They could jump out at any time, but there never comes a time when their little brains judge it's time to jump. So they cook.

I looked into her earnest, translucent eyes, and tried on her hopeless, empty version of the future, filled with plagues and hunger, flies buzzing over corpses, thick-necked men with guns.

Could things really just keep getting worse? Could the economy really collapse? Now I wasn't sure.

"This could be terrible," was all I could think to say.

She checked the readout, softly nodded agreement. "I'm sorry I dumped this in your lap. It's not why we're here. But you asked."

She took a deep breath, and smiled at me, showing all those teeth.

"Actually, I think what you asked for was financial advice," she said. "Put all of your money in ammo."

I laughed, and for a moment I thought *maybe*. There was something about her that gave me a warm, almost nostalgic feeling.

We sat in silence, listening to the patter of the fountain.

"So," she said, clearing her throat. "Know any jokes?"

I laughed. "Yeah. There was this guy who could be kind of a jerk…"

Maya faded away, which was fortunate, because I didn't know how the joke ended.

A new profile came up. It was hard for me to concentrate on it. Danielle, thirty-one, Energy Consultant (whatever the hell that meant), a daughter, twelve years old. Widow. I wanted time to think.

Danielle materialized across the table.

"Jasper, so nice to meet you!" she said, wobbling her head enthusiastically. She was very bubbly, attractive in an Italian sort of way. Really nice lips.

I tried unsuccessfully to keep up with her enthusiasm, and she didn't seem to notice that I was speaking from inside a black funk. She asked about my job, I asked about hers. She dropped some flirtatious lines that I fumbled. I wondered how her husband had died.

When I was young I'd taken for granted that, while there might be intermittent wars, disasters, economic downturns, overall things would remain about the same. But people had always inflicted suffering on other people, pretty much unceasingly, since the beginning of history. So as better ways to inflict suffering were developed, of course more suffering would be inflicted. Once biotechnology advanced to the point where a bright amateur could devise and release plagues on a shoestring budget, of course some would.

And all of a sudden it seemed obvious. I was living through an apocalypse. I was at a dating service in the middle of a slow apocalypse. Things weren't going to get better like the government said, they were going to keep getting worse.

Danielle told me that she'd really enjoyed meeting me; I said me too, although I had no idea whether I'd enjoyed meeting her or not. There was a song spinning in my head now, some really old thing about how when the world was running down, make the best of what's still around. It's funny how apropos songs find their way into your head without you realizing.

As Danielle faded, I looked at the water nymph stretching toward the sky, the plume of water pouring from her mouth. Her wings were too small for her body, giving the impression that if she were to fly, it would be a strenuous ordeal—not the soaring freedom of a gliding eagle, but the mad flapping of a fruit bat.

The next few speed-dates went by in a fog. There was Savita, a tiny Indian woman with big doe-eyes and long black hair that she draped over one shoulder the way Indian women do. Keira, who had raccoon shadows under her eyes. I struggled to hear them over the winding-down of the world and the sound of tearing photos.

Then came Emily, who made bad jokes and oozed desperation.

Most people can't stand being single. I see people get divorced, then immediately implement the "best available" strategy, desperately seeking the most viable single person they could find in the course of, say, three months, and then marrying that person. They can't stand the idea of not being with someone. It's like the light is too bright. They race to the nearest shade.

When you're unattached, you live life closer to the edge. A partner gives you a sense of security, and I think it can lead to complacency, to life-laziness, if you're not careful. You don't feel the need to live vividly. Being single means there's no safety net. It's riskier. If you lose a leg stepping on a street-mine, you won't have a wife to wheel you around. If you drink milk laced with clotting factor and have a stroke, you won't have a wife to wipe the drool off your chin. Despite my avid desire to meet a woman, I was proud of my ability to live in this time as a single person, to have the courage to wait for Ms. Right instead of running to the shelter of Ms. Best Available.

The next woman's name was Bodil Gustavson. Thirty-three, artist. She materialized. My heart started to pound, slow and hard.

It was Deirdre. Jesus Christ, it was Deirdre.

"Oh, this is going to be good," she said. She was sucking on a green lollipop. It brought back images that I quickly shoved aside.

Her cute little hands were fidgeting, as always, part of that child-like quality she had that had melted me like a creamsickle on a July sidewalk. But she was not childlike, not really. I reminded myself of her collection of 911 recordings—people screaming into the phone, people dying into the phone, six-year-old kids telling the 911 operator that mommy's face had turned blue and foam was coming out of her mouth. Plus there was the song she wrote about my tribe.

"So tell me—Jasper, is it?—what are you looking for in a woman?" she said, pointing the lollipop at me.

"What did you do with my photos?"

"Fuck you, Jasper." The day I broke up with her, I'd been shocked by the anger Deirdre could express with her eyes. She gave me that same glare now.

"So tell me, do you miss these?" She pulled up the conservative floral-patterned turtleneck shirt she was wearing and shook her breasts at me. I drank them in like a heroin addict welcoming the needle.

"Do you still have my photos? What did you do with them?" She dropped her shirt, smoothed it back into place.

"All those pepper seeds we planted on the balcony?" she said. "They all came up. Red ones and green ones and purple ones… they were pretty."

That had been a good day, Deirdre planting peppers naked, strips of sunlight filtering between the slats of the fire escape stairs.

And for the briefest instant, I considered getting back on the horse and riding the chaos that was life with Deirdre, surrendering to her dark charm, allowing my personal life to mirror the violence that was all around me. If nothing else, I could stop feeling guilty for dumping her.

I realized that as soon as I sleep with a woman I feel responsible for her happiness. Pretty much for the rest of my life. I've no idea why that is. Two or three years of therapy would probably uncover the reasons.

I thought of the 911 collection, of her complete lack of distress as she played calls for me. It was a soothing methadone that killed thoughts of reconciliation. Besides that, Colin and Jeannie would never speak to me again if I got back with Deirdre.

"I'm sorry," I said.

And Deirdre was gone.

I downloaded her bio-vid. I couldn't resist. How would Deirdre present herself to a prospective date? Would it be raunchy sex scenes? Footage from one of her flash concerts? I wasn't sure she'd emphasize the rock star part of her life, given what had happened at her last concert.

I couldn't wait—I played her bio-vid during the sixty-second break before my next date. It opened with an eleven- or twelve-year-old Deirdre squatting in a little garden on the side of a garage, a wood pile in the background. She pulled a big red tomato and held it up, grinning. The scene drifted into another: An eight-year-old Deirdre sitting cross-legged on a hardwood floor in pajamas, working on a puzzle, pieces spread all around her. Then Deirdre buried in Christmas gifts and torn wrapping paper, sitting beside my sister, Jilly, in front of our tree, both of them grinning wildly. Deirdre, getting on my school bus on the first day of kindergarten, waving goodbye to my mother. Pedaling a three-wheeled bike, my cousin Jerome standing in the big basket on the back, his hands on her shoulders. On vacation with my family in Puerto Rico, sunburned in a restaurant with half a dozen leis around her neck. Sitting on the porch of my childhood home, before a hurricane tore it apart.

It was beautifully done, brief moment drifting into brief moment, all of them happy, nostalgic, all of them scenes adapted from my photos, with Deirdre in my place.

I cried as I watched. It was so pathetic. My heart broke for her. Suddenly I wished I could give her some of that childhood—that garden, that puzzle, that vacation, instead of whatever it was she'd really gotten. I didn't like to imagine what she'd gotten. I'd once asked her about the little scar under her chin, and she said it came from the button-eye on her teddy bear, when her stepfather hit her with it. Maybe she was actually doing well, given the memories she was trying to keep crammed into the basement of her mind. I don't know.

As the images faded to black, I thought again of my conversation with the wheelchair woman, whatever her name had been—Maya. There would be no more childhoods like that for anyone, not when a kid had to carry a gas mask, pass through security checkpoints, run from a hungry stray dog out of fear that someone had surgically implanted a bomb in it.

A lovely red-haired woman materialized. I was a wet, sobbing mess. I wiped my eyes. She tried not to notice.

"I'm sorry," I said, "I'm not feeling very well. I'm going to discontinue. No offense."

I terminated my session.

The room seemed dingy and scuffed after the virtual garden. I went on crying. I felt my hope for a better tomorrow, for blue skies and a button-nosed girlfriend, slough off like dead skin, leaving me pink and raw.

I felt like I'd been struggling in every aspect of my life for a hundred years—struggling to earn enough money to survive, struggling to find love, struggling to not die a violent death. The weight of all of that was crashing down as I considered the possibility of things actually getting *worse*.

The selection screen dropped down, startling me. For a long time I just stared at the little pictures of all the women I'd met. Then I started tapping profiles. I didn't look at any of their bio-vids, I just started tapping away at the women I would be interested in dating. Danielle, the Italian happiness-machine; Savita, the Indian princess;

three, four, five others.

I hesitated at wheelchair woman.

I sniffed, wiped my nose on my sleeve, stared at her smiling picture.

I had a connection to her. She was my sensei—she'd whapped me with a stick, and I'd awakened to the truth. I tapped her profile. What the hell.

Then I came to Deirdre's profile.

I didn't tap it, and my tape of neurotic Deirdre-thoughts didn't start playing. I felt a warm sadness—that was all.

I read somewhere that we choose to date people for reasons that are lost in our personal histories, and we keep making the same choices—the same mistakes—till we figure out why.

The Civil Defense alarm went off while I was walking home. I pulled out my gas mask and flipped it over my nose and mouth in one deft motion, a gunslinger fast on the draw. People raced indoors—their masks (in a wide variety of colors and styles) and their tight, hunched shoulders made them look like strange chimps.

Six boys in red-brick camouflage ran by clutching short, square weapons that swung from their fists like lunchboxes. I stepped out of their way. Shit, they were recruiting them younger and younger. I had no idea who they worked for—police, CD, Jumpy-Jump, fire department. They were all pretty much the same now—gangs fighting for power.

I walked on, enjoying the sun on my face, the light afternoon breeze. I realized that my mood had shifted—I felt light and empty. I took a deep, easy breath. I fished my phone out of one pocket, the printout of phone numbers for my speed-date matches out of another.

"That was quick," Maya said.

"I don't think I can handle the wheelchair; I want to be honest about that and I hope it doesn't hurt your feelings," I said. The honking of the alarm went on in the background.

"Okay. Is that what you called to tell me?"

"I just don't want to waste your time. I don't want to hurt anybody. I—"

I wanted to tell her that the world was fleeting and beautiful. I wanted to tell her that the white windmills on the roofs of the exhaust-blackened buildings were all turning in unison, and that somehow she was responsible for me seeing this.

"I'd like to ask you to spend some of your time with me. If you give me some of your time, your precious time, I won't waste it."

She didn't answer. I heard a sniffle and thought she might be crying.

"I'm good at that part—the now part," I added.

I was right, she was crying. It sounded like she was wiping her nose with a tissue. Then I realized that wasn't possible.

"I think I'll pass," she said.

"Fair enough," I said, both disappointed and relieved.

"I'm looking for someone I can count on. I've had enough of casual to last a lifetime."

So was I. It was the wheelchair. It was dumb in a way, rejecting someone out of hand for being in a wheelchair. I'd never dated someone in a wheelchair, how did I know I wouldn't be fine with it?

Because I knew. I didn't want a woman of these times. I wanted Ms. Right.

"I'm sorry," I said.

"No problem." She hung up.

I stuck my phone in my pocket and headed home.

There was a crowd gathered in Chippewa Square. I peered through the heads into the open space by the statue of Oglethorpe, and felt a sick sinking sensation: they were carrying out executions, right near my home. Six or seven members of the DeSoto Police—the local segment of the Civil Defense that was controlled by "Mayor" Duck Adams—were conducting them. (Three or four other "Mayors" had control over smaller sections of the city, last time I checked.)

A fat DeSoto thug with a flattop shoved a gas gun—the kind with a black mask on the end of the barrel—into the screaming face of an old lady while two other gas-masked DeSotos held her. The gun squealed; the old lady went stiff as a board, then dropped to the cobblestones, twitching and jerking like all the muscles in her body had spasmed at once (which they had). Her mouth formed a rictus "O"; her eyes were rolled up, exposing red veins on white.

"Wicked shit," a kid next to me who couldn't be more than thirteen said with a mix of disgust and excitement in his voice. "She probably figured she was gonna die of a heart ailment or something."

White foam gushed out of her mouth, spewing five feet, hissing and steaming on the pavement.

"What the fuck could that old lady have done to deserve that?" I said, keeping my voice low. It was sick, everyone standing there watching people get gassed.

"It's what you say, not what you do," the kid said.

"Yes," I said. "And what you know." Right now Savannah wasn't a healthy place for educated people, especially those who wrote articles for the underground papers, or made milk-crate speeches in the squares.

"The wolves are always at the doors," the kid added as the DeSotos picked up the old lady's body, carried it to a flatbed truck, and tossed it on top of a pile of twisted corpses.

"This isn't right! This isn't right!" a guy with out-of-date two-pocket pants and a button-down shirt shouted from the group still to be gassed. A DeSoto chopped him in the neck with the butt of his gun; he fell into the guy in front of him, grabbed hold of the guy to keep from falling. I turned to leave, then paused. The guy who'd shouted seemed familiar. I turned back and studied him, trying to think of how I might know him. It had to have been a long time ago.

The guy sniffed—a nervous habit—and suddenly I had it: he'd been a teacher at my high school. Mr. Swift, my English teacher in eleventh grade. That had been a million years ago, in a time when there was always enough food in the refrigerator and you let the crystal-clean water keep running and running out of the tap while you washed your hands. Mr. Swift had been a nice guy, had taken a liking to me. That had been rare. I'd been a quiet student, bright but not at the top of the class, and not ingratiating enough to draw attention from my teachers. Mr. Swift had been the exception—he always seemed to pay special attention to me, and it had felt good.

Mr. Swift looked toward the crowd. "Somebody help us. Somebody stop this." Nobody moved.

Then he looked right at me.

"I know you. Don't I? Please." Thirteen, fourteen years later and he still remembered my face.

"Is he talking to you?" the kid next to me asked.

"I don't know," I muttered. I felt awful. There was nothing I could do. If I opened my mouth I could very well end up in line behind

Mr. Swift. So I just stood there, too ashamed to simply turn and walk away, watching them pull people from the little crowd of condemned until it was Mr. Swift's turn.

"This is tyranny!" Mr. Swift shouted as they dragged him out. He got a face full of the vapors.

Poor Mr. Swift. There wasn't a bad bone in him. The wolves were always at the door—that was the truth.

I left the edge of the crowd, my mood pitch-black. Had I really just been to a dating service? How could there still be dating services when people were being murdered in the streets?

The wave of hopelessness I'd felt at the dating service returned, pounded me so hard that I sank to the curb, pressed my palm on the hot, gum-stained pavement to steady myself. Was this it? Was there nothing ahead, nothing but heat and boredom, viruses and bamboo? Just more and more of this and then everything would collapse completely? What could I do? I forced myself to get up, and moved on.

I accidentally kicked a bony, blue-veined ankle as I stepped around a group of sleeping homeless people spilling out of an alley onto the sidewalk.

"Sorry," I said. My victim didn't answer, just drew her ankle under a black plastic tarp that was her home.

I passed the coffee shop, the Dog's Ear bookstore.

I paused, backtracked to the window of the bookstore. The display was mostly gardening, DIY manuals, cookbooks, but there were a few others: *Existential Philosophy: An Introduction*, *Socialism Revisited*, *Light of the Warrior-Sage*.

Years ago Mr. Swift had told me that whatever I do, keep reading. I'd read in college, but after that I pretty much stopped, except for newspapers. I rarely saw people reading books any more. Maybe I should do some reading, in memory of Mr. Swift.

The bookstore was closed—permanently, by the looks of it. I went into the alley, stepping between people sleeping out the heat of the day, and climbed in a broken bathroom window in the back. The bathroom was beyond odious; the toilet looked like it had been used a hundred times after the water had been turned off.

I hurried into the bookstore, opened the blinds on a side window, and held books up to read the titles by the sunlight streaking through. Most of the dusty books were in heaps on the floor, but they were still pretty much sorted by classification. I didn't know what I was looking for; I just wanted some way to get Mr. Swift's voice out of my head.

I gave the store a careful once-over when my eyes had adjusted to the dimness. Rough wooden beams and fat pipes ran the length of the ceiling. Pipes. It blew my mind that they used to be filled with drinkable water.

Books reminded me of Ange. She'd always had a book in her hand when she was in grad school. I dug around in anthropology, tossing titles over my shoulder, stacking a few possibilities to the side.

I picked up a book titled *A Field Guide to Medicinal Herbs and Plants of Eastern and Central North America*. I opened it at random; the names of the herbs were bolded in the text: **Echinacea**, **Golden Seal**, **Eucalyptus**, **Feverfew**. In the back were lists of herbs and their medicinal uses. Pain relief. Inflammation. Enlarged prostate. Ruplu was finding it impossible to stock medicine, and no one could manufacture it locally. We hadn't had any aspirin in two years. I wondered if there was a market for this sort of stuff, or if I could create one? Back in the day, herbal remedies had been sort of a rich yuppie thing, but that was when all you had to do if you had a headache was grab a bottle of Tylenol.

The last thing I grabbed was *Light of the Warrior-Sage*, from out of the window display. I liked that phrase, warrior-sage. I found a plastic bag behind the counter, stuffed the books into it, and took off.

As I turned onto Jefferson Street I caught a whiff of the river. Even ten blocks away, when the wind was right the stench of dead seafood and ammonia cut right through the city's default smell of piss on brick.

When no one was watching I pulled open the steel cellar hatch in the sidewalk in front of a burned-out storefront. I ducked down the steep staircase, crossed a damp basement, pushed out another hatch, and popped out into my secret retreat—a little courtyard surrounded by four-story walls which shaded the tiled floor most of the day. It had been part of a bar many years earlier. I tipped a mattress that was leaned up against a wall, spread my books and lay down to do some reading.

Mostly I read about medicinal herbs. Some of them grew wild. I imagined making forays out of Savannah to hunt for them in the vast bamboo jungle beyond. I'd have to learn how to prepare them—I knew nothing about herbs, I didn't know if you dried them, or what.

My phone jangled. I checked the number, wondering if Maya was calling back. No—it was Ange.

"Hey," I said.

"Hey, sweetie! How *are* you? I was just thinking about how I never see you any more. I miss you!"

The words felt so good. I wanted her to say them over and over. "I miss you, too," I said.

"You doing anything right now? Want to hang out?"

Yes, I did. I asked where she wanted to meet.

Chapter 6:
Street Hero

Fall, 2032 (Two years later)

"**S**low your roll, Slinky, we ain't walking you down," Cortez shouted as Slinky's skinny, cheekless ass disappeared around the red brick corner. I always felt out of place around Cortez's street friends. They weren't bad guys, it was just that we were so different.

There was a touch of gray in the newly grown mustache that Dice kept licking, yet he still acted like he was twenty, his arms splayed as he walked on the balls of his feet like a gangster. Slinky had long, greasy hair and always wore a faded baseball cap. Somehow Cortez could easily straddle my world and these gritty streetballer types, but I couldn't.

"Hey, appears we got us some buckwilders," Slinky said, pointing out a couple sitting in the back seat of an old Toyota parked across Broughton. It didn't look like they were buckwilding to me; they were just sitting, the woman with her arm around the guy's shoulder.

Slinky scampered over, giggling, and peered in the window, his hands cupped around his face to block the glare.

"Shit!" he screamed, leaping away from the car like he'd burned himself, pulling on the mask dangling around his neck.

"What is it?" Cortez asked, pulling on his own mask and squatting to look in the window for himself. I followed suit.

The guy was dead. His jutting tongue was swollen to three times its normal size, his sinuses and adenoids bulging like water balloons under his skin. Some sort of designer virus.

The woman had it too—she looked like a basset hound. Her eyes were closed, her breathing labored. She was just sitting with her man, waiting to die, practicing good virus etiquette with the windows cranked up tight in the blistering heat. It broke my heart to see it, but there was nothing I could do. I was no doctor. There were no doctors downtown, period, even if I had that kind of cash.

"C'mon," Dice said. He tried to resume his cool-walk, but it had lost much of its bounce.

We cut through Madison Square, which was right near Cortez's apartment house. Twenty or thirty vagrants were making a camp in the square. I'd never seen such destitute people in my life. You couldn't even call what they were wearing rags—more like patches, pieces of material stitched together, half the time not even covering the spots that people typically covered. There was a teenage girl running around topless. She was probably good-looking, but it was hard to tell because she was so filthy. I felt for them; I'd been in their shoes (although they weren't actually wearing any shoes).

They were chopping low-hanging branches off the Live Oaks and leaning them against the base of the Revolutionary War monument to make lean-to shelters.

"That kills me," Cortez said. "Makes me sick to my stomach, seeing that beautiful square corrupted like that."

"Somebody should call the berries on them," Slinky said, snickering.

"They'd have to be hacking limbs off babies before the public police would come," Dice said, glancing at Cortez to get some appreciation for his wit.

A skeleton of an old lady was pulling Spanish moss off branches to fire the cooking pots. It *was* upsetting to see the trees molested like that. The Live Oaks were the only beautiful thing we had left. The moss was what gave Savannah its particularity; I loved the way it made the trees look like they were melting.

"I'm gonna go talk to them," Cortez said. He pulled his Eskrima sticks out of his sock, tucked them into the front of his pants, probably so they'd be nice and visible. Displaying exotic weaponry likely gave people pause. Most people probably knew to stay away from a guy carrying Eskrima sticks (unless they had a gun), because if someone is carrying Eskrima sticks, chances are they know how to them use them. Cortez did know how to use them.

Dice glanced down at the sticks. "You anticipating blood and guts?"

"I just want to have a talk. I can't put up with this desecration."

We crossed the street and wandered along the brick walkway, through the center of the camp. When we hit the end of the square Cortez doubled back, probably expecting someone to tell us to get lost, but they just went on doing what they were doing. Finally, Cortez approached the biggest and strongest guy.

"Ho," the guy said, smiling and nodding.

"Where you coming from?" Cortez asked, hands on hips. I hovered behind him with Dice and Slinky.

"Bamboo forests to the West," the guy said, pointing. He had a peculiar accent; bamboo sounded like bumpoo. His beard was so shaggy you could barely see his mouth, his skin leathered from too much sun.

"You mean the sacrifice zone past Rincon and Pooler?" Cortez asked.

"I don't know towns. West. Good hunting there."

"Good *hunting*? What the fuck do you hunt in the bamboo?" Dice asked. Slinky laughed.

As if on cue, there was a squeal in the grass behind us. A squirrel twisted on the ground, a little wooden arrow jutting from its side. The topless girl ran to it, squatted, and brained it with a half-brick. She picked it up by the tail and took it to a steaming pot.

"Shit, that's just odious," Slinky said, lips pulled back from his big square teeth.

The guy just shrugged. "What's those?" he asked, pointing at Cortez's Eskrima sticks.

"Weapons," Cortez said. He pulled them out and assumed a karate pose. He launched into a display, filling the air with blurry sticks, sometimes veering decidedly close to the vagrant. The guy flinched, but kept smiling. When he finished, the guy dropped his hands back to his sides and nodded vaguely.

I think Cortez had figured on a circle of spectators, a little shock and awe, and I was guessing he felt a little stupid now, because no one had stopped to watch.

"You mind taking it easy on those branches?" Cortez said to the guy, still breathing hard, wiping sweat from his eyes.

The gypsy squinted, shook his head like he didn't understand.

"The tree branches, would you mind not cutting them?"

"It won't kill the trees," he said.

"No, but it looks bad, and we live here."

The guy stared up at the trees, then back at Cortez like he was whacked.

"This is a park," I said. "The reason the trees were planted was to make the park look nice." I loved those trees, the way their gnarled branches formed shady roofs over the streets. I also loved how tough they were—they survived the climate shifts and chemical dumps, while the crepe myrtles and azalea, the little yellow songbirds, those little green frogs that stuck to windows had mostly died. They had turned brown or blue and rotted. Brown and blue, the real colors of death. Who made black the color of death? Black was the color of night, and the potential of a cool breeze.

"Just don't cut any more branches, okay?" Cortez turned without waiting for an answer. He turned to Dice and Slinky. "Dudes, I gotta bounce. If I don't put in a few ticks hauling dirt to the roof for the garden expansion, the old man is gonna toast my biscuits."

"I thought we were going to the blanket district," Dice said.

"Another time."

As Dice and Slinky took off, I waved goodbye to Cortez, but he gestured for me to stay.

"I just didn't feel like having those guys around right now," Cortez said when they were out of earshot. "They're good guys and all, but you can't really talk to them, you know?"

I nodded. We headed toward his place, hugging along the buildings to stay in the shade as much as possible.

"You know I'm thirty-four years old today?" Cortez said.

"I didn't," I said. "Happy birthday."

"Yeah, thanks. But it's weighing on me." He sighed heavily, shook his head. "Thirty-four years old and I'm still beating the sidewalks with my friends like I'm fifteen, sitting in that sauna apartment staring at the TV when we can get a signal, hauling sacks of dirt to the roof to try to keep from starving."

"It's not where we expected to be by now, that's for sure," I said. "I kept expecting things to improve, and that our opportunities would improve with them." I had to admit, though—Cortez's prospects were even bleaker than mine. He had no real job, just a high school education.

"Yeah. I just keep thinking if I'd been born in an earlier time, before you needed boats to navigate the streets of LA and shit, that I could've been somebody, could've been a legend at something." He looked at me, maybe waiting to see if I was going to laugh. "I don't know, a martial arts champion, maybe a major businessman. You know? Now I'm just one step above those gypsies in the park."

"Hey, you seen this?" An old guy in the doorway of Pinky Masters gestured into the bar. We peered in, saw he was specifically gesturing at the TV. One of those Breaking News Special Reports was on, with flashing red all around the borders of the screen.

"Christ, what now?" I said. We stepped into the bar. Every eye in the place was on that screen.

A guy with a prosthetic eye that was too big compared to his real one shouted at the screen. "Nuke 'em all. What are we waiting for? Take 'em out."

"What happened?" Cortez asked the old guy at the door.

"They nuked Lake Superior, made all the water undrinkable."

I felt a falling sensation in my stomach. "Who did?"

"North Korea. They said it's because we sink their fishing trawlers."

"They send those giant fishing factories right up our coast, of course we're gonna sink 'em," the guy with the bad eye said.

The U.S. Navy sank pretty much any non-U.S. fishing boat they found within two hundred miles of our shores, even though international waters technically started twelve miles out, but I wasn't going to say that out loud. But hell, the why didn't matter. Lake Superior had been nuked. I didn't know what the implications of that were, but I knew it wasn't good. The biggest body of fresh water in the country, poisoned.

Cortez touched my back. "Unless we're gonna get drunk, let's get out of here. I can't take this right now."

"I can't afford to get drunk in a bar," I said. "Plus, I should get home."

A dog was dying in the gutter a block from Pinky's, flies buzzing around its eyes, its lip pulled back in a death snarl. It was a puny thing, mostly ribs. The eye facing up fixed on us, then started to go unfocused. Its little chest stopped rising and falling. Now it would turn blue.

"What next?" Cortez asked, sitting on the curb.

I looked up at the apartment building rising beyond the dog, the rusted black bars on the windows, vinyl siding broken off in places, exposing splintered plywood underneath.

"A few years ago an economist told me things were just going to keep getting worse. She said that when there isn't enough food and water and energy, everyone will fight over what's left, and the losers of those fights will get desperate, and will do desperate things. It's starting to look like she was right."

"*Starting* to look? Hell, we've been fighting for enough to eat for the past eight years."

He had a point.

Cortez heaved a big sigh. "I can't stand the thought of going home, facing my old man's sarcastic bullshit."

"Well, come on home with me."

"I can't. I gotta get this work done."

Cortez stood, saluted the little fallen dog and walked on, past the row houses with their busted railings and rotting wood, trash piled up on the sidewalk where it'd been thrown out the windows.

I was eager to get home to watch the news and talk to Colin and Jeannie about what was happening. What good did it do anyone to irradiate our water? The U.S. had been doing some ruthless shit around the world that made me awfully uncomfortable, but at least it made sense. Our navy quietly sank fishing boats because that left more fish for us to catch, but they didn't dump poison in the Pacific to kill all the fish. It was as if entire countries were acting like Jumpy-Jumps.

As we got closer to Cortez's house we heard that telltale cracking, like ice underfoot or twigs snapping. "*Oh shit*," I said. We hurried toward the sound, which was also toward Cortez's place.

It was the yellow variety—not as bad as the green, but worse than the black—and it was coming up right outside Cortez's apartment house. Some of the stalks were already three feet tall, trembling and popping as they grew. The asphalt in the road was broken into a thousand fragments as nubs of new stalks pushed through. How the hell had it gotten inside the rhizome barrier that'd been sunk around Savannah? That barrier went down ten feet.

Private Civil Defense people (I didn't recognize their insignia, but this wasn't my neighborhood) had cordoned off the area. Technicians were at work tearing up the street with road-eaters, trying to set up a rhizome barrier to contain the bamboo before it spread.

Cortez's place was inside the perimeter. Inside the sacrifice zone. His father owned the place—Cortez had been born there—and just like that, they were letting the bamboo have it.

"There's my old man," Cortez said, sounding utterly defeated. His father was standing in a crowd that had gathered on the sidewalk. He was shaking his head, making angry gestures at no one in particular.

"No way this made it through the barrier," he said when we were within earshot. "God damned biotech punks carried it in and planted it, I'm telling you. Or terrorists—damned Jumpy-Jumps."

Cortez and I nodded. Let his dad go on thinking it was some adolescent bio-tinkerer who'd originally loosed the bamboo to impress his friends. I didn't know how the bamboo had jumped the barrier, but I knew it wasn't biotech punks who'd set it loose in the first place, and so did Cortez.

"You seen Edie or Pat yet?" Cortez asked. They lived in the apartment next door, or used to.

"Nah," his father said. He walked off without another word.

"Do you have a place to stay?" I asked Cortez.

He was staring glassy-eyed at the apartment. He was in serious need of a shave. "That fucking bamboo. It's coming back to bite my ass good."

"I wonder if it's actually doing any good. It didn't stop North Korea from nuking Lake Superior, but who knows? Maybe this whole city would be dust without it."

"I don't know about that, but one thing I do know—if I find out who planted this patch right in my back yard, he's gonna be one sorry son of a bitch."

"I'm glad it wasn't me," I laughed. "So, do you have a place to stay? Want to crash with us?"

"Hey, thanks, J—I appreciate it."

Colin met us on the porch. "Did you see what happened?"

"About Lake Superior? Yeah," I said.

"Did you see what happened to North Korea?" Colin asked.

We picked up our pace. "No, what?"

Colin held open the screen door, nodded a greeting to Cortez. "It's gone."

The news was showing aerial images of a silent, smoldering city. The gray, twisted wreckage reminded me of a heavily used ash tray.

"They bombed all the major cities and military installations. Some North Korean troops surged into South Korea, and they're still fighting, but that's it, besides survivors in the countryside."

I didn't know whether to be happy or sad. None of my friends seemed to know either. It was a relief, but it was scary. I couldn't imagine what those survivors were experiencing right now.

The red *News Alert* banner flashed at the bottom of the screen. "We're just now receiving this update," a blonde anchorwoman said. "It has been confirmed by sources within the Pentagon that all U.S. troops currently serving overseas have been ordered back to U.S. soil."

Their military analyst, a bald colonel with no right arm, explained that the military trained for this sort of mobilization, that it even had a name: Operation Repatriation. The troops would destroy any large weapons they couldn't take with them, then they would be readied to deploy across the U.S. to reestablish order if that became necessary.

"I'm not sure if that's a good thing or not," Colin said, "assuming they're really deployed."

"They can't be worse than the police or the Civil Defense goons," I said.

"Maybe we'll find out," Cortez said.

Cortez slept in the kitchen, between the counter and the table, because my bed was in the living room and he said he didn't want to crowd me. By the time I woke, he was gone—he'd left a note saying he was going to salvage what he could from his apartment, and would see us later.

After breakfast I wandered into Pulaski Square, where the tribe was still camped. They had so few possessions: machetes, cooking pots; one kid was clutching an old action figure. From what I could see, no one was in charge. Most of them were sprawled on the lawn dozing; a group of older men were playing some sort of gambling game that involved tossing carved stones.

"Where is your friend with the sticks?" I turned; it was the topless girl. Her accent was like the man we'd talked with yesterday—she pronounced Ws like Vs.

"He's at home," I said. I didn't figure it was worth trying to explain all of the nuances in that statement.

"Was he playing a game with them?" She made a strange, scrunchy facial expression, almost like she wasn't aware other people could see her face.

"It wasn't a game. They're weapons, for protection."

She made a grunting sound that I took to mean she understood. I glanced at her chest. I couldn't help it, her breasts were right there. Her nipples were puckered, her areolas as big as silver dollar pancakes.

"Why doesn't he just have a gun?"

I opened my mouth to answer, then saw that she was grinning. I laughed, and she laughed with me. We stood there looking at each other, only I realized after a moment that she wasn't looking at me, she was looking off over my shoulder. I turned to see what she was looking at. It was the bamboo outbreak.

She smiled, suddenly looking almost like any city girl.

"It's beautiful," she said.

"I guess you could say that."

It occurred to me that these people were like modern hunter-gatherers. A few years ago I'd watched part of an old documentary about a hunter-gatherer tribe in Africa. These people were so much like them—they loved nature, no one seemed to be in charge, they kept moving and seemed to live almost totally off the land. I wondered if they'd been out in the woods since my tribe had been out there. That would be eight years, a long time to be wandering around in the woods.

"Hey, Jasper!" It was Cortez, jogging toward us. He waved briefly to the girl and then pulled me aside.

"Remember yesterday when I told you that I felt aimless, that I didn't know where my life was going?" He didn't wait for me to reply—he was excited, talking at high-speed. "Now I know. I found this book on your shelf..." He fumbled in his pack, pulled out a softcover book. It was *Light of the Warrior-Sage*, one of the books I'd salvaged from the abandoned bookstore after seeing Mr. Swift executed. I'd never gotten past the first chapter. Cortez shook the book. "This book showed me my path." He leafed through it, opened to a page he'd dog-eared, and read:

"*The warrior-sage keeps a silent quest in his heart. This quest keeps him vital, lubricates his mind and spirit, keeps him poised and alert in the luminosity of his soul. His quest is selfless, for the warrior-sage recognizes that the boundary between self and world is illusion, that alleviating the suffering of the world and alleviating the suffering in his own heart are one and the same.*"

As Cortez looked up from reading, I was surprised to see that his eyes were filled with tears. "It's like those words have always been inside me, waiting to come out. A warrior-sage—that's what I am."

"Hm." I nodded, as if I were thinking about what he was saying. It was good to see him so up a day after his house had been bambooed.

Cortez dug back into his pack and retrieved an old Batman comic. "Yesterday I was rereading this. I've always admired Batman. I was thinking that the Caped Crusader would sure pull a full shift if he were working in these times, and then it all came together. All this time honing my martial arts skills, my weapons technique... it was all leading to this."

"To what?" I asked.

Cortez held up a finger. "I'm going to devote myself to helping others. Maybe I can't stop the Jumpy-Jumps and the CDs on a large scale, but I can stop some crime, at least. At least I can do something." He gripped my shoulder, spoke almost in my ear. "And I know just where to start. I found out who's responsible for releasing that bamboo."

"Really? Who was it?"

Cortez cocked a thumb toward River Street. "There's a guy who sells drugs and fences stolen merchandise out of an abandoned building on MLK. I found out he also handles bamboo. I checked the place out. It's a small-time operation. I'm going to straighten them out."

"I'd love to see that," I laughed.

Cortez's eyes got wide. "Hey! Come with me!"

"Oh, no, I wouldn't be a good Robin. I have no crime-fighting skills whatsoever." I neglected to add that I'm a coward. Before the depression, when battles were fought with words and lawyers, I would have been a much more effective fighter. Fists and guns are not my weapons of choice.

Cortez put an arm around my shoulder. "No, I'll take care of the enforcement—it would just be nice to have some company. You can just hang."

I had the impression that Cortez mostly wanted a witness. What's the point of exacting retribution if no one sees it? "What are you going to do, exactly?"

Cortez waved a dismissive hand. "I'm not gonna hurt anyone. I'll just confiscate their drugs and bamboo and grind it all under my heel, then tell them they're closed for business."

I wanted to say no, but Cortez was giving me this imploring, expectant look, his eyebrows raised. It seemed important to him that I go. It probably wouldn't entail much risk. I'd watched him dismantle two knife-wielding thugs who were ready for him, and that was years ago—his skills had improved since then, and he'd have weapons of his own this time.

"Sure. Why not?"

Cortez beamed. "I'll come get you tonight around ten."

Cortez was dressed all in black. A fat knife was sheathed at his calf, and his Eskrima sticks were in a pouch at his waist.

MLK Drive was bustling now that the sun was down. An Asian woman stood on the corner in a faded green felt skirt, looking to turn tricks, her children sitting at her feet playing with bottle caps. One of her arms was nothing but bone and scar tissue; she'd danced with the flesh-eating virus, but she'd survived it, lucky lady. Cortez's mother hadn't been so lucky, along with maybe a hundred thousand others.

A bunch of uniforms were standing outside the boarded-up Lucky 7 mini-casino checking IDs, probably for no reason except to exert their authority.

An old tour trolley, stripped down to wheels and a floor, rumbled by. "Right over there, a particularly bloody stiletto went down," a red-haired guy in an old navy jacket said into a crackly microphone. "Dude stabbed another dude seven, eight times in the face, till his blade got stuck in the eye socket and he couldn't get it back out."

"Where's the harm in that?" someone shouted from the back of the trolley, a bottle of home brew clutched in his fist. We watched the murder tour roll by.

"Have you ever read that book I borrowed, *Light of the Warrior-Sage*?" Cortez asked.

"No, I never got around to it. When I have free time I've been reading about medicinal herbs."

"How's that going? Your apothecary business?"

"It's going okay. I'm able to stock about two dozen different herbs. I make foraging day-trips into the country."

"That's great."

"Yeah, I enjoy the foraging expeditions. It's peaceful in the bamboo, and fun to hunt for the herbs, kind of like a scavenger hunt. Once I started selling them people started coming into the store to consult with me about what they should take, you know, for a toothache or to help them get pregnant."

Two guys stumbled past. "Look at the moon! It's glowing in the dark!" one of them said, pointing. The other cackled. Stoners shot up with something, probably godflash.

"You making some good cheese?" Cortez asked me.

"Not a lot. People can't afford to pay much, so if I want to sell it, it's got to be cheap. Plus it's Ruplu's store, so he gets a cut."

We stopped behind a battered Prius, in front of what was essentially an empty lot with a door and a roof tucked between two buildings. Blackened bricks and heat-tortured steel lay scattered and piled, casting long shadows. "This is it," Cortez said. "Dude's name is B-Bob, or something like that." A tug boat hooted in the distance; overhead a bat flapped mad figure-eights around a lamppost.

I followed Cortez through the doorway, into a big, dark, empty space. In the far corner there was light, created by dozens of candles, their flames burning in a rainbow of colors. B-Bob sat on a stool behind a bruised Formica counter, his back to the brick wall of an adjoining building. A girl leaned up against the wall, arms crossed behind her back, purse dangling from her shoulder, talking to B-Bob.

"She's got some train wreck going on at her place," the girl was saying as we approached. I recognized her: Tara Cohn. I'd gone to school with her. She'd hung out with a different crowd, but she'd been okay. Always chewing gum.

"Freeze," Cortez said. He was holding a gun. Tara shrieked; B-Bob nearly fell back on his stool. Cortez lunged, grabbed the automatic pistol sitting on the counter, stuffed it in his belt.

"Take it, take it," B-Bob said, hands in the air. "We got no problem."

"Yeah, we do got a problem," Cortez said to B-Bob. "Put everything on the table. Now."

Hands shaking, B-Bob pulled piles of baggies and bright-colored pills out from behind the counter, laid them on top. Then he put his hands back up.

Cortez pushed the drugs into a pile, pulled a little can of lighter fluid from his pocket and squirted it over the drugs.

B-Bob stared at the pile, wide-eyed. "What the fuck? You just going to flunk them all?"

"I ain't no thief," Cortez said, fishing a matchbook from his pants. "Where's the bamboo? I want that too."

"What bamboo? I don't got no bamboo."

"Don't bullshit me," Cortez said.

"I just hold it to pass on to somebody once in a while. I don't got none right now."

"Well, your fucking bamboo cut up the wrong guy's home," Cortez said. "All you bastards bleeding the block, wrecking this city. This is my home, god dammit."

"I don't sell to kids," B-Bob said. "I don't do no harm, I just help people escape for a little while. It's the only vacation most people around here can afford."

I heard a metal click. "Drop the gun." It was a man's voice, behind Cortez.

Cortez put his hands up slowly, turned halfway around. Before I understood what was happening, he planted a side kick under the guy's armpit, followed by a spinning hook kick that caught the guy square in the jaw and dropped him. He was so fast—I couldn't believe it.

Out of the corner of my eye I saw Tara fumbling in her purse.

"Look out!" I shouted at Cortez. He spun to face Tara as she pointed the pistol at him, clutching it in both hands.

"No!" Cortez shouted as she drew a bead. "Put it *down!*" He pointed his pistol at her. Tara hesitated, then closed one eye like she was at a fucking rifle range.

Cortez shot her twice in the stomach.

She grunted, fell back into a sitting position, stared down in disbelief at the blood, which looked black in the dim streetlight.

She looked up at Cortez. "You suck."

"I'm sorry," Cortez said. "Why didn't you listen? I didn't want to hurt nobody."

I was swimming in a dream world. I couldn't wrap my mind around what was happening.

"Bobby," Tara whimpered. "I need help. It's starting to hurt." She gagged; blood leaked out of her mouth and down her chin. Bobby squatted beside her, drew her head to his chest.

Cortez grabbed me by the arm and yanked. I stumbled, almost fell. "Run," he said. I let him jerk me along as I looked back at the seemingly frozen scene of B-Bob holding Tara to his chest, until the doorway flashed by around me, and the scene was snuffed out.

"Run!" Cortez shouted. I ran. I've never run so fast.

I finally stopped not because I was out of breath but because I couldn't see where I was going through the tears. I stopped in a deserted alley, pushed my face against the bricks. Cortez leaned up against the wall across from me, then slid to a sitting position, his head dangling between his knees. He sniffed.

What had we done? We'd shot Tara Cohn, who used to sit in front of me in biology class. For what? For what reason? She'd told Cortez he sucked, like he'd taken her last French fry or something.

"She might be okay, we don't know," Cortez said, his voice thick from crying.

"She's not okay," I said.

I turned and stared out of the alley, into a square a block away, at the Spanish moss dripping from the branches of the oaks, the moonlight peering through. "I think I need to be alone for a while. Will you be okay?"

Cortez nodded. "I'm sorry I got you into this. I'm so sorry."

"I know," I said. I couldn't look at him. I walked off.

I walked until daylight. I didn't want to go home and have to explain what had happened when Colin and Jeannie saw my face. By morning I'd stopped crying, but I still felt so twisted inside that it was hard to take a full breath.

I found myself thinking about the other killing, when we'd stabbed the men who were trying to rape Ange. That had been a more understandable killing—a noble murder, almost. We hadn't felt noble, and I still had occasional nightmares about it, but I never regretted it. I would regret Tara's death every day for the rest of my life.

I wandered into Madison Square. The primitive tribe was breaking camp. The girl waved when she saw me. I realized I hadn't even asked her name, like she was an animal not worth that courtesy. This morning she looked strong and certain, like she was the one who had it right, who knew how to live, and I was the clueless one.

"I don't know your name," I said, trying to smile.

"Bird," she said.

"Jasper."

"I like you," she said, staring at the ground, looking like a fifteen-year-old with a crush. It occurred to me that I didn't know she *wasn't* fifteen, though I suspected she was more like twenty. It felt good to have someone say something nice to me just then.

"I like you, too," I said. I blinked tears away.

"Why don't you come with me?"

"I can't," I said. She nodded, let her shoulders drop in disappointment.

It occurred to me that I could go if I wanted to. I imagined myself in the bamboo, hunting for herbs and roots, sleeping under the stars, maybe not sleeping alone. That would be nice. Why couldn't I just go for a week or two, maybe a month? No guns, no viruses, nothing to think about. Noble savagery. The urge to flee, to get out of the city, was overwhelming.

"Could I come for a little while, maybe a few weeks? Would that be all right? I can't come for good." I didn't understand these people's culture, and didn't want to mistakenly give her the impression we were getting married or something.

She shrugged. "Sure."

"Would they let me?"

"Would who let you?" Bird asked.

"Your… people. Who would I ask?"

Bird shrugged, squinted. "Why would you ask anybody?"

No one was in charge. What a refreshing concept.

Two naked kids ran between us, giggling, one chasing the other.

"I'd like to come with you for a while," I said. Bird squealed with excitement, jumped up and down.

"I need to go get some things. I'll meet you back here?"

She pointed at the ground. "Right here."

"Right." I jogged out of the park, up Whitaker to East Jones.

Colin was on the roof, working in the garden. I told him I was going on an extended herb excursion with the tribe in the square, that I might be gone for a few weeks. I'd done a few overnight jaunts, so he didn't think too much of it. I didn't tell him about Tara Cohn. I knew I would eventually, but it was too fresh right now, it would take too much out of me, and I was so tired. My eyelids burned from dirt and tears and lack of sleep.

I packed some toiletries, a change of clothes, two wild herb books. I threw on my collection vest, its pockets like a dozen little drawers in a curio cabinet, and headed to the square.

Back in the square Bird grabbed my arm, led me to a little pile: a cooking pot, bow and arrow, machete, a black plastic bag tied with a string. "These are my things. Can you carry the machete and bow and arrows?"

I nodded, picked them up. Bird grabbed the other things, and we left. Just like that.

By afternoon I was drenched in sweat and exhausted. I hadn't slept in thirty hours, and I'd been an accomplice to a killing since then.

We reached the foot-high plastic wall that marked the perimeter of the outer rhizome barrier, and pressed into the bamboo. It was like another world. In most places the stalks were so tight that you had to squeeze between them; you chose your path like you were in a maze, trying to look ahead, avoid the areas where you had to hack with the machete, seeking out the more open areas where you could walk normally. It was a perfect distraction, a mindless task that occupied most of my attention.

I liked watching the kids. They navigated the bamboo so effortlessly. Not only were they smaller, but they moved like they were born to it, which they probably were.

There was a constant cracking. The cracking seemed to rise and fall, louder, then softer, but that may have been in my head. The long, narrow, striped leaves added a dry rustling whisper to the cracking when the wind blew.

It was hard for me to think of the bamboo as something beautiful, but I had to admit, it was beautiful in its way. There were a few birds and squirrels and other little animals around—most of the animals seemed to have died out, but there were some, if you watched. There were also lots of small plants, especially where the bamboo didn't grow too thickly.

I spotted a clump of senna growing in the shade of a cherry tree along the bank of a little stream. I squatted and plucked it.

"What are you doing?" Bird asked, squatting next to me.

I wasn't sure how to describe it to her. "I collect herbs that you can use as medicine." I held the senna in my palm so she could see it. "This is a laxative—it helps you go to the bathroom."

Bird scrunched her eyebrows, then turned away, evidently unimpressed.

When we camped for the night I called Ange. I told her I was on an herb expedition, and I told her about the tribe, but I didn't tell her about Bird, or Tara Cohn. Maybe Ange would bump into Cortez and he would tell her, but they didn't socialize much, and I guessed Cortez might not tell anyone about it.

I described the tribe, though, and Ange laughed and said it sounded like I'd joined a cult, and that my ass would be back in my apartment in two days, when I was tired of playing Tarzan and needed a fucking shower.

It was a "one-night" camp, which meant we found a reasonably open spot, put our shit down, sat on the ground, and we were camped. A few people went off to forage. Bird took my hand and led me a little ways off, and pulled me down into a bed of fallen bamboo leaves to make love.

It was obviously not her first time. Her breath was bad, but she wasn't all that interested in kissing anyway. It felt good and natural, having sex in the wilderness with this sweet, easygoing girl.

When we rejoined the tribe, no one looked at us like we'd done something wrong. No convoluted moral code, no guilt. They weren't playing at this, I realized. It was like they didn't know how to think about things the way most people thought about them.

Dinner was wild onions and blackberries, and canned corn beef. There wasn't much of it, but I ate without complaining. I didn't want to play the role of soft city boy. I was a city boy, but I wasn't all that soft. It wasn't my first time sleeping outside, or eating whatever scraps could be gathered.

After dinner, people lounged around while Sandra, the white-haired skeleton of an old lady, told a story. I recognized the story—it was a bastardized version of an old movie from the late 0s, *King of Our Engine*. Good flick, so-so in story form.

I wondered what was in the garbage bag Bird had been carrying. I grabbed it and pulled it over to me. I was starting to get the hang of this place: you didn't ask permission to use other people's stuff, you just took it if you wanted it. They were true socialists, way more than my old tribe, which had shared food and energy, but not personal belongings. These people barely had any concept of personal belongings. I untied the bag and peered inside, instantly recognizing the contents.

Bamboo shoots, with black-and-white-striped stalks, the roots wrapped tightly in burlap. I closed the bag, suppressing a smirk. I'd never seen this variety before, but I would never forget the day that Sebastian pulled shoots much like these from his bag of tricks in Ange's living room. I knew what they were for, even if I didn't know why this tribe had them. I couldn't ask Bird about them now, because the old lady was still telling her story, so I sat cross-legged and listened.

A little girl, two or three years old, came over and sat in my lap. She threw her head back and looked up at me, grinning. I ruffled her hair. She giggled. You couldn't tell whose kids were whose—they wandered from person to person like they were happy orphans, and it occurred to me that I had no idea if any of these people were Bird's parents or brothers and sisters.

When the story was finished, I thought I'd start up a conversation. "So how long have you been doing this?"

"What?" said the strong-looking guy Cortez had approached in the park that first day.

"Living in the wilderness, not living in houses."

"Most of us a long time, a few a shorter time," Sandra piped in. "The children, their whole lives. We don't talk about our city lives much. We prefer happy stories." She didn't sound pissed off at me for bringing it up, just matter-of-fact.

"So why do you visit the cities at all?" I asked.

"There are things we need there, food mostly, and things we need to give to them," Carl said. He was a fifty-something guy with an overbite. He didn't have as much of an accent as most of the others, so I guessed he was a recent convert.

"You trade with them?"

A couple of people laughed.

"We give them what they need, we get what we need," Carl said.

I smiled and nodded. I understood more than they thought I did, and that felt kind of nice. "Are you speaking in riddles because my ignorance is entertaining, or because you don't want to tell me? If you don't want to tell me, you can say so."

Some of the smiles faded; a few people picked up weaving projects and other things they were working on.

Carl tossed a bamboo shoot he'd been whittling at my feet. "We give them these."

I picked it up, held it in my palm. "You started the outbreak near the square, didn't you?" I looked at Bird. She smiled like a gremlin and nodded so vigorously her breasts bounced. I was with the people who had wrecked Cortez's home. Ironic.

"Are you working for the scientist in Atlanta?" I asked. "Do you know a man named Sebastian?"

Carl seemed surprised. "So you know."

I flashed a big smile. "I was there for the very first planting."

We sat and smiled at each other for a while. Another thing I was learning about these people was that they were comfortable with silence. Long lulls in conversation were not uncommon.

"We're not wandering aimlessly, are we?" I asked, finally.

"We're heading north," the big guy said. "To slow things down up there."

With a newly engineered variety that thrived further north, clogging the highways and airports, slowing the spread of brand-name products even more. Maybe throwing them back into the Stone Age. I still wasn't sure if that was a good thing. I had no way of knowing what the world would have been like by now if it wasn't for the bamboo, and Doctor Happy, and any other disruptions that'd been created that I didn't know about.

A week in, I had no idea where we were. We reached the top of what passed for a hill in South Georgia, and there was nothing but bamboo and sandy blank patches and scattered stands of scrub pines as far as I could see in every direction. It would take the tribe months to make their way north (not that I planned to be there that long), but the tribe didn't seem to be in a hurry. I was filthy, thirsty, and bored. Sand gnats buzzed around my face, relentlessly landing in my ears and the corners of his eyes, but I wasn't ready to go home yet. Maybe I was doing penance for what I'd done, or maybe I just wanted to prove Ange wrong about how long I could play Tarzan. I turned and waited for Bird. She was dragging, sweating even more than me, her mouth pulled down in a grimace that made her look confused. Usually she was egging me on.

"You okay?" I asked.

"I ate something wrong. I have to poop." She pulled down her rags and squatted right there. I was getting used to it. I turned and walked a respectable distance. Three guys moseyed past, saying hello to her as she squatted there, her face red from straining.

Suddenly she turned her head to one side and puked. I ran to her, put a hand on her shoulder. "You're really sick." I put my palm on her forehead, and hot as it was outside, it was still obvious she was pulling a fever. "Shit, you've got something." I automatically reached to yank my mask over my mouth, but I'd packed it away days ago, and it was way too late in any case if she'd caught anything designer. I thought of the woman with the giant tongue, panting in the car, and my bowels went loose. I turned in the direction of the guys vanishing into the bamboo. "Hey! She's sick! Call a stop."

They called, and the call repeated, further away each time.

"I have something that will help with the nausea." I wrapped my arms around Bird's waist to help her to the ground. She cried out in pain, like I'd stuck an arrow in her, and grabbed her stomach, low, on the right side.

Appendix. As soon as I saw her grab that spot, I knew. I had nothing in my pouches to help that.

The tribe was gathering, a few at a time.

"We need to find a doctor! She's got appendicitis." It had never occurred to me to wonder what would happen if I fell and fractured my skull while I was out here.

"There are no towns near here. No doctors," an old guy missing his front teeth said.

"Well what do we do?" I asked. Bird was whimpering in pain.

"Nothing to do," Sandra said, shrugging. "We'll camp here till Bird's strong enough to walk, or till she dies."

"I don't want to die," Bird said.

I needed a consult. I pulled out my phone, dialed the Phone Doctor number. A recorded voice prompted me to type in my credit code. Wincing at the thought of what this would cost, I did.

"Andrew Gabow, M.D. How can I help you?" a clean, rested voice said over the phone. I felt a wave of gratitude, just to hear that tone.

"I've got a woman here who I think has appendicitis. We're way out in the wilderness, there's no way to get her to a town. What do I do?"

"Describe her symptoms."

I went through them; the doctor asked follow-up questions about the exact location of the pain in her abdomen. He sounded miffed that I didn't have a thermometer to get Bird's exact temperature.

"You're probably correct—acute appendicitis. I'll give it to you straight, Jasper—she's in real danger. You're not going to carry her out of there in time, and when her appendix bursts, the infection will spread, and chances are she won't survive. Not out there. Probably not even in a hospital."

"What do I do?" I asked.

"You've got one option. Perform surgery on her."

"*Me?*"

"Whoever in your party has the most medical experience. Is there a nurse with you, a paramedic? Nurse's aid?"

I asked the tribe; a dozen heads shook. Shit, half of them probably didn't know how to read. Most of the rest had probably forgotten.

"There's got to be another way," I said to the doctor. "What about a helicopter?"

The doctor laughed. "Will that be cash or charge?"

"Oh god," I said. I felt like I was separating from my body; I heard my voice saying "oh god," but it sounded far away, coming from someone else.

"Build a fire," Doctor Gabow said. "I'm going to do this for a hundred dollars federal, because you can't afford what I should be charging, and because I'm a nice guy."

"Thank you, Doctor," I said. "Somebody build a fire!" *Who was that scared little boy who just yelled that?* a calm sliver of my mind asked.

When the fire had been built, we heated water. I plunged my hands into the pot of scalding water and held them there as long as I could. Then Carla did the same—she was going to assist. Carla put a knife in the water, then held it over the flames before handing it to me. My hand shook so badly I could hardly hold the knife. The children had been moved out of hearing distance. Four people held Bird down, one for each arm and leg. The doctor suggested we put her in a stream to cool her and reduce the bleeding, but there were no streams around.

"Don't make the cut too deep," the doctor said. I had activated the hands-free element on the phone. "About a half inch down, two across. There's going to be a lot of blood, but don't worry about that. We'll handle that later."

Tears poured down Bird's cheeks as I held the knife over the spot we'd washed and doused with moonshine. The knife was shaking so badly it was blurry. I held it there a long time; twice I brought it down just short of Bird's soft skin, and twice I pulled it back up.

"Make the cut, Jasper," the doctor said.

"I can't do this," I said. "Somebody else, please. Somebody do this." I wasn't an action guy. Cortez was the action guy—if he was here, he would have done the cutting without breaking a sweat. I'd never cut anything in my life that wasn't on a dinner plate.

"I don't want to die," Bird whimpered. "Please. I don't want to die."

With a howl, I cut her. She screamed in agony, bucked violently, trying to break free of the people pinning her down. Like an animal. Blood welled up where I'd cut her, filling the incision and pouring out. "I can't do this, I can't do this."

"How deep is the incision? What do you see inside?" the doctor said, so calm, so far away in his comfortable air-conditioned office.

"I don't know." Reluctantly I pulled the skin apart with my thumb and forefinger to see how deep it was. "There's just red tissue, I can't see anything."

"You're still in muscle. You have to cut again, deeper."

"Oh, god. Not again." Tears poured down my cheeks; I was trembling all over like I was freezing cold.

You suck, Tara Cohn's voice said inside my head. I sobbed.

"Cut, god dammit. Cut her. Do it now," the doctor shouted.

I screamed, and kept screaming as I cut, wider and deeper. Bird thrashed, but the fight was bleeding out of her. She seemed only half-conscious, only the whites of her eyes visible.

"What do you see?" the doctor asked.

I pulled on the flap I'd made, and it tore a little wider, exposing something gray and puckered, a fat snake folding in on itself. It was an organ. Christ, it was her liver or gall bladder or something. I described it to the doctor.

"Good boy, Jasper, that's what you want. That's the colon. Fish around, find the bottom of it, where it meets the small intestine.

You're looking for a small, tubelike appendage attached to the colon."

I poked around inside Bird, trying to ignore the moist squishing sound, the blood pouring down her side, dribbling onto the tan bamboo husks that littered the ground.

"I can't find it," I said.

"Get your damned hand in there and move the colon around. This isn't some dainty parlor game. Get your hands bloody."

I dug, squeezing my fingers between the slimy tubes, pushing one section up with my finger. Behind it was something that looked like a swollen maggot. I described it to Doctor Gabow.

"Cut it off and pitch it away, Jasper."

I cut it off. Sandra sewed the end of the colon closed while I held the knife over the flame, getting it good and hot. Then I pressed the flat end of it against the wound, to cauterize it and stop some of the bleeding. Bird didn't flinch as the knife hissed against her insides; she'd passed out somewhere along the way. Sandra held the edges of the wound closed while I sewed. Doctor Gabow explained that someone needed to get to the nearest town and buy antibiotics, or Bird would likely die of infection, and all his good work would go to waste.

People slapped my back as I stumbled out of the camp. I found a quiet copse and collapsed onto my back, staring at the half-moon through the narrow leaves. I felt… strange. Calm. Like a buzzing had turned off in my brain for the first time in years. I held my hand in front of my face, looked at the blood covering it, starting to dry and cake. I'd done it.

I closed my eyes and let myself drift off to sleep, thinking that I'd had enough of the simplicity of the hunter-gatherer life. I wanted to go home.

I caught a whiff of jasmine, waited at a crosswalk as a cluster of men pedaled by on bicycles wearing helmets with built-in gas masks, semi-automatics dangling from their belts.

Across the street, a tattered teal awning read: *Francis McNairy Antiques and Collectibles.* Yeah, right. I'll trade you my mint condition *Spider-Man* number one for your slightly used bottle of Cool, what do you say?

A block further I could see my house, its porch looking inviting to my aching feet. I put my head down and trekked the final few yards, then plopped into a chair on the porch.

The screen door swung open almost immediately. "How was your trip?" Colin asked, unfolding a mildewed lawn chair and joining me.

"Do I have a story for you," I said.

"Really?" Colin scooted his lawn chair until it was at a ninety degree angle from mine. "I could use a good story; the TV's been out for three days."

I told him the good stuff, where I was the good guy, saving a life.

"So, you've decided the right woman for you is a semi-primitive, illiterate teenager with bad breath?" Colin asked when I'd finished.

I shook my head, blew out a long breath. "I just needed some affection. She offered, and I took her up on it." I stared off toward the far end of the porch, at a weight-lifting bench that had been abandoned by some previous tenant. Padding jutted from the rotting vinyl fabric. We should really throw the damned thing out.

Then again, it added a certain character to the porch. I felt a sudden wave of affection for our crappy little apartment, and the people I shared it with. It was good to be home.

Chapter 7: Smithereen Sonata

Spring, 2033 (Six months later)

From our seats in the upper deck the players looked like tissues dropped in the grass, yet it was so quiet I could hear the shortstop scuff his foot on the infield dirt, smoothing an invisible divot.

I fished for a peanut. Even the crackle of the cellophane bag seemed loud, as if we were in a movie theater. I half-expected someone to shush me as I cracked the peanut under my thumb, peeled off the top half of the shell, popped one red-skinned peanut into my mouth, reached over and fed the second to Ange. She closed her lips over my fingers, grinned when I glanced over at her. Lately Ange had been way more affectionate than she'd ever been before. We'd been through so many waxes and wanes; at times I'd felt certain that we had drifted so far apart we would never again be more than acquaintances who'd once been close, but we always seemed to drift back into our not-quite-dating netherworld. I'd long ago given up thinking about the possibility of a real relationship, squashed any romantic feelings I had for Ange so that what I felt for her was a (somehow workable) mix of lust and brotherly affection.

The pitcher wound, threw a high fastball. The lanky batter swung and missed, and the inning was over. No one clapped. The Macon Mets took the field, and the pitcher began his warmup tosses.

"Whatever that shit is in the atmosphere, it sure makes the sunsets pretty," Ange said.

"Mmm," I said. The sun was setting over the left field fence; the clouds were a gorgeous pastel of pink, peach, indigo, violet.

On the first pitch the Sand Gnat batter yanked the ball into the right field corner. The right fielder took a few listless steps after it, then gave up. He squatted on his haunches and watched it roll. He covered his face in his hands as the ball rolled to a stop on the warning track. The center fielder trotted over to him, put a hand on his shoulder, said something. The right fielder shook his head.

The batter trotted to second base and stopped, probably figuring that's where he would've ended up if the play had been made. Winning didn't mean as much with so many people dying.

"His family was in D.C. All dead," the man in the row behind us said. I glanced back at him. His face and neck were a swirl of burn scars, and his right arm ended in an uneven stump. A China War veteran, probably.

"Shame. I'm surprised he's playing," An older man beside the scarred man said.

I wanted to tell them to shut the hell up. I didn't want to think about D.C. That's why I was at a baseball game instead of watching fucking CNN.

"I wonder if the people who killed the president had propped him in the chair for effect, or if he died in the chair," Ange said.

"I bet they propped him there," I said.

CNN kept replaying the video of the president in the oval office, behind his desk, his head rolled back, his tongue huge and black like he'd choked trying to swallow a tire. He'd been a Republican; the vice president had been a Democrat. That was supposed to change things. The man on the videotape they kept showing on CNN was neither a Republican nor a Democrat, but he claimed to be in charge. Or not in charge. It was hard to understand him because he talked fast and used a lot of Jumpy-Jump slang. The newscasters weren't sure anyone was in charge. They looked scared. The streets of D.C. were a madhouse, and some of the other big cities didn't seem far behind.

It wasn't clear whether the teams were going to finish the game. The managers and umps were standing near the first base coach's box, arms folded across their chests, talking.

Over the left field wall, there was a flash, and a hot boom. People in the stands screamed, leapt to their feet. The ballplayers sprinted for the dugouts, looking back over their shoulders at the explosion, which was a good thirty blocks away. It looked like an expanding rainbow of colors, like ripples in a candy pond.

I looked at Ange. "Shit," she said.

It could be anything—chemical, biological, nuclear, or an accident at a crayon factory.

We waited for most of the stampeding crowd to exit, figuring their panic could kill us as easily as chemical weapons, then we fled.

The streets were filled with the sound of breaking glass and shouting, which was not unusual. There was something else, though—a thrumming that registered deep in my stomach, like the beating of drums. Mortar fire, or maybe tanks, far away. Closer, we heard the pop of gunfire, which was also not that unusual, only there was more of it than usual.

Screams rose from the direction of Waters Avenue, cutting through the other noises. Ange's phone rang.

"You guys okay?" Ange said. I could hear Colin's voice in the phone. "Shit," Ange said. She turned to me. "Your building's on fire."

I started running.

"Hold on. It's okay, they're out, they're safe," Ange said. She grabbed my sleeve, slowed me down.

"Jeannie's okay?" I asked.

"Jeannie's fine. Baby still on board."

"Where are they?" I asked, relieved to hear that Jeannie hadn't lost the baby. With no access to a doctor, her pregnancy was such a tenuous thing.

"Outside your building," Ange said. She told them we'd meet them there.

We passed a building with red flames licking out of a boarded up window. A siren wailed in the distance. It wasn't the wah-wah siren of an ambulance, and the police never used their sirens any more—they didn't want people to hear them coming.

"I already called the fire department," an old guy standing on the sidewalk said, seeing us peruse the flames as we hurried by.

"You called the fire department?" I said.

"They're on their way." Purple veins blossomed on the guy's cheeks and nose. He was probably a drinker, passing dull nights in his apartment sipping moonshine while he watched old TV shows where cops solved crimes and firemen ran into burning buildings to save crying babies.

We picked up our pace. "They're bad news. Get away while you still can," I shouted back.

The crack of gunfire and the booming of explosions was every-where. Something was happening.

A baritone honking announced the big red truck before it careened around the corner. It was crawling with firemen, their faces painted red, their helmets festooned with illustrations. The truck was im-maculate, the polished chrome blinding in the sunlight.

We cut into an alley. It was packed with homeless, milling around, looking ready to bolt if they could only figure out which direction to go. I thought of our apartment burning with all of my possessions in it. I didn't have much to lose, but when you don't have much, it sure hurts to lose what you have.

The pop-pop of gunfire was constant. Crowds of people were run-ning in every direction. A helicopter roared overhead, just above roof level. In the east, where the explosion had been, the horizon glowed red—it looked as if everything in that direction was on fire now.

We spilled out onto Drayton. A tight cluster of Civil Defense guys with machine pistols rounded the corner and headed in our direc-tion. We ducked into a doorway, stared at the bricked pavement until they passed. I had no idea what the rules were, what might get us shot, who might do the shooting. I struggled to understand, to put a label on this thing that was happening. It was a war, the city was at war—that was clear. But wars had two sides, and this had twenty sides, or fifty, or maybe no sides.

We cut down another alley, past people hiding behind a green dumpster. Others stared down at us from the safety of open windows in locked apartments. Above them, on the roof, were flocks of boys with guns.

Ange's phone rang again. "Where are you?" she said, plugging her free ear.

"It's Sebastian," Ange said to me. "He says we need to get out."

"Out of the city?"

Ange nodded.

"But Jeannie's eight months pregnant!"

Sebastian said something. Ange held up a finger. "Okay, see you there." She hung up.

"He said we don't have a choice, things are going to get bad."

I thought of what that economist in the wheelchair had said three years ago, during our speed-dating session. *It's not going to turn around; it's going to get worse, and then it's going to collapse completely.*

Sebastian was going to follow the railroad tracks out of town. That made sense, to get off the roads, but the thought of the railroad tracks sickened me. It reminded me of our tribe days.

A woman screamed in one of the apartments above us. She screamed again, forming the outline of a word. It sounded like "help." She screamed a third time, and this time it was clear she was calling for help.

Ange called Jeannie back and got them moving in our direction.

"I should warn Ruplu," I said. We made the two-block detour to Abercorn Street, and turned the corner into an inferno. Flames roared over the roofline of the Timesaver. Ruplu was nowhere to be seen. I called him.

"It's gone, Jasper," he said. "Everything we worked for is gone."

"I know. I'm so sorry." I spotted Colin and Jeannie up ahead, raised my hand. They waved back. "Listen, we've been told by our scientist friend that we need to get out of the city. It's not going to be safe here."

There was a long silence on the other end. "Are you sure?"

"Pretty sure, yes. This guy has friends in Atlanta. They say things are going to get very bad."

"All right, then. Thank you, friend."

I suggested he and his family meet up with us, but Ruplu said if he needed to leave, his uncle had a little boat, and they would head down the coast to stay with relatives in Saint Augustine. That seemed like a good plan.

We joined up with Colin and Jeannie and headed toward Thirty-eighth Street.

My phone rang: I recognized the number, but I couldn't connect it with a face. I answered it, too breathless to do more than gasp in lieu of a hello. We'd stopped running and were hugging the edge of doorways.

"I need you," Deirdre said. She was crying. A tingle of shock ran up my balls.

"I can't," I said.

"You can't *what*?" she said. "I don't know where to go. There's no-body…" she trailed off, crying. It was an angry, outraged crying.

"I can't get to you. I'm not home," I said. "We're leaving."

"I'm coming with you." I didn't respond.

"Please!" she added.

"Who is it?" Jeannie asked.

I covered the mouthpiece of the phone. "Deirdre. She wants to come."

"Oh Christ! No. No way," Jeannie said.

"What can she bring?" Colin said. It was a shock to hear Colin put it so bluntly. If you bring a keg, we'll invite you to our party. But given the situation I guess he saw no choice but to be pragmatic. I've heard a lot of people say that having a child changes you.

We were crossing Thirtieth Street. We had to step over a body stretched across the sidewalk, covered with bloody bullet wounds.

"What can you bring if we let you come? Do you have money?"

"Three thousand," Deirdre said. "A gun. Two kils of energy."

I turned to Colin. "Money, gun, energy." He nodded, and so did Ange. Jeannie cursed.

"Tell her to bring water filters if she has any," Colin said.

"Get to Thirty-eighth Street," I said into the phone. "Follow the railroad tracks east out of town until you catch up with us. Bring water filters if you have any. We'll move slowly, but you'd better move your ass, because we won't move slowly for too long."

"I'm coming," Deirdre said. "Fuck you," she added before hanging up.

We jogged as fast as Jeannie could, through a roiling tide of people fleeing in every direction, past looters climbing into shattered store windows, past tanks rumbling down Habersham Street. Eventually we stopped running and hugged the edge of doorways, trying not to be noticed. We cut through an alley and had to step over three bodies, probably dragged from a car that was bent around a telephone pole. One had been shot in the eye, an old black woman.

There was a long burst of gunfire nearby.

"Oh jeez," Colin said. A block away, on Lincoln Street, men with automatic weapons were executing dozens of people kneeling, hands behind their heads, in front of an apartment building.

We turned into another alley, behind Liberty, and ran headlong into four soldiers in MOP suits and gas masks. Federal government soldiers. The cavalry had arrived. With the president dead, I wondered who they were taking orders from. The VP? The secretary of defense?

"Let's go," one of them said, motioning with a gun "you're being evacuated.

"Evacuated where?" Ange asked.

"Move," the soldier said.

We were taken a block over and directed into a section of Bull Street that had been barricaded with cyclone fencing topped with spirals of silver barbed wire. There were thousands of people milling around inside the fence.

We sat on the edge of the sidewalk, in the shade.

"I'm going to go up front and see what's happening," Colin said. "Stay here."

People were standing quietly, in bunches. "We'll be safe soon," someone said nearby. A mother was stroking her crying child's hair. She lurched forward suddenly and vomited into the sewer grate between her feet. The people nearest scurried away, giving her a wide buffer. The woman barely noticed; she was staring between the rusted iron bars of the sewer, into the wet darkness below.

Colin came back at a trot. "I don't like this. They're separating people into groups—old people in one, one for younger men, another for younger women, a fourth for anyone who doesn't speak English."

"Why would they do that?" I asked. My pounding heart made me think that the answer was something awful, and that maybe deep down I knew what it was.

"None of the answers that make sense are good things," Ange said. We had to get out.

We walked the perimeter, trying not to raise suspicion, looking for a way out. Up the street in Forsyth Park, three big semis were pulling out, one after the other to form a convoy.

"I think there are people in there," I said. "I think the young males are being conscripted into the Army."

The holding pen we were in was thinning as people were sorted into categories and disappeared through a gate at the front, near the park. Soon we'd be corralled toward the front, and then Colin and I would be separated from Ange and Jeannie.

We finished our walk back near the woman who'd vomited. She hadn't moved; her head was still hanging over the sewer.

The sewer.

I retrieved a mangled bicycle handlebar from a trash heap. "Guys, stand so you're blocking me from the soldiers' view." I pried open the manhole in the center of the street. "Come on." I climbed down the slimy rungs of a ladder. Ange was right behind me, her red sneakers in front of my nose.

We waded down the main sewer tunnel through ankle-deep effluence. A dozen others had followed us, but they were lagging behind and keeping to themselves.

Striped sunlight filtered through sewer grates intermittently. Far ahead was a brighter area; harsh engine noises echoed down the pipe from there.

I turned right, into a smaller pipe where we had to bend at the waist.

"Do you know where you're going?" Ange asked.

"No idea," I said. "I just want to put some distance between us and those soldiers."

"You think we can we take this all the way to Thirty-eighth?" Jeannie asked.

That was a great idea. If there was another juncture I could turn left and follow Drayton six blocks to Thirty-eighth.

We found the juncture and turned left. The tunnel ahead seemed to be partially blocked. As we drew closer, we could see that it was blocked by a pile of bodies. We pressed along the damp concrete wall as we went around the pile. There were a dozen or so bodies heaped in a twisted tangle. They looked to be Civil Defense. Above them, light filtered in along the edges of a steel grate.

"The federal soldiers must have killed them," Ange said.

"Help me," a face buried in the pile whispered. A woman, strands of her hair spilling over a booted foot. Her mouth was caked in white foam and blood. One of her arms jutted from under the leg of a hairy man. Her hand opened.

Jeannie grasped it, staring at the pile of bodies on top of the woman.

"I'm sorry, we can't," she said. She squeezed the woman's hand. We hurried on, the woman's pleas fading in the distance.

I counted six blocks, then climbed a ladder and strained to unseat the manhole cover. The first thing that came into view was a street sign: Thirty-eighth.

We crossed Thirty-eighth and hit the tracks, scurrying like roaches fleeing the bathroom light. The tracks cut through back yards and vacant lots. As we reached each intersecting street we sprinted across. Sebastian had chosen well—there wasn't much going on around the tracks. We passed an abandoned loading dock surrounded by heaps of rusting kitchen appliances. Families were ducked down among them, hiding.

"Are there other people we should call and offer to let them come with us?" I asked. Most of our friends had their own families, their own housemates.

"Cortez?" Colin said.

Cortez. I hadn't seen him in six months, since the night of the killing.

"He's big and tough, and we can trust him," Colin said.

"Yeah," I said. I called Cortez.

He was way ahead of us, already on I-16. He'd traveled the last thirty blocks out of the city in a sewer. He agreed to swing back and meet us on the tracks outside the city.

"Good call," I said to Colin as I hung up. I'd felt a rush of affection when I heard Cortez's voice. Yeah, it would be good to have him with us.

We walked on, watching for Sebastian, gravel crunching underfoot.

"We should call Sophia," Jeannie said. The name jolted me; it must have registered on my face. "She was good to us when we needed help, we should see if she needs our help now."

Colin looked at me and shrugged. "Do you remember her number?"

Of course I remembered her number. I took a deep breath and punched it in, put the phone to my ear, listened to the ring as if it were the cry of some mythical beast.

"Hello?" That unmistakable island lilt.

"Sophia, it's Jasper."

Pause. "How're you? It's been a long time."

"Alive," I said. "Are you all right? We're leaving the city. We wanted to see if you needed help."

She said they were barricaded in their condo in one of the gated communities. Their police force was in a pitched battle, trying to repel gangs storming the walls.

They were barricaded. Hopes I hadn't even felt welling up were dashed. And now that I was conscious of them, I felt like a sick bastard for hoping that her husband had left her, or died.

I filled the others in.

"They've got to get out of there," Ange said. "Sooner or later the mob will get in, and they'll kill everyone."

"There's no way out!" Sophia said, her voice hitching. She'd heard Ange.

We'd used the sewers, and so had Cortez. The gated communities must use the same sewers as the rest of the city, if nothing else. "I think I know a way. I'm going to have Cortez call you and guide you out. You remember Cortez?"

She did. "Jasper, thank you for thinking of me," she said before she hung up. I called Cortez. He promised to get her out. He told me not to worry. I fought back tears, glad I'd called Sophia.

"There they are!" Jeannie said, pointing. Up ahead, Sebastian was sitting on the rail. He shimmered a little in the afternoon heat.

When Sebastian spotted us he ran to meet us, laughing, his arms spread for hugs. "Look, a little good luck." He pointed ahead. Good luck, indeed. We were near the perimeter of Savannah's rhizome barrier—ahead of us lay a wall of bamboo, broken only by scattered pines. But a train had been through recently, slicing away the bamboo that had grown in the tracks. As I watched, a dozen people hurried up a ridge from the roadway and fled along the tracks. We would make good time as long as the trains kept running. They'd better keep running—they were the only transport in and out of Savannah.

"Where are we going?" I asked no one in particular.

"We should head to Athens," Sebastian said. "They're establishing a communal setup there—cutting edge, very cool. Most of the smaller towns are grown over, and all the cities are going to end up like Savannah if they haven't already."

"This all part of the master plan?" I asked.

"We are the master plan, Jasper," Sebastian said, clapping my back and giggling. The Zen virus bastard always had a koan ready.

"I always wanted to be a master plan," Colin said.

"Remember what they taught us in fifth grade?" Sebastian said, holding up a finger. "We can be anything we want, if we work hard enough and believe in ourselves."

"They really taught us that horseshit, didn't they?" Ange said.

"Hold on," I said, still looking at Sebastian. "I really want to know: did you expect the bamboo to spread like this?"

He chuckled. "No. No one expected this. But nothing works exactly the way you planned, and it's still probably better than the alternative." Sebastian started walking toward the tracks, and the rest of us followed.

"What exactly was the alternative?" Jeannie asked.

"World war. Countries will always choose war over starvation if forced to choose."

He made it sound like he and his egghead friends had a crystal ball. The bamboo screw-up made it clear that they didn't know half as much as they thought they did. It hadn't slipped past me that for the first time Sebastian had inserted the word "probably" into his claim that the bamboo was helping rather than hurting.

"That's all well and good," I said, "but is anyone planning to fix the royal fuck-up that this bamboo has turned into?" I asked.

"People are working on it. It's a tough problem, though—the bamboo is engineered to be resistant to herbicides, and even if you can design an effective herbicide, the root systems are engineered to disconnect after a time, so you can only kill a tiny cluster at a time."

"Wow, look at that girl run!" Colin said, pointing.

Deirdre was sprinting toward us with her head down. Dread, and a little lust, washed over me at the sight of her. She glanced up, spotted us, and immediately slowed to an easy walk. She was wearing plain old shorts and a t-shirt. It was so un-Deirdre-like to see her dressed down. There were more people on the tracks behind her—more refugees fleeing the chaos. We wouldn't be lonely.

By the time Deirdre reached us she wasn't even breathing hard.

"So let's get the fuck out of here," she said by way of greeting, and walked right past us. We hoisted our packs.

Deirdre. Sophia. It was as if my past was collapsing in on me.

"I'd forgotten how charming she was," Colin said as we followed her into the narrow tunnel cut in the bamboo. "I don't understand why you broke up with her."

Walking on train tracks is a pain in the ass. The gravel in between the railroad ties is rough and uneven, and the nubs of the cut bamboo didn't help, so your instinct was to walk on the ties. But they're never evenly spaced, so you're constantly adjusting the length of your steps. Every so often I would resolve to ignore the ties, pick up my head and just walk, but my gaze kept drifting down, hypnotized by the ties underfoot, and I'd find myself stutter-stepping again.

Within an hour we hit patches where the bamboo was growing back through the tracks, and that added to the challenge. And then there were the insects—sand gnats buzzing in my eyes and ears, little dragon mosquitoes biting my ankles.

"Anybody have insect repellant?" I asked.

"I do," Sebastian said, reaching to pull his pack off without slowing. But Deirdre beat him to it, tossing a tube over her head without turning. It landed on the tracks in front of Jeannie, who retrieved it, squeezed a blob for herself, and passed it on to me.

"Thanks," I said. No answer.

For once, I realized it wasn't hard to understand what Deirdre was feeling. She resented having to ask me for help. She didn't like asking anyone for help, and our history made it worse. But at the same time, she felt she owed me. So she hated me and felt grateful at the same time.

We hit a steep bend, and suddenly there was Cortez, lounging in the middle of the tracks, his back propped on an enormous pack.

"Ladies. Gentlemen," Cortez said.

Everyone shouted out and hurried to greet him. More hugs ensued.

"Is Sophia out?" I asked Cortez as I hugged him.

"She's underground. We're meeting them about five miles ahead."

"Hey, I know you," Deirdre said.

"I worked for you five, six years ago," Cortez said, shaking her hand. "Good to see you again."

Deirdre looked off toward the tops of the pine trees. "Shall we onward?" she said. She squeezed past Cortez and walked on. The rest of us followed.

"So what are all those federal troops doing in the city?" I asked Sebastian, since he seemed to know everything.

"The feds are trying to retain control of the country. Remember last year when all U.S. troops were called home from overseas, after

Lake Superior was nuked? That was the first step. The fed has decided we're at the tipping point, and drastic measures need to be taken to keep us from slipping into chaos."

"To *keep* us from slipping into chaos?" Cortez said. "I think that ship has already sailed."

Sebastian gave him a little grunt of a laugh. "You ain't seen nothing yet."

I didn't like the sound of that at all.

"To your left! Your left!" Cortez called to a ragged group ahead of us. A woman carrying a crying baby glanced back, called out to her group in Spanish. They drifted to the right, letting us pass. The tracks allowed us to walk two abreast, but no more; we had to go single-file when we passed someone.

"Speaking of chaos, did anyone hear about what happened in New York City on Thanksgiving?" Cortez asked.

"What?" Ange said.

"Word spread that the parade down Fifth Avenue was going on, for the first time in six, seven years. Thousands of people showed up—moms brought their kids to show them the big floats, everyone was feeling a little hope, a little lift that things were getting better."

Cortez bit at one of his fingernails, spit the sliver out. "Then the parade comes. The floats were awful nightmare things, the marchers covered in blood. Some guy was walking holding up a dog's head with the eyes gouged out. Kids were crying and screaming. The Jumpy-Jumps had put the whole thing together."

"I don't believe that," Colin said. "It sounds like an urban myth. It's got to be or we would've heard about it on TV or the radio."

"Maybe, but how much of this shit do you think they're still putting on the air?" Cortez said. "That just helps the Jumpy-Jumps."

Nobody answered.

We walked in silence, lost in our own thoughts and fears. Colin was half-carrying Jeannie, sweat pouring down his temples. She was awfully pregnant.

They were leaving me even further behind, I realized, moving on to a different phase of life. The grownup phase. I was stuck in perpetual late-adolescence, going over the same ground again and again.

All of us were moving backward, I realized. We were homeless nomads again. Everything we had worked for, all of the progress we'd made had been torn from us in a single afternoon. I didn't even have a jacket, and I'd worn my old sneakers to the game. It had all been so sudden that I couldn't wrap my mind around all of the implications.

Up ahead, two people were heading the wrong way on the tracks. Her walk was unmistakable: the quick sway of her narrow hips, the short steps, as if she were walking downhill. The energy of it, the eagerness, despite having just hiked two or three miles through a sewer. She waved, started running toward us. Her husband trotted behind, not looking as eager. Ange shouted her name, then Jeannie. They ran ahead. The three of them met in a triple-hug.

I guess I was expecting Sophia to keep her distance from me, out of respect to her husband, but even while she huddled with Ange and Jeannie she was looking past them. She came right to me and hugged me. "How're you?" she said in my ear. It felt good to be in her arms. Way too good; I felt a familiar tingle of electricity, a fluttering in my stomach.

"I'm okay," I said.

"For sure, for sure?"

"For sure, for sure," I replied, an old island saying we'd made our own, long ago. I let go, drifted back as others greeted her, as she and Jean Paul were introduced to Sebastian.

I was suddenly afraid the feelings I'd had for her so long ago would resurface, along with all that pain. It would be easy to do if Ange and Cortez hooked up. It's easy to fall into unrequited love if it's the only kind available. I looked hard at Sophia, testing myself, ready to flee inside myself if I felt those feelings blossom. Not too bad, so far. Maybe the Jasper who'd fallen so hard for Sophia was gone—bludgeoned with a shovel, shattered by a gunshot, choked by a cat fetus.

We camped on a trestle, thirty feet above a sluggish stream—high enough that the bamboo couldn't reach us. The stream wasn't moving fast enough to generate any energy, and the sun was down, so we kept our ancient solar blanket and river skimmer packed. Cortez pulled a huge hunk of cooked meat wrapped in a plastic bag out of his pack and sliced it up with a scary hunting knife while Sophia and Jean Paul brought out some bread, peanut butter, and cookies they'd manage to grab as they fled. Colin and Jeannie retrieved water from the stream and hooked the water filter to the energy pack. The filters were one thing we hadn't had in our first stint as nomads that would make this trip a little easier. Ah, progress.

We sat along the edge of the trestle, our feet hanging over the edge, and ate dinner. And lunch, for that matter.

"What is this?" I asked Cortez as I worked to dislodge a piece of meat jammed between my back teeth.

"Just eat it," he said, his voice low.

"I just like to know what I'm eating," I said.

He sighed. "Dog, okay? You're eating dog."

"Okay." I was hungry enough that dog was fine. I just wanted to know. "Thanks."

Below us, oil glistened on the black water.

"It sucks to kill a dog," Cortez said.

An image flashed in my mind, of Cortez holding out food, luring a dog to him, then cutting its throat, then butchering it. I hadn't realized he'd gotten that destitute since losing his place. "I bet it does."

"It sucks to kill anything," he added.

"Yeah," I said. I knew what he was referring to.

"Boy, what I wouldn't do for a moist towelette," Colin said to no one in particular, wiping his greasy fingers on bamboo stalks.

When it got dark we lay in the tracks, our asses and elbows dangling over the stream between the ties.

"Somebody tell Deirdre to turn off her music," Colin said. "She's had it on for half an hour."

Deirdre was on her back, eyes closed, her arms cradling the back of her head. From ten feet away I could hear the buzzing of her music pod.

"Deirdre," Cortez called. Then again, louder. Deirdre didn't flinch. Cortez dragged himself up, went and tapped Deirdre on top of her head.

"What?"

"We need you to turn off the music. We've got to conserve our energy."

"Fuck you, I brought most of it." I recognized the music bleeding out of Deirdre's earphones. It was her own.

"I know you did," Cortez said, "but when you're part of a tribe, everything is community property. We all take care of each other."

Deirdre sighed loudly. "Fine." She rammed the pod into her pack.

"Is anyone's phone working?" Ange asked.

"Nope," Colin said after a pause. "Ours is dead. Nothing."

Cortez had a radio. Most of the stations were off the air, but a few were still broadcasting. While we prepared to travel, we listened to a report. New York was in flames. Seattle was in flames. Los Angeles and a few other cities were under the control of federal troops, but elsewhere federal troops were battling various warlords, gangs, corporate entities, police, and fire departments that had claimed control of territory ranging from city blocks to entire states. General Electric had claimed ownership of a chunk of upstate New York and declared it a sovereign nation. At least that's what the radio said. They didn't sound all that certain. The feds had announced that all males between the ages of eighteen and forty-five should report for military duty. Evidently it was written somewhere that they were allowed to do that during an emergency. The radio guy sounded more certain about that.

"Let's be ready to move in about ten minutes," Cortez announced. "Statesboro's about twenty miles. It would be nice to make it there by tonight." He turned to Jean Paul. "Please don't take this the wrong way, but it would be safer if you changed clothes."

"What's wrong with my clothes?" Jean Paul asked. He was wearing a green designer jogging suit.

"You don't look poor. It's best if we look like we have nothing worth killing us for."

"Excuse me, but who exactly put you in charge?" Jean Paul said, balling his fists on his hips. The immature part of me perked up, hoping Jean Paul would make the mistake of provoking a fight, which he would lose badly. The mature part of me knew it was every tribe member's job to make sure there was peace and harmony within the tribe.

"We did," I offered. "Not exactly in charge, I guess, but he chairs the 'keep us alive' committee."

"He's also in charge of wardrobe," Colin added.

Jean Paul didn't look at us. He just pulled off the jacket and squatted next to his pack, muttering something under his breath as he dug through it.

As we trudged forward, the ties glided by beneath our feet, the bamboo giving the illusion that we were moving briskly. Occasionally there were breaks and patches in the bamboo; these were usually filled with groups of refugees. As we passed them, many begged for food. In some places an entire half-acre might be relatively bamboo free, but for the most part it was omnipresent.

"So," Cortez asked, joining me. "You got a girlfriend these days?"

I laughed at the absurdity of the question, given our current situation. Cortez grinned. He was clearly trying to lighten me up a little.

"No, not really. How about you?"

"I'm taking a break. A spiritual celibacy fast."

"Really? Why's that?" That would mean he was out of the Ange business, at least for the time being.

He struggled for words. "A lot of reasons, I guess. One of them you know about."

"Yeah. Can't say I've been feeling very romantic myself these days. But I'm also tired of being alone, you know?"

"Yeah."

Up ahead, Sebastian shouted. He, Colin, and Ange had stopped. They were eyeing a huge trailer park buried ass-deep in bamboo.

"What is it?" I called. Sebastian waved us on. He wasn't smiling for a change.

Then I noticed the smell.

I'd seen a lot of dead bodies—everyone who doesn't live in the elite enclaves has—but I'd never seen anything like this. There were thousands of them, maybe tens of thousands. Men, women, children, filling a dried pond between the tracks and the trailer park, a tangle of arms and legs and faces and muddy clothes, the occasional bamboo shoot pressing up between them.

"They all look Latino," I said.

Sophia's eyes went wide when she got in sight of them. She put her hand over her mouth and began sobbing. Jeannie put a gentle hand over Sophia's eyes and led her away.

"Foreigners, probably," Ange said. "People don't take kindly to strangers competing with them for food when there isn't enough to go around."

"I don't think locals did this—not this many people." I thought of the holding pen we'd recently escaped, how they'd separated out the foreigners.

As if on cue, a train whistled in the distance. We pushed into the bamboo and waited.

The engine was rigged with a long, low, V-shaped blade, like a snow plow for bamboo. The cars rumbled by, drowning out all other sound. Federal troops armed to the teeth stood on top of many of them. There must have been a hundred cars.

"Supplies for the troops, coming from Atlanta," Sebastian said. "That's where the closest push packages are stored."

"Push packages?" Colin asked.

"That's what the military calls them—packaged supplies for troops, stored for years for just this sort of occasion. Each one might contain upward of a million bottles of water, a hundred thousand MREs, generators and fuel to run them, tents, everything the well-dressed soldier might need."

"And when that train gets to Savannah, they'll fill the empty cars with bodies, and dump them in that dried-out pond," I said. No one argued. If the government was willing to sink foreign fishing boats to cut down on the competition for food, it was capable of dealing with the illegals pouring over the border by killing them by the trainload.

When the train had passed we squeezed back onto the tracks.

I found myself walking beside Deirdre. I hesitated, considered acting like I had something to say to Cortez or Colin and rushing ahead, but it was too late, it would be too obvious.

"So how've you been?" I asked.

"Swell," she said. "Just Georgia fucking peachy." The receding train's whistle blew in the distance. "It doesn't appear that you found Ms. Right at that little circle jerk where I bumped into you."

"Nope," I said. I was tempted to point out that she'd been at the same circle jerk, but I thought it best not to pursue that little nugget.

"Let's get something straight," Deirdre said. "Just because you let me join your little gang doesn't mean I'm going to let you fuck me."

"I understand," I said. "I could never keep up with you in bed anyway. You were too much for me."

Deirdre glanced at me, checking for sarcasm. "Damn right." She smiled. Just a little, just with the edges of her mouth, but it was nice to see.

"Jasper," Colin called from behind us. I stopped to wait for him. Deirdre kept walking.

"I thought you might need rescuing," Colin said when he caught up.

"That was an astute assessment. Thank you."

"My pleasure," Colin said. "So, you ever been to Athens before?"

I nodded. "I was friends with a guy who went to the University of Georgia. Jack Stamps, you remember him?"

"Sure. Tall guy, curly hair."

"I visited him there once. Nice town. Pretty downtown area, right alongside the university campus, which is huge."

"I wonder if it's still intact, or if a lot of it has burned."

"Sebastian probably knows," I said, jerking my thumb toward Sebastian, who was walking alone, chuckling to himself like a mentally ill derelict.

Colin slowed, tried to work something out of his shoe, then continued. "Shouldn't we be getting used to all this? Being dirty, not having laptops?" Sweat was pouring down his cheeks, disappearing into three days' growth of whiskers. There was a hint of white in the whiskers.

"I think we get used to improvements in our lives," I said. "I'm not sure we ever get used to having those improvements taken away."

"Ever?" he said.

"Only until we die. Whatever you do, don't let your kid know how good things used to be."

The pine forest opened onto a hot blue sky; up ahead a series of tall grain silos and an octopus of long silver tubes were the first sign that we were close to Statesboro. A flash of red from a stop sign filtered through the bamboo.

"You know what I miss?" Colin said. "Fat people. I miss variety in the size of people."

"Have you noticed that fat women seem a lot hotter than they used to?" I asked.

"In poor countries fat women have always been hot, because almost no one could afford to get fat," Ange said.

Colin and I both glanced over our shoulders. Ange was two paces behind us.

"Hey, this is top secret guy talk," Colin said. "Chicks aren't supposed to hear this."

"I promise not to tell any other chicks. I'll take it to my grave."

"Well, all right then, you can listen," Colin said.

I spotted a good plant. "Hold on a sec." I trotted down the embankment, squatted at the base of a hardwood tree and examined the leaves on it.

"What is it?" Ange called down.

"Stinging nettle. It's edible," I said. I gripped it close to the ground, below its prickly armor, and pulled it.

"It doesn't look edible. It looks like a rank old weed."

"It's all in how you cook it." I carefully folded it into one of my pockets. I'd been focused mostly on medicinal plants, but I could identify the ones that you could eat as well. That knowledge was probably going to come in handy; I didn't think it would be long before we'd be desperate for food. I'd keep my eyes peeled for pokeweed, dandelion, sorrel, arrowroot, wild onion, mushrooms, along with the medicinals.

We passed an abandoned warehouse with "*Southern Pecan Company*" stenciled on the side, then a green Raco gas station sign *advertising unleaded, with the price blank except for the final "9," and farther away a Shoney's sign poking out of the wide green sea.*

"Looks like your bamboo even took out the bigger towns," I said to Sebastian.

"It wasn't the bamboo, it was the gasoline shortage," Sebastian said. "I know for a fact that Statesboro set up rhizome barriers and cleared the bamboo out of the town at some point, but these towns aren't self-sustaining; without a cheap way to bridge them with Atlanta or Savannah, they die. Their only hope was to switch over to food production in a hurry, but people think they can ride it out, keep their dry cleaning and tanning bed businesses going until things turn around. Most of the people probably left looking for food and work. When there weren't enough people to hold back the bamboo…" He made an exploding gesture with both hands.

Sebastian seemed to have an answer for everything, at least when it came to the monsters he and his friends had unleashed. "You know, ever since you started spreading this god damned bamboo, I've been wondering something. Why didn't you engineer it to be edible?"

There was a long pause. I glanced back, wondering if he'd heard me.

"They couldn't," he said.

"Bullshit," I shot back.

"They couldn't. There has to be some die-back in the population—the resources left on the planet can't support anything close to the current population."

"So, you *purposely made it inedible?*" *I stumbled, clutched at a clump of bamboo to keep from falling and fell anyway, the bamboo bending to slow my descent to comic slow-motion. I'd tripped over a curb. Sometimes you didn't know where the road was until you were on it.*

"Welcome to Statesboro," Sebastian said. "And to answer your question, yes, they did it on purpose. As I've been saying all along, one to two billion people are going to die by the time this is over. The idea is to keep it from becoming four or five billion."

I told Sebastian that the whole thing sounded like demagoguery to me before falling into angry silence.

We passed a guy in a hammock who was either sleeping or dead. He didn't open his eyes to look at who was passing, so he might have been dead, but he wasn't sallow or decomposing, so he might have been sleeping.

Ange picked out an old Southern mansion on Main Street for us to squat in for the night. She loved old houses. It had a wide green porch and a massive magnolia tree in the front yard, and it sat in the shadow of the town's massive water tower, a fat kettle wearing a conical hat resting on five legs.

The front door opened into an ornate living room—gold stuffed chairs with flower patterns, a huge mirror with a rococo gold frame. A table was covered in framed family photos, some of them recent, some ancient. Sometimes it was easy to forget that people had lived entire lives in these houses.

The biggest photo was also the oldest, maybe from the late 1800s. A family of seven were posed outside this exact house. Dad was seated in the center, scowling, hands on knees, in his Sunday best. Two older women, one probably his wife, the other maybe a sister, were seated on either side of him. One woman was holding a book, the other a sorry little bouquet of wildflowers. A row of teenaged children stood behind them. No one was smiling; the two teenaged girls had stark, haunted eyes; the others just looked exhausted.

Most of the color pictures were happy ones: a father with a round belly holding a toddler at the beach; a woman dressed in black regalia accepting a degree; a new bride clutching a colorful bouquet of roses. Everyone looked bright-eyed and ridiculously healthy.

There were only a few recent photos. The people in them looked a lot like the people in the oldest photo, only in color.

"I wish we had a chance to talk. There are so many things I want to say to you." Sophia said softly. I turned away from the photos to face her. She glanced toward the hallway.

"Maybe we'll get the chance," I said, knowing I should discourage any suggestion that something remained between us, but nonetheless dying to know what Sophia might want to say to me.

Cortez put his duffel on the coffee table, then disappeared into the kitchen. He came out clutching eight stemmed glasses and set them around the table.

"Hey guys?" he called. "Everyone?" People filed into the room, and Cortez encouraged everyone to take a seat. He pulled a nearly full bottle of gin from his pack.

"You are a god," I said as he started pouring. "Where's Deirdre?"

I called, but got no answer. Two or three others shouted her name, including Sebastian, who sang her name more than called it.

"What you want?" she said. She was standing at the top of the stairs wearing a silk nightgown, munching on a chocolate bar, a bottle of pills in her other hand.

"That's my nightgown!" Jeannie said.

"Hey, that's our chocolate!" Jean Paul said.

Deirdre took a big bite of the chocolate. "No, we're a tribe, so it's all our stuff. Look at all this great stuff I found stashed in the bottom of people's packs! Ange even had some Valium to share."

"You went through our stuff?" Ange said. "You piece of shit."

"Oh, I'm the piece of shit? I can't use my own energy because it's for the tribe to share, but you can have your own little personal stashes of chocolate and drugs hidden in your packs? Fuck you all." She disappeared down the hall.

"We were going to share that chocolate," Jean Paul said. "We were waiting for the right time, like Cortez with his gin."

"You don't need to explain yourself, we trust you," Cortez said. "Let's not let Deirdre poison us. Let's drink, and have a good time."

I lifted my glass. "To Cortez, who brought us booze, and dog."

"To Cortez!" everyone said.

"Dog?" Ange said. "Fuck, were we eating dog?" She took a long swallow from her glass.

We had a good evening. We played a game of Truth or Dare by candlelight, and found out that Cortez had had the most lovers in his life (about forty, he estimated) and Colin had had the least (four—that's what happens when you married at twenty-six and were a dweeb in high school). We learned that Jeannie thought her best feature was her boobs, and Sebastian thought he had perfect toes.

It felt bad to be laughing and having fun while Deirdre sat alone, listening to us, but three different people (Sebastian, then Cortez, then I) made pilgrimages to her door and implored her to join us. Her answer was the same each time: Fuck you.

Jean Paul didn't play either. He hadn't said a word to me since they joined us. He hadn't even looked at me. I think he'd enjoyed confronting me at that nightclub years ago because he'd been in his element, among his friends. Here, he was the outsider.

When the Truth or Dare game petered out, Jeannie got everyone singing. I felt like a little moonlight and solitude, so I slipped out the back door.

The swimming pool was empty, and filled with bamboo, but there was a concrete patio that must have been poured extra-thick, because the bamboo hadn't penetrated. I stared up at the sky. I loved the night sky, because the moon didn't have chipping paint or rust and wasn't sprouting weeds, and the stars weren't flickering out due to a lack of power. On the contrary—the stars had been growing progressively brighter as the lights on terra firma went out, and now the night sky was breathtaking. I could see the Milky Way, a spectacular swirl of silver tinged with blue and red.

"Isn't it beautiful?" Sophia said behind me.

I took a sip of gin. "It's the one thing that gets better as everything else gets worse."

"For sure," she said. She moved up to stand beside me. The crickets chirped in the bamboo, their cadence cold, almost mechanical.

"It's been a long time since I last saw you," I said. "You haven't aged at all, it's remarkable."

"Thanks. You haven't either." I knew that was a kind lie. I'd lost one of my bottom teeth since I last saw Sophia, just for starters. "And actually, I've seen you a couple of times since then."

I looked at her, questioning.

"When you first moved back to Savannah, I found out where you lived from Ruplu's father," Sophia said. "Once in a while I would drive past your apartment and watch for you. I saw you a few times, walking to work or going out with your friends."

"Why didn't you stop and say hello?" I asked.

"Because you asked me to stay out of your life, and I owed you that much." There were four white plastic lawn chairs around a plastic table on the patio. Sophia pulled one out and sat. "I never got a chance to say how sorry I was for what happened the night I bumped into you at that bar. I wanted to go after you when they threw you out. I felt terrible."

I chuckled.

"Why are you laughing?" Sophia asked.

"That same night I was dragged into an alley by Jumpy-Jumps and watched them murder a half-dozen people. They held a gas gun to my face, and as far as I can figure the only reason they didn't kill me was because I was poor." And then of course there was the part about them making me eat a cat fetus, but I figured I'd skip that.

Sophia looked stricken. "I'm so sorry."

I shrugged. "It was a long time ago. I laughed because being kicked out of the bar doesn't really register on the stress meter from that particular evening." I took another big swallow from my glass.

Sophia stood. "I'd better get back inside." She left out the obvious: before Jean Paul sees me out here with you. "I just wanted you to know that I never stopped loving you." She hurried inside, giving me no chance to respond.

I swallowed the rest of my gin, those long-dormant feelings twirling in my stomach. With an effort that felt almost physical, I squashed them. I headed back inside. I got into bed feeling a perfect buzz—not enough to set the room spinning, but enough to kill the existential hum, enough to tuck me in and tell me everything would turn out just fine. Drinking always made me feel better, and made me think nice thoughts.

My door opened with a soft whine, then squeaked shut.

"Hi." Ange said.

"Hi."

"Is this okay?" She ran her fingers down my arm.

"Yes. Perfect."

"I don't want to be alone right now."

"Me neither." I ran my hand over her hip, down her thigh, pushing away pangs of guilt that Sophia might hear us. The guilt was spectacularly stupid—I realized. I owed Sophia nothing. What had been between us was long over, and had been nothing but mist and daydreams to begin with.

"You sure you don't want to crawl into Sophia's bed instead? Or maybe Deirdre's?" She laughed.

"I'm sure," I said, wondering if she'd seen us on the patio. I kissed Ange's neck, her jaw. She had an incredible flaring jawline. It was too dark to see the blaze of tattoos that covered her ribs, but I could feel them, making the skin there slicker.

Later, we lay tangled together, dozing. A dream-image of a leering Jumpy-Jump floated into my mind and I jolted, waking Ange. She rubbed my arm, reassuring. It was nice having someone there in the dark when nightmares came.

"It's kind of amazing how long we've been fucking around without screwing up our friendship," Ange whispered drowsily.

"It's hard to believe," I said. "People say it can't be done, but we proved them wrong." What would my life have been like without Ange? I didn't even want to contemplate it. It's much more bearable to be single and alone when you're not really alone.

"I've always wanted to ask you about something," I said. "You once said that if a guy didn't have the nerve to ask you out point-blank, you knew there was no way it could work with him."

"Mm. I don't remember, but I can see myself saying that."

"Hypothetically, if I'd had the confidence to ask you out back then, would you have tried the boyfriend-girlfriend thing with me?"

Ange rolled over, scooted up against the headboard. Outside, a dog was whimpering. "You really want the truth?"

"*Yes.*"

She folded her arms under her breasts. "You were sweet, and interesting, and fun, but you were too much of a boy. Those are all good traits in a friend, even a fuck friend. But not a boyfriend."

"Fair enough. I can see that." I think I'd even seen it then.

For a moment I considered asking Ange if she wanted to try the boyfriend-girlfriend thing now. If I wanted to pursue a relationship with Ange, now was the time to ask. But even as I thought it, I knew I was years too late. Regardless of the sex part, she played the part of the female friend who gave me advice on how to get the girl. She couldn't also be the girl.

It was more than that, though. When times were good, it was worth the risk to fall in love, because the risk was low. People died of cancer, got hit by cars, but mostly they lived long lives. Now, falling in love was a sucker's bet. The odds were long, and favored the house.

"You know, I think you're tied for my best friend in the world," I said.

"Me too, sweetie." She took a deep breath, let it out, scooted down and rolled over.

I drifted off to sleep feeling hungry, but good.

I was out of bed and in the hallway before I was awake enough to register that someone was screaming. Deirdre was screaming. Her door flew open and Sebastian ran out, chased by Deirdre, who had a knife. She slashed at Sebastian, cutting his upper arm wide open before he got clear of her and down the stairs. She stopped, crazy with anger. Cortez and I, the first to reach her, kept our distance.

"What happened?" I asked.

"He stuck me with a needle while I was asleep." Deirdre said, probing a spot on her neck with trembling fingers. "Oh god, I think he infected me with that fucking virus." She looked past us; there was an awful fear in her eyes. She screamed and charged for the stairs; I ducked into a doorway to let her pass, but Cortez stood his ground. He grabbed Deirdre's wrist as she went by, and twisted. Deirdre's feet came out from under her as if by magic; the knife thumped to the floor. Cortez dropped to his knees and wrapped his arms around her from behind as she struggled. I grabbed the knife.

"Calm down, calm down," Cortez said, but Deirdre went on screaming. Her screams were deafening—it brought back memories of her flash concerts in the squares.

I went downstairs, past the others, who were trying to figure out what the hell was going on, and shoved the kitchen door open. "Did you infect her?" I shouted at Sebastian. He was examining his wounded shoulder. Blood was dribbling off his elbow, splattering on the floor.

"Oh, yeah," he said. He looked up at me, grinning like a loon. "How could I not? Every minute is excruciating for that poor girl. Can't you see it? I alleviated the suffering with one pinprick." He snapped his fingers.

"It's not up to you!" I said. "You don't get to decide that for her."

He shrugged. "I did, though." A few drops of blood dripped onto the tile floor. Sebastian tisked and shook his head, still smiling. "Don't worry about it. She'll thank me in a few hours."

"You'd better take a walk until we can calm her down." It was Ange. Sebastian nodded, grabbed a kitchen towel and headed out the back door.

"I'll kill him," Deirdre shouted from the next room. "I'll fucking kill him. I don't want to be like *you!*"

"Not good," Ange said.

"No, not good." We went into the living room. Cortez had Deirdre in a full nelson.

"Did he really infect her?" Colin asked.

Deirdre grew still and looked at me, eyes wide. When I nodded, she threw her head back and let out a squeal of such terror and anguish that I stumbled backward. Cortez slowly released his grip on her and let her sink to the floor.

I went outside.

The morning was surprisingly crisp for March. A light breeze rattled the bamboo. Jeannie and Ange were already out there, talking in low tones.

"Sebastian's got to go," I said, shaking my head.

"That's what we were just saying," Jeannie said. "As soon as he's physically able, we need to send him packing."

"What a nut case," I said. "I think all of these Doctor Happy people are a little off-kilter." I twirled my finger near my temple. "That virus might make you happy, but it also makes you a little crazy."

Ange and Jeannie nodded agreement. Inside, Deirdre was sobbing.

"It's probably not a nice thing to say, but she's probably better off with the virus, though," Ange said. "Not that I'm condoning what he did."

I smiled, kicked my toe against the steel porch rail. Maybe she did, but I still felt a sick dread at the thought of what she was going through in there. It must be terrifying, thinking of that virus racing around in your brain changing the chemistry, changing your personality, the way you think about things.

There was no way we could travel with Deirdre in the state she was in, so we waited. Sebastian kept his distance, lounging on the porch two houses down, his feet propped on the rail, humming, sometimes bursting out laughing for no apparent reason.

I spent some time in my room, some exploring surrounding houses looking for salvage. After five or six hours, the living room had finally grown quiet, so I ventured in to see how Deirdre was doing.

Cortez was still with her; they were sitting on the hardwood floor, a couple of glasses of water beside them. Deirdre was staring at the floor, her eyes wide. Cortez nodded a greeting as I took a seat on the couch.

"How is she?" I asked.

Deirdre looked over at me. "Why are you asking him?" I felt a chill as I looked at her face—her new face. It was nothing like the old one. The belligerent eyes and the withering, sarcastic twist of her mouth had vanished. Instead she was a mix of wide-eyed amusement… and something else. It ran like a ripple just under her skin.

She threw her head back and laughed as if I'd just said something absolutely hilarious. She laughed and laughed, finally subsiding into keening gasps and the occasional giggle.

"How do you feel?" I asked.

Deirdre considered the question, running a hand through her hair. "I feel… just peachy. Like the cherry on top of the sundae. Like the apple of every boy's eye." She patted Cortez's calf. "Thanks for being my designated driver." She stood, twisted at the waist to the right, then the left, like a runner getting loose.

"I think I'll take a walk," she said. We watched her saunter out the door.

Cortez and I looked at each other. "Wow," I said. "She didn't say 'fuck' once."

"I know. Eerie."

I followed her out, wondering how one takes a walk when the world is clogged with bamboo. From the vantage point of the empty front stoop I scanned the block. The bamboo was thrashing halfway across the street. The disturbance continued in a crooked line. A giggle drifted on the breeze, just loud enough for me to hear.

It was hard to grasp the notion of a happy, carefree Deirdre. There would be nothing recognizable left of her.

Across the street I spotted her rising out of the bamboo, climbing the ladder on the water tower. She was moving fast, a huge smile frozen on her face, her little legs stretching to reach the rungs.

Cortez joined me on the stoop.

"Where the hell is she going?" I said, pointing.

Cortez spotted her and grunted surprise. "I don't know. Maybe she's gonna climb to the top and sing songs about lollipops."

I cupped my hands around my mouth. "Deirdre! You won't be able to get down." I know she heard me, because she paused for a second, but she kept climbing. More tribe members came out, alerted by my shout.

"What is she doing?" Jeannie asked.

"I have no idea," I said. "She said she was going for a walk. I didn't understand the old Deirdre, let alone this new one."

"Deirdre!" I called. "Please come on down." She was up high now, thirty or forty feet. The top was at least fifty. It made me dizzy just seeing her up that high.

"Deirdre," Ange shouted, "it's too high! Come down!" She put her hand over her mouth.

Deirdre reached the top, a narrow catwalk that skirted the bottom of the tank. She reached up, pulled herself onto the catwalk and turned to face out. She was still laughing, her chest and shoulders heaving with the violence of it. At least I thought she was laughing; from this distance laughing and crying would look about the same.

She lifted her leg and swung it over the railing.

"*No!*" everyone screamed in unison. Everyone but me. My lungs were frozen; my heart had stopped. Deirdre swung her other leg over so that she was sitting on the narrow rail.

She pushed off into empty space.

She looked like a little doll, a doll a naughty little girl had hurled over a railing. Her clothes flapped in the wind as she fell.

I was the first to reach her. She'd landed in a dry drainage canal, on a bank covered with stones. I pulled her head into my arms and held it. The others broke through the bamboo in ones and twos, and cried, or cursed, or asked Deirdre's lifeless body why.

Sebastian came last, his arm bandaged with white socks.

"Pack up your stuff and get out," I said.

"She just needed to give it time," Sebastian said.

"*Go,*" I screamed.

Sebastian shrugged, turned away. "I'm so sorry," he said as he disappeared into the bamboo.

I felt a hand on my shoulder. It was Ange. I put my hand over hers and squeezed. Another hand clapped my other shoulder. Cortez.

"Everyone?" It was Colin, shouting from the house. "I think the baby's coming."

"Go on," Cortez said. "I'll take care of Deirdre." He gave my shoulder a hard squeeze, then nudged me toward the house.

I pulled myself up, my legs wobbly, and headed toward our temporary home.

Jeannie was on the couch in the living room with Colin kneeling beside her, holding her hand. Colin looked up. "Can you help me?"

I wanted to argue that I didn't know anything about delivering a baby, but I could see in his expression that he wasn't asking because he thought I'd be any better at it than anyone else. He just wanted me by his side.

I knelt beside the couch.

Ange grabbed Colin's wrist, pulled him up, and repositioned him at Jeannie's head. "Your job is to be up here with your wife. We'll worry about this end."

Ange looked at me. "Ready?"

"What do we do?" I asked. I was so disoriented; I needed time to deal with what had just happened.

Ange shrugged. "We'll figure it out."

I turned. Sophia was kneeling behind us, her cheeks stained with tears. "Can you and Jean Paul build a fire and boil water?"

"Have you ever done this before?" Jean Paul asked.

"I'll do it," Cortez said, glaring at Jean Paul. I hadn't seen Cortez return.

"Try to find some clean towels, too," Ange suggested. "If there aren't any, clean clothes."

I think we were just lucky. The baby's head was pointing straight down, and we didn't have to do much except catch him when he came out.

Colin and Jeannie had a son. I both envied and pitied them. What would it be like, to be sick with worry every minute that something awful is going to happen to your child?

Chapter 8: Pig Thief

Summer, 2033 (Two months later)

Ange rocked gently, one foot planted on the wood porch, the other tucked underneath her on the swing. We could see much of downtown Swainsboro from this vantage point—a dress shop, antique store, pawn shops huddled together in a row of red-brick buildings made this place feel deceptively small and old-fashioned.

There were people foraging in the music store across the street, their voices and the clatter of things drifting out of the broken store window. I considered going over and seeing if they had any news that we didn't, but it wasn't worth it. They wouldn't know anything we didn't.

People had been fleeing the country for the safety of the cities in droves for the past few years; now the cities weren't safe either. But there was nothing out here to eat. There was nowhere to go.

Five or six people were relaxing on the wide white steps of the courthouse, their heads propped on their packs, a water bottle passing among them. They were young, and reminded me of our tribe back in the early days of the depression.

Music bleated in the distance. It was familiar. It grew louder, and

I recognized it as a classic rock tune by the Young Mozarts: "Carry My Heart Around with You." The song was a little too saccharine for my taste, but under the circumstances it gave me a warm feeling as I watched the sun reflect off the shards of broken glass in the upper window of the Dragon Fire Tae Kwon Do studio. The music got louder. Ange stood, and I followed suit, peering down the street in the direction of the sound.

There was a placard bobbing up out of the bamboo, the person carrying it hidden. The banner read "Free Meal! Ask me how!"

"What the hell?" I said. Ange pulled open the screen door and called to the others to come out. They flooded onto the porch. I pointed to the sign.

"What the hell is that?" Colin asked. "It must be the fed army, looking for recruits."

The kids in front of the courthouse were standing and staring at the sign. One of them shouted and waved; the sign changed directions, heading toward them. Two people approached on the steps—a man and a woman. The man laid the placard down. The kids formed a semi-circle around the couple.

Hungry as we were, we weren't stupid. We watched the people for a few minutes.

"What do you think the catch is?" Sophia asked.

"I say we find out," Cortez said.

"What, just waltz into an obvious trap?" Jean Paul said.

Cortez shrugged. "There are only two of them. I'm gonna check it out, you guys can stay here."

"They're probably armed," Jean Paul said, "and have two dozen friends nearby."

Cortez pulled a pistol out of his pants pocket. "I'm armed, too."

"I'll go with you," I said, mostly because Jean Paul was against the idea. We climbed down the porch steps and slid between the waxy bamboo.

"That guy really has a stick up his ass," Cortez said.

I chuckled. "He doesn't seem to grasp that he's not in an office building surrounded by private security any more."

We stopped fifty feet shy of the steps, hoping to catch some of the conversation before deciding whether to proceed, but it's difficult to move through bamboo without announcing your approach.

"Sounds like we've got more visitors," The woman said. "Hello in there!" she called.

Cortez called a greeting in return; we pushed the last few yards and broke onto the white marble steps. The crowd was welcoming, especially the couple with the sign. They told us and the six kids (who I could now see were actually quite young, mostly in their mid-teens) how to get to the empty Bi-Lo where their tribe was camped, that their tribe would indeed provide us with a meal, no strings attached. Cortez and I probed them with questions. We didn't want to seem ungracious, but we were still skeptical, despite how well-intentioned and harmless the couple seemed.

They explained that their tribe was looking to grow, to create a larger community and carve out a new town where they could all be safe and live a civilized life. It sounded nice, but my bullshit meter was in the red.

"What do you think?" I asked Cortez as the teens set off toward the Bi-Lo.

"Let's play along for a while," he said.

We could smell pork barbecue before the Bi-Lo was even in sight. The place was doing a fairly brisk business, considering there probably weren't a hundred people within twenty miles of here. A man with kind eyes greeted us at the door. He didn't have to introduce himself.

"Hello, Rumor," I said.

He no longer looked like a Jumpy-Jump—he was dressed in a pair of tattered blue jeans and a green t-shirt—but as he hugged me like a long lost brother and cried that I was the man who had let him see the light, the singsong accent was the same.

"Come, come, you look hungry," he said. "Let me prepare you a plate." He guided us toward white plastic chairs with a gentle hand on my shoulder blade.

Cortez and I each accepted a paper plate of pork with a side of corn.

"Enjoy your food," Rumor insisted. "When you're feeling good and plenty we can catch up, and chat a little about what we have to offer you."

"What you have to offer us?" Cortez said, eyeing the food warily.

Rumor waved at the plate. "There are no tricks here. My trickster days are long behind me. Eat, then we'll talk."

Cortez and I looked at each other. I shrugged.

"Can we get our friends?" Cortez asked Rumor.

Rumor assured him that by all means he should fetch our friends. Cortez went to get them while I ate.

I willed myself to eat slowly, to savor the wonderfully juicy meat, despite the urgent cries from my stomach that I eat faster.

The concrete floor of the Bi-Lo was scattered with tents and sleeping bags. Here and there people sat conversing in white plastic chairs, always in twos, one person holding a Styrofoam plate and mostly listening.

"How have you been doing?" Rumor asked, handing me a paper cup of sweet iced tea. He swung a chair around and sat so our knees almost touched.

"I'm not dead, so, better than most I guess."

"Are you happy, though, Jasper?" Rumor asked. It surprised me that he remembered my name. Of course, I *had* been the one who'd let him see the light.

"No. I'm hungry and scared, and people are dying all around me. Of course I'm not happy."

"I once offered you happiness," Rumor said.

I didn't get what he was saying, then I remembered. "Ah, the vial of blood." I paused in my eating, eyed the food on my fork.

"Exactly, the vial." Rumor pushed his palm toward my plate. "Eat. I can see you tensing, like a deer who's just heard a branch crack. I gave you my word, there are no unexpected seasonings in the food."

I ate. It was too late anyway. But I couldn't help distrusting this guy. I'm not sure I could ever forgive someone for doing what he did. That he was regretful for killing Ange's dog now, after I infected him with Doctor Happy, did not seem to merit absolution. I've never been a huge believer in giving people a pass for hurting other people just because they're sorry about it later, and when that regret is virus-induced, I'm even less inclined.

"So that's what this is all about? You're recruiting people to the virus?"

Rumor laughed merrily. "Yes, of course!"

"But it's not in the food?"

"We don't trick people. We invite them here and offer them an opportunity to join our tribe. If we were going to introduce you to the virus by force, wouldn't it be easier to surprise you with a needle as you walked in the door?"

That was true. "If you want to spread the virus, why don't you just do that?"

"Is that how you would do it?" Rumor asked.

"No."

He shrugged. "That answers your question. We respect people's rights, as long as they respect others' rights."

I didn't say anything. If they were so damned ethical, why hadn't the people with the sign told us they were infected with Doctor Happy right up front? And then there was Deirdre. Sebastian hadn't given her any choice.

Outside, Cortez appeared, trailed by the others. I waved them in. Baby Joel was sleeping in Colin's arms, still looking too small to be real.

Rumor went straight to Ange and hugged her fiercely; he was so much bigger than her that she almost disappeared inside the one-way hug. "Little Peanut! So good to see you again."

Rumor led everyone to the food table. I followed and shamelessly fixed myself seconds. As we settled into chairs, Rumor came and stood in front of our little group. "Can I give you my patter? Then if you decide not to join us, you can all fly away with food in your bellies."

"Sure," I said, my mouth full. "But I doubt you're going to find any converts here." I thought of Deirdre, falling end-over-end to her death.

"That's fair enough." He covered his mouth with his palm, considering for a moment. "I have to alter my pitch, because you already know so much. You know this virus was engineered by scientists. These scientists realized that if the human race was going to survive, we have to take the next leap in evolution ourselves. What do we need to survive? We don't need more hands, or two heads, or to fly. We need to be healed. Our violence, our sadness, our loneliness, our fear... they are a sickness that is killing us." The cadence of his speech was mesmerizing. It was like listening to a good sermon.

"Look at what's become of the world under yesterday's people." He swept his hand around the room with a flourish, as if all the suffering and death in the world were spread out before us. "What do you think? When the ashes settle, shall we let the same people have another try?" He laughed. "Would you like another helping of the same rotted stew?"

No one responded. Rumor went on.

"We are the future, my friends. We're going to build a world based on loving kindness, not ego. We convert violent people every chance we get, against their will if we must. If you're violent, you forfeit your right to choose. But for others like you, it's your choice. We offer you food, companionship, a safe home. We offer you the future."

"Hold on," I said. "This safe home—it wouldn't be Athens by any chance?"

"It would indeed."

"Son of a bitch!" Cortez said. "Everyone in Athens is infected?"

Rumor bowed his head. "Only the converted are permitted to live there."

"Sebastian, you bastard," Cortez muttered.

"When did he plan on telling us?" Ange asked. She looked angry enough to pull Sebastian's ears off if he'd been there.

Rumor spread his hands. "Can I finish, please? What questions do you have for me about joining us? Why are you so angry? Tell me your doubts."

Sophia spoke up. "I'm happy the way I am. I'm not killing anyone; I'm not filled with hate."

"Clearly you're a good person," Rumor said, moving to face her directly. "But don't we all strive to better? Don't we all want to reach our greatest potential? This will lead you toward that self-actualization. It's like an extremely nutritious vitamin, only for your mind instead of your body."

He waited for Sophia to respond, but Sophia only crossed her arms and shook her head.

"There are thousands of foreign entities already in your bodies! Consider all the helpful bacteria in your digestive tract. And this virus won't change you. I'm still me." He pointed at his chest. "I'm more me than I was before I felt the needle's song. Only in my case it was not a needle, it was a water gun!" He laughed merrily. "The virus freed me to be far more me, far less of the streets I grew up on. I'm still me, just a much friendlier version of me."

I looked around at my tribe, gauging their reactions. You couldn't help but get a little caught up in Rumor's words. But it was irreversible, and there was Deirdre to consider. What if it wasn't as pleasant as it seemed from the outside? The scientists behind this had also created the bamboo, and that hadn't turned out all that well. Who knew, maybe over time Doctor Happy would drive its hosts insane.

"Isn't it also important for people to remain human in the full sense of the word?" Jeannie asked. "Being human means experiencing both the good and the bad, feeling both happiness and sorrow."

Rumor laughed. "The fundamental human experience has led to ruin. Yes, humanity is both good and bad, but the good has not adequately balanced the bad, and probably cannot. The bad must go."

The more I considered it, the more it seemed like giving up. Maybe one day I would be ready to give up, but not today. "You're a good salesman," I said, "but I don't think we're your target audience." I put my hands on my knees and leaned forward. "Now, is that your patter? Are we free to go?"

Rumor sighed. "Jasper, your wings can carry you wherever you like, after my patter or before. You are a free bird." He came over to me, put his hand over mine, his rough palm touching me gently. I resisted the urge to pull away. "We mean well. I hope you believe that."

I pulled my hand away and stood. "We do, too. We appreciate the meal, and the offer." The others gathered up their stuff.

"Where are you going to go?" Rumor asked. "You're not going to survive anywhere but in Athens, I promise you."

We looked at each other. "We'll do the nomad thing for a few more months, then go back to Savannah and see if things have settled down," I said.

Rumor shook his head. "There is nothing for you in Savannah. The Jumpy-Jumps cut off the federal army's supply route. Their push collapsed quickly after that. The soldiers who aren't dead are thirsty like everyone else. And don't head northwest from here, whatever you do."

"Why's that?" Cortez asked.

Rumor frowned. "You haven't heard about Redstone?"

"What's Redstone?" Jean Paul asked, impatient.

"Redstone Arsenal, outside Huntsville, Alabama," Rumor answered. "Millions of rifles are stored there—literally millions. The governor of Alabama conscripted the unorganized militia, which means that every male between the ages of eighteen and forty-five was to report for military duty to restore peace and quiet. The problem was, no one told the Jumpy-Jumps, the Civil Defenders, the city-block warlords that they should stay home when the rifles were passed out."

We digested this little nugget. There were a million rifles running around northwest of us.

"Well, we'll figure something out," Colin said.

With that, we left the Doctor Happy recruiting station.

There was a path of sorts through the bamboo—we squeezed around three people heading toward their free meal and patter.

"Good luck," Jean Paul said as they passed.

I woke from a dream in which I was walking on cookies. Lots of cookies—enough to carpet the ground. That's it, not much of a dream, not very profound or insightful. Dreams become less insightful, less draped in deep symbolism, when you're hungry.

Ange rolled onto her stomach. Her eyes had that bleary just-awake look, where dread was still raw and refused to be closeted.

"Morning," I said.

"Hungry," she said sleepily.

I wondered what she'd dreamed. Maybe popcorn falling from the sky like snow.

The Doctor Happy cult recruitment meal we'd had ten days earlier had been our last decent one. Since then there had been days when we ate nothing at all. We gave Jeannie much of what food we could find so baby Joel could be nourished.

Something had to give, and last night as I was drifting to sleep, I'd gotten an idea. There was another Young Mozarts song that I liked better than the one the Doctor Happy recruiters had been playing. One of the lines in it was *Chances are before you're done, you'll beg, you'll borrow, and surely you will steal*. I'd never stolen anything in my life. Of course I'd killed someone, so it was a giant step backward as ethical transgressions go. I decided I wouldn't involve my tribe, just as Cortez didn't broadcast that he'd killed someone's ex-pet to provide the first meal on this shitass journey to nowhere. I dressed, stuffed a few things in my pack, and stood on the stoop of our current domicile with the crickets still chirping.

"Where are you going, exactly?" Cortez asked.

"I won't go far," I said. "I spotted a place that looks like a good spot to find wild mushrooms. I may be a while if I find a bunch."

"I'm coming with," Ange said.

"No," I said. "You'll be bored."

"Of course I'll be bored. I'll also be bored if I stay here." She shrugged on her pack. I tried to think of a better reason why she couldn't come, but drew a blank.

"Ready?" Ange asked. Cortez handed me a pistol. I couldn't get over how much the guy had changed since I'd first met him. Back then he'd been one of those guys who had an exaggerated tough-guy walk that he'd clearly rehearsed in his bedroom mirror. Now he seemed so comfortable in his own skin, and in this world.

As soon as we were out of hearing distance of the others, I turned to Ange and said, "I'm not really going to look for herbs."

"I kind of sensed that. So where are we going?"

"We passed a farm on the way in, about a mile back down the tracks. I want to try to steal some food."

I looked at Ange, gauging her reaction. She nodded tightly. "Okay."

"I don't like stealing," I said.

"I know you don't. You just realized that the rules have to change if we're going to stay alive. The rest of us need to get our heads out of our asses and realize that, too."

And that was that. Ange and I moved quickly. She had a knack for finding the path of least resistance through the bamboo. Once we hit the railroad tracks we made better time.

The farm was just a few acres of cleared land, a house, silo, a few animal pens, all surrounded by a rhizome barrier. There were a couple of dogs asleep in the shade of the house.

I handed Ange the pistol. "We're less likely to get caught if there's just one of us. I'll be right back." My heart racing, I sprinted through a clearing before Ange could argue. I stopped behind the silo, scanned the yard for signs of people, then went around to the front of the silo and ducked inside.

It was empty.

I'd been picturing it filled with grain of some sort—I had a shopping bag in my pack that I'd been planning to fill. I didn't know anything about farms, about where the food might be.

Outside, a pig screeched.

I snuck back around behind the silo and eyed the animal pens. Crap, I didn't want to kill a little pig or a chicken. But what else was there that wasn't actually in the house itself?

"Put your hands in the air." The first thing I saw was the rifle. The guy holding it was about twenty. He was a big guy—big calves, big neck, had a big guy's swagger as he came out of a pecan grove. I put my hands up.

"I'm sick of you thieves." The tone in his voice, the disdain, was so familiar. I was a gypsy again.

"I'm sorry, we're just very hungry," I said.

"That doesn't mean you can steal from people!"

"I know. I'm sorry. It won't happen again," I said.

"I'm sorry, too," he said. He wiped his mouth with one hand. It was shaking badly. "If there were police, we'd let them take care of you, but the way things stand we shoot looters on sight."

He lifted the rifle and pointed it at me.

"No!" I threw out my hands as if I could ward off the bullet, clenched my eyes shut as if I could hide. I shrieked as the gun fired once, twice. I was gone for a moment, my ears buzzing, the world spinning away.

I opened my eyes, looked down at my chest. I couldn't understand why I wasn't on the ground, why there was no blood.

The guy with the gun was on the ground.

Shouts rose from the house. People came running out. They had more guns.

"Run!" Ange said. I was grateful for any guidance, given how confused I was. We broke into the bamboo. It was hard to run—the stalks pounded me in the face, yanked at my arms.

Voices shouted behind us. I heard a hiss of labored breathing, glanced back to see three men close behind. I ran harder, but that only made things worse.

Heavy hands ripped at my shoulders, yanked me to the ground. I landed ear first, felt a knee dig into my back.

"She shot Danny! She shot my Danny!" a woman shrieked. "My Danny's dead. Oh, Jesus, my Danny's dead."

"Gun! Gun!" the man on my back shouted.

"Here!" another guy said.

The muzzle of a pistol pressed into my neck. I was yanked to my feet. The guy holding the gun on me was in his sixties, with a silver goatee and beady blue eyes.

"Get her!" a white-haired woman shouted. She had both of her hands on top of her head. I followed her gaze.

Ange was still running, clutching the gun. A guy was right behind her; he jumped at her and they both went down in a tumble of dust.

The guy dragged Ange toward us by one foot. Danny's mom ran at her; she kicked at Ange's head, screaming incomprehensible curses as Ange wrapped her arms around her head to ward off the blows while kicking her foot to try to break free.

"He was going to shoot me!" I said. "I wasn't resisting and he was going to shoot me."

"What did you expect?" the man pinning me said. "An invitation to supper?"

"I'm sorry—" Ange said.

"Shut *up*!" Danny's mom screeched, kicking at Ange frantically until Ange shut up. She was an ugly woman, with a hound dog's droopy face and deep ragged creases in her forehead. Breathless, she tottered back to Danny, knelt, slid her hand under his head. Danny's tongue was poking from between his lips.

Jesus, we were in bad trouble.

"I say we find a good crackling spot," the dad said.

"That'll fix them," an acne-stricken teen said, probably Danny's brother. His voice was filled with grief.

They dragged Ange to her feet.

"Danny was gonna—"

"Shut up!" The father hit me in the side of the head with the pistol. "Don't say nothing, either of you!"

It was quiet then, except for the mother's crying, and the crunch of dead bamboo leaves underfoot. My ears buzzed, and I had a terrible headache. I wanted to look in Ange's eyes. I don't know why, just to have contact, or to thank her for saving my life, but Ange was ahead of me. I had a wild, irrational moment of hoping someone in our tribe had followed us and would save us, but I knew it was just wishful thinking. I felt a wet dribble of blood down my neck. They were going to kill us—that had to be what was going to happen.

"Quiet," the dad said. Everyone stopped. I didn't hear anything, except the rustling of bamboo leaves in the breeze. "That way." He pointed. They moved us on, faster. I didn't want to go, didn't want to know where they were taking us. Something bad was going to happen, and not knowing what it was made it a thousand times worse. Every time we paused I thought they were going to line us up and shoot us, or throw a rope over a branch. Only they didn't have a rope with them.

We reached a clearing with only a few scattered patches of bamboo.

The crack and snap of new growth lit the air.

"This looks like the place," one of the brothers said.

"Over there," the father said, pointing. The two older brothers dragged Ange into the clearing while the rest of us remained at the edge. Ange began to struggle harder, so they grabbed her arms and legs and carried her to the spot their father was pointing to. They put her on her back, pinned her arms and legs. Ange twisted and bucked.

I thought they were going to rape her, right in front of their parents, but they just held her down. I didn't understand what was happening—they were just pressing her to the ground.

And then I realized what they were doing.

"No!" I screamed. I lunged, broke free of the father's grip, took two steps before being slammed to the ground. I clawed blindly at his face, trying to find an eye, a lip to tear off. Something hard hit me in the face. I knew instantly that my nose was broken—I'd never felt such pain before. Again, at the same spot, I heard a crunching. Again. Again. Finally it stopped. "Turn him over, he's gonna watch this." They rolled me over. Someone pulled my hair so my head lifted.

Ange was still twisting and thrashing.

"Help them," the father said, waving a finger toward the clearing. A third brother ran over and pressed Ange's hips to the ground.

It was a bluff. It had to be. They were going to scare her, then let us go. That had to be it; they couldn't really mean to do this.

Ange screamed, thrashing her head back and forth.

"Please don't," I said. I could only see out of one eye.

Ange's eyes clenched shut, and the pitch of her scream changed. It went on and on, broken only long enough for her to take quick breaths, drowning out the crackling of the bamboo, and my screams.

Could this really kill her? Could a bamboo shoot really grow right through her, or did it just hurt badly because it was ramming against her back? Surely that was it. Later I'd give her some antimicrobial Goldenseal and she'd stay put for a while and heal.

Ange stopped screaming abruptly. A bird sang brightly nearby. Ange looked at one of the brothers hunched over her.

I couldn't seem to string my thoughts together; the blows to my face had left me disoriented, my head literally spinning.

"Please get it out of me," Ange said. "Please." He looked off into the distance, one of his fists closed over her wrist, the other on her breast. "I'm really sorry. Please let me up."

There was a fluttering under her shirt, as if a moth were trapped there. A green shoot poked out near her collar bone.

"Can I have a drink of water?" Ange said.

One of the brothers slid a hand under Ange's shirt. He squeezed her breast, stared at his hand beneath her shirt, mesmerized, his mouth hanging open.

"Let me get her a drink of water," I said.

The father hit me on the side of the head with the gun.

I couldn't see the green shoot grow, but every time I looked at Ange lying there, the shoot seemed bigger. Soon it was jutting a foot over her, pointing straight at the sky. Ange groaned, and cried.

"I'm so sorry, Ange," I cried. "It's my fault. I'm so sorry."

"Shut up!" The butt of the gun slammed into my cheek, whipping my head sideways.

"It's not your fault," Ange said.

"Yes. It is."

I was hit again, harder. "Every time you open your mouth, you're gonna get hit," the father warned.

"I love you, Ange." Another blow landed; I heard a crunch. One of my back teeth had been knocked out. I felt it sitting against my tongue and tried to spit it out.

"I love you too," Ange murmured. She made a strangled choking sound, and didn't speak again after that.

When it was over, three fledgling stalks trembled over her, streaked pink, their bright new leaves still tucked.

The brothers stood; one brushed the knees of his jeans.

The father got off me, pushed the pistol back into my neck. He gripped me by my collar and shook me hard. "Are you next? Huh? You gonna be next?" My head swung back and forth; the ground spun in a sick blur.

"No, please," I said. "I'm sorry. I'm sorry for your loss."

He held me still for a long moment.

"Go on," he said, shoving me. The youngest brother started to protest, but the dad cut him off. "Tell your friends what happened. Tell them we'll do the same to anyone who tries to steal from us."

"Go on," he said, motioning toward the bamboo forest. "Before I change my mind."

I ran, my face wet with tears and sticky with dried blood, leaves whipping my face, until I tripped on a fallen tree and tumbled to the ground.

One day I was going to go there and kill every single one of them. But what did it matter? Ange was dead. I would never wake up beside her again.

I crawled to my feet and walked on. "She was shot," I said aloud, sniffing, wiping my runny nose. I winced as my hand touched my face. "Ange was shot. They shot her. She died right away." That's what I would tell the others. That's how I wanted to remember it, if I could convince myself. I didn't want to remember the truth; I wanted it gone, stripped from my mind.

Cortez was on the porch. He leapt up as soon as he saw my face. "What happened? Where's Ange?"

"Ange is dead," I said.

Cortez covered his face and sobbed.

"What happened?" It was Jean Paul, standing in the doorway. "What happened?" I only shook my head.

The screen door squealed and Colin appeared. "Oh, jeez," he said. He raced out, grabbed me by the elbow to help me inside.

"Ange is dead," I said. Colin froze, his expression melting from concern to despair.

"What happened?" Jean Paul repeated.

I told the story as it had happened, except I told them that they shot Ange in the clearing.

Cortez disappeared upstairs, reappeared a moment later armed to the hilt—gun, knives. No Eskrima sticks. "Where is this farm?" he asked me.

"No," Sophia said, grasping Cortez's arm. "Let it go. They're all armed. We don't need anyone else dying today."

"She's right," Colin said. "We need you here, we can't afford to lose you." Colin glanced at me. I didn't care. I wanted to be unconscious.

Cortez stuck the gun into his belt. "They murdered Ange, and we're just going to walk away?"

"Yes!" Sophia said. "We just walk away. Killing them isn't going to bring her back."

Cortez turned and stormed out. As the screen door slammed, I was already on the stairs, weaving like a drunk, heading to my bed.

Chapter 9: Gunslinger

Fall, 2033 (Three months later)

The faded purple neon sign by the road read "Paradise Motel," and "No Vacancy." There was an empty pool in front, between the highway and the parking lot, surrounded by a cyclone fence choked with kudzu. The roofs on the last four units had collapsed, but the others looked to be in decent shape—a few even had glass in the windows.

An ice machine was tucked between two support poles, a toppled and partially crushed snack machine next to it.

"I hope they have plenty of ice," Colin said, "I could use a cold one." Baby Joel, his head lolling, was asleep in the makeshift carrier on Colin's back.

"It feels strange not having the bamboo around. I feel exposed," Sophia said, hugging her elbows. The bamboo had tapered off just past Midville, though we knew it was just a patch—an area the scientists and eco-terrorists hadn't bothered to target. The bamboo would make it here eventually.

"We got dibs on this one," Colin called, peering into a room with his hand on the door knob. "There's even a mattress, sort of."

I opened the door to the next room down.

A woman was standing inside, a machete raised over her head. I cried out in surprise.

"I don't have any food," she said. "I don't have anything of value. Just leave me alone."

She was wearing a big floppy hat over wild, tangled auburn hair, Khaki shorts, and a white button-down sweater like my grandma used to wear. Still, she had a machete.

I raised my hands. "Okay. No problem."

As my heart slowed I noticed that the woman was so scared the machete was shaking. She had a pretty bad cut on her shin—it was straight and fairly deep, like a slashing knife wound.

"We're just looking for a place to—"

Behind her, the bedside table was adorned with knickknacks. A postcard of hula dancers caught my eye. The caption read *Everything's Better in Metter*. It reminded me of something: I'd bought a postcard just like it once, at a convenience store when I was on a date.

A tingle washed over me—an honest to god tingle. I studied the woman carefully.

"Phoebe?"

Her look of surprise was priceless. She looked at me carefully; her eyes grew wide.

"Jasper, right?" She lowered the machete.

The rest of the tribe had rushed over when I cried out, and were crowded around the doorway and the big glassless window. I introduced everyone. Of course she'd already met Colin, Jeannie, and Cortez, but that was briefly, eight years ago.

She hadn't changed much. She still had pretty green eyes and (despite the grime) refined, aristocratic features—high cheekbones, a perfectly shaped nose, a long, elegant neck. She could have been a young Harvard lit professor who specialized in Milton. She had nice legs—lean, shapely runner's legs. Greyhound legs.

"That's a pretty bad cut," Colin said.

"I did it while hacking through the bamboo." She looked chagrined. "I'm actually not as spastic as that suggests."

"I'm sure the other ten thousand hacks were works of art. We all know what it's like to swing that thing for hours." We didn't actually use a machete—we'd decided early on it was too energy-ineffi-cient—but it seemed like the right thing to say. I took another look at the leg. "I hate to say this, but I think it needs to be stitched."

Phoebe went a little white. "Really?"

"Definitely," Cortez said. "It's not going to heal right like that. Stuff will get in it. It'll get infected." He clapped my shoulder. "Colin and me will boil some water to clean the cut. I've got a needle and thread you can use to close it up."

"Me?" I protested.

Cortez nodded. "You've performed major surgery. Compared to that, this will be a piece of cake."

Phoebe looked confused. "You performed surgery?"

"I removed someone's appendix once," I said, feeling a blush of pride, but trying not to let it show.

I told Phoebe the story while the water boiled, then I cleaned out the cut with a bath towel. Colin had found a hundred of them in a linen closet in the manager's office.

I picked up the needle, which Jeannie had dipped in the boiling water, thread and all. I may have done it once before, but I hadn't enjoyed it, and I was still horrified at the idea of sewing up somebody's skin. Someone had to do it, though. "I'm guessing this is going to hurt."

Phoebe just nodded.

I poked the needle through clean, white skin. Phoebe hissed and squeezed her eyes shut. I had to resist the urge to close my eyes as well. I ran the needle under the skin on the other side of the gash, brought the needle out through the skin and pulled the thread through.

The rest of the tribe left to give Phoebe some privacy. I got her talking to take her mind off what I was doing. It got a little easier after the first stitch.

Phoebe had been living for the past couple of years in a little co-op carved out in Twin City, but had a falling out with her boyfriend and left. These details were conveyed in small pieces, punctuated with winces and a few tears. I filled her in on the low points of my life, then cast about for distractions.

"What are all those things on the night stand?" I asked. Beside the postcard, there were photos, little stuffed animals, figurines, a book, all carefully arranged.

"It's my stuff," she said, smiling sheepishly. "It calms me. Everywhere I stay, I arrange these things in the same way to make it feel more like a home."

"What about if you're sleeping outside?"

She gave an embarrassed shrug. "I still do it."

I pictured her sleeping on a bed of leaves, her curios arranged on a cleared rectangle of ground beside her, a talisman against the icy blasts of loss and uncertainty.

"Familiar things help me cope with the anxiety. Even before things went bad I was anxious." She squeezed her eyes shut to the pain. "Ouch. Sometimes it's like I'm drowning—like there's no air to breathe." She blew a puff of air that brushed back a lock of her insanely curly hair. "I'm sorry, I don't mean to unload on you. I've been alone for a long time and I think it's making me weird."

"No, no, it's fine," I said. "Just keep talking. I'm almost done."

I glanced at her curio table. There was a photo of a girl and an elderly woman. The girl was in a numbered jersey, and they were at a sporting event of some sort. "Is that you?"

Phoebe looked over my shoulder. "Mm hm. With my nana, at a track meet."

"There," I said, leaning back and letting my aching shoulders relax. The needle dangled against her leg on the end of an inch of thread. I cut it with a pocket knife Cortez had left beside me, and taped some gauze over the wound. We didn't have any bandages.

"Thanks, Doctor," she said. "I don't have my checkbook with me, but you can bill me to this address."

"Have you been here long?" I asked.

"A couple of days."

I picked up a little stuffed pig from the night stand.

"Sir Francis Bacon," Phoebe said.

I tapped the postcard with my fingernail. "I'm touched that you kept my gift in your memento collection."

Phoebe laughed. "Yes, it's almost like having it on display in a museum."

Memories of those days washed over me—the music playing in the camp, the first Polio-X victims, the cops chasing us out of town. I'd been so conflicted about that date, because of my "relationship" with Sophia. Ironic that the woman I'd been so hung up on back then was right outside. I didn't feel like I was old enough to be nostalgic for an earlier time, and those certainly weren't good times, but I still felt an indescribable longing.

"I can't believe we didn't even recognize each other," Phoebe said.

"It was, what? Ten or eleven years ago?" I said.

"It feels like such a long, long time," she said. "Can I really be only thirty-five years old?"

"My mom once told me that I'd be shocked by how fast life flew by," I said. "I don't think that happens when you're scared most of the time."

Phoebe stood. "Shall we join the others?" We went outside.

We all lounged in the parking lot talking for a long time. Phoebe told us about Stephan, her husband of sorts who'd ditched her in the middle of nowhere, trading her in for a relationship that bordered on pedophilia. We told her about Jeannie's delivery, and Ange, though not everything about Ange.

Finally, Jeannie stood, and the rest of us followed suit and went off to sleep. I went to my dark, empty room and sat on scraps of carpet, among the components of a smashed TV. Right before bed was the worst time. The first few months after Ange's death had been filled with flashbacks of the killing—images I kept from everyone else. The flashbacks had grown less frequent, but I still missed her terribly. I missed talking to her, having her there. I had never really loved her, nor she me, but that didn't diminish the incredibly strong friendship we'd had.

Colin knocked on the door frame. "So, what do you think?"

"I think we should invite her to join us, if it's okay with the others. She has nobody, and she's a good person."

He nodded. "I'll ask them." I'm sure he could hear the depression in my voice. "Nothing else, though?"

He didn't need to lay it out for me. I knew what he was getting at. "You know, you never see love stories set in concentration camps, and I think there's a reason for that."

He nodded. "You might feel different in a few months. You never know."

I shrugged. "I doubt it."

Colin left me alone. I stared at the wall. Laughter drifted in from a few stragglers leaving the parking lot. There was a thrumming in my eardrums, a pressure. I wanted to sleep, but I wasn't tired.

The morning was hot and smoky, the aphids buzzing in the wild grass out past the parking lot.

Cortez leaned in my window. "We took a vote. We want Phoebe to join us. You want to ask her?" I took a big, sleepy breath and nodded.

When I stepped into Colin and Jeannie's room, Phoebe was telling them what she'd heard about Athens. It sounded like the Doctor Happy crowd had lured thousands to join them. Maybe they could establish a beachhead to get things stabilized in the region, who knew? As long as they didn't come my way with their needles, that was fine with me.

"I'm going to get some air," Phoebe said after a while. She grabbed her sweater and headed for the parking lot.

"She's such a sweetheart," Sophia said. "I came in to check on her last night, and we talked for a long time. I told Jean Paul if we didn't take her with us, I was staying with her." Jean Paul smiled sardonically.

"I'll go ask her," I said.

Phoebe was sitting on a concrete step, her knees pressed together, her feet pigeon-toed, reading an old waterlogged book: *Midnight in the Garden of Good and Evil.*

"You don't see many people reading these days, except the newspaper," I said.

"They don't know what they're missing," she said. It had to be in the 80s, but she was still wearing her sweater.

"You read a lot?"

"I read all the time. I always have."

"What are you reading?"

She looked down at her lap, marked her spot with a finger, held the book up so I could see the cover. "It's about Savannah, back in the nineteen nineties."

"Really? Is it good?"

She wobbled her head. "It's okay. I've read it before—I like that I know most of the places he writes about."

"Hm. Maybe I could borrow it when you're done."

Phoebe knotted her eyebrows at that.

"We'd like you to join us, if you're interested."

Her eyes filled with tears. "That's really kind of you." She looked directly at me, something she didn't do very often. "Thanks," she said. "I was hoping you might ask. It's difficult being alone out here."

We ate a hellish mix of bitter grass, wild onions, and mint leaves I'd harvested since we got clear of the bamboo and there was more biodiversity. Afterward we relaxed in the parking lot. Cortez settled on the tailgate of a truck, plugged our energy pack into the radio and took his daily stroll up and down the dial.

We all bolted upright when a voice leapt out of the static.

"The Wasteman was having a bubble, I tell ya." The speaker had a Jumpy-Jump accent mixed with a southern twang. "Told her he was issuing a batybwoy warning on Paddy."

A second adolescent voice laughed raucously. "Paddy's always using a toe to do a thumb's job."

They rambled on, gossiping in their incoherent slang about the Wasteman and Paddy, about who better watch out, and who should represent themselves physically at the radio station.

"Come on, say something helpful," Jean Paul growled.

More crap. Termite was working for the firemen, so he needed to be drenched.

"At least it tells us there's something left of Savannah," Colin said.

"Let's go home," I said. "I'm tired of this."

"It could be worse there than here," Cortez said.

"The last I heard when I was still in Twin City was that Savannah was a very bad place to be. We were in short-wave communication with people there," Phoebe said. "Of course that was almost six months ago."

We fell into disappointed silence, listening to the two boys talk about killing.

"I don't care," I said. "I'm sick of these ghost towns."

"Where would we live if we went back?" Colin asked. "With so many people dead, there might be more places to live, or there may be less because so much was burned, but it doesn't matter, because we have no way to pay rent."

"The Poohbah's making a zigzag that's likely to terminate Twig's hall pass," the broadcaster said.

We looked at each other; we looked at the floor.

"Well, if Savannah's infrastructure is intact, I can certainly provide you with all the money you need to get started," Jean Paul said. "But I doubt that's the case."

I guess I could have interpreted that as a generous offer, but to me it reeked of condescension.

"Why don't we just head in that direction?" I suggested. "We don't want to head west toward Athens, or Atlanta, which is bound to be worse than Savannah. South is going to be hotter and dryer. North is where all those rifles are. We can scout out Savannah, and if it's bad we could head north up the coast."

No one had any better ideas, so we headed in the general direction of home.

"There is no such word as 'jerkin.' I've never heard or seen the word 'jerkin' in my life," Phoebe said as she jumped from the roof of an SUV, crashed through bamboo stalks and onto the hood of a sedan.

"There is," I said. "It's from back in Conan the Barbarian times—it's like a leather vest. You can store your quiver of arrows in it."

"I'm going to find a dictionary. You want to make a bet?"

"It won't be in a little pocket dictionary, but if you can find one of those giant dictionaries that could fell a charging ox, I'll bet you. I wish there was still an Internet. We could just Google it."

I caught a glimpse of color in the distance, felt the stirrings of a thrill deeply conditioned in me from childhood. Bright multicolor flags, red-and-white-striped awnings. A Ferris wheel, stretching high above the bamboo. "Oh my," I said. "The carnival is in town."

Phoebe looked confused for a moment, then she saw what I was looking at and broke into a big smile. "Oh man, do I love a good seedy carnival."

"Me too," I said. "You think the owners left any good salvage when they abandoned it?"

"Probably not. They were probably traveling light, moving from town to town." She slapped at something behind her ear, looked at her hand. "Then again, the only way to know for sure would be to make a quick trip over there."

"Good idea," I said. "Yes, maybe a quick reconnaissance trip is in order."

"And maybe one quick trip down that gigantic slide."

There was indeed a gigantic slide, with three progressively bigger swells. "Let's go," I said.

We started at a squat snack stand that promised *candy apples-cold drinks-popcorn-cotton candy-soft serve*, but it was cleaned out. Most of the games were shuttered. We opened the Baseball Toss: prizes still hung from the ceiling, and all the hairy but deceptively thin trolls were lined up to be thrown at. I vaulted over the counter, and Phoebe followed. A huge crate of worn rubber baseballs sat beneath it.

"Looks like they took off in the middle of the night," I said. "Cost too much to transport the show, so they just ditched it."

"Yeah," Phoebe said, holding a baseball in each hand, not sounding particularly interested in what I was saying. She climbed back over the counter. "Get out of the way."

Phoebe could throw hard. Her arms were long and as thin as twigs, but sinewy. A little knot tensed on her triceps as she drew the baseball back and fired it, brushing the fringe of hair but missing the elusive meat of the troll.

"Damn!" she whispered.

"You're an athlete," I said.

She smiled. "Track and softball in high school. I sucked at softball, but I was good at track." She grabbed another ball, tossed it in the air and caught it, getting a feel. "You're all going down," she shouted at the trolls. "I have plenty of baseballs here, and they aren't costing me a dime. You can't run, because you have no feet, and you can't hide, because, again, you have no feet." She whipped the ball, laughing. It sailed right between two of them. "Crap!" she shouted, still laughing. She wiped a tear from her cheek.

"You cry when you laugh," I said. "Not just when you laugh really hard, but whenever you laugh."

"Shut up," she said, laughing harder. "I do not." More tears welled up in the corners of her eyes and rolled onto her cheeks.

"You do!" I pointed at her cheek. "I've never seen anything like it, it's like those birds who can't help but make a peeping sound with every flap of their wings."

She laughed harder, and more tears came. "Liar," she said, swabbing her cheeks with the sleeve of her sweater.

"Shall we to the slide?" she said when her laughter had settled down to intermittent bursts.

"We shall," I said, motioning ladies first. It felt so good to be laughing, to be having fun and goofing off. Phoebe was so quick-witted; I didn't remember her being like that when we met all those years ago. Of course, we'd only spent a couple of hours together.

"Did you go to traveling carnivals a lot when you were a kid?" I asked as we picked our way across what had once been the midway.

"All the time. It's hard to imagine a time when things were that easy. You worked, you bought groceries, you took your kids to the carnival." She shook her head. "It's like some fairy tale world."

Phoebe grasped a rung of the ladder, looked up. "I didn't realize it was so *high*." She craned her neck to look back at me, hand still clutching the rung. "I'm afraid of heights. We could have just as much fun sitting on the merry-go-round horses, don't you think?"

"They won't move, they'll just sit there," I said.

"That's okay. They're pretty, and I'll make horse noises."

I pointed at the ladder, laughing. "You promised we'd ride the slide, and it's the only ride that works."

"I didn't *promise*, I just *suggested*."

"The promise was implicit."

Phoebe huffed. She grasped the rungs and looked up. "All right, but you may have to call the fire department to get me down."

I laughed. "They'd get you down, all right. With a high-powered rifle."

I caught a glimpse of Phoebe's white calf as she climbed, remembered her long legs, how perfect her knees were when I'd seen her in shorts that first day in the motel. Phoebe never wore shorts around us, always jeans.

It took a bit of coaxing to get Phoebe to slide down. At first she clung to the sides and braked herself every few feet, but the first steep drop made that impossible, and gravity ruled the day.

Phoebe clung to her hat so it wouldn't blow off, which, along with her auburn hair snapping in the wind, made her look like a woman in a Jane Austen novel.

There was something about her very proper, demure nature that was extremely sexy. There was no denying it. But the thought of the emotional part, the thought of love, the negotiation of what the physical part meant… I had no stomach for that, so better not to try to cross that bright red line between a hug and a kiss.

Phoebe shrieked her way down the third and steepest drop. So strange. Wasn't this what I'd always hoped for? I was with a funny, attractive woman, and we got along effortlessly. We'd met only a few weeks ago, and already we were close friends.

I slid down while Phoebe shouted an undecipherable mix of encouragement and taunts. I hit the steep drop, and felt that tingly falling-feeling in my intestines. It felt great, simulating emotions I hadn't experienced in a long time.

"What say we check out the World's Smallest Woman exhibit?" Phoebe said as I climbed back to solid earth. "My parents would never give me the extra three dollars to go in. They said it was a scam."

"I doubt she's home," I said.

"Still, I'd like to go through her tiny dresser and look at all her tiny shoes." She led the way.

The World's Smallest Woman's tent was a bust. It was an empty husk—no tiny dresser, no tiny kitchen appliances.

"Well damn," Phoebe said, letting the tent flap fall.

I wondered if, given a different past, this afternoon, in this abandoned carnival with Phoebe, could have been one of those magically romantic days that you never forget.

"You okay?" Phoebe asked. "You got quiet suddenly."

"I'm fine. I just got thinking about something that happened to me a long time ago," I said, covering my trail.

"What was it, if you don't mind my asking?"

"Why don't we stop and eat, and I'll tell you?"

We ate wild mushrooms and nettle in the merry-go-round, in a chariot. Cherubs in silver diapers and women in flowing burgundy robes were carved into its sides. The carvings were exquisitely detailed, though the fingers on one cherub's hand, which was reaching toward the sky, were missing. While we ate I told Phoebe about my first encounter with Rumor, at the art gallery. It was the first thing that came to mind to mask what I'd really been thinking.

Phoebe reached out and stroked the hoof of the horse closest to her. Its front legs were curled under it in mid-gallop, its mouth open, tongue jutting out between square teeth.

"I can see how that would haunt you, even after all these years. The bad things get tattooed on your brain, don't they? Even though they're in the past, it's like they're not, like they're still happening somewhere."

"They do," I agreed. "I wish I could take just three or four days of my life and cut them out. I would feel so much better."

Phoebe continued absently stroking the hoof. "I know what mine would be." She looked off into the carnival, her face turned away from me.

"Which would they be? Unless you don't want to say."

Phoebe didn't say anything for a long time.

"I haven't told anyone," she finally whispered.

"If you want to tell someone, I'm a good listener." I waited, studied the red Tilt-A-Whirl choked with weeds.

Phoebe laced her fingers together, looked down at her feet, and began a story.

"After I left Stephan, the guy who wanted me to share him with a fifteen-year-old, I went off to find my parents. I hadn't seen them in over ten years, since the day I left home to live with Marlowe, a black guy, and they effectively disowned me. It took me a month to reach my parents' house, and when I got there I found my mother in worse shape than I. She had just carried on as if nothing was happening—planting flowers in her garden, watching crap on TV, until there was no more food or power. I took her out of there, but of course I had no idea where to go. We headed east, toward Savannah.

"She hadn't changed much in ten years. All she did was complain. Her feet hurt, she was hungry, why had I taken her out of her home to drag her across the countryside. All day long she complained.

"Then one day we were walking through the main drag of a small town, and the McDonald's had a cardboard sign up in the window that said 'Open,' so I left Mom in the shade, because I wasn't sure it was safe, and I went inside.

"The man inside was selling hamburgers made with some sort of critter meat, but he didn't accept cash, only precious metals or guns and the like. I didn't have anything like that, and I started to leave, and he suggested—"

She choked up. I considered putting a reassuring hand on her back, or squeezing her shoulder, but sensed that wasn't the right thing, so I just waited.

"He suggested a trade: he'd give me the hamburgers if I'd sleep with him. I told him no and hurried out, but I was starving, and my mother was starving." She wiped her eyes and sniffed; her nose was badly clogged. "So I did it. Behind the counter. I tried not to cry, but I couldn't help it, and he said to me, 'Just think about how good those hamburgers are going to taste.'" She laughed, although it was partially a sob, and now I did press my palm to her back and rub just a little to reassure her, and it seemed to work. She took a few deep breaths and calmed down.

"Two times after that, I left Mom somewhere, telling her I was going to buy food. Then I would approach a man with food and offer sex for food.

"The last time, the man did it, then called me a whore and threw me out without giving me the food."

Phoebe wiped something from the side of her nose with a trembling hand. I wanted her to look up, to see that I was hearing her, that I wasn't judging her, that she'd done nothing wrong, but she kept her eyes on her sneakers.

"When I went back to my mother that last time, she told me that she had figured out what I was doing to get the food. She said it was disgusting. When I asked her if she'd rather starve, she said yes, she'd rather starve.

"The next time we stopped, I sat her in the shade under a tree…" Fresh tears rolled down her cheeks; her shoulders heaved. "I told her I was going to look for food." She struggled to get the words out. "And I left her."

She looked up at me. "I left my mother."

I nodded, simply nodded understanding. I wasn't sure how to respond, didn't trust myself to respond, because it seemed like any response would be either trite or judgmental.

She leaned back in the little seat, looked up at the wood-slatted ceiling, her cheeks wet with tears. "She walked so damned *slowly.* Each step seemed to require this huge effort. So I left her." She sniffed, wiped her nose on the sleeve of her sweater. "Half a day later I couldn't stand the guilt any longer and I went back to look for her, but she was gone."

I had to respond; I couldn't leave her hanging there on those words, but I felt like I'd been struck mute. So I reached over and hugged her. She hugged me back, tightly, and we went on hugging until it wasn't a hug any more, it was more like a seated slow dance. I rocked her ever so slightly while she cried into my neck.

Finally, we separated, looking off into the mad decay of the carnival. I peered up into the steel framework of the Ferris wheel towering nearby, a series of shrinking Xs, thinking about the courage it had taken for Phoebe to tell me what she had just told me, and realized what my response should be.

I took a ragged breath, and began my own story. "One day two years ago I got it in my head to steal a pig from a farm." I choked up almost immediately. I wondered how I would get through the story if I couldn't even make it through the first sentence.

I did get through it, though. I told her what really happened to

Ange, something I'd never told another living soul. I cried through most of it, but when it was out the relief I felt surprised me.

I didn't stop there. I told her about how Cortez had killed Tara Cohn, and my part in that, and the time we stabbed the men who were raping Ange, and got through both of those without any tears. I was all cried out, and besides, awful as they were, neither of those events tortured me the way Ange's death did.

We just sat for a while then. I felt drained to the point of numbness.

"I love the word 'calliope,'" Phoebe finally said, sounding far away. "It's so festive."

"Mmm," I said.

"But it's not a cheap, simple, primary-color sort of festive, like 'confetti' is."

"No. Never."

Phoebe fidgeted with a button on her shirt, her gaze far away. She had such beautiful, delicate wrists. "When we went on that date all those years ago, I was a virgin. I was a virgin until I was twenty-six," she said. "That's who I am."

"That not hard to believe, given the sweaters and all."

Phoebe laughed. "I can't help wondering, though: is that *really* who I am? I never thought I was capable of doing what I did to my mother. Now that I know I am, how can I still think of myself as the person I thought I was?"

I nodded understanding. "You wonder if doing something awful makes you an awful person, even if you didn't have a choice," I said.

"Yeah."

"I'm so afraid sometimes, that this world has turned me into a monster, capable of horrible things. Or it's exposed me for the monster I am."

"Yeah, that's it. Exactly."

Someone had gone through and smashed a lot of the mirrors in the Hall of Mirrors. Outside, the facade was painted with huge clown faces. One had a long, pointed head, another, a fat round one.

We went on talking—about our fears, about the pain we felt for the things we'd done. It felt good to have someone listen without judging.

We didn't realize how late it was getting until the light began to

wane. Phoebe raised her arms over head and stretched. As she did
so one of her nipples was just barely visible through her shirt. It was
like glimpsing a rare bird, obscured by thick foliage and then gone as
she dropped her arms. She was a beautiful woman. I wondered if my
capacity to love wasn't as far from the surface as I thought. Maybe
I was afraid of those feelings, or embarrassed by them, or felt guilty
about having them. Or all of the above.

"I can't handle any more emotion in my life," Phoebe said, as if
reading my thoughts. "My tank is empty. I can't handle any more
love, no more tearful breakups."

"Me neither," I said.

She looked at me with those turtle green eyes. I leaned over and
kissed her, lightly, almost not at all. I didn't intend to do it—I just
did, without thinking. To my surprise, Phoebe didn't protest. To my
further surprise, a light spring breeze blew through me, lifting me
just high enough to see beyond the despair I'd felt for so long I could
barely remember ever feeling anything else.

Neither of us said anything. We headed back as if it hadn't happened.

On the walk back I realized that in my entire life I'd never had a
conversation like the one I'd just had with Phoebe. I hadn't even
been able to talk like that with Ange.

I was staring at a wall of thick kudzu and suddenly realized that
there was an entire house hidden in that tangle of green. A wren
squeezed into a crack between the slats just below the roofline.
Looking further off, I spotted another house.

"Did anyone notice that there are houses right there?" I asked,
pointing.

Everyone turned and looked. Phoebe laughed. "I hadn't noticed."

We'd spent the night sleeping outside, thirty feet from shelter.
I finished rolling up my bedding, stuffed it into the duffel bag I'd
salvaged at one house or another.

Phoebe was putting away her knickknacks. Each night we seemed
to lay out our bedding a little closer together.

"How did your parents die?" Phoebe asked.

"In the water riots in '21," I said. "I don't know the specifics, just
that they were alive before the riots and weren't after." I plucked a

bamboo shoot off a stalk, twisted it between two fingers. "How did your father die?"

"My mother said he choked on a chicken bone."

"Wow." It seemed an anachronistic death. But even with all the awful ways to die these days, I guess some people still choked on chicken bones.

"We should get moving," Cortez called out.

"Whatever you say, boss," Colin called back. Cortez gave him a "don't make me kick your ass" look.

I shrugged on my pack. It felt a little heavier each day we continued on our survivalist diet.

Two men ambled out of the brush. One was dressed head to toe in camouflage, the other in a crisp, white Atlanta Braves baseball uniform. Each cradled an assault rifle in one hand.

"What have we got here?" the guy in camouflage asked. His close-set eyes were nearly hidden by a wiry black beard.

"We're just passing through," Cortez said.

"Yeah? To where?" the one in the baseball uniform asked. It reminded me of a Jumpy-Jump outfit. Had the Jumpy-Jumps made it this far out of the city? Anything was possible. He went over and pulled the corner off the tarp we'd tied over one of the big packs that held our community property. He had a meaty bully's face, the kind of guy who was a second string linebacker on his podunk high school's football team and never got the girl.

"Savannah," Cortez replied.

He turned back toward us. "Tell you what—why don't you all drop those packs?" He looked Phoebe up and down.

I knew this script, I knew where it went even though it had only begun to play out. *Eat this.* I didn't want the script to play out that way.

With a calmness I never would have imagined I was capable of, I reached back and pulled a pistol out of my belt, aimed it, and started firing.

I just kept pulling the trigger; I hit one man square in the mouth, then shot the other high on the chest, then in the side. They were blown backward like extras in an action movie, their eyes wide with surprise.

The gunshots subsided. There was a moment of stunned silence, then Joel started to cry. My heart was pounding so hard that I could feel blood pulsing in my neck. "Jesus," Colin said.

The big one, who I'd shot in the chest, was taking ragged, hitching breaths. The other guy had stopped breathing the moment I shot him.

For a change my heart wasn't pounding from fear—it was pounding with rage. The emotion was pointing outward instead of inward, and that felt good.

"What did you do?" Sophia said, her eyes wide. "We don't know if they were going to hurt us." She squatted next to the guy who was still alive.

"They were going to hurt us. You know it and I know it," I said.

"They may have been soldiers of some sort, or police. They only asked us to drop our packs. You can't shoot people for that."

"I'm not letting any more of my friends die," I said, my voice trembling. "If that means shooting strangers before they let on whether they're killers or just assholes, fine."

The guy I'd shot coughed a spray of blood, then made a choking sound.

"Somebody help him!" Sophia said.

"We can't," I said, not taking my eyes off the man. "He's dying."

"What's happened to you?" Sophia said, tears rolling down her cheeks. Her eyes spoke volumes. *You're not the man I thought you were. How could I have ever thought I loved you?*

"I haven't been fortunate enough to spend the last ten years behind a gate, guarded by mercenaries. That's what happened to me." Jeannie tried to interrupt, to defuse the situation, but I talked over her. "I've been terrorized by men like these every day of my life. I had to watch someone I loved be tortured by men like these. That's what happened to me. Go figure."

I'd like to think it just came out, that I'm not so eager to win an argument that I would pull out the truth of Ange's death and thump Sophia with it. But Sophia had just called me a murderer.

"Okay J, calm down," Cortez said. "Why don't you give me your gun, okay?" He held out his hand.

I put the gun back in my belt.

I felt a hand on my back. It was Phoebe.

"Come on," Phoebe said, leading me by the elbow, "let's take a walk." I saw Cortez look at Phoebe and nod, telling her that's what they needed to do to handle the guy who'd clearly lost it, the guy who'd gone all shell-shocked on them. I let her lead me away, down a deer trail, to a wide pond that was mostly dried mud.

There were fissures in the dried mud, long jagged cracks in the parched earth that reminded me of the bark on the Live Oaks that lined the streets in Savannah. I stared at them, feeling like there was some significance there, some symbolic importance that my emotionally exhausted mind couldn't reach.

"Here," Phoebe said. I felt her hands slathering insecticide on the back of my neck. I hadn't noticed any mosquitoes.

"Thank you," I said.

The receding water had revealed a cornucopia of debris that had been thrown into the pond over the decades: rotted soda cans, bald tires, fishing line, two bicycles, a license plate.

"You okay?" Phoebe asked.

"Yeah," I said. I walked out onto the dried pond, pulled up one of the bicycles with my toe. It made a sucking sound as it came loose. The brand was still etched in the crossbar: Hard Rock. "Was I wrong? Were they going to walk away in another minute?"

"No," Phoebe said. "You were right."

I spotted some bones further out, near the oval of rusty water at the center of the mud flats. They looked like they might be human. I headed back toward Phoebe. "It felt good in a way though, and that scares the hell out of me. It's like what we were talking about just yesterday. I *have* changed. I'm not who I thought I was."

Phoebe considered. I was tempted to tell her that her eyes were the color of those little turtles you bought at the pet store, back when there were pet stores, but clearly it was not an appropriate time.

"Maybe the change is temporary," she suggested. "Maybe you've had to bury your true nature for now, because you have no choice." She nodded, as if she was convinced she was on the right track. "Like a soldier. The soldiers who fought the Nazis didn't lose their humanity, even though they had to do awful things."

I kicked at the dry mud. I wasn't in the mood to see myself as some sort of honorable soldier. The more time that passed, the sicker I felt about the two bodies lying a hundred yards away.

"I don't know. I think something died in me when they killed Ange. I don't know what it is, but it sure feels like my humanity, and I don't think it's coming back."

Phoebe's eyes filled with tears.

"Guys, we need to move!" It was Cortez. There was no mistaking the urgency in his voice. As we raced back toward him, we heard distant voices through the bamboo, maybe a hundred yards away.

We gathered our stuff (Cortez grabbed the two automatic rifles) and headed down the railroad tracks.

We'd gone a few hundred yards when shouts erupted behind us. I glanced back; one of the figures in the clearing raised a pistol and fired a shot that kicked up gravel ten yards short of us. We ran harder.

Another shot rang out. I half-expected to see one of my friends drop on the tracks, but no one did.

"They're chasing us. Keep running," Cortez said. I glanced back again. There was no point—Cortez had just informed us that they were coming after us, but I needed to see it for myself, see how fast they were coming, whether it was a half-hearted trot or a hard sprint.

It was a hard sprint. One of them was holding a walkie-talkie to his mouth as he ran, probably alerting a bunch of others, maybe the families of the two guys I'd shot.

"Drop your packs," I said. We couldn't outrun them carrying fifty pounds each. I shrugged mine off, felt suddenly light as a feather. The others followed suit, but we were still limited to how fast Colin could run carrying Joel. He was cradling Joel's head so it wouldn't roll around.

I looked back again. The men were no more than a hundred yards behind us. "They're gaining," I said.

"Keep moving," Cortez said. He pulled one of the automatic weapons off his shoulder and dropped to one knee. A deafening burst of gunfire followed.

I realized I should help him. After all, I was the gunslinger who got us into this catastrophe. I stopped, pulled the pistol out of my belt, realized Cortez was in my line of fire and ran back toward him.

By then the men were gone. Cortez leaped up, looked surprised and somewhat annoyed to see me standing behind him. "I hit one," he said, breathless. "The others carried him into the bamboo. Come on, I'm guessing they'll be back."

We caught up with the rest of the tribe.

"We should get off the tracks," I said, pointing into the bamboo to the right, the opposite side of the tracks from where our pursuers had gone.

Cortez took one look back, then broke off the track and into the jungle. "Come on."

We tore through the bamboo. If it hadn't been so serious, it would have been comical: seven of us running single-file, at times hitting bamboo so thick we had to back up like a seven-car train and seek another way through. Eventually we slowed to a brisk walk, but we kept moving, and no one talked except to suggest a route through the tangle. Joel was crying now—he was probably hungry.

An hour into our flight, long after I'd decided we were safe, we heard a shout behind us, and then an answering shout.

"Shit," Colin said.

We ran again.

"How can they know which way we went?" Colin asked.

"They must know how to track—broken branches, footprints," Cortez answered. That was the last of the conversation. It was grueling; my lungs ached, my legs were rubber. Joel cried in earnest in Colin's arms, his face red with outrage at being jostled so roughly for so long.

We kept running until the light began to wane, then slowed to a walk again.

I heard sniffing behind me, turned to see that Jeannie was crying. "I can't believe it," she said. "We lost everything. We're out here with nothing."

Nobody responded. I was true, and there was no sugar-coating it, no bright side.

"What now?" I asked.

"I guess we look for shelter," Colin said.

We were heading in the wrong direction—northwest, away from Savannah.

We walked on, everyone in a black mood, until we came upon a neighborhood choked in bamboo and overgrown with kudzu. It wasn't so much a neighborhood as a cul-de-sac set with half a dozen duplexes. Cortez kicked down the door of one and we took shelter inside.

"I don't think we should stay until morning," I said. "Let's rest an hour, then keep moving."

Nobody argued, although nobody agreed either. There were two bedrooms; Cortez suggested the two couples take them while the rest of us rested in the little living room.

We had no bedding, but we found some clothes in the closets and used that. It was growing dark. Phoebe lay along a wall, a half-dozen feet from me, hugging a pile of t-shirts.

"I'm sorry you lost your keepsakes," I said.

She shrugged. "You can always buy me another postcard the next time we visit a Timesaver."

"But Sir Francis Bacon…" I meant to strike a jovial tone, but it came out flat.

Phoebe smiled grimly. "Maybe one of the people chasing us will give it to his kid." She closed her eyes, took a big, sighing breath. There was a ragged cut on her wrist, but it wasn't too deep. Probably just some thorns.

Exhausted as I was, I couldn't just drop off to sleep. I felt responsible for the mess we were in. I knew how Sophia felt about what I'd done, but I needed to know if the others thought I'd acted irresponsibly, or even criminally. I got up, knocked on Colin and Jeannie's door.

Colin had pulled off his shirt and stretched it along the windowsill. Two rows of ribs ran down his back in sharp relief. He didn't yet look like someone rescued from a concentration camp, but he was getting close.

"Was I wrong?" I asked.

They looked at each other, deciding who was going to tackle the question.

"No," Colin said. "It was just so…" He struggled for the right words.

"Like I murdered them? Something like that?" I suggested. "But if I'd waited long enough to be sure, I probably wouldn't have been able to catch them by surprise, and we'd all be dead."

"No, I agree with you—" Colin said.

If you'd have told me when I was eighteen that one day I would debate whether or not I'd murdered people or shot them in self-defense, I'd have been spectacularly surprised.

"Japer, we're not criticizing you," Jeannie interrupted. "You saved us, and you saved our son, and we'd do anything to protect Joel. We were just surprised that *you* did it. If Cortez had done it, I don't think we would have been shocked."

"Exactly," Colin said.

I nodded. "Fair enough." I turned to go.

"Jasper?" Jeannie said. I turned back. "What happened to Ange?"

I sat on the edge of the bed and told them the truth. Cortez heard me telling the story, and came in. Phoebe hovered in the doorway. Difficult as it was, when it was over I was glad it was out. Secrets eat at you; they're nothing but lies in drag.

"Hey, Jasper," Colin said as I stood to go. "Thank you for saving my son."

I nodded. That was all I needed.

The door to the other bedroom was partly open; Sophia stood holding a blanket she must have found in the closet. Our eyes met for a moment before she turned away.

Until last year, I'd carried my memories of Sophia as proof that true love was possible—but for her being married, we would have been together all these years, blissfully. I think Sophia had been doing the same, and now I had shattered her illusions, leaving her with nothing but cynical Jean Paul. My illusions had already been shattered, though not by her. I was sorry to take hers away, although maybe it was for the best in the long run. In any case, I was at peace trading those bullets for her illusions.

"Oh, crap," Cortez hissed. He was peering out an open window. Hushed voices drifted through the window; a beam of light filtered through the bamboo.

I ran to get the others. We huddled in the living room, listening as the people outside went from door to door, searching.

Cortez handed me one of the automatic weapons. I took it, but shook my head. "If we get pinned in here, they can just wait us out, call a dozen more people on their walkies."

Cortez nodded, motioned for us to follow him to the back door. Outside we heard rustling leaves and low voices no more than two dozen feet away.

"I'm going out there. Hopefully I can surprise them. Wait for my signal, then run." Cortez turned the knob soundlessly, pushed the door open a foot. "If you need to shoot, aim lower than you think you should, and spray." He showed me, sweeping his weapon left to right and back, then he handed his assault rifle to Phoebe, pulled a pistol from his pocket and squeezed out the door, immediately disappearing into black leaves.

We waited, squatting by the door, barely breathing. The assault rifle was heavy. I slid my finger over the trigger to make sure I could find it if I needed to. The safety was already off. Safety was a luxury.

There was a meaty thump, a shout of alarm that quickly morphed into a gargled choke, then three gunshots.

"Now," Cortez shouted. I ran outside, stepped aside and covered the others while they passed, then ran like hell after them, my hands splayed in front of me, the automatic rifle bouncing wildly against my hip. Shouts erupted from the other side of the house. A bamboo stalk hit me in the forehead; I raised my hands higher. The bamboo leaves blocked most of the moonlight—all I could see were gray shapes on a black background, then, from behind me, a light. This was no good, I realized—if they had light and we didn't, they'd be able to outrun us easily.

I stopped, dropped to one knee like I'd seen Cortez do. I pointed the automatic rifle lower than I wanted to, then pulled the trigger and sprayed blindly.

It was hard to hold the rifle in position—it bucked like I'd hooked a marlin. The staccato roar was like a Harley revving an inch from my ears. I released the trigger.

"Hold it. Stay," a man's voice said. "It's too dangerous." Relieved, I turned and ran.

"We'll get you, you fuckers," the same voice shouted after me. "Don't you worry, we're coming for you."

Someone shouted my name. I followed her voice, caught up with Phoebe, grabbed her hand. Others were just ahead; we followed, weaving, blind. We moved as fast as we could, given the darkness, and Joel. I'd never been so thirsty, and hungry, and tired.

Soon the first hints of sunrise were blooming behind me. I could make out Phoebe's sneakers, the tangle of her hair.

But it hadn't been more than an hour since sundown! I glanced back, saw an orange glow on the horizon.

Then I smelled smoke.

I slowed. "Hold on."

Phoebe slowed, called the others to a halt. We stared at the orange glow filtering through the forest. Now that it was quiet, I could hear the distant roar of the flames.

"Does anyone know what to do?" Cortez asked. "I don't know anything about fires."

Silence.

"If we hole up in a house, the fire will burn it down," Colin said. There were no spaces anywhere—the bamboo touched everything, and so would the flames.

"Can we outrun it?" Jeannie asked.

"I guess we have to," Colin said.

We ran. Within minutes the air was hazy, and smelled like roasting chestnuts. My back felt vaguely warm.

"This isn't any good," I said, maybe not loud enough for anyone but me to hear.

"Wait," Colin said. I bumped into Phoebe, who had stopped. Colin pointed at a steel dome rising out of the bamboo. A grain silo. "What about that? That won't burn."

"Come on." Cortez broke for it.

The door was locked with a fat padlock. Cortez pulled the pistol and shot it; it burst apart. He pulled off the remnant and threw open the door and we all hurried in.

It was a round, empty space, maybe ten feet across. It was too dark to see the domed ceiling maybe thirty feet above us. Cortez pulled the door closed. It was dark, and stiflingly hot. Joel began to wail.

The silo wasn't airtight by any means, so there would be smoke. I wondered how much. I knew that most people who died in fires died from the smoke, not the fire. "When it comes, stay on the ground with your mouth as close to the floor as possible," I said.

We waited in silence for a few minutes, and nothing happened—no roaring outside, no smoke.

"Maybe the wind shifted and it missed us?" Colin suggested.

"Why don't I check?" Cortez said. "Everybody move away from the door." A bright crack of light formed, then a big square. The light flooding into the silo was tinged orange, and thick with smoke. Cortez slammed the door. "It's coming. Everyone down."

I got on my stomach, cradled my face in my arms and closed my eyes.

Twice in my life I had been certain I was going to die. The first had been when the Jumpy-Jumps pulled me into that alley, the second when I was caught trying to steal from the farmers and Ange had saved my life. Now, as I lay in a silo hoping to ride out a forest fire, I suspected that this might really be it.

I crawled on hands and knees over to Phoebe, put a hand on her wrist. She turned her hand palm up, took mine in hers.

There was a squealing, like air leaking from an inner tube. The smell of roasting chestnuts grew heavier.

"How long will it last?" someone asked. No one answered. I didn't think it would be too long. Didn't forest fires travel fast? Off on the other side of the silo, Joel was crying. Poor Joel, with his fresh little lungs.

The squealing grew deeper, or maybe a deeper sound drowned out the squealing. It became that roar that could never be mistaken for anything but fire.

Someone coughed. I tried to press my face into the crook of my elbow to create a little pocket of oxygen, but I could already feel a tickle in my lungs. I coughed.

The roar became deafening. I took a breath, felt my lungs fill with hot smoke. I coughed uncontrollably, nearly gagged. Joel screamed—a piercing cry of outrage that was followed by frantic coughing. I hadn't noticed that it was getting hotter, but suddenly my clothes were so hot they felt like they were burning my skin. I wanted to pull them off, but that would involve exertion, and then I would have to breathe. I didn't want to inhale again. I lingered on the outbreath, expelling the smoke, willing the fire to pass.

When I finally did inhale, it was agony. The smoke was hot; it singed my throat, made me cough so hard it was more a full-body spasm. I was burning up—the heat both outside me and in. I heard Phoebe's coughs in my ear, clutched her hand like a lifeline.

Around us others were coughing and gagging in the darkness. I tried to inhale, but it felt as if my lungs had collapsed, like I was trying to inhale with something clamped over my mouth. The sounds around me receded. I was losing consciousness. I was suffocating. My legs drew up of their own accord, putting me in a fetal position. Fetal, as in fetus, but not a cat fetus, which I once ate. I was fairly sure I was dying, receding into a swirling blackness punctuated by swirls of even darker blackness that popped into my vision with each cough. Although I knew my arms were up near my head, I had the sensation that they had drifted up behind my head and were twisting and stretching. Far off, someone was screaming. It may have been Ange.

I felt a squeeze on my hand. I coughed. It felt like I'd been gone. I coughed again. It hurt like hell. My throat was raw, like someone had peeled all of the skin out of there.

Phoebe's coughs returned, or I returned to where I could hear them, then I could hear the others coughing as well.

There was a blinding light. I lifted my head, saw Cortez curled up by the door, which was now ajar. Red light filtered in, along with heavy black smoke. Cortez closed the door.

I coughed, and this time the cough felt more productive, making me feel slightly better instead of worse, so I let my spasming chest go, let myself cough.

Joel began to scream.

I gave Phoebe's hand a final squeeze and let go, then sat up, tried to rub the smoke out of my eyes with fists that were just as smoky. I crawled over to the door.

"I guess we should wait until the worst of the smoke has cleared," Cortez said.

We stepped out into a different, completely alien place. Instead of bamboo leaves right in front of your face no matter where you turned, the landscape was a vast black desert covered with charred spikes (the remnants of the bamboo) and black, naked trees. In the mix of starlight and the red glow radiating from the horizon, it was a chilling sight.

We stared off at the burned land. The assholes pursuing us had probably assumed we were dead, and had gone home, so there was probably no need to hurry. We had no supplies, no food or water, no tents, no clean clothes.

"Which way?" I asked. We'd come from the north, so that was out. The fire was moving south, so we'd only hit more devastation that way, so it was east or west. I crossed my arms, pointed toward the east and west simultaneously. "That way is a very nice way."

It was a lame joke, but I got some laughs.

"Of course people do go both ways," Colin said absently.

"Hey, Scarecrow, how about a little fire?" Phoebe said, doing a decent Wicked Witch of the West impression that got people giggling.

Cortez began to sing, "Ding-Dong! The Witch Is Dead," and a few of us joined in. If we'd had more energy, maybe we would have tried to do that special skip that Dorothy and her companions used when traipsing down the yellow brick road, but our giddy relief didn't extend that far. We left it at "Ding Dong! The Witch Is Dead," then grew serious again. We weren't nearly out of the woods yet.

"I guess the first priority is finding abandoned houses that are not burned, to salvage some clothes and whatever else we can use," I said.

"East or west?" Cortez asked.

"Colin and I vote west," Jeannie said. She was bouncing Joel, who'd quieted down. His little head bobbed languidly as if nothing had happened.

But what was west? Athens, then Atlanta. Atlanta would likely be a bigger mess than Savannah, and we weren't welcome in Athens.

"Why west?" Cortez asked.

"Because we're going to join the Doctor Happy people in Athens," Jeannie answered softly.

I dropped the rifle. I looked at Colin. He met my gaze for a second, then looked away. "It's the only way to keep Joel safe."

Cortez squatted on his haunches, his head hanging.

"What about the virus?" I asked. "You're going to let them infect you? And Joel?"

Colin shrugged. "There are worse things. Like starving."

I felt rising panic. I could barely imagine being separated from Colin and Jeannie. Yet I also couldn't imagine infecting myself with Doctor Happy.

I stared off into the charred landscape, watched smoke rise off a blackened scarecrow of a tree.

"That's where we're going. We'd like it if you all came with us," Colin said.

I looked at Phoebe, then Cortez. Cortez shook his head. "I'm going east."

I looked back at Phoebe. She just stared at the rifle I'd dropped.

I've heard that you have to have a kid of your own before you truly get it, but, looking at Joel, tear streaks in stark relief with the dirt and soot covering his face, I understood why they had to go to Athens. He was probably going to die if they went anywhere but Athens, and it was unimaginable that such a small child should die. I guess Doctor Happy was a small price to pay for his life.

Infecting myself, on the other hand, filled me with a dread that went right to my bones.

I looked at Phoebe, gauging her reaction to this. Under my exhaustion and anxiety at talk of the tribe dividing, I found one sparkling bit of clarity: I wanted to go where Phoebe went. I didn't have time to think too deeply about this, but it afforded me a mooring in the chaos.

"I hate the thought of splitting, but maybe that's best at this point," Cortez said.

"Hold on," I said. "We're going to split up, just like that?"

"It's not 'just like that,'" Cortez said. "Colin and Jeannie have clearly thought this through. I respect the choice they're making, but it's not for me. Period." He gestured at the assault rifle slung over his shoulder. "I'll take this for me and whoever else is going east. Whoever's going west can take the other. Fair enough?"

We stood like rival gangs in a standoff, no one moving.

My guts tensed. "Hold on," I said, buying time. "Let's think this through." We needed to stay together; I felt that with absolute certainty. "Colin and Jeannie can't make it to Athens on their own. If this is what they want to do, we owe it to them to help them get Joel there safely."

Phoebe bent and picked up the assault rifle. "I agree." She looked at me, then at Jeannie. "I'll help you."

"Thank you, Phoebe," Jeannie said.

Cortez put both hands over his mouth and sighed through his nose. He stared at the burnt ground, his eyes fixing on one charred spot, then flicking to another, and another. "Shit," he finally said. "You're right. I was only thinking about myself." He nodded tightly. "Okay, if that's what you want to do, I'll go with you, but then I'm going to Savannah."

"We won't be joining you," Jean Paul said. He seemed to be trying to sound regretful, but it came out sounding mostly angry. "We're heading back to Savannah."

There was an uproar of protests, entreaties that Sophia and Jean Paul stay with the tribe. Jeannie all but begged, which got Sophia crying but did not shift their resolve.

I'd noticed that Jean Paul and Sophia had been standing a few dozen paces away from the rest of the tribe, pointedly separating themselves as we deliberated. They hadn't joined in on the Wizard of Oz antics, or done more than crack a smile. I suspected they were leaving to be rid of me, not because they'd rather go to Savannah than Athens.

Cortez held the assault rifle to Jean Paul, who waved it off. They said their goodbyes; Sophia hugged Colin and Jeannie. She nodded to me, mumbled goodbye. I mumbled goodbye back.

I caught Sophia glancing back once as they walked away; I winced at the pain in her swollen red eyes. I glanced back a few more times, watched her shrink into the distance, remembering how once, in another time on another planet, I'd kissed her in a movie theater, and my heart had nearly stopped.

I glanced at Phoebe walking beside me, and revisited the feeling I'd had a few moments before—a feeling that was very real and fresh. When I imagined Colin and Jeannie disappearing into crazy Athens, it was like pulling something out of me, some organ or some sense that would leave me permanently disabled. It was easier to imagine Cortez trotting into the brush, because that's where Cortez belonged. He was a cat, he was meant for this life. When I imagined losing him, it felt like losing my big brother, the person I looked up to, the person who kept the monsters in the closet.

I couldn't imagine Phoebe leaving at all. I couldn't picture her disappearing into the bamboo, couldn't envision her white sweater growing fainter until it merged with green stalks. Just couldn't imagine it, and that shocked me.

Something broke open inside me. My eyes filled with tears; I looked off to my right so Phoebe wouldn't see if she happened to look my way. It felt so good to walk beside her. I wanted to reach out and take her hand, but I wasn't sure how she'd react.

As the rays of sunlight painted the burned landscape, the ground beneath us began to stir. Here and there little green nubs pushed up out of the earth. It would probably take weeks for the bamboo to reestablish completely, but it was already growing restless. Those jackass scientists had designed it well.

I glanced at Phoebe again, and this time she looked back at me. "What?" she asked.

I touched her elbow, motioned that I wanted to let the others get further ahead of us.

"I was just thinking about how much I enjoyed that afternoon at the carnival. It'd been so long since I had fun. When we get to a town, can we go hang out somewhere alone for a while? Just go for a walk, maybe find an abandoned movie theater and look at the posters, or an abandoned Dairy Queen and make fun of the names of the sundaes?"

"Sure," she said. She had a puzzled look on her face, maybe mixed with a little whimsy.

"What?" I asked.

"Nothing."

"Come on, what?"

She burst out laughing. "I'm sorry, it's just that a few hours ago we were almost barbequed in a grain silo, and I'd swear you just asked me on a date. Am I right, are you asking me on a date?"

"I guess I am." I nodded. "Yes, that's what I'm doing. My timing may not be perfect, but if you think about it, when would be a good time to ask? When we're not barbecuing in a grain silo, we're in a shootout, or hacking our way through bamboo, or eating bugs. There really is no opportune time to ask someone on a date any more."

Phoebe wiped laughter tears from under her eyes with the back of her hand, which was as sooty as the rest of her hand. "I see your point."

"So, will you go?"

"I already said yes," she said. "But don't expect a kiss, because my toothbrush is lying on the railroad track next to Sir Francis Bacon."

"Fair enough. Can we hold hands?"

"We can hold hands."

Chapter 10:
Athens

Fall, 2033 (Three days later)

We weaved through the bamboo until we came to one of those blissful, enigmatic blank patches, then we walked side by side, holding hands.

"A mockingbird," Phoebe said, lifting her head to look for it.

"You know the sounds different birds make?"

"Just mockingbirds, because they're easy. They learn songs from other birds and sing them one after another. Listen."

We listened. Sure enough, it went through a whole repertoire of different songs. We followed the songs of the mockingbird to a little house on a dirt road and headed down the driveway, trying to spot it.

"It has white spots on its wings," Phoebe said. She stopped short.

The mockingbird was perched on the branch of an elm tree, in the back yard. A man and a woman were hanging from a low branch of the tree, beside a picnic table. The woman twisted slowly in an imperceptible breeze, the rope creaking. It looked as if they'd been dead about a week.

The mockingbird went right on singing.

We turned around without a word and continued our walk. We were avoiding any talk of bad things, which was a challenge with corpses hanging from trees, especially if you haven't eaten anything except wild herbs and bugs in two days, and nothing beyond that except the occasional bird or squirrel for the past few weeks.

The tiny strip of businesses that passed for Elberton's downtown did not include a movie theater, nor a Dairy Queen. There was a hair salon called Shear Perfection, a restaurant called Kountry Kooking, and a few long-vacant storefronts.

"So, what position did you play on the softball team in high school?" I asked, putting my arm around Phoebe's waist.

"Third base," she said. She eased toward me, allowing her hip to press against mine.

"That makes a lot of sense, with your rocket arm. I miss sports. I hope professional baseball comes back."

"I miss new things. Shrink-wrapped things that have that brand-new smell."

What we both really missed was food. I wondered what this date with Phoebe might feel like if I wasn't so hungry. I was certain that I would be floating, that I'd be butterflies-in-the-stomach in love. My stomach was too empty for butterflies to survive, but as it was, I still felt like the dials on all of my senses had been turned up. I felt like I belonged next to Phoebe with a certainty I'd never felt before.

"This is going pretty well, considering. Don't you think?" I asked.

"No complaints. Best date I've had since you took me to the Time-saver. We should start heading back, though. It'll be dark soon."

We passed Kountry Kooking again. There was an illustration of a piece of partially shucked corn on one side of the sign, an ecstatically happy pig on the other.

A walking skeleton who could have been a man or a woman pushed out of the bamboo into the clearing and crossed in front of us. Two starving children with haunted eyes trailed behind him or her. As they disappeared back into the bamboo on the other side, the smaller kid glanced our way. It was easy to forget that there were still people here. Not many, but a few.

"I'm worried that we're going to be too weak to walk all the way back to Savannah once we get to Athens," I said to Phoebe. "It's a long way."

"I had the same thought. We won't have many options, though. Either we try to make it to Savannah with Cortez, or we join Colin and Jeannie."

"Do you consider Doctor Happy an option?" I was almost afraid to ask; I didn't want to think about that possibility, unless there turned out to be no other options.

"Yes. But I'm scared. It scares me to think about it," Phoebe said.

"Me, too. I don't know what to make of Doctor Happy. Look what happened to Deirdre." I swept a spider's web out of the way with the back of my hand.

"Why do you think Deirdre did what she did?"

"I've thought a lot about that." I gestured toward a house with a porch swing. "Want to sit a while?"

We sat on the swing, sitting closer than friends but not as close as lovers. Phoebe gave us a push with one foot; the swing squealed, but swung nicely. She looked at me, waiting.

"I think Deirdre decided she'd rather be dead than happy."

Phoebe looked taken aback by the idea.

"You had to know Deirdre," I said. "Happy Deirdre is about as easy to imagine as clean filth."

Phoebe laughed.

"I swear, it's true."

"And you went out with this woman?" Phoebe asked.

I gave the swing a push. "I *know* I can't explain that one."

"I'm sure it had nothing to do with her breasts," she teased. It had slipped my mind that Phoebe had met Deirdre that one brief time at the beach. "So you think she couldn't stand being in her own happy skin?"

"Yeah, I do." I considered for a moment. "There was something in her eyes when the infection first kicked in; something I couldn't quite place. The more I think about it, the more I think it was terror."

Phoebe wrapped her hands across her upper arms. "God, that gives me chills. Do you think that reaction was just because of who Deirdre was, or do you think everyone feels it when they get infected? I can't help but wonder if there's an underside to Doctor Happy—if it's not all sunshine and lollipops."

"I once asked Sebastian about being infected, and he said it gives you a glimpse of the infinite, and a glimpse is enough, because if you could see any more you'd probably go mad."

Phoebe considered. "That does sound terrifying. But not the sort of terrifying that makes you jump off a building... more like you're tightrope walking without a net. Terrifying, but exciting, too."

"Maybe it was just Deirdre, then," I suggested.

A bird landed on the porch railing. "Ooh. Mockingbird," Phoebe said. We stayed still, letting the swing slow. The mockingbird opened its little beak and belted out a remarkable series of chirps and twills and tweets before turning and taking wing over the bamboo.

"The funny thing is, I actually don't mind Doctor Happy people. I sort of like them," I said.

"Me, too," Phoebe said. "I'm just not sure I want to be one." She gestured that we should get moving. We headed back toward camp.

"What if we lived *near* Athens?" I suggested as we pushed into the bamboo. "If that's the new cradle of civilization, maybe we could be their semi-civilized neighbors. The Sparta to their Athens."

"Ooh, keep using historical metaphors. That'll win major points with me."

"What do you think, though?" I was pretty sure I was blushing from her compliment.

"What would we eat? I'm guessing the area surrounding Athens is pretty much like this."

I thought about it. "We could salvage things to trade with Athens, go on foraging trips into the outlying towns to find things they need."

"Can't they do that themselves?" she asked. She tilted her head to one side. "I guess it's possible, though."

We returned to the back yard of the house where we were staying and found the tribe in good spirits. Cortez had shot a squirrel with the assault rifle. We could smell it roasting over an open spit. There weren't many squirrels around. I wasn't sure if that was because of the bamboo, or climate change, or because hungry people were eating them all.

"I'm going to make soup," Cortez said as we joined him. "Goes further that way."

While we ate in the kitchen, I laid out my sketchy idea. The tribe picked up the thread and ran with it, and we hashed out a plan. By the time we'd sucked the marrow out of the squirrel's bones, it was dark, and we could barely see one another.

When we topped a ridge and saw the mass of buildings that used to comprise the University of Georgia, it was like seeing the Emerald City. After tramping through wilderness and abandoned buildings for so long, civilization looked shiny and magical.

Much of the bamboo had been cleared, although there were copses here and there worked into the landscape as if it were an ornamental plant. The town was ringed by a high wall that looked to be constructed of red clay blocks. Guard towers stood at strategic points along the wall, and each housed a big steel thing that resembled a satellite dish. Inside the city, the old brick and concrete buildings were interspersed with new buildings made of the same red clay. The clay buildings were rounded, and snaked crazily through the campus.

We circled the wall until we found a gate. It was open; people were going in and out. They were all so absurdly clean. By pre-collapse standards they weren't that clean, but by current standards they were like walking moons.

Attempting to look like we knew what we were doing, we went right up to the check point.

"We'd like to speak to whoever's in charge of trade," Cortez said.

"Trade?" the guard asked, shaking his head. He had the inevitable shiny eyes and easy grin of a Doctor Happy carrier.

"Yes," Cortez said. "We have goods we'd like to trade."

"Hold on," the guard said. He ducked inside a little round booth that was also made out of red clay bricks and got on a walkie-talkie.

The guard came back out. "Someone will be with you in a moment."

"Can it possibly be this easy?" Phoebe asked, her voice low.

"Looks like we're about to find out," Jeannie said.

"Get a load of this," Cortez interrupted, gesturing beyond the gates.

I followed his gaze. Sebastian was running toward us with open arms, laughing like a lunatic, eyes wide. "You made it, you made it." He roped an elbow around my neck and leaped, wrapping his legs around my waist so that I had to catch him or fall over.

"We made it," I said as I held him.

Sebastian dismounted, suddenly got serious. "I don't see Ange."

I'd forgotten that Sebastian hadn't been there when we lost Ange. So much of the past was a hungry blur. I shook my head. "Ange didn't make it."

"Ah, fuck," he said. He teared up, looked up at the rafters for a moment. "I'm sorry to hear that."

He cheered up almost immediately and rubbed both of my shoulders. "But I was sure you were all dead by now, so this is a net gain."

It was a sobering idea, that Sebastian had simply assumed we were all dead. It was a reasonable assumption, I guess. How many people who'd been living in Savannah (or any other city, for that matter) were still alive? Less than a quarter, easily. It could be as little as one in ten. Was it just luck that we were among the survivors? Cortez certainly had a lot to do with it, but maybe I wasn't giving the rest of us enough credit. I'd never thought of myself as a survivor, but we had survived a lot, had defied the odds in staying alive.

"We haven't made it yet, though," I said. "We've made it to the gate. We need your help to make it the rest of the way." He raised his eyebrows. "We have a plan for how to live on our own terms. Help us convince your people."

I explained our plan to set up a camp nearby and establish a trade relationship with Athens. Sebastian moaned theatrically, rolled his eyes as I laid it out.

"You always have to do it the hard way," he said. "One little pinprick!" He reached out and poked Cortez with his index finger. "One little pinprick and all will be vascular." I couldn't help but feel annoyed by his antics; we were tired, near-starving. This was no joke to us.

"That's not the way we roll," Cortez said. "Will you help us?"

Sebastian shook his head. "What you're suggesting just isn't possible."

My heart sank. "Why not? Why isn't it possible?"

"Because people have been planning this for five years," Sebastian said. "They thought out these communities very carefully. One of the fundamental guidelines is that the community be homogenous. No exceptions."

Communities? So there were others forming.

"I don't have any more influence than anyone else here, until my turn comes up to be on the decision board," Sebastian went on, "and that's not likely to happen any time soon."

"Can you get us a meeting with them?" Colin asked.

"They're just going to tell me to tell you to join the community. And that's not how you roll." He waggled his head, gently mocking.

"Will you at least ask?" I said.

He shrugged. "Sure, I can ask. I can also ask them to form a human pyramid and sing Christmas carols."

An hour later Sebastian returned. As he approached I tried to read his expression, hopeful that he had succeeded in convincing them to at least talk to us, but he was always smiling, so it was impossible to glean anything from his expression.

He shrugged. "They're just not interested."

I felt like crying. I was so tired, so hungry.

"They said that besides the homogeneity issue, we have teams who go out on salvage runs every day. We don't need to trade."

"How are you fixed for medicines?" I asked. I grabbed some of the samples I'd put together. Instead of being stuffed into pouches, each was in a separate pill container with a child safety cap. We'd found them in a medicine cabinet in Watkinsville, all empty. I opened one, tipped some of its contents into my palm. "Chamomile. For inflammation. It also works as a mild sedative." I opened another, wiped a bit of the goo that oozed out onto my palm. "Aloe vera. For burns and—"

Sebastian shook his head. "We've got it all growing in our greenhouses, and herbalists to work with our doctors."

I wiped the aloe on my pant leg.

"Look," Sebastian said, "why don't I show you around the town, and we can talk about what Athens has to offer."

"No, thanks," I said.

Sebastian shrugged, looking perplexed. "Okay. Suit yourself. I'd better get back to my work. I'll check up on you when I can, see if you change your mind. I hope you will."

We set up camp twenty yards from the gate, at the edge of where they'd set up their rhizome barrier. We had no tents, so we used sheets we'd salvaged from houses along the way. Once we were settled, we initiated plan B. Each of us chose a trade item and took up a position outside the gate.

"Tampons. Who needs tampons?" Colin shouted without embarrassment. He held a box of tampons in the air, two more under his arm.

"Soap. I've got soap," Jeannie called, while a dozen steps away Cortez was hawking water filters. Actually we only had one spare water filter—a happy find in the basement of a house in a little town called Washington. It didn't matter—the plan was to establish ourselves, then we could seek out more trade goods.

It didn't work. No one even approached to see how much we were asking for our merchandise. We got plenty of attention, though. One smart aleck shouted, "Blood! I've got blood that will solve all your problems." That got some hearty laughs from the residents.

The steady stream of residents passing in and out of the gate was supplemented by the occasional group of new recruits coming to join the community. Some of these groups were small, others consisted of forty or fifty starving people led by one Athens recruiter. I kept expecting to spot Rumor leading one of these groups. Cortez had scouted the entire perimeter of the city, and reported that they were expanding the city on the far side to make room for all of the new recruits. I imagined they were already planning for a day when their community wound through the bamboo for miles in every direction.

After about an hour, we gave up.

There was no plan C.

Sebastian came out as the sun was setting. He squatted beside us, pulled a flat, round loaf of bread from under his shirt. We stared at it with wild, wide-eyed hunger. It smelled incredible.

"It's all I could hide," Sebastian said apologetically.

We took the bread behind a tent, out of view of the citizens of Athens, and Cortez divided it up with his hunting knife, giving Joel a double share.

"So good," Colin said between bites. He was clearly trying to eat slowly.

A tear rolled down his cheek. I don't know if he was crying with relief, because it tasted so good, or out of despair that we had fallen so far that eating a loaf of bread was like a thousand Christmases rolled together. Whatever the reason, it spread, and soon all of us except Cortez were crying softly as we ate.

As the sun set Phoebe and I crawled into the same tent. We hadn't discussed it; it just flowed from the bonds that had been building between us. I lay there with my eyes closed, listening to Phoebe's breathing, so grateful that she was here with me.

I don't know why it took me so long to find her. Maybe it makes sense that it would be difficult. What does love look like when the world is falling apart? Your one true love might appear when your heart is so badly wounded that you can't possibly bear for someone to touch it, and her heart might be in the same shape. Now that I'd finally recognized that this was the woman I'd been searching for, though, I was afraid that we might never get the chance to see where it might lead.

"We're running out of time," I said, keeping my voice low. Joel seemed to be shrinking, turning back into a newborn, unaware of the outside world, sometimes unable to recognize his mother.

"I know." Phoebe took my hand under the blanket. We listened to the crickets. "If Colin and Jeannie join them, what will you do?"

I'd been thinking about that all day. "When I told Sebastian that Ange was dead, did you notice that he got really sad for a second, then he cheered up?"

"Yes, I did notice that."

"They haven't been scrubbed of all their negative emotions; they still feel sadness, probably fear and anger as well; it's just toned way down. It makes it seem less like getting a frontal lobotomy."

"So you're thinking of joining Colin and Jeannie?"

"I don't think I can go back into that jungle." I couldn't quite bring myself to say yes directly.

"Me neither," Phoebe said. "I think we're on the same page." She squeezed my hand. "But I'm scared."

"Me too." Every time I thought of that pinprick, I felt like I was falling into a dark, unknown place.

We spent the next day doing nothing. Cortez made a few forays into the bamboo looking for food, but came back empty-handed. Phoebe and I had only slightly better luck, returning with a stingy handful of stinging nettle and some beetles. The rest of the day we sat and stared at the gate, watched the well-fed populace go about their lives.

Around noon, Colin and Jeannie crawled out of their makeshift tent with Joel in tow and their few possessions in plastic bags. Colin's face held the grim resolve of a soldier going off to war. Jeannie's eyes were red from crying. She went over and hugged Phoebe.

"Give it a few more days," I said, stepping between Colin and Athens.

"What will a few more days buy us?" Colin asked.

I had no answer.

I felt a hand on my shoulder. It was Phoebe, coming to join us.

Colin gestured toward Athens. "That's the only way forward. We've ruled out every other direction. They're all dead ends. Literally."

"I don't disagree with what you're saying, but shouldn't we take more time to think it through? There's no going back once we make that decision. Why don't we step back, talk about it some more?" I gestured toward a spot in the grass.

"We've been thinking it through for months," Jeannie said. "I just want to get this over with, and get some food for my baby."

I took a deep breath, brushed hair out of my eyes. I wasn't ready for this. I didn't want these to be my last hours as me, the way I was used to feeling and thinking. I looked at Colin, could see in his eyes that they really meant to go, now. My heart was racing.

A hundred yards away, half a dozen federal soldiers in tattered combat fatigues slipped out of the bamboo. They were led by a bright-eyed, smiling black guy in tan shorts. The black guy spread his arms and said something to the new recruits before leading them on toward the gate. The gate to nirvana, to Valhalla. Shangri-La.

"Come with us," Colin said. "We don't want to do this without you." He shrugged. "How do we know it's not going to be great? A couple of hours from now we might be laughing, wondering why we'd made such a big deal about it."

I had no doubt we'd be laughing. I had no idea what would be going through our heads, though. I wasn't ready. Maybe in a day or two, but not now.

"We came all this way with you," I said. "I'm not saying you owe us anything, but I'm asking you to give it another day or two. That's all I'm asking."

Colin and Jeannie looked at each other. Jeannie nodded reluctantly.

"One more day. I don't see what good it'll do, but if that's what you want…" He shrugged.

"Thanks," I said, feeling a rush of relief. I didn't know what good it would do, either. I just knew I wasn't ready.

Late in the afternoon, Sebastian came to visit. I was disappointed to see that he didn't bring any food with him.

"Let me show you around Athens," he implored us. "Come on, what do you have to lose?"

"We'd like to see it," Colin said, meaning him and Jeannie.

I looked at Phoebe.

"Why not?" she said. "I'm curious to see it up close."

Cortez said nothing, but as we turned to follow Sebastian, he followed as well. Sebastian reached around me and pulled the pistol out of my waistband. "Leave this here, if you don't mind." He gestured to Cortez. "Yours too, please." We stashed the guns in our tents and rejoined him.

There were no angles in the newly constructed buildings. Everything was curved, and many were open to the outside.

"We don't like to be closed in," Sebastian explained.

It was difficult to see where any one building left off and another began; they snaked into each other, in some places rising up to wind through the trees. The overall effect was pleasing to the eye, the colors a variety of soothing pastels.

"Are those weapons mounted on the outside walls?" Cortez asked.

"Non-lethal weapons, yes. They're heat cannons—when you activate them and point them in a general direction, everyone in a ten-acre area will have the sensation that they're extremely, extremely hot. Very unpleasant." He fanned his face, chuckling. "But the heat cannons are only our most visible defense. We've got others—all non-lethal, but I wouldn't want to be a hostile trying to take Athens unless I had tanks and fighter planes."

We passed a wide, canopied space where a hundred people were eating, or lined up to eat. I couldn't help suspect that he was leading us past the dining hall on purpose.

"Why is it you have food when nobody else does?" Colin asked.

"Like I mentioned, we've been planning for years," Sebastian said. "Most of our cleared land is dedicated to food production, and everyone puts in some work in the fields every day. No meat—meat takes up too many resources to produce, plus nobody would want the job of killing the animals."

Interesting as all this was, I was having trouble caring at the moment. My mouth was watering.

The clatter of a dropped bowl rang out. "Phoebe?" an old woman in an orange house dress was tottering, bow-legged, toward us.

"Mom?" Phoebe cried. She raced to meet her mother.

"Phoebe, I can't believe it. I thought you were dead." She gripped

Phoebe by the shoulders, looked her up and down. "I'm so sorry I didn't wait for you, but these people came by with a sign that said 'Free meal, ask me how,' and I was *so* hungry, so I followed them and had a meal, and then after my meal we went back, but you weren't back yet, and we waited, but we couldn't wait all day because we had to come here." She buried her face in Phoebe's shoulder and bobbed up and down. "I'm so glad to see you. My Phoebe, I can't believe it."

Phoebe looked over her mother's stooped shoulder; it looked like the weight of the world had been lifted from her. She caught my eye; I nodded, the only person there who really understood. Everyone in the dining area had stopped to watch the reunion, now a few clapped, then they returned to their meals.

Phoebe introduced me to her mom. "Is this your boyfriend?" she asked. She had one of those voices, sort of shrill and whiney, and she talked fast. Although most Doctor Happy people talked fast.

"I sure am," I said as I took Phoebe's mom's hand.

As Phoebe introduced her mom around, I watched people eat. Everyone seemed friendly as hell, joking with each other, laughing. Even when nothing funny was being said people just burst into spontaneous laughter, occasionally propelling food from their mouths with the force of it.

Phoebe's mom was astonished when she learned that we were not necessarily here to accept the Doctor Happy needle and be saved (forever, amen), but judging from Phoebe's reaction I got the impression that this was nothing compared to how her old, non-Doctor Happified mother dealt with disagreements. Phoebe promised to find her mom again as soon as she could, and we moved on.

As we walked it occurred to me that Athens was pretty much scrubbed of any reminders of the outside world. There were no movie posters outside the theater, no ads, billboards, no stuffed Disney characters in the gift shop we passed. They seemed serious about making a new start. "So what is the plan for this place?" I asked. "How is it going to be so different from the past?"

"Well, we're decentralizing power, for a start," Sebastian said. "No crooked politicians for us. We're borrowing a lot from other places that tried to make a clean start, looking at what worked and didn't. External things, like shorter work days and a de-emphasis on material goods, is crucial, but we're also working on the internals as well."

"Such as?" I asked. I was truly interested in what they were putting together. In a sense, we could be living in year zero, seeing the beginning of something new. Assuming the Jumpy-Jumps didn't plow the whole thing under.

Sebastian pulled a spiral notebook out of his pocket and held it up. "This is my liar's notebook. Every time I tell a lie, I write it down. Everyone has one."

"You're all nuts," Cortez said.

"What's nuts is what's going on out there," Sebastian said, pointing over the city wall.

He led us through the old part of the university campus, where tall oak trees shaded a long stretch of lawn. People were lounging around like they were killing time between classes. It seemed so anachronistic, a scene from the time before everything went wrong.

"Everyone gets one day off a week," Sebastian said. "Once everything is established we'll start bumping that up, until it's three or four."

Colin and Jeannie were surveying the scene with the look of house hunters about to pull out a tape measure to see if their favorite sofa would fit.

As the last light bled out of the sky, Phoebe and I were tired, but couldn't sleep.

"What happens now?" Phoebe asked.

"I don't know."

"Me neither."

Murmurs drifted from the next tent, where Colin and Jeannie were also not sleeping. I wondered what they were saying. Joel let out a pathetic squeal of hunger. It was a heartbreaking sound, an intolerable sound. I would not ask them to wait another day; I felt guilty that I had asked for this one.

It was hard to think with my stomach so empty. What I really wanted to do right now was to clutch Phoebe to me and tell her that I loved her. I wanted to vanish the last bit of distance between us so we could face this together. But we hadn't known each other long enough for that.

"There are things I wish we could talk about," I said, hesitantly, "but they're the sort of things you talk about when you've been together much longer than we have."

Phoebe was quiet for a long moment. "Maybe we should talk about them anyway, given the circumstances?"

"Okay." For a moment, my old, familiar insecurities reared up. Would I blow it by professing my undying love? Was Phoebe feeling the same for me, or was I just any port in a storm? Off in the distance a whimpering dog serenaded us; my psyche given voice.

The hell with it. What did I have to lose?

"I'm afraid Doctor Happy will change how I feel about you. If you love everyone, how do you parse your feelings for one person out of that giant vat of love?"

Phoebe laughed hysterically. For an instant I thought she was laughing at my profession of love. "Giant vat of love?"

"Yeah. Haven't the Doctor Happy people told you about the giant vat of love?"

"No," she said, wiping her eyes. "But I know what you're saying, and I've thought about it too."

"You have?"

"Mm hm. I'm afraid I won't feel the same way about you if Doctor Happy changes us too dramatically."

One of our stomachs growled. I was pretty sure it was mine.

"On the other hand," Phoebe went on, "if we didn't lose each other in the giant vat of love, Athens is a place where we could stop worrying about starving or being shot. It might give us the space to be together in a real, normal way. Out here it takes all of our energy just staying alive."

"So, you do want to be together?"

"Yeah. I do."

A flush of warmth swept over me. I wrapped my arms around Phoebe and kissed her.

"We're not so broken," she whispered. "The people we thought we were are just waiting for a chance to come back out."

She was right. The evidence was right there—the two of us, falling in love, still able to fall in love after all we'd been through.

I was up most of the night, thinking, trying to sort through a tangle of conflicting emotions.

Early the next morning, music drifted across to us from Athens—something classical, with a lot of string instruments. It sounded live. Somehow it didn't surprise me that Athens had accomplished musicians. They had everything else.

Phoebe and I crawled out of our tent with our possessions in plastic bags. My stomach did a flip, like I had just hit the big drop on a roller coaster. This was it, I realized.

Cortez was squatting beside his tent, the assault rifle across his thighs. I pulled the pistol out of my waistband and looked at it, thought about the two men I'd shot with it, thought about Ange screaming in pain while those boys held her down, about Tara Cohn telling Cortez that he sucked. What was so nuts about wanting all of that to stop? Maybe Sebastian was right, maybe they were the sane ones.

"You want this?" I said, holding out the pistol. The words seemed to come from a distance, somewhere over my head.

Cortez ignored the gun. "You're going in?"

I nodded.

Colin and Jeannie crawled out of their tent. When he saw our stuff packed, I thought he might hug me. "Good. Great. The tribe will stay together." He turned to Cortez. "How about you, Cortez? Come with us."

Beyond the gates a trumpet rose out of the softer strings. It was a beautiful, golden sound. It had been so long since I'd heard live music that clear.

"Come on, take the leap." I tried to smile, but the muscles in my face were stiff with fear. The edges of my mouth began to twitch and I gave it up.

Cortez folded his arms, shook his head. "I probably would take a leap. Off a water tower. It's not for me. You all go ahead."

"But what will you do?" Jeannie asked.

The trumpet bleated triumphant, soaring toward a crescendo. Cortez paused, waited for it to recede. The song was almost over. Funny how you can tell a song was ending, even if you've never heard it before.

"I'll head home," Cortez said. "Choose the sanest gangsters and join them. In these times there's always work for warriors." It made sense. Cortez was the only one of us who had the right resume now that civilization had collapsed.

One by one, we said goodbye to Cortez. When it was my turn, I hugged him fiercely and said, "You've been like a big brother to me, watching out for me, showing me how to get by. We'd all be dead if it wasn't for you."

He pressed his face against the side of mine. "Don't get me crying," he said into my ear. I handed him the pistol; he tucked it into his waistband.

We watched as Cortez hefted his belongings, turned, and slipped into the bamboo.

"He'll make it," I said to the others, fighting back tears. "Somehow he'll make it." Unable to put it off any longer, we turned toward the gate.

"I'm scared," Phoebe said. Her hand was cold.

"Me too," I said.

The music ended, leaving the valley quiet.

"We're going to be at the start of something new—the year zero," I said.

"And they're good people, honest and kind," Jeannie added.

"Hell, we're going to get to eat in that food tent three times a day," Colin said. "No more hunger, no more bugs."

In my college psychology class I learned that bettors are more confident about the horses they pick after they place their bets. I knew that was what we were doing; if you're going to drink the Kool-Aid you might as well throw your head back and chug.

As we approached the gate, I realized that some part of me had known for a while that this is how it would turn out. We were survivors, after all. If this was the only game in town, then we'd play.

Besides that, it felt good not to have the weight of that gun in my waistband.

We reached the gate and asked the guard to fetch Sebastian. I took a deep breath. Fine. Time to meet the future. Phoebe squeezed my hand; I squeezed hers back.

When Sebastian saw our expressions he hurried, wrapped his arms around each of us, whispered that we'd made the right decision. His eyes were bright, and just a little wild.

He led us through the gate, and this time I looked at the town through different eyes. This was going to be my home. It was such a strange notion.

"In here," Sebastian said, sliding open a door made of yellow bamboo. We stepped into a big hall with long, narrow windows draped in wheat-colored fabric. The close end of the hall was squared, the far end rounded. Two people, a man and a woman, greeted us.

"These people are joining us today," Sebastian said. "They're friends of mine. We go back a long way."

I thought of Cortez, pushing through the bamboo, and had a moment of panic. Couldn't we do it, the six of us? Couldn't we figure out a way to survive out there?

Maybe for a few weeks, but no more. I thought of Sophia and felt a terrible sadness. She should be here with us, safe. She was probably dead by now. I hoped she had died quickly. By gunfire, maybe.

"Ready?" The woman put her hand on my back and coaxed me toward a curtained cubicle. Inside there would be a little vial of blood and a sterile needle.

I paused. "We want to go together." I looked back at Phoebe, who nodded.

Jeannie, who was also being led to a cubicle, paused as well. "We do, too."

Her escort smiled. "Sure. We can fit two to a room. Or two and a half." He touched Joel's bald head.

The woman transferred a chair from one cubicle into another. They led Colin and Jeannie inside. The pungent, familiar odor of Colin's unwashed self hit me as he passed. We must smell terrible to these people—it was amazing that their pleasant smiles never dropped, were never replaced by a wrinkled nose of disgust.

Phoebe and I stood at a respectful distance, waiting our turn. We heard murmuring in the cubicle, then a little cry of rage from Joel that tapered off after a few inbreaths.

Colin pushed back the curtain. He held up his arm, displaying a little round band-aid on the inside of his forearm. Jeannie followed, carrying Joel. Her eyes were red-rimmed. She didn't show us her band-aid, or Joel's.

"Next?" the woman called, poking her head out of the cubicle.

My bowels loosened. My heart was hammering like crazy. I looked at Phoebe; she took a quavering breath, tried to give me a brave smile. "Ready?"

"No," I said.

"Me neither."

We walked to the cubicle holding hands.

It was a tight fit; Phoebe's thigh was pressed against mine. The man and woman, wearing yellow surgical gloves, sat facing us, their knees almost touching ours. It felt strangely intimate. I wondered if people in Athens shared a special bond with the person who infected them, the way Rumor seemed to think he and I shared a special bond because I squirted him in the eye with a water gun after he killed my friend's dog.

The woman rubbed alcohol on the white underside of my forearm.

"Can you poke us at the same time?" I asked.

"Sure," the man said.

"Relax," the woman said, probably seeing the panic in our eyes as she unwrapped a needle from its packaging. "You'll be so glad. I promise. You're going to feel better than you've ever felt before."

I hoped it was true. I so wanted this to be our happily ever after. We deserved a happily ever after, after all we'd been through.

They dipped the needles into vials of deep red blood. Was blood always that red? The neutral colors in the room probably created a contrast.

The woman held out her hand. I laid mine in it, palm up. Phoebe did the same.

The man and the woman looked at each other with bright, eccentric eyes. They weren't crazy eyes, really. Eccentric was a better description. "Ready?" the woman said to the man, grinning. "One. Two…"

I looked into Phoebe's lucid green eyes and willed myself to always love her in exactly the same way that I loved her at that moment.

"Three."

She was very gentle; I barely felt the needle prick my skin.

Acknowledgments

First and foremost, thank you to my wife, Alison Scott, for her encouragement and love, and for reading and commenting on this novel, which is nothing like the Jane Austen novels she usually reads.

I'm deeply grateful to Laura Valeri, Sara King, Joy Marchand, Tom Doyle, and David W. Goldman, my friends and fellow writers, for providing truly indispensable feedback. Also Walter John Williams, Kelly Link, and my fellow students at Taos Toolbox 2007.

Special thanks to my father, Brigadier General William F. McIntosh, for advice and information regarding how the military might react to a soft apocalypse.

Thanks to Andy Cox and the people at *Interzone*, who published the short story on which this novel is based. To the Clarion Science Fiction Writer's Workshop, and my teachers Jim Kelly, Maureen McHugh, Scott Edelman, Nalo Hopkinson, Richard Paul Russo, Howard Waldrop, and Kelly Link. Thanks to my friends Colin Crothers, Doris Bazzini, and Angela Ogburn for inspiration.

Finally, many thanks to my agent, Seth Fishman, for believing in this book.

Although I created a nightmarish version of the city of Savannah, I hope a glimpse of its real beauty and charm has shone through. If you haven't been to Savannah, come visit and wander the squares.

Night Shade Books Is an Independent Publisher of Quality SF, Fantasy and Horror

ISBN: 978-1-59780-221-5, Trade Paperback; $15.99

YOU ARE BEING WATCHED. Your every movement is being tracked, your every word recorded. One wrong move, one slip-up, and you may find yourself disappeared—swallowed up by a monstrous bureaucracy, vanished into a shadowy labyrinth of interrogation chambers, show trials, and secret prisons from which no one ever escapes. Welcome to the world of the dystopia, a world of government and society gone horribly, nightmarishly wrong.

In his smash-hit anthologies *Wastelands* and *The Living Dead*, acclaimed editor John Joseph Adams showed you what happens when society is utterly wiped away. Now he brings you a glimpse into an equally terrifying future. *Brave New Worlds* collects 30 of the best tales of totalitarian menace. When the government wields its power against its own people, every citizen becomes an enemy of the state. Will you fight the system, or be ground to dust beneath the boot of tyranny?

Night Shade Books Is an Independent Publisher of Quality SF, Fantasy and Horror

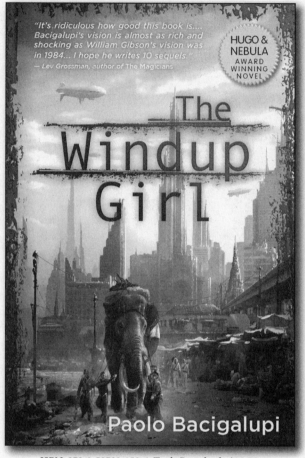

"It's ridiculous how good this book is.... Bacigalupi's vision is almost as rich and shocking as William Gibson's vision was in 1984... I hope he writes 10 sequels."
— Lev Grossman, author of The Magicians

HUGO & NEBULA AWARD WINNING NOVEL

The Windup Girl

Paolo Bacigalupi

ISBN: 978-1-59780-158-4, Trade Paperback; $14.95

Winner of the Hugo and Nebula award for Best Novel.

Anderson Lake is a company man, AgriGen's Calorie Man in Thailand. Undercover as a factory manager, Anderson combs Bangkok's street markets in search of foodstuffs thought to be extinct, hoping to reap the bounty of history's lost calories. There, he encounters Emiko, the Windup Girl, a strange and beautiful creature. One of the New People, Emiko is not human; she is an engineered being, crèche-grown and programmed to satisfy the decadent whims of a Kyoto businessman, but now abandoned to the streets of Bangkok. Regarded as soulless beings by some, devils by others, New People are slaves, soldiers, and toys of the rich in a chilling near future in which calorie companies rule the world, the oil age has passed, and the side effects of bio-engineered plagues run rampant across the globe.

Night Shade Books Is an Independent Publisher of Quality SF, Fantasy and Horror

ISBN: 978-1-59780-213-0, Trade Paperback; $14.99

Fallen angels and The Fey clash against the backdrop of Irish/English conflicts of the 1970s in this stunning debut novel by Stina Leicht.

When the war between The Fey and The Fallen begins to heat up, Liam and the woman he loves are pulled into a conflict invisible to most humans—a conflict in which Liam's father fights on the front lines. This centuries-old battle between supernatural forces seems to mirror the political divisions in 1970s-era Ireland, and Liam is thrown headlong into both conflicts.

Only the direct intervention of Liam's father and a secret Catholic order dedicated to fighting The Fallen can save Liam from the mundane and supernatural forces around him, and from the darkness that lurks within.

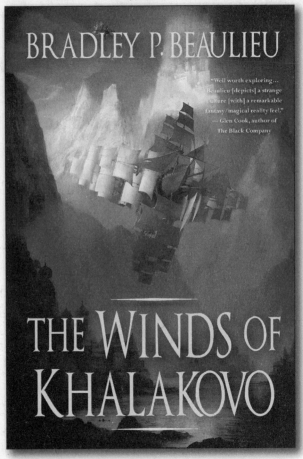

"Well worth exploring... Beaulieu [depicts] a strange culture [with] a remarkable fantasy/magical reality feel!"
— Glen Cook, author of The Black Company

BRADLEY P. BEAULIEU

THE WINDS OF KHALAKOVO

ISBN: 978-1-59780-218-5, Trade Paperback; $14.99

Among inhospitable and unforgiving seas stands Khalakovo, a mountainous archipelago of seven islands, its prominent eyrie stretching a thousand feet into the sky. Serviced by windships bearing goods and dignitaries, Khalakovo's eyrie stands at the crossroads of world trade. But all is not well in Khalakovo.

When an elemental spirit attacks an incoming windship, murdering the Grand Duke and his retinue, Prince Nikandr, heir to the scepter of Khalakovo, is tasked with finding the child prodigy believed to be behind the summoning. However, Nikandr discovers that the boy is an autistic savant who may hold the key to lifting the blight that has been sweeping the islands. Can the Dukes, thirsty for revenge, be held at bay? Can Khalakovo be saved? The elusive answer drifts upon the Winds of Khalakovo...

Night Shade Books Is an Independent Publisher of Quality SF, Fantasy and Horror

ISBN: 978-1-59780-214-7, Trade Paperback; $14.99

Nyx had already been to hell. One prayer more or less wouldn't make any difference... On a ravaged, contaminated world, a centuries-old holy war rages, fought by a bloody mix of mercenaries, magicians, and conscripted soldiers. Though the origins of the war are shady and complex, there's one thing everybody agrees on—

There's not a chance in hell of ending it.

Nyx is a former government assassin who makes a living cutting off heads for cash. But when a dubious deal between her government and an alien gene pirate goes bad, Nyx's ugly past makes her the top pick for a covert recovery. The head they want her to bring home could end the war—but at what price?

The world is about to find out.

About the Author

Will McIntosh is a Hugo Award winner and Nebula finalist whose short stories have appeared in *Asimov's* (where he won the 2010 Readers' Award for short story "Bridesicle"), *Strange Horizons*, and *Science Fiction and Fantasy: Best of the Year*, and many other venues. In 2005 his short story "Soft Apocalypse" was nominated for both the British Science Fiction Association and the British Fantasy Society awards. His story "Followed," which was published in the anthology *The Living Dead*, is currently being produced as a short film. A New Yorker transplanted to the rural south, Will is a psychology professor at Georgia Southern University, where he studies Internet dating, and how people's TV, music, and movie choices are affected by recession and terrorist threat. In 2008 he became the father of twins.